Peter F. Ryan

Peter Ryan M.A. (Oxon) has had a varied career in business and the United Nations in Africa, UK, Austria, USSR, Eastern Europe and the Caribbean.

He was commissioned in 33rd Airborne Artillery Regiment and later served in 21st Special Air Service Regiment.

After a business career in Africa and Europe, he joined in 1972, the newly-formed United Nations Industrial Development Organisation, UNIDO, in Vienna, Austria.

He worked as a senior diplomat mainly in East Africa, Middle East, S.E. Asia and Latin America. During the 1980s he led teams which established Industrial Development Corporations in Kuwait, Oman, Saudi Arabia, United Arab Emirates and Yemen. He speaks five languages including Ki-Swahili.

From 1983-1990 he represented UNIDO in the Caribbean, based in Barbados. Since then he has worked as a management consultant in some twenty five countries.

He is Vice President of FEMOZA – World Federation of Free Zones – Geneva.

I speak of Africa and golden joys.

Henry 1V. Part 2. Act 5 Scene 3.1

THE GREEN
FIELDS OF AFRICA

Peter Ryan

The Green
Fields of Africa

Vanguard Press

Cover illustration © Gina Foster

The Prayer by Zirnfeld
By kind permission of Mars& Minerva

Looking for Trouble by General Sir Peter de la Billiere
By Kind permission of HarperCollins Publishers Ltd

Extract from FIGHTING FOR PEACE by General Sir Michael Rose
published by The Harvill Press. Used by permission of The Random
House Group Limited

A CIP catalogue record for this title is available from the British Library
ISBN 1 84386 204 2
Vanguard Press is an imprint of
Pegasus Elliot MacKenzie Publishers Ltd.
www.pegasuspublishers.com

First Published in 2004
Revised Edition 2004

Vanguard Press
Sheraton House Castle Park
Cambridge England

Printed & Bound in Great Britain

Dedication

This book is dedicated to all those soldiers; African, English, Irish, Scots and Welsh, many long forgotten, who died in small wars and emergencies in Africa in the last half century.

Introduction

"One rule for survival in war – when someone is out to kill you, you had better get him first, or at least keep out of his way – otherwise you will not be thinking about the problem very much longer."

General Sir Peter de la Billière.
'Looking For Trouble'

PART ONE

FIRST SEVEN DAYS

CHAPTER ONE

BLUE ON BLUE

I bring this prayer to you, Lord,
For you alone can give
What one cannot demand but from oneself.
Give me, Lord, what you have left over,
Give me what no one ever asks you for.
I don't ask you for rest, or quiet,
Whether of soul or body.

I don't ask for wealth,
Nor for success, not even for health.
That sort of thing you get asked for so much,
That you can't have any of it left.
Give me, Lord, what you have left over;
Give what no one wants from you
I want insecurity, anxiety,

I want storm and strife.
And I want you to give me these
Once and for all,
So that I can be sure of having them always,
Since I shall not have the courage
To ask you for them again.

Give me, Lord, what you have left over.
Give me what others want nothing to do with.
But give me courage too, and strength and faith,
For you alone can give,
What one cannot demand but from oneself.

André Zirnheld
Free French paratrooper of the Special Air Service.
Killed at Sidi Hannisch, Libya, 1942.)

The C.O. had wanted to see for himself how the national servicemen were getting on out there in the mountain forests of the Aberdares. New to the fighting conditions in Kenya, he noticed that they were mostly townsmen, unhappy to be stuck out there at seven thousand feet above sea level, with strange noises all around, especially at night. With them there was a hard core of regulars, with battle experience in Korea, Malaysia; and before that in North Africa, Italy, France and Germany. There were men there, who, like himself, had survived the battle of the bridge at Arnhem. He knew that he could rely on them in any conditions. It was the raw recruits that worried everybody. They needed them to make up the numbers. They had all been selected for the commando by passing a rigorous two week survival course. Less than a third of every intake had passed. But the Colonel wanted to see for himself. He led the patrol, striding out hard, as he always did.

Even Regimental Sergeant Major Rory McTaggart, who had been with him since 1940, through El Alamein to Tunis, D-Day through to Berlin, could only just keep up the pace. The rest of them just had to run now and then. As they had done in Korea two years ago, before he was captured. But then, being the man he was, he had escaped, jumping into the half-frozen Yalu River, and swimming for it. Many of the captured did not survive the two and a half years in Chinese prison camps.

Sean Chaber O'Neill was a hard man. His nickname, "Ironballs," expressed the soldiers' wry exasperation with the way he drove them. Always from the front. He was the right man to lead this commando, drawn from the South Irish Rangers, from the slums of Dublin, Limerick, and Belfast; from farms north and south of the border. To make up the numbers, after the casualties in Korea, they had to take some British national servicemen who had, at least passed the commandos' selection course. The Irish, whether from Ulster or from the Republic, were volunteers to a man.

"What's a commando?" the recruits would ask. The selection team told them. "Infantry regiments have mortar platoons, machine-gun platoons, signals units, transport Sections, maintenance and repair sections, a padre, a doctor, cooks and admin clerks. We do not. We travel light. We travel fast. We learnt this from the Boer Commandos fifty years ago. 45th Marine Commando raided France in the Second World War. Lord Lovat lead them ashore on D-Day. We don't have companies and platoons. We have two Sabre squadrons with two troops in each. Everybody is his own scout, artificer, cook and bottle washer. Every man fights. Got it?"

That day they had already inspected two strong-points, set on well-known paths where gangs of Mau-Mau had been seen to go down to the villages in the Reserves to gather food. These bashas were all well camouflaged, set on small hilltops. Bren guns were set on fixed traverse, so that the risk of a surprise attack was minimised.

The men manning them had an easy job in daylight, with scouts out left and right. But when the night came, it was a different story. There were all manner of animal noises. Monkeys foraging; hyenas; sometimes rhino or buffalo. The bullfrogs and, in dry weather, cicadas, strumming their monotonous whirring and scraping, which masked other noises. Birds let out sudden insane cacklings, startling the townsmen.

It didn't bother the old hands, who were accustomed to long lonely watches in all weather conditions. They knew how to keep warm and dry. And to stay awake when "on stag." They knew the penalty for being caught asleep in an active duty station. The NCOs, sergeants and corporals drummed it into them night and day.

The new commanding officer wanted to see three posts. But it took longer than he thought to get from the start point to the first two and down again. They were supposed to finish before darkness, but they reached the third and last well after sunset.

The Bren gun that fired down on them, was set on a fixed traverse aimed at the path up to the basha. Sean got at least four rounds of 303, just below his neck and instantly he knew it was terminal. He didn't die at once. As they fought to try to stem the fierce arterial bleeding he gasped. "Don't punish that man. We didn't train him well. Our fault."

"What a bloody awful waste," Rory commented bitterly, the

tears pouring down his seamed, strained face as they staggered downhill with his body slung in a blanket. "Sod all national service nig-nogs." In camp he had the body laid out in the guardroom on a table under green cloth with the union flag at one end, the tricolour at the other. The men filed in all day to pay respects. Four sergeants stood at the corners, rifles reversed. There were plenty of volunteers to relieve them while the paper work and the telephoning went on.

This was in their eyes a tragedy akin to the death of Michael Collins in West Cork, ambushed by anti-Treaty guerrillas in 1922. As sad as the death of the rebels, executed by the British after the Easter Rising in 1916. They all knew the names: Padraig Pearse; Thomas Clarke; Thomas McDonagh; Joseph Plunkett; Edward Daly; William Pearse; Michael O'Hanrahan; John Macbride; James Connolly; Sean MacDiarmada.

They all knew O'Neill's record from North Africa with 45 Commando under Shimi Lovat. Campaigns in Greece, in Crete. Raids with the Special Boat Service in the Dodecanese. With 2nd SAS at the invasion of Sicily. In the hand-to-hand fighting at Monte Cassino, where he won his second Military Cross. And then after D-Day, behind the German lines in France and Germany when he won the DSO – Distinguished Service Order; the Croix de Guerre and several American awards.

Most of them knew that his father had been killed in Belfast in 1923 as an independence activist. It was only one of the many tragedies played out in that time of The Troubles. No one ever knew whether he had been killed by the RUC, the Royal Ulster Constabulary, or by British troops.

Now at his death, they were all angry at the waste and the stupidity of it. The anger hung around the base camp like an invisible black mist. Men who normally moved with the joy of youth slouched and sat bowed over cups of tea. The NAAFI ran out of beer and spirits. All the officers and NCOs wore a black arm band for a month.

When they took his body to the military cemetery, Pipe-Sergeant Major Seamus O'Sullivan led the cortège. The African trackers from the King's African Rifles asked to be bearers and took the coffin out of camp. They stayed with it and lifted it on to a gun carriage. Only reluctantly, once through the gate, they handed over to the six officers to carry it through to the gravesite, with the whole commando following in slow march, to the strains of the pipes playing a lament. The invited diplomats, military attachés, press, air force crews, civilians: all stood stock still, heads bowed as the buglers from the Rifle Brigade, the King's Own, the Devon's blew their slow, high piercing notes of the Last Post.

As the last sad notes died on the still, silent air, O'Sullivan started on a long slow lament, the pipes skirling and whining with a piercing, plangent keening. The trackers stood grim faced to attention. The guard of honour, to a man, and most onlookers let the tears flow down their faces as they listened to that age old sad Celtic air, which seemed to embody all the tragedies of the Scots and Irish battles of the past.

Later that month they all subscribed to a monument, a two metre high slab of polished limestone, set very firmly in a wide concrete base. They dug in four stout pillars and hand-forged iron chains to link them and to keep animals and vandals at bay. That made sure that it would be left there standing out in the scatter of monuments, when they finally went home. The inscription reads;

"We Irish soldiers,
Called to fight against evil.
We gave our bodies to Africa;
Our souls to God;
And our hearts to Ireland."

Below it were listed the names of the twenty-six officers and men of the commando of South Irish Rangers who died in Kenya between 1952 and 1955. It is still there amongst the leleshwa bushes, partly covered now where the rain and sun of half a century has nurtured the grass and weeds. There are coffee shambas all around it, but no land-hungry farmer has disturbed this long forgotten memorial to the bravery and rugged persistence of these foreign soldiers who died doing their duty, protecting farmers from their tribal enemies.

CHAPTER TWO

ARRIVAL

"We are the pilgrims, master; we shall go
Always a little further: it may be
Beyond that last blue mountain barred with snow,
Across that angry or that glimmering sea."

James Elroy Flecker
(Adopted as the motto on the memorial in Hereford for all Special
Air Service soldiers who have been killed in action since 1945)

The inside of the aeroplane was a dark corridor, its four Merlin engines throbbing and roaring. As he opened his eyes he saw a single reading lamp glowing over a seat across the gangway. It was nearly 6.00 a.m. and they had been flying for over 24 hours with stops in Rome, Cairo and Khartoum. Jonathan Fitzpatrick, aged 19, Second Lieutenant, South Irish Rangers Commando. Posted to Kenya where the Mau Mau "Emergency" was two years old, he had been sent, to replace casualties, on a commercial flight, in civilian clothes.

His skull pulsated in rhythm with the engines, and he regretted having taken the advice of the husky, sunburnt farmer who had got on at Rome. "A couple of codeines, washed down with brandy." It had knocked him out then, at 1.00 a.m. leaving the midnight heat of Khartoum, but now he felt he needed another dose.

Stumbling back to his seat after sluicing his face, he saw that the face under the lamp was the elderly Englishwoman who had boarded at Cairo. She was on her way home to Tanganyika, she had told him. "Good morning," she said softly, "I'm waiting for the sunrise." She had pulled down the shade and was staring out of the window. He bent over to hear what she was saying. "You don't often see it from so high up." Twenty thousand feet, he thought, sitting down in the empty seat beside her. They were somewhere over the foothills of Ethiopia, where they shelved down towards the Equator.

At 6.15 a.m. a pale light began to thin out the velvety darkness below. Tania Phillips put her book away calmly and began to watch. The light spread quickly, flushing the sky with yellowish white on one side, without defining the horizon. The ground below was still invisible, giving an eerie sensation of disembodiment, of flying with no sense of speed or height or direction.

The sun thrust up suddenly, small, blood-red and strange, so far below. It squeezed up, defining the horizon, between a gold and pomegranate sky and a still dark earth, glowing like a white-hot coin, unreal in its swiftness. Then the whole sky flamed as it roared out, swelling and burning, rolling away the darkness, and it was a full incandescent orb of eye-piercing light. The whole visible sky blended with it in a few seconds, taking colour and shape, through deep mauve and light-shot purple, to a dazzling white and turquoise to full day. Far down near the ground a few small clouds floated in the sudden daylight, rising like steam, puffy and isolated. Then huge whirling clouds obscured the view.

He looked at the old woman's face. She was smiling contentedly, and turned to him conspiratorially. "Now I am really back in Africa," she said. "What are you going to do in Africa, young man?"

Slightly miffed by the "young man," he could not resist it. "Fight your Mau-Mau for you, so I'm told."

But she didn't blink, just looked a bit sad. Under her breath she murmured "Or get yourself killed." Like her father, her husband and two of her brothers. In other wars. In other lands.

"Why are you not on a military flight?"

"None available ma'am. The RAF stop at Aden. Too slow by sea, I suppose."

"National service?"

"Yes."

She smiled. "You be careful down there."

He laughed. "It's all right. I'm a country boy. Guns I know about."

"God bless you, then. I'm Tania Phillips. Come and see us. Everyone knows our farm."

He went back to his seat and dozed, thinking of the sunrise. Remembering muzzily about the Little Prince, whom St Exupery wrote, he had met in the Sahara. The Little Prince attended, not just watched, several sunsets a day from his asteroid. Joanna had been very fond of Le Petit Prince, with his sheep who would eat the thornless roses unless they were kept under glass bowls, and the baobab trees whose roots threatened to split the asteroid. Whenever he saw baobab trees he would remember about Joanna in England, which would be a little sad, like Le Petit Prince. On the other hand the Mau-Mau probably didn't watch sunsets. He was not looking forward at all to meeting them.

In the next seat Frank Hullyer woke and they had breakfast. The view from the windows changed from a uniform green fuzz to a glaring buff-white, rock-strewn plain, with only threads of green in the hollows of meandering, spidery ravines. "Northern Frontier District," Frank told him, "Sand, Somalis and bugger-all." Later, he pointed out Lake Rudolf over the western horizon, a long leaden strip, merging hazily with the sky. "Two hundred miles long," Hullyer said. "Full of Nile perch and crocodile. Three hundred miles from anywhere. Northern parts in Ethiopia. North-west shore the Sudan border. El Molo tribe live at the Kenya end. The most God-forsaken, desolate place left in Africa."

"Funny place to have a lake," Jonathan mumbled through his corn flakes.

"Part of the Great Rift that starts with the Red Sea. Goes through Ethiopia, splits Kenya in half, goes slap through Tanganyika, forms Lake Nyasa and finishes in Portuguese East. We live on one side of the Rift Wall. To get to Nairobi we go down four thousand feet, along the valley, up the side of the Rift again to seven or eight thousand to the Kikuyu Highlands, then down to five and a half thousand."

He screwed up his eyes, gazing out of the window. When his face relaxed the deep-etched lines around his eyes stood out, white against the boot leather shade of his skin. His forehead was pale where his hat shaded it; as pale as his palms against their mahogany backs.

"Mount Kenya," he said, and there were two jagged peaks with featherings of cloud floating around them. The shoulders of the mountain spread out enormously on either side and then sloped down wider and wider into the surrounding emptiness of the plains. As the aircraft drew nearer he saw snow glittering on the peaks, glinting in the strong sunlight amongst the clouds. "You'll see that close-up." That sounded ominous. "Bags of Mau-Mau down there," he added with a grin.

They passed over the north east east shoulder. The land on the south side was at a higher level than the plains behind them, thickly forested, dotted with groups of beehive huts and patches of cultivation. He could see roads like thick ochre ribbons snaking southwards. "Kikuyuland," Hullyer said. "From here to Nairobi. Best of luck, mate, with that lot down there." Jonathan shivered.

Half an hour later they were wheeling over the city, the glittering buildings like chunky, sawn-off skyscrapers scattered bizarrely amongst thick clumps of trees and bare, open squares. The outskirts were dotted with red-roofed bungalows and square grey blocks, looking equally strange and raw in the burnt sienna of their surroundings. As they began the run in to the airfield he could see the plains again to the south, stretching endlessly into the glaring distance, an eternity of dry scrub, thorn trees and dried up wadis.

They walked unsteadily down the wobbly steps, held in place by two Africans in blue jerseys, khaki shorts and red fezes. A black policeman stood by the entrance to the wooden reception building, shouldering a rifle over his navy-blue greatcoat. He wore a mulberry-coloured helmet with a silver badge, puttees and enormous boots. A crowd of Africans, laughing and shouting, trundled a luggage trolley up to the plane. Their legs, he noticed, were not black but a purply-red, and their feet, that splayed out, bare in the dust, were grey with pink soles.

Then he saw Tim Collins standing there in crisp khaki-drill, his gleaming Sam Browne belt dark against the light cloth, legs stout in puttees with the dark green regimental hose-tops of the South Irish Rangers just below the knees. He smiled under his wide bush-hat, his teeth white against his brown face; he raised his shillelagh in salute. Joanna said he seemed to be all muscle, tensed like spring steel. Yes, true.

Seeing the Harp and Sword badge that pinned up one side of the hat's brim, Jonathan Fitzpatrick realised fully that he had arrived, a soldier in civvies. That he was in Africa, a few miles from the Equator, on a plateau nearly six thousand feet above sea-level. He hoped the uncertainty he felt did not show. He would give his soul for a large mug of hot black coffee.

CHAPTER THREE

FIRST PARADE

"For all men would be cowards if they durst."

John Wilmot
Lord Rochester. 1647-1680

They queued behind two families of Indians for the immigration formalities. Hullyer had protested at the delay and as a Resident had been cleared, but Jonathan was considered as a tourist and told to wait. He passed the time by studying the Indians, who had fascinated him since they boarded the plane at Cairo. They were Muslims, Hullyer told him, on their way from a pilgrimage to Mecca. They were a strange mixture of East and West, with European jackets and coats over their pilgrims' robes, a travel bag in one hand, and a three decker brass curry container in the other. They certainly did not look as though they could afford the fares, but Hullyer had looked at him pityingly.

"You'll soon find out how business gets done around here. Most of them from around Bombay," he went on, "originally coolies, sweeper class untouchables and night-soil removers, brought in to build the railway in the eighteen-nineties. Some became merchants and brought in their relations, and now there's ninety thousand of 'em. Against about thirty-five thousand Europeans. Most Muslim Indians are colonisers. They build houses and stay very often wherever they settle and never go back to India."

After five minutes, Tim Collins took his baggage tags and left him to queue alone, with the cryptic remark, "Good for you to find out how the local officialdom operates."

Jonathan stared, wondering at the difference between the Muslims before him and the few Indians he met at home.

"Poor Hajis," Hullyer had said, "Hard to love them because they make money and their breath smells of onions and garlic. I like them a lot, because they give me credit in their shops. When I'm skint they wait months for me to pay,"

Eventually he was confronted by a Sikh official who handed him a document stating that if he remained in the colony as a visitor he could do so for three months only, on payment of two hundred pounds as a security bond. Another sheet said that if he applied for a Temporary Work Permit, and it was granted for two years only, then after six months, he would be liable for military service with the Emergency Security Forces. Would he prefer, it enquired, to serve as a private in the Kenya Regiment? Or if he spoke Ki-Swahili, had been commissioned, and had active service experience, he could apply for the King's African Rifles. Or if he knew Kenya well he could become a temporary Sub-Inspector of the Reserve Police. If a qualified pilot he could fly with the Police Airwing. If he could ride very well, the Police Mounted Section. Finally, if he had a thorough knowledge of the Kikuyu, he might become a temporary District Officer (Kikuyu Guard).

Jonathan took a deep breath and again produced his Military Identity Card and a note from the War Office (Postings Dept.), to say that he was a Second Lieutenant, attached 22nd Commando Brigade, South Irish Rangers. This puzzled the bearded and smartly turbaned Sikh official more than a little, and he retired with a pained expression saying, "I go now to see Number One."

Ten minutes later he was still sitting there, rather dazed, pondering on the inscrutable ways of bureaucracy, and wondering why in mid-1953, with Mau-Mau in full revolt, a soldier was a surprise. Tim returned, counselled patience and went back to the restaurant. "Maguire has your bags," he said with a grin.

Jonathan reflected on his first impressions of Africa. Most striking was the fact that there was evidently little money available to provide lavish public buildings. He found, after a search, two doors opposite each other, one marked "European Type Lavatory," and the other marked "Asian Type Lavatory." Out of sheer cussedness he pushed open the door of the Asian convenience. He was slightly startled to find only a white enamelled hole in the floor and a water tap on the wall. Comfortably seated in the European type it occurred to him that he had read somewhere that Asian ritual in these matters differed, and it was therefore probably not a question of hidebound colour prejudice.

Emerging, he noticed on his way back to the Reception that among the African staff there were a good many Indians about. He recalled Hullyer saying in Khartoum that an old Masai elder once told him. "We are like zebra. Skins black and white. Indian fellow is dust all over skins."

So I asked him "What of Arab?" But he knew nothing of them. What is odd is that the Arabs ran the slave trade. "Only a hundred years ago we Europeans took a hand in it. That brought Christian missionaries. Fifty years ago, we brought the Indians here to build the railways. Now they are mainly shopkeepers. You have to accept that, but some folks are jealous of them."

Eventually the official returned and with a flourish of stamps, released him. On his way to the restaurant he noticed an acrid, slightly burnt, strongly animal smell wafting through the windows along the corridor.

"Does Africa always smell like the smell in the corridor?" he asked. Tim looked puzzled. "Oh, the cats. Look." Jonathan looked. In the square of beaten earth formed by the buildings, dozens of cats and kittens roamed or dozed in the shade under the raised floors. "I'm glad it's not typical."

"Smells you will get accustomed to, like officials." Jonathan thought the remark a little acid for Tim's placid nature. "Had a good safari?"

"Interesting, if a trifle long. I'm a Doctor Barnado's case. I trust you have a big bed in a cool, airy room with apple-green walls?"

Tim turned to look at him. "We have a nice stuffy tent not too far from the vehicle repair lines. Another breakfast?" Jonathan nodded. "Please." Tim led the way to the airport cafeteria.

"Mayai na Bacon-i moja," he said to the "boy," who looked at least fifty.

" 'My-eye na bacony moja?' " What sort of language is that? Not this Ki-Swahili stuff in my E.U.P. book."

"Forget that. It's Ki-Settla, old boy. Up-country as opposed to the pukka coastal stuff, which is corrupt Arabic anyway. It's easy, you'll learn. Tell me about the Auld Country, about Joanna. How is everybody?"

Where to begin? He hadn't see Tim for years, since they were kids on neighbouring farms. Tim, as a regular, had been briefly in Korea during 1950, where he had been mentioned in despatches and in Malaya in 1951-1952, where he won the Military Cross. The purple and white ribbon, started a row on his chest that continued with the General Service ribbon and the two blue and white ribbons one from a grateful United Nations for Korea. Now in 1954 he had been in Kenya for only six months, and had been 'mentioned' again for doing something which Jonathan considered, if it had been anyone else, would have been either thought crazy or deserving a VC. Perhaps such things were expected from Tim. The only fear he had in him was of hurting somebody's feelings, or boring them.

"Julia sends love. She will qualify, as you know, in eighteen months."

She was studying medicine at University College, Dublin. If she had any sense she would then marry Tim. But they were not engaged because Tim didn't want to tie her while he was abroad for so long. She agreed because she knew she would always want him whatever happened and thought it unfair to expect a young officer to be an angel for three years in foreign parts.

He gave the news about their families; farming in County Meath where they had both met as boys, and about his summer and winter in the ranks and at OCTU. Tim wanted to know about how he had managed to get through the selection course into the Commando. What Joanna had thought of his going to Africa for national service, and what he was going to do afterwards?

"Joanna and Africa,? You might well ask. She said it is obviously more interesting to serve in Africa than somewhere like England." He left out the bit where she said, "particularly when you happen to know Tim, and he's the ruddy adjutant, and got you recommended for the regiment."

"She wasn't very enthusiastic about it. Father had muttered something about settlers being tax-dodgers. Almost everybody else told me stories about all the potty people they knew who lived there; remittance men, ex-gaolbirds and eccentrics all."

"Huh. Most of them will turn out either to be dead, gone somewhere else, or actually living in Rhodesia or South Africa."

"Joanna was scornful about the whole thing. 'Out-dated imperialism,' she said. And 'About time Africans got their freedom.' But even *her* geography was faulty. She's a funny mixture. So left wing and so…"

"So posh." Tim grunted. "Likes supporting underdogs, she does."

"She's a one off," Jonathan admitted.

When they had first met at Oxford, she stood out amongst all the clever and the plain girls. She was a fey, wild creature brought up in a dozen countries by her widower father. She had been reacting partly against his suave, slightly bored character. She was moulded in the blasé world of international art-dealers. At first all blue jeans and sloppy joes, she had matured surprisingly fast. She achieved a balance that Jonathan sometimes found infuriating, which he tried occasionally to undermine in self-defence. She taunted him about being feckless and irresponsible, enjoying all that undergraduate nonsense. When he was called up and slogging though the Officer Cadet School she said "You're just a soldier, with no worries, mate. I am living an adult city life. I am growing," she added, "seriouser and seriouser."

They fought about the future of Africa. He read it up.

"You can't lump Africans all together. Apartheid, Afrikaners and the Dutch Reformed Church, being South African, have nothing to do with East Africa," he told her. She, in common with most people he met, was vague about the Federation and the three High Commission Territories of Kenya, Tanganyika and Uganda. The same solutions would not suit them all, he argued.

They talked too about what he would do when he returned. "I read Law," he said, "so I guess I'll be a boring old lawyer."

When he appeared in the uniform of his new regiment for the first time, she stared at the badges and said, "What the hell is this Irish Commando? I never heard of it."

"It's like the Lovat Scouts, or the Irish Fusiliers. Only smaller. The Wild Geese. Do you know about them?"

"No."

"1791. Patrick Sarsfield, fighting for the Catholic King of England, James the Second, surrendered to English troops at Limerick. They let him go providing he took his 7,000 men with him, sidearms, flags and drums only. Being Roman Catholics they went to fight for Spain, France, Austria mostly. So, there are Fitzpatricks in Madrid, Paris, Vienna, to this day. Those left behind, for lack of space on the first ships were sent away in crates marked 'Wild Geese.' "

"Relevance?"

"Many wars later it occurs to the British that they have valuable assets in the shape of Scots and Irish cannon fodder. But now they need to make sure they are all on their side. So they put us together. Scots in the Argylls, the Inniskillings and the Black Watch. Us in this lot. In the Boer War they got troops from Australia and Canada. But the Irish fought with the Boers. Bet you didn't know that?"

They met a *Times* reporter one day, just back from Africa, who told them that he had been amazed at the huge differences, even in the natives, in each country. "Kenya," he said, "is like Ireland and the West Indies, poor and happy-go-lucky, without the coal, iron, copper and factories of the Rhodesian towns."

"There is," he told them, "a middle-class, nouveau-riche snobbery, and white workers frightened of losing their jobs to natives, but no more so than in Birmingham. In Kenya, there is nothing much except farming and Indian traders, but on the coast the natives are strongly influenced by the Arabs, originally from Zanzibar, and before that from Oman."

The reporter went on, "Don't think the natives there resemble the West Indians or say, American Negro servicemen, because they don't, no more than we resemble Laplanders. In

Kenya they are mainly Bantu. But the Kikuyu, who are behind Mau-Mau, are very different from, say Nigerians. The Nigerian who has been in contact with white men for two hundred years, is also very different from an English-speaking, educated Jamaican whose forebears left West Africa two hundred years ago. I don't envy you your job with the Mau-Mau, Jonathan. When I left Nairobi they had just moved thirty thousand of them out of town. Not all active members maybe, but all Kikuyu. And, not one speaks English."

Jonathan sensed a quick stab of excitement, and wondered if it was fear.

"So that's how home is. And Joanna, and Julia," Jonathan said. When he left, the February Aldershot sky had been a cold grey strip between the tall buildings, a sky thicker than the old rain-worn sheets of lead on Home Barn where he and Tim had climbed as boys.

Trooper Maguire forced the Land Rover through the civilian cars to the pile of baggage, guarded by a policeman. He leapt out and flashed a razor-sharp salute. "Bloody hell," Tim said. "Is that all yours? Oh. This is Marty Maguire. Mr Fitzpatrick." Another fierce salute and a growl ending in "Sorr."

"Well you said to bring shotguns and fly rods. And Julia sent your polo sticks, and some other kit of yours."

"How are things here?" Jonathan asked, as they clambered in. "Bad?"

"They've settled down now. The towns and reserves are fairly clear and we go patrolling while the police deal with local upsets; the gangs that are left are in the forests. Now it's cattle raiding mostly. The Kikuyu are fed up with it. Mau-Mau killed about five thousand of their own people and now they have mostly done a cleansing ceremony to clear them of the Mau-Mau oath they took. The other tribes didn't join it of course, because they knew that the Kikuyu would just pinch their land."

"But why did it start? Are the settlers such a gin-sodden, bullying lot?"

"I think they were just careless. They aren't a bad crowd. A bit old-fashioned, of course, but they didn't have the police or enough supervision in the reserves. If anyone is to blame, it's the administration for not spending enough money on schools, village facilities and police. Jomo Kenyatta organised it as a Free Kikuyu Church and his trade union directs it. They should never have let him back here. He became a communist at the London School of Economics, did a two-year postgraduate course in agitation in Moscow. It was quite simple. He told the Kikuyu that Christianity was all very well but one wife was nonsense. The women do all the work, literally. So they joined his Free Church, and the witch doctors and Labour Union boys went around oath giving and there you were. They haven't published the various grades of oath because five out of seven include, among other delightful obscenities, cannibalism, bestiality, forced homosexual acts and public fornication. The idea is to cut off gang members from Christianity and all tribal traditions as well. He's a bright spark, Kenyatta, a genius at it. And after all that high cock-a-lorum he got seven years. But about 1960 he'll be out for another try."

"Ours not to wonder why."

"Don't say that in the Mess, old chap. Might think you were scared." He followed that with a sharp dig in the ribs and a frown.

"We know it isn't exactly a glorious war dammit. But it's a glorious country, there's plenty of shooting, and horses are given away. Our national servicemen on patrol can be heard a mile away, and they're no trackers. They're more scared of rhino than of the Micks. That's Mau-Mau, not Irishmen. But thank God, there are no hostile aircraft or artillery, no mines. Ambushes, yes. You'll see, when we get out of this horrible town."

"Can't wait to see the countryside." A lorry, heavily loaded, passed them on a hill, its engine roaring.

Then Tim dug him in the ribs again. "Look at me," he whispered so that the driver could not hear. "Don't be so bloody airy-fairy," he snarled. "If you are going to survive here you have to get serious. You get me?" In a loud voice he said to Maguire," Foot down, man. We're dawdling."

Shocked by the harsh words, Jonathan gulped and just nodded.

"Now listen," Tim said. "Today's wednesday. so we have

the weekend to settle you. I need you on patrol as soon as possible. Two national service officers have just left. Two regulars got killed in a car crash. I'm short handed. There is no mess night until next friday, so I'll introduce you around quickly to the key people. You heard about the C.O?"

Jonathan nodded.

"Bloody tragedy that, but the second-in command is a good hard man. Cormac O'Riordan. He's a bit gloomy, as you tend to be after fifteen years of it. And he was due for staff college next month. He was a Chindit, then SAS. I'll explain more later, before you meet him. And, by the way. Don't talk politics with anyone."

CHAPTER FOUR

NAIROBI 1953

"War is nothing but a continuation of politics,
with an admixture of other means."

Karl Von Clausewitz
1780-1831

The midday sun was fierce outside but the air had a thin, strained quality from the altitude, and its alpine dryness made the temperature reasonable in the shade.

They had driven through the half-empty African town where the shanties had been burnt and only the Municipal Council houses remained, heavily fenced with barbed wire. "Keeps the Mau-Mau from getting at the Kikuyu who remain," Tim explained.

The bazaar area, looked like any film-set of a Far Eastern bazaar except that there was a sickly-sweet smell of spices and cheap incense on the warm air. All the shopkeepers were Indian, and Africans stood about in tattered shorts and singlets, or sat outside working sewing machines. They were making shirts and shorts mostly, but Tim said they never seemed to wear anything new, except on Sunday.

"Why do the Mau-Mau come into town?"

"Food and to raise money. Steal guns if possible."

Strains of high pitched, discordant Asiatic music and shrilling Arabic came from the radios inside the shops. They passed a garishly painted petrol station on a triangular island, its walls splashed with red mud to a height of two feet, into another area of Indian shops. This time they catered for Indians and some for Europeans. The names were all Verjee, Shah and numerous Patels.

"The Patels seem to be a great family for trading," Jonathan commented.

"It's a tribe. Gujerati from Bombay. Thousands of them. They can starve in India, and few countries will let them in. The Brits brought 'em here to build the bloody railways. Now they come here with their British passports and say they have relations here. I suppose it's tricky to disprove it. But make no mistake, the Sikhs, Bengalis, Rajputs make good soldiers. Not afraid of your cold steel. Lot of them here with the police. Horrible job, but they do it well and in remote places. The Gujeratis, are not soldiers, but tradesmen."

"They didn't seem too anxious to have me. The Immigration, I mean."

"Oh no, you have to have a job as a European."

"But I could get a job here."

"No, you might not. Then you'd be an embarrassment. And you can't do a job, say on a farm, that an African could do."

Jonathan gave up, and gazed at the buildings. The old corrugated iron-roofed, verandah-fronted wooden buildings on stilts were sandwiched in between square concrete blocks. Here and there among the unused building sites and clumps of trees were new, six storey office blocks, some of them in ultra-modern style, with all glass fronts, coloured tiles and ground floors cantilevered out over the pavement. The biggest block was where the High Commission was. "The Administration," Tim explained, "administer the services that are common to the three territories. Uganda and Tanganyika share railways, roads and organisations like Desert Locust Control with Kenya. The result, oddly enough, is that the railways were nationalised, and the Government could control not only roads and railways but all Crown land as well. It's called the colonial system, they tell me."

"No wonder the Kikuyu got fed up," Jonathan said. Tim said nothing.

Out of the commercial area there was a more spacious

effect of tree-lined avenues and statues, all peculiarly British-looking. "You should see those jacarandas in October," Tim said. "Every tree is a cloud of dusty blue. And those coral trees bloom when there are no leaves, so you just see the orange-red blossoms."

Jonathan said, "I think I am going to enjoy the place. Not the town so much, but the trees and perhaps Africans. Nice hilly-billy atmosphere." The town did have that frontier air about it, a special alpine, African ethos of its own. Somehow the hopeful new buildings growing up amongst the oleanders, poinsettia and bougainvillaea creeper saved it from being raw, from being just an overgrown suburb, by the brightness and swift, prolific vitality of the old, savage beauty of Africa itself. Anyway, it didn't fit any of the clichés about boom towns and it didn't look nouveau riche or Americanised like the photographs or newsreels he had seen of South African and Rhodesian towns.

"Don't look too bad at all!" Jonathan said.

"Could be a lot worse. There's a good crowd here, with guts, and it's a damned shame this happened to them. I spent my leave last month down south and there they're all self-conscious about the blacks, but here there's a slap-happy sort of attitude, and none of that nonsense about separate cinemas and separate counters in the post office and the bank."

As they went slowly along the street there was the oddest mixture of people Jonathan had ever seen. There were men in suits and men in khaki shorts and bush jackets, mingled with Sikhs in turbans and women in saris and bright frocks. Among them were Africans in every stage of clothing from office suits and uniforms to ragged, patched shorts and vests, with a few, obviously from the bush, with a mud-coloured blanket and very little else. His eye was caught by a pretty young white woman who carried one child in her arms and was dragging another along with her free hand. Around her waist was a thin leather belt with a tiny holster dangling from it, looking strangely out of place against her flowered frock.

"Don't they use prams here?" he said, pointing. Tim had stopped the Land Rover and was watching a native policeman who, standing on a box at a crossroads, was waving his arms like a bookie's runner at a race meeting.

"Dunno. I suppose they come into town in a car and they can't leave the kids at home. You couldn't get a pram into a small Ford." Jonathan lost interest as he watched a very fat African woman in a tawdry skirt and huge high-heeled shoes waddle past, with her enormous buttocks swinging from side to side. Behind her came an old Indian with bow legs wound around in two sagging triangles with swathes of what looked like muslin. "What on earth is that?" he asked.

"What? Oh, that's a dhoti. Some peculiar Hindi sect who don't think it's nice to wear trousers. Some of the women wear long silk trousers under their skirts. Indians are like anyone else, they all want to be different."

"Cor," Jonathan said. "All part of life's rich pattern." Tim frowned, and he realised he was being too flip.

As they went around a traffic island there was a statue Jonathan noticed, perched in the middle, surrounded by a ring of flowering shrubs. It was a bronze statue of a sharp nosed man in slacks and shirt, who sat with his knees crossed negligently, an expression of fierce aggressiveness on his compact face. "Who is that?"

"Delamere. Pioneer peer chappie who started farming the place. They tell me he kept Whitehall in order in his day, but nowadays the Colonial Office have got themselves dug in, in style." Tim waved towards the new plain fronted buildings of the Administration. "They divide their time, I'm told, between arguing with the natives and arguing with the settlers."

Maguire swung around another traffic island with a sub-tropical rockery built on it, and they were on a wide double carriageway, edged with a boxed thorn hedge and handsomely flanked by jacarandas. In the centre grass strip, bougainvillaea proliferated to left and right of a low hedge, spilling lavishly onto the turf in every shade of red from a bright crimson to a deep orchidaceous purple. "I have a feeling that the Governor might be fond of flowers," Jonathan said, and Tim chuckling replied, "Well it's a tarmac road after all, even if it isn't very even, so it's worth setting out prettily."

"I like it." Jonathan said, as they swung off the tarmac and started the climb up to the camp.

"Shit awful roads," Tim said. But the tarmac went all the way out to the camp, although Jonathan saw what he meant in that most of the roads leading off the main one were just compacted earth.

"Fortunately," Tim explained, "there's plenty of murram about, which forms a sort of ironstone after it's rained on. Where it doesn't occur naturally they spread it, with rocks, over the soft stuff. Wait till you see blackcotton soil. Boy, it's just like trying to drive on black, spongy treacle. The snag with murram is, it corrugates and shakes hell out of your suspension, and sharp stones crop out and rip the tyres."

The camp was like any army camp anywhere. The surroundings might have been Ireland, except for a powerful sun that already, at ten o'clock, was almost vertically overhead in a cloudless sky. Some wooden huts had supplemented the rows of tents, and a few that followed the native pattern of poles and mud with a reed thatch, except that they were square. There were watchtowers at each corner and triple barbed wire all around, with slit trenches and gun pits ten metres back from the wire.

The area had been a farm and the owner had built a big stone house, looking like a stockbroker's place in Surrey. It was now the officer's mess on one side, sergeants on the other, with kitchens built on behind. There was a wood behind it, to the rear of the camp, which was surrounded by barbed wire, and faced along the road.

The men were clad in "jungle-green" denims and a peculiarly inelegant matching waterproof hat, which could be twisted and shaped by the individual to resemble anything from a pork-pie trilby to a coon-shooters cap. Among the British troops there were a few black faces in the same uniforms who, Maguire explained, were trackers.

Tim went off to his office. As Adjutant, he had done a big favour to a new greenback.

Jonathan unpacked and donned his best khaki drill, Tim had told him to report at once to meet the acting C.O., Major Cormac O'Riordan.

"Send someone to tell me when you're ready. I want to

check your turn-out before I risk you with the boss."

Tim inspected Jonathan's turn-out, rejected his boots and yelled for his batman to come and polish them better. Trooper Maguire appeared.

"I've warned him. In camp smart. Outside it – optional. At no time, shit order."

"Are there no locals I can hire for this?" Jonathan asked.

"None. I told you, just trackers. Marty, please try to keep Mr Fitzpatrick smart at all times."

"Sorr," said Marty, in a Belfast burr. He was a wiry, whippety man, with that Ulsterman's grim expression. But he could smile. Jonathan lay on his camp bed and waited for his boots.

Tim marched him in. After very brief pleasantries, the major said, "Indoctrination course for you, me lad. Have a hard look at you. If OK after three days, allocated to a troop for patrol work in the forests." He didn't mention that he would be in front of all patrols with the tracker or trackers.

Tim had warned him.

"Cormac was in Burma with Wingate. Bit eccentric like all those Chindits. Got two DSOs."

Jonathan looked and saw a thin, wiry major with a rat trap mouth, and grizzled grey hair that resembled the stuff you used for cleaning cooking pots.

He looked as though he hadn't had a square meal for months. He spoke in short, sharp bursts and a thick Belfast accent.

"Most interesting part of indoctrination is a gruesome session with one of the Intelligence boys and one of the Chief's sons, on atrocities and the Kikuyu generally. Then there's a bod called Lerrick who lectures on patrolling, who is usually more concerned to tell you not to disturb the game than anything else. Any questions?"

"No, Sir," Jonathan zapped out. There were a million, but he knew this was not the time or place.

"What do we call you?"

"Er, Jonathan. Jon will do. Er. Sir."

"Good luck, Fitzpatrick. Dismiss."

Jon threw up his best salute, wheeled and stamped his feet in the brand new boots. He missed the patient smile, on Tim's face, mirrored in the majors'.

Outside, he asked, "Was that all right?"

"It'll do. Go and get some kip. Report to me at fourteen hundred."

"Sir!" Jon yelled, feeling slightly dizzy. He marched off to his tent. Found one that looked like it, but wasn't. Finally made it and collapsed on the truckle bed, boots and all.

Jonathan woke three hours later, laid back and listened to the cicadas. It was hot in the tent, although Maguire had lifted the flaps to let air circulate. He was going to enjoy Africa. Brought up to go shooting every week between October and March, he was accustomed to killing game. Gutting rabbits and hares, plucking pheasants and duck were things he knew instinctively. His uncle Seamus had survived the First World War he claimed, because he heard the sound of a German trench grenade, or the clink of a rifle on a water bottle, just that fraction of a second quicker. He didn't explain how he avoided the shell burst and machine guns enfilading the stumbling infantrymen. But survive he had. "Keep your eyes open, lad, and your ears," Seamus said, "and you'll be fine."

Africa was full of game and the country, he knew from reading Hemingway, was full of different conditions, from forests to open plains. He was ready for the heat and the sweat, and the wild animals. He was fit and toughened up by six months at the Officer Training Unit. The only worry was that he knew that much of the Commando had battle experience. He was going to have to stamp his authority on men ten years older who had fought in France and Germany. And maybe before that, in Italy and North Africa.

He went to the office sharp at two o'clock. The notice on the door said "Captain T.S. Collins M.C. Adjutant."

"Sit." He was report-writing. A clerk came in and removed the documents. Tim looked up. "Tea?" He banged a bell on the desk. An African in a fez came. "Leti Chai tafatali."

Jon sat, waiting. Sensing that he was not to speak first. Tim got up, went over to a couch, sat and started filling a pipe. He waved at a battered easy chair. Silence continued.

Tea arrived. After a long pause Jonathan risked a question.

"What's the game like?" Having forgotten to quiz Hullyer on that point.

"In the forest, buffalo and rhino. No snakes or lion anyway. Do not try shooting at them. Outside it you can get deer and gazelles, zebra and giraffe, but not much of anything at the higher levels. The RAF has been bombing to scatter the gangs, which I think was bloody mad myself, and it's driven the elephant away, and the buff out into the plains. We've had a couple of men gored by rhino, though."

"A nasty, unaccommodating beast, I'm told." He quoted Hullyer.

"What about social life?"

"Wild. Girls all spoilt. Shocking shortage. Tell you what though, this chap Lerrick asked me to lunch tomorrow, and I told him you were coming, so he asked you too. Now his sister really is something. Got a big tough boyfriend, of course, but wow-ee."

"Sounds good."

"But she may be out. They usually are. We'll probably just talk shop. Micks and the Administration. We can always get Tom Lerrick on to game, though. He's done a bit of hunting and game wardening in his time. Hard man. Ex-SAS with David Stirling in North Africa. He leads a pseudo Mau-Mau gang. Very dangerous thing to do."

"Wow. Sounds fierce."

"He is. You be careful."

"Don't worry, I'll be good. Mix in with the natives, that's it. Our civilising mission – a drop of culture to go with the old Gatling gun – that's me." Tim frowned and looked up sharply.

"Watch it, lad. I don't know what they'll make of an educated subaltern," he said wryly.

There was a pause. Somewhere Jon had read that soldiers should know what they were dying for. He didn't. But he was reluctant to ask.

"Why are we here?"

"Big subject. Tell you later."

"Am I going to make it here?"

"We'll see." To himself he said, 'Omigod. He's so green. Have to watch him.'

"Go and check the mess cooks know you are here for dinner. As soon as you want to, after that, go and get some kip. You'll need it. I'm short-handed this week."

As Tim lit his pipe he recalled his father telling him about the Fitzpatricks. One of them, a cavalryman in India in 1899, had stopped off in Capetown during the Boer War. A group of Irish officers had resigned en masse and joined the Boers. Of the British Empire at that time, they had had enough. Somewhere he had seen a photograph of those Irish renegades.

"Terrible hard man, that," Marty was saying to Jonathan in his tent. "Wasn't his father C.O. in the 'Skins?"

"If you mean the Inniskilling Dragoon Guards, yes. And his granddad the same in the Crimea."

"Aye," said Marty. "We make good fighters, drunk or sober."

No answer to that, Jon thought.

There was a screech outside. A bird? A hyena? Maybe a monkey. It was going to be fun finding out which was which.

CHAPTER FIVE

JEHA AND SAMSON

"Enter rumour, painted full of tongues."

Anon.

Jeha never felt at ease with Samson, the neopara, and headman on the coffee shamba. Previously he had felt a little jealous of Samson because, although he was one of the 'watu,' who worked outside, and he, Jeha, ran the house, Samson was a Christian and somehow a white man always seemed to trust a Christian more than a Mohammedan or a pagan. But now his uneasiness had more foundation, for he knew that Samson had refused to eat even the first oath, and so his son, who had been a teacher in the reserve, had disappeared, and no one knew his fate. He, Jeha, had eaten the oath, against his will, for both his sons were safe, one a policeman and one a soldier in the King's African Rifles. He had paid the tax to Mau-Mau too, after his judgement was clouded at a beer drink. Solemnly, he had sworn to kill one European when the war-horn sounded, and paid his two thousand shillings for a share in Bwana Lerrick's farm. But the war-horn had never sounded, and when Kabero, the gang-leader who he remembered as a milk delivery boy, had come that night with his gang to give more oaths, Bwana Tom had already wired in their huts and built a watchtower with a light which shone all night. So there were no more oaths, and he had confessed to his oath taking and went to the river with the others and was cleansed of it.

Now, when Samson came and leaned against the kitchen door and asked to speak with Bwana M'Kubwa, Jeha thought he detected scorn in his voice. They lived in different parts of the compound and now they had to go at night into their huts and could not sit out in the centre around a fire and talk about the old days and the price of goats and cattle. Samson, he thought, looked scornfully at him in his white kanzu and red fez, with the silver embroidered blue jacket that denoted his status. But just as he had never spoken against the Mzungu before, so Samson never spoke now against all those who had sworn. But he knew that he, Jeha, would now not be able to buy himself another wife when he went back to his village, and that he would be an old man before he saved his two thousand shillings again. The knowledge was bitter. The Kikuyu had brought a curse on themselves with the secret oaths, that were taken against the accepted custom, and it was hard to bear the scorn of other tribes. And any night the oath giver might return, with sharp pangas. (Machetes.)

Now a man could not go freely into the town to the beer halls and Indian stores. He could not walk about after dark, or even leave the compound without that nagging fear of being set upon by thugs. If a man planted mealies or sweet potatoes outside the compound wire in the accustomed places, he would not harvest them, for others would come by night and steal them. It was not safe to graze animals out of sight. Times were frightening and a man had no peace. So when Samson came with his grave face and his unpierced earlobes and dirty clothes and stood by the door, Jeha was inclined to be surly.

"Jambo," Samson said, "Habari ya kasi yaku?" How goes your work today?"

"Kasi mingi sana. There is much work," Jeha replied curtly, but he who was wont to expand on the subject of how much work there was, had not the spirit to discuss it now with Samson.

"Ay-ee. There is much work on the shamba also. I must speak with Bwana M'Kubwa." Jeha mumbled, "Yes," without enthusiasm. There was in fact extra work that day, with two extra people for lunch. Also it annoyed him that very often nowadays when he entered a room his employers stopped talking. He knew that that was because they discussed Mau-Mau, and were not quite sure how much English he understood.

Once he had said to Memsaab Kidogo, the Bwana M'Kubwa's daughter, "You know, Memsaab how much of your language I understand. I can say 'It is time for bed' and 'It is time for food', and the names of your food, but truly I know little else."

The Memsaab laughed. "What you did not hear will not hurt you, Jeha," she said in Kikuyu.

But it made his heart heavy to know that he was not trusted completely as before, for he had once been entrusted with the children, with Bwana Tom, Bwana Colin who had been killed in the Europeans' war. And with Memsaab Gillian, whose name he could never pronounce.

As he went down the corridor to the verandah where he knew his master was sitting, he thought for the thousandth time that he did not know when he took it, how serious the oath was. Jomo Kenyatta had not spoken the truth to his people, for now there was war among the Kikuyu and more killing than in the old days when the Masai came from the plains to steal cattle and wives. Kenyatta was as cunning as a leopard that would snatch a dog from out of a hut, but after all his promises and threats, nothing had happened except that thugs raided the villages, Kikuyu against Kikuyu, and there were police everywhere and many questionings. No good had come of it, only evil. And already he was feeling tired and now he could not go home to his village if he wanted to, until all the trouble was finished.

Sometimes he felt his heart in him like a stone when he thought of the place where he was born, where he had a good hut and a shamba that might now be burnt down. It was when he saw Samson, who had no trouble in his heart that, he felt he could see the place before him, the huts and the valley and the mountain. His own heart ached for the mountain where the god of the Kikuyu who was a piece of the sky, Kerinyagga, lived, making the top of the mountain white like Baraf, the cold stone that the Mzungu put in their drink.

He opened the door noisily and said, "Bwana, Samson is here to speak."

"Tell him to come round into the garden," the old man replied.

From where Tom Lerrick and his father were sitting on the back verandah of their house they could see right out over the garden and the rows of coffee trees to the hills in the distance, that blended with the clouds on the horizon. The lawn sloped down, flanked by flower beds to a small stream that flowed through an area that had once been swamp. It sloped upwards in regular, drained terraces to the coffee that covered six hundred acres and represented thirty years' work.

"I wish Jeha didn't sound so bloody miserable all the time."

"Bad conscience." Tom said.

"Mourning his lost savings more likely. I wonder what they stung him?"

"We caught one treasurer with five hundred quid on him, and he'd probably spent half that again. Will you give him a pension?"

Old Lerrick grunted. "If he behaves himself. But he'll have to cheer up a bit if he's going to stay. Depressing old bastard." He put one blackened finger into his pipe and made that face that was half a puff and half a self-deprecatory expression signifying that he was not quite satisfied with what he'd just said. Tom smiled. His father was always making concessions nowadays, in the spirit of the times, and it went a little against the grain. In his lifetime in Africa he had had a long hard struggle against the climate, the soil and falling world prices and it was only since the war that he had begun to succeed. He had seen in his own time Africans progress from savage to politician. He, who had seen cannibalism die out and revive, had also seen Africans return from Europe with degrees, from universities to which he could not afford to send his own children.

Tom had just been telling his father about an incident that had taken place in the town during the night. A fight had developed outside a hotel between some British troops and Kenya-born servicemen, during which one of the locals had been razor-slashed. Later a British soldier was found, tarred and feathered, lashed to a pillar outside the hotel. Old Lerrick could not restrain a smile, which he quickly replaced with a look of gravity. "This pommie versus bushwhacker stuff will have to stop," Tom said severely, and his father crossed one long khakitrousered leg over the other uncomfortably, looked out into the garden and mumbled, "Mmm."

Tom knew that to his father it was just a part of the old story of friction between the local colonial and the disinterested foreign whites; like Boer versus Roinek. Old Lerrick was no Afrikaner, but he had no love for those of his fellow-countrymen who came to spend a year to two in Africa, wasting their time telling him what to do, and then returning to England criticising how he had done it.

Their conversation turned to the effect the Emergency was having on Jane Lerrick. There was no doubt that Tom's mother had taken it badly. So badly that at first she despaired and gave up her ceaseless work of trying to improve living conditions among the labourers. Despite the disappearance of several of the younger men, and numerous murders in the district, the daily queue for medicines had not stopped and soon she began again to go around the compound. But a much postponed trip to Europe had been cancelled and she refused to reconsider it until things had become more normal.

Part of the trouble was that Tom's sister, Gillian, had then only just returned to Kenya from England, when the Emergency began, a little over two years before and she was not anxious to go back. But the main problem was that, since Tom went out on patrols from time to time with the police reserve, there was nobody to help run the farm. So discussion often turned towards means of persuading Mrs Lerrick to take a holiday. Tom had frequent conversations with people who had heard of a possible manager to stand in for six months.

Samson appeared at the foot of the verandah and the old man heaved himself out of his chair with a "Jambo, Samson," and, knocking out his pipe, went down the steps to talk with him. Tom left them and went to the dining room where his mother was.

"I'm working with the Irish Rangers' Commando." Tom said. "I invited Tim Collins, the adjutant, to lunch tomorrow, if that's OK. He asked to bring a friend."

"Boy or girl?" His mother asked.

"Boy. But I asked Alison too."

"Oh, good," she said, glancing up at him.

She was arranging an armful of flowers with Wambai the girl she was training, who was holding the vase steady. Tom was grateful that his mother had not become the hard-riding, hard-swearing, up-country farmer's wife, and that she did not spend most of her time in trousers. She had preserved the English graces of her upbringing, and although she had been in Africa for more than thirty years she had not lost her subtle sense of humour or her affectionate scorn for unnecessary discomforts. For she had been brought up in a capital city and still from time to time she would threaten to return to London if such and such a member of her family did not cease such and such a barbaric, colonial habit.

"Who are these two chaps, Tom?" she asked, stepping back to eye the effect of gladioli and poinsettia leaves in the white vase. "I think you'll like them, and perhaps even Dad might. One of them only arrived yesterday. I think we should be a bit more hospitable. Reduce this anti-British army guff. Anyway, this lot are Irish, mostly."

Tom watched as one hand stretched out deftly, the long tapered fingers touching a stem, gripping and moving it.

"It's just jealousy. They are professionals, just doing a job." Gillian had inherited her mother's low, soft voice that could be made to drawl so infuriatingly impishly.

"You know, Dad said they had the same effect as dropping bombs. Said they just stumble about making so much noise that it keeps the gangs on the move."

His mother looked at him and smiled. "Mzuri, Wambai," she said to the girl, who picked up the cuttings and left the room. "I expect they're just bored," she said. "Our boys are a bit thick at times and they don't understand that national servicemen just don't care. Anyway, I hope these two aren't dull. Gillian ought to meet a few more civilised people than Sammy Webb and his ilk."

"Is she going to be in for lunch tomorrow?" Tom asked.

"She didn't say. Isn't Sammy coming at the weekend?"

"Don't know," Tom said. Poor Sammy wasn't very popular. He was the tough, bushwhacker type. So far he had refused to settle down to develop a farm in the approved manner and had

had a series of jobs, mostly connected with living in the bush killing things. Having learnt to fly, he was currently in the Kenya Police Airwing.

"Did you tell Jeha about lunch? It's not fair on him to leave it to the last minute."

"No, but shall I tell him six."

"Who's the sixth?"

"Alison Lindbern."

"Sorry, I forgot you said that already. Good." There was that quick, almost shy look of pleasure from her. She was always pleased when he brought girls to the house. He had been away so much ever since he had come back after the war, she rarely saw the few girlfriends he had. Alison was approved of even though she was a newcomer, or perhaps, in his mother's eyes, because she was. Certainly he found most of Gillian's girlfriends boring and it had to be admitted that there was not much choice in Nairobi. It seemed to require more time and energy than he had to spare, to find a wife in the narrow field that existed.

"Who's Tim's friend?"

"Junior officer. Chap called Fitzpatrick, who's just arrived. I met him briefly in the guardroom today. He has your type of nose and that smoo-ooth pommie look."

There was a Lerrick tradition to call all foreign soldiers "poms." Something he had picked up from Australian troops.

"Lucky fellow. There's nothing so becoming as a delicately arched Roman nose. He might do for Gillian. I just don't trust young Webb. And Tom, don't call them poms if they are Irish."

Jeha appeared noiselessly through the open door of the dining room where they were standing.

"Ngapi Wangeni ta-kuja jumamosi?" he asked in his slightly ungrammatical Ki-Swahili. "How many guests for Saturday?"

"Six." Jane said. "Let's go to the kitchen, Jeha, so we can see what there is to eat. I think they might also stay for dinner."

CHAPTER SIX

GILLIAN

"My darling came home in the twilight,
with white snowflakes in his hair
My darling is no longer mine.
There is another there."

Inger Hagerup

Gillian Lerrick sat in front of her typewriter, staring at the little notice pinned on the wall that gave the prices of cakes to go with tea. It was noon, and she had asked for a long weekend. She had only been there an hour, but she was bored. There were lists to be typed, of tea, coffee, sugar and sisal fibre prices, but she told herself that Mr K.W. Walker, commodity broker, could go and jump out of the window. She picked up the phone, wondering, as she listened to the buzz, what he would say if she told him to do so. "I've got to go and take Mrs Dwent to a dentist. Her husband's on safari." There was a mumbling sound, so she said, "See you on Monday," and put the phone down. He'd probably meet Dwent at his club at lunch time, but what the hell.

Nairobi was crowded with farmers, contract policemen and temporary district officers, shopping, going to the bank, or just down from the reserves for a binge. She cruised around Lord Delamere's statue twice, looking for a space, forced an Indian in a shiny new Chev into the kerb and then saw a police Land Rover waiting as a car backed out of a space. But the gears on her M.G. were faster and she beat him to it.

"Manners," he snarled.

"I bet you aren't on duty, driving that thing in town," she said cheerfully and walked away as he gave his opinion of her in the flat, broad accents of northern England.

As she strode into the foyer of Torr's Hotel, two men in slick new khaki shirts and slacks with square pockets and flaps grinned at her. She looked through them and walked over to the rack where messages were left. There were offers of lifts to Tanganyika and Uganda, requests for lifts to the Congo and Rhodesia.

A note for her said, "Please collect me Nairobi West at one. Races tomorrow. O.K? Sam."

She strolled out to the lounge which was full of bare-kneed men with Padgett or Sten guns slung around them or revolvers in various styles from regulation Smith & Wesson to Colts with ivory handles slung on the thigh. They sipped coffee and exchanged news, ogling the few girls, waiting for the bars to open. It was a pity she thought, because even she could remember the days when, if you failed to recognise someone here, you went up, introduced yourself, and exchanged invitations to come and stay for a week or two. Now there were hardly any among the shiny red faces and crew cuts to whom she could put a name.

Ian Gredling saw her before she noticed him, and stood up and called her. She went over and said hello and asked after his parents. "Had a raid last week," he said, "So Ma's a bit on edge, but we caught 'em. They slashed six cows and killed three of the boys and a bibi."

"Sorry to hear it. I must go, though. See you later." Ian was all right, but he was never organised and she didn't want to have to refuse any invitations in front of his friends.

As she went out she spotted another man she knew getting out of a jeep, so she cut across the grass to her car, stepping over the low-cut Mzeiga box hedge. As she got into the car she noticed the olive green thorned leaves were free of dust, so that it must have rained. She liked the Mzeiga, with its tiny red flowers at the base of the long sharp spikes. Who was it said it was really called Christ's Thorn? Mother? Poor mother was worried about Sammy again. There was always something.

Swinging out into the traffic, forcing another Indian in a pink Pontiac to brake sharply, she remembered about the rains. Of course they weren't due for a month, until mid-March at least. It was the new corporation street cleaner she had seen for the first time last week from the balcony of the "Green Door." Wow, she must have been late – three? four a.m.? Poor Mama.

June Dwent lived in a bungalow, a new one, that wasn't quite suburbia because the road was still badly rutted and ridged with wash-outs, and the nearest shops were two miles away. No postman ever called, no laundry van, no milkman, no dustbin collector, and no one ever delivered groceries or the newspaper. The shamba boy dug a hole for the rubbish he could not burn and the house boy laundered after his fashion. The nearest hourly bus would be a mile away, so everything was collected in the car. When June wanted to go out she rang a friend. Her husband hadn't paid for his own car yet, so she wouldn't get one for some time.

Gillian let out a loud "Damn" as her car's sump scraped a stone. She was very proud of the car, although it really belonged to her brother, with its cream paint and scarlet upholstery, with zebra skin mats that Sam had given her, and a jaunty 'QUE SERA SERA' painted on both sides of the bonnet. She tootled the horn as she entered the narrow gates, noting that the garden looked bare and forlorn, with a few parched looking frangipani and withered bushes. She had always imagined June as living on a farm, but she had always got what she wanted, and now apparently this husband of hers, with his six months leave in England every four years, was what she wanted. June said he was awfully clever and all she could say was that an official like that ought to be, because they were a feeble bunch in her opinion.

The walls were rough stone and a creeper was sneaking up near the door already. A wild clump of gladioli flourished outside the kitchen window, nourished by water from the open drain. It looked almost as bad as England, she thought, all prissy and artificial and cramped. There wasn't even a verandah on these modern bungalows, built by Asian contractors, and the rain scuffed up the red murram soil, staining the steps and the bottom of the walls. So that even when new, they had a tatty, dingy look, like the frayed hem of a long dress in the sharp light of morning.

Marriage seemed to Gillian something of a tremendous, final importance, but June seemed to regard it as a huge joke. She often wondered if Henry Dwent knew about all those men she used to go out with. There was that grim Swede, Lars something, and a couple of white hunters, in whose house she had practically lived. Even "Boy" Hummel, who must be nearly sixty. Her penchant for going out with what Gillian thought of privately as unreasonably old, paunchy men was inexplicable. But again, thinking of it now, perhaps it was part of the same thing as this odd marriage. She had got her way in everything but that vital question of going to school in England, and that had never come off, as her parents seemed to spend so much time fighting, that the farm never did very well. "Miaow," she said to herself as June appeared in the hall in tight pants and a man's shirt, with her hair down.

"Hello, darling," she sang out. "lovely to see you." She babbled away about never getting married, look what domestication did to a girl. But Gillian knew that behind the gush was a forceful little mind that had things all worked out, and she never listened to it. But the hard, methodical June she was aware of made the marriage seem more intriguing still.

"My dear," June was saying, "We had a mortar battle down in our little valley yesterday. A hell of a row all day. I'm sure the houseboys round here feed gangs all the time. Last week old Hetmer came home and found his place ransacked, and got so mad he emptied his gat in the air. The cops came and charged him for breaking the peace. *The peace* – I ask you. And they fined him fifty shillings."

"Silly bugger." Suburbia, Gillian reflected, Nairobi style, wasn't yet quite Cheltenham. Maybe that was what June had meant her to think. Or am I being bitchy? June skipped in front of her through a bedroom and into another.

Gillian had only been to the house once before and she looked at it critically now. The main part of the house was the usual lounge with the dining room at one end of it. Through the

French windows she could see right across the lawn and a rough patch of vlei to a tarmac road. It must be terrible, she mused, to live near a tarmac road and traffic noises. The sun blazed through the windows on to the polished floors. The contractor hadn't bothered to build wide overhanging eaves to keep the place cool. There was something bare and unfriendly about these bungalows. There was none of the friendly litter of outdoor life, the sticks and boots, hats and old coats hung about the place, no skins on the floor, no native mats and stools, no heads or horns on the walls. Even the furniture stood about on the unnaturally level floors without seeming to belong to the room or to give it anything. It didn't look natural or filled up as a result. Everything looked ready to move, to be transplanted.

June hadn't bothered much with it either. Her flat used to have a gloss to it, a shiny, modern decor with slick lines and smart bright colours. Her husband hadn't stamped anything on the place either. But then that was the puzzle: nobody knew him, so if he wasn't rich or forceful what chance would he have, long term, with June?

As she walked through the first bedroom she couldn't make out whether it was being used or not, but it looked like it was, and passing into the room where June was lying doing her nails, it looked as though that room was used too. "Do you use alternate bedrooms, dear?" Gillian asked with a grin. "More or less." June said. "This is the bridal suite really, and the other is where I go when I get bored with Henry, or where he goes if he comes home late. He hasn't yet," she added with a giggle. Then, as if she knew what Gillian was thinking. "Yes, I know, my dear. If you could just see your face. Just like my mother's. But the idea of starting a child at a time like this. It's ridiculous. Sitting at home clutching a pistol with these idiot houseboys feeding every Kyuke who appears at the door. And how many baby sitters do you know who'd be willing to mount guard over a brat while Mum and Dad go to the movies? Besides, Henry's due for leave in under a year." She returned to her nail-painting with concentration, leaving Gillian to her thoughts.

Yes of course, six months in England, and then one day Henry might be left a house in England. Not all government servants were penniless. The English regarded that sort of career as almost a duty, before they went back to England to retire. Did that explain June's choice, this house, this way of life?

"The boys," June was saying. "You've still got some Kyukes, you just don't know. We used to get the lake tribes on the farm sometimes, Luos, but they were intelligentsia compared with this lot. The so-called mpishi uses half a pound of fat to fry an egg and as often as not they forget to heat the plates. And the shamba boy. I told the little brute to dig a new pit last week and on Friday I found him asleep in a hole you couldn't have hidden a pig in."

Boys, cars and babies. Gillian's mother said, were the only things that Nairobi housewives ever did talk about. She examined June's face, half expecting to see that marriage had affected her in some other way. But the face still had that tautness despite the plump cheeks. The mouth seemed to open on springs, the right upper lip drawing back a fraction more than the left when she laughed. Her skin was good, as it tended to be in the Highlands despite the dryness, as long as you never washed it, of course. Kleenex and skinfood, no matter how young you might be, unless you had a very oily skin, in which case you'd be as dark as an Indian. Her eyes had always moved quickly in flashes, but you couldn't expect that to change either. Finishing her nails, she moved her tongue from where she had put it, the tip pushed out between her pursed lips.

"Going anywhere tonight?" she asked.

"Don't know. I'm collecting Sam at one at Nairobi West. He's flying down from Nyeri."

"Well we're theatreing with one of Henry's high-ups. Honestly, they do treat each other like a lot of old women. I mean, what farm manager takes the shamba boss out? Do these subalterns take their senior officers out? These Admin boys go for it in a big way. Still we can always leave 'em later and go to the Green Door or the Travellers. I hear someone's opening another, Golden Horn or something."

"Where? That place where the Greek ran off with the funds last year?"

"Where the '300' was. Greeks run off with the funds every

year, dear. Don't forget you've only been back a year. Still, it does make a change. The old Croc's been bust three times and it never moves, which is a bore." Blowing on her fingers, she bustled out to the living room. "Kahawa tiari?" she yelled, and a voice answered in a deep bass tone from the kitchen, "Ndio, Memsaab," yes, coffee was ready. An untidy, fat tribesman brought in a tray, baring his brilliant white teeth at Gillian. "Jambo, Memsaab," he mouthed ponderously, and when she responded the shambling, awkward figure, pathetically anxious to please, said "Ndio" again, for no reason at all. "Have you every wondered," June asked briskly, "Why it is that if you stub your foot on a chair or drop something, these bush natives always say 'Sorry,' in English, as though they had caused the accident?"

Gillian said she never had wondered. She thought it was just their eagerness not to hear the sharp tone of anger in the voice, the note that a dog cringed at, when the words meant nothing to it. "Well," June said, "since having this lot around I have thought about it and the only reason I can think of is that the average English Memsaab out here nowadays is so damn bad-tempered. Not the Kenya born, mind you, the others – that if a Native apologises to a mistake they've made, they'll accept it to soothe their ruffled dignity. How the hell else can they have all learnt to say it in English? No one says sorry to them. It's understood that they were either in the way or they dropped whatever it was through their own fault."

"What's the Swahili for 'Sorry'?" Gillian asked thoughtfully.

"You might well ask what's the word for atom bomb or psychology or faith, hope or charity," June said, pouring the coffee.

"Oh, it's not as bad as that, you know. We failed to educate them, that's all," she said to herself. She's anti-bwana and anti-Munt, as she would call it, both at the same time. Marriage was supposed to make you sweet-tempered, wasn't it? To herself she said. "It's like the old story about thank-you in Swahili. You never hear it. That's our fault because we never say 'tafatali,' and they never do because they never hear us say it."

"Sammy had a good story about a boy who said 'Tafatali'

once," June mused. Gillian thought all right, touché, but I can't blame Sammy just at the moment when he's lost four of his squadron flying into hillsides in cloud, dropping food to units chasing demented Kikuyu around Mount Kenya. But even he doesn't call them Munts. Kyukes are "those black bastards," and the others he's rather fond of in his way. "Yes," Gillian said quietly, "I remember."

We haven't discussed cars yet anyway, Gillian thought. She wondered what it had been that had attracted her to June. It must have been just that June, being a few years older, had represented sophistication. But she had never been to Europe, and since Gillian had returned, somehow June's sophistication had become very imperfect, so that at times, like now, Gillian felt sorry for her.

The thought remained throughout the morning as they trailed around the crowded Indian shops in the town centre. They were such pitiful shops in comparison with the Oxford Street that June would see very soon. Gillian tried not to sound too condescending when asked for her opinion on a purchase. They met quite a few people they both knew, and June waved gaily to the men Gillian recognised as her ex-boyfriends, making cutting comments on them sotto voce. Just before noon, Gillian dropped her at Torr's to meet her husband and thoughtfully hooted her way through the traffic to Wilson airfield.

Poor Sammy, she thought as she wrenched her car round a roundabout, listening with pleasure to the satisfying tyre squeal. After this morning, she told herself, I'm not as sold on this marriage thing as I thought. Not, of course, that Sammy was either. This phoney war of theirs tended to make the boyos feel they were more entitled to a little mixed and unlicensed doubling. Well, she had seen enough of that in London, and she wasn't going to get into the sort of tangle young Lalage, Sammy's sister, had got herself into at the ripe old age of twenty two. "No," she murmured as the needle crept past seventy into the eighties, "Momma says no. Not now, anyway."

She parked in a swirl of red dust behind the hangars and walked through the wooden customs shed and waiting room to the bar. Ignoring the whistles of bored maintenance men she went out onto the verandah. Sammy was late, and she stood with her back to the sun, looking out over the strip, past the control tower to the Game Park beyond. Over the fence was nothing but that park, the enormous emptiness of Masailand and all the endless, aching distance down to the steaming green coast. She sighed and turned, shading her eyes, searching the sky to her right. And after a few minutes there he was in the blue Piper Cub, losing height over the dam. She watched the tiny plane bank, to see the green light in the control tower, circle and swoop down on to the strip. He taxied right over, switched off and clambered out as a couple of bare-legged Africans ambled over to him and "Jambo'ed" profusely before pushing the plane away.

She watched with a smile as he strode over. His uniform was just the strip of blue tape on the shoulders of his shirt, and even then, but for the wings in gold wire pinned on his pocket, he might have been any young farmer down on a quick trip for tractor spares.

"How's the Memsaab?" he said as he took her hands. His face was very burnt with the long hours patrolling with the sun striking straight through the aircraft's windscreen. "Memsaab's very well," she said determinedly. Poor Sammy. One day she would probably be a disappointment to him.

"Come on," he said, hurrying through the waiting-rooms, "I'm as dry as a stick, man, let's get into that Long Bar quick."

"And how was your long week dropping hand grenades on the poor Micks?" she asked as they raced towards Nairobi. "Didn't see a one," he answered, "Ruddy food drops to lost poms, that's all. Tell you something, though, that brother of yours is right about the buffs. They're being driven out of the forests by those R.A.F. types' bangs. When they've bred up in the plains they're going to play hell with the maize around Nyeri."

"Ever known Tom to be wrong about game?" she asked with a sweet smile. Her father said that hunters were as temperamental about each other as ballerinas and Sammy's expression tickled her as he grunted.

The Long Bar of Torr's was as packed as usual with farmers

and their managers, young temporary district officers and combat police. Gillian was one of the few women in the place and she always moved Sammy on as soon as he had got the news from his cronies. "Got anything up your way?" was the question, and the answers were a few cattle slashed and maimed, a few villagers bodies found in the bush, a cache of home-made guns found here, and a handful of grimy gangsters with unkempt hair caught, there. The pattern was the same now, with a total of two dozen Europeans and a dozen Asians murdered since the thing began and now the monotonous senseless killing of thousands of Kikuyu, by Kikuyu. For their part, the security forces had lost some twenty men in firefights and accidents. So far, three Police Airwing pilots.

"Where are we going tonight?" Gillian asked when she had dragged Sammy out to the dining room. All she meant was, were they going to one of the three or four eating places or hotels alone, or was there a party somewhere, or was Sammy broke, in which case it meant food at home? If the Emergency had damped down normal social life, it had certainly accelerated an almost war-time fever of young men in pursuit of relief from the boredom of isolated outposts, and the tension of this war where your prisoners were murderers and guerrillas forced to swear to kill any white man they could.

"Said I might go up to your place for a shauri with Tom," he mumbled laconically. "I've got a shilling or two for later," she told him with a slow sideways smile, but he didn't respond. "Well, we ain't staying there all night, Webb my lad," she added as she began her melon.

CHAPTER SEVEN

SHAMBA

"The naked earth is warm with Spring,
And with green grass and bursting trees
Leans to the sun's gaze glorying,
And quivers in the sunny breeze."

Julian Grenfell
"Into battle."

Jonathan spent his Thursday morning being administered, meeting the RSM and a succession of other faces. He tried to memorise the key ones. In between he gazed around him, never ceasing to think how really it was just like any summer's day in Europe without the rain. Green hills softly curving to the horizon. He could understand now the story of the film chief who after taking a five minute look at Kenya told his camera crew to "Get us some place else where it looks like Africa."

He would lead Red Troop, he was told. He met the lieutenant in charge of Blue Troop, a gawky Dublin man, Seamus O'Malley. He kept looking at Jonathan shyly. He was a recent arrival, a regular with two years of Sandhurst behind him. He seemed rather nervous and bumped into Jonathan in the stores, where they were drawing weapons, in the motor pool, and then in the horse lines.

He walked around the lines and then sat with the sergeants and corporals to get to know them. The Commando, he knew, judged young officers by the reports these men made after any kind of action. Good idea to get to know their quirks in advance.

He was taken to the stores to meet the quartermaster, draw

more kit and listen to the gossip there. The atmosphere was cheerful. Kenya was a cushy place by the standards of Korea or Malaya. The Mau-Mau were nasty, he was told, but they didn't have much weaponry, and, as Maguire put it, "They're crap at ambushing."

He met more people and read accounts of recent fighting. Major the Lord Wavell, son of the famous general, had just been killed in a minor skirmish, but otherwise casualties were low. Accidents seemed to have claimed half the military casualties. The farmers in remote locations had suffered almost as badly as the Kikuyu villagers who had refused the Mau-Mau oathings. Many of the gangs had been broken up. Prisoners were being sent down to the coast near Mombasa. There would be a long period of re-education, so the reports from the Colonial Office said.

The day went by in picking up the do's and don'ts. RSM Taggart explained tersely. "This Commando's not keen on square bashing. Spit and polish is for weapons. Bullshit baffles brains. We try to teach the new lads fieldcraft, weapons handling. Bit of bush cunning. Marching raw lads about doesn't teach them teamwork. No place here for polished brass bits. Sunlight hits 'em. Enemy sees you first. No good. Our men must be alert and keen. Not polished all over. We mix the old hands in with the national service blokes, so they can learn how to stay alive. Lucky for us, most Mau-Mau lousy shots. But we cannot afford more casualties."

The RSM's craggy Highland face looked fierce. Of course he had to keep his distance. Both from young officers, and from the men. It must be a worry for him wondering if this new sprog officer was a liability or a fast learner.

Jonathan took his troop to the ranges to practice snap shooting. He got MacNamara to throw a loaded Bren gun at him. Grabbing it, he loosed off half a magazine from the hip, blowing the centre out of the target. That showed them that he could handle weapons. Next he had to show them that he could handle men.

At lunchtime he nearly burnt his hand on the paintwork of Tim's car, and he had to find a newspaper to insulate his shorts before he could bear to sit on the seat. "Can't they knock you up a shanty to keep this in?" he asked indignantly.

"Too busy building 'em for the horses," Tim replied. "We acquire most of the unwanted polo ponies in the colony. You'll see. Never admire a hack or you'll find yourself owning it. This Lerrick lass, by the way, rides across the coffee there at the back of the camp occasionally. If only the girls were as plentiful as the horses. Let's go."

After a few minutes they turned onto a dirt road and before Tim accelerated, Jonathan felt the hammering bumps through the wheels. Hullyer had told him what to expect of corrugated murram roads. They drove through an area of neatly cultivated coffee, the fields unfenced and interspersed with planted windbreaks of wattle trees and blue gums.

"The Lerrick's place is surrounded by reserve now," Tim told him, and the road started to twist and the terrain on either side altered to patches grazed by goats and sheep-sized cattle, with straggling plantations of mealie and banana. There were small deep valleys and the slopes were roughly ridged along the contours. Here and there washaways scored the lower slopes where there were obviously no storm drains amongst the tilled patches. On the ridge backs the bare bones of the earth were showing through, a rusty red under the brilliant sky.

Then suddenly the slopes were covered thickly with neat rows of vivid green coffee and at a crossroads a wooden sign with an arrow had the name 'Lerrick' painted on it. At the top of a rise Jonathan could see the thatched roof of a house protruding over a belt of trees growing on the slope. A little further along the road Tim turned into an opening in the coffee and fifty yards along it they were stopped by a gate set in a tall fence reinforced with barbed wire. An African inside the fence leant his spear against the wall of a mud hut and gave a jerky salute that set the copper ornaments in his distended ear lobes in a jangling swing. His face was patterned with greyish scars and Jonathan noticed that his nose flared from a high bridge unlike the Bantu he had seen so far, while his mouth was small and thin-lipped.

"Jambo, jambo, effendi" he said as he swung the gate open and the long sword-like knife in his belt swung against the side of the car.

"I got a phrasebook," Jonathan said "Mostly stuff like 'My postillion has been struck by lightning' and stuff. Jambo is hello, isn't it?"

"Yep. Sort of greeting. 'Effendi' is military 'Sir.' 'Bwana' is civilian. That poor chap Seamus O'Malley thought that 'Jambo, bwana' meant "Good morning," and he went round camp, his first few days, saying 'Jambo bwana,' to every cook and bottlewasher he met. His nickname now is 'Jambo.'"

The Lerrick house was in fact a large, rambling bungalow. It looked as though it had grown in stages at different times, as it had. The originally open veranda that ran right round it under the wide overhanging reed thatch was now framed and wired in. A wired-in corridor running to a smaller building to one side. Although Jonathan knew that it could only have been there for a generation, the house fitted in with the pattern of the country, not looking like those in the town, as though they had been transplanted. The garden did not riot with exotic growths, but the grass was a luxuriant green and old, blackened cedars threw pools of shade that gave an English air to the unfamiliar plants. Nandi flame trees held out their brick-orange flames on leafless branches and just at the side of the house the bougainvillaea swarmed forty feet up over a towering cascade of tall bushes. Jonathan identified jacaranda with the last of its turquoise-blue powdering of blossom clinging to it, a clump of eucalyptus and a stubby, green-grey euphorbia candelabra that looked exactly like a huge cactus.

"Wow," he said softly as he got out of the car and looked up at the pale blue creeper that hung from the roof over the gate in the wire of the verandah. Bougainvillaea poured over gables in an explosion of scarlet, purples, pinks. It wasn't the Africa he had expected, this lush upland country, revived by the November rains, it wasn't the humid, sweltering atmosphere he had imagined. But this half-Europe, half-tropics that seemed filtered and strained with altitude in a manner that had something of alpine clarity in it. This was a lot better than fog and frost of an English or an Irish winter. Even plodding through the forests after gangsters was better than wasting two years in dreary barracks back there. That brought a momentary flash of Joanna muffled against the February cold, her face framed in a fur collar against the frosted glass of a pub screen.

Tim introduced Jonathan to Tom Lerrick. They had only met briefly in camp. His face and arms were tanned the shade of boot leather and a scar on one forearm showed up as a greyish weal on the skin's surface. His dungaree slacks and shirt showed hard flat muscles underneath, and there was a service pistol in a leather holster on his hip. He took them through the large central room of the house to the verandah at the back of the house where his mother and father were sitting with a tall fair-haired girl who was introduced as Alison Lindbern. Jane Lerrick bore little resemblance to her son, for whereas he was over six feet, thin with dark hair and eyes, his mother was a foot shorter with fair hair, almost white and pale blue eyes in an untanned plump face.

Lerrick senior was a great bull of man, a thickset edition of his son. When he had heard all three speak, Jonathan, glancing from one to the other noticed, after the similarity in their voices, how Tom, born in the country, differed from his parents. It was intriguing. Tim had told him, "Don't try too quickly to pick out the effect of Africa on people."

Still, he couldn't help noticing that Alison, apart from her paler complexion, obviously hadn't been in the country long. He didn't know exactly how he could tell. There were inflexions in the voice and perhaps that she looked around her as he did. Then, of course, from the way she put things when she spoke.

When they went into lunch Jonathan smelt curry, and glancing at Tom's father he trembled slightly, for it would surely be what his father called "Ko-hai curry." Indian style, as hot as the devil. But when it came he found it was palatable enough, and with a galaxy of chopped onion, tomato, banana, pineapple and coconut as well as chillies to scatter over it.

Jane Lerrick talked to him of Ireland while Tim discussed the economics of coffee farming with Tom's father. The table they were sitting at, she told him, had been made by Italian prisoners of war, cabinetmakers from Milan, who were supposed to have been working on the shamba, but spent their time making furniture. When he commented on the roads she laughed and said, "Yes, as colonists the Romans seemed to have learnt the knack, but we haven't acquired it. There's a hundred miles of tarmac road" she said, "in the Rift Valley built by Italian POWs except for one strip of a few miles in the middle, where the two teams nearly met. There, you still have to slow down for five miles to twenty miles an hour to get over the regulation bumps and holes left by the Public Works Department."

In all her speech Jonathan noticed how she had a more vigorous and frank approach to life than his mother, safe in an Irish farm without the daily concern with a primitive people and all the concomitant difficulties of climate and soil. That too he had expected to a degree, but when he asked what she would do if the farm was attacked, she replied, "You mean what did I do? The first time I locked the boys I trusted in a drying shed with their families, but the second time I just let them get on with it and sewed them up in the morning."

"My husband," she told him, "came out originally just before the First World War. He started when he returned in 1920 as a tractor driver on one of the first farms. I've been in the country since 1925. I have only been to England four times since then, three times since 1945. I ran the place during the last war. When we started to make a profit for the first time since 1928," she said with a smile. "We get £400 a ton for maize nowadays, 12½ acres to the ton and we have 400 acres. But it wasn't always like that, and already labour costs us £4000 a year, believe that or not."

"We are farmers," he told her, "but I don't think my Mum knows what the labour bill or profits are." When he told her that he had two sisters she asked where they went to school and grumbled about the schools in the colony. She didn't give him time to say that Grainne was married and Fiona was a vet.

"We couldn't afford to send either Tom or his younger brother to school in England, but thank goodness we could afford it by the time Gillian was twelve. I do think that girls should know a little more than how to dose cattle and break in foals. A little chic and a whiff of perfume go better on the raw colonial scene than jeans, chaps and a polo whip. Don't you agree?" Jonathan smiled and said he did.

Tim was telling a story about an evening a week ago when

he had been in a Nairobi night club and some locals in the Kenya Regiment had been turned away because they weren't properly dressed. Apparently they had gone meekly enough and twenty minutes later several smoke bombs had come sailing over the balcony overlooking the street, followed by two thunderflashes. People who panicked and rushed down the stairs to the street found the door blocked by a Jaguar that had been lifted bodily onto the pavement.

"What did you do?" Tom asked, looking at Tim's expression closely.

"Opened the window and went on drinking." Tim replied, and Tom's father grinned and kicked his son under the table.

"Just let me catch them, that's all," Tom said severely. "I got a gang report last week which turned out to be some of those boyos shooting over the heads of some picnicking Indians."

"Oh, I'm sure you get some fairly odd reports from our lot," Tim said, "But it's refreshing for our lads to have a little enterprise without the next day's papers being full of pompous sermons on law and order."

Jane Lerrick changed the subject, asking Alison about her father, and Tim went on quizzing Bill Lerrick, leaving Tom to talk to Jonathan. "Your blokes," Tom said, "are in the habit of taking pot shots at dangerous game at long range. The buffalo and rhino in the forests, and occasionally elephant, are inedible anyway. It doesn't improve their tempers to have half a magazine of Bren-gun ammunition sticking into their hides. Later, when they charge a patrol at close range a .303 Service rifle will not stop them. The point is," Tom explained delicately, "if left alone, the animals would hear the patrol and move off. The snag is that it's one of my jobs to train patrols to move quietly. Even so game will scent them first in most types of country."

Sitting on the verandah after lunch, Jonathan looked out over the garden, over the orderly rows of coffee to the mountains beyond, that blended with the clouds on the distant horizon. The dazzling vertical sunshine seemed to fade all colours until they disappeared into a neutral haze. He blinked and told himself that less than three days ago he had been shivering in an icy street.

He closed his eyes and searched for something that was missing, and not finding it he had a sudden moment of almost panic, and opening his eyes again he felt for the first time a little dazed and lost.

Then it came to him. Amongst all the strangeness, and after all the travelling, it was really the same world in another setting. It was a summer's day on the farm at home, tea in the garden. Nothing was foreign about it all. Everything was basically familiar, the voices speaking English, the food and the furniture, the customs and the ideas.

"It's so European here," he said. "I thought it would be like the Africa you see in the cinema. All jungle and rivers." No one replied. "I mean, after moving five thousand miles, everything is the same."

"Don't be too sure, lad," Tim said.

Alison Lindbern was in the next chair to him. "Father," she explained, "is in the Legal Department of the Administration. We came here from Hong Kong." She spoke quietly and her habit of looking straight at the face of whoever spoke to her gave her an air of interestedness. Jonathan guessed that she was younger than she seemed and not as serious. Her face was slightly too angular for beauty, her jaw a little too large, but she had attractive eyes with long sandy lashes that veiled them whenever she turned towards the sunshine. "Nairobi," she said, "is a little raw after the sophistications of Hong Kong." Jonathan tried to draw her out on the subject, but she seemed rather conscious of Tom at the other side and was non-committal.

He wondered whether Jane Lerrick would have passed on her refreshing outspokenness and lack of social pretences to her daughter. Or would her years in England have put on her that patina of reserve and silly snobbery that made him cross? Again he thought of Joanna, realising with renewed force that her attraction for him lay in just that frankness and that she said what she thought, did more or less what she liked and was never for a moment boring.

But at that moment Tom went over to his father's chair and after a few words with him excused himself. Jane Lerrick too said that she had to issue rations and left Mr Lerrick talking to Tim on the far side of the verandah. Jonathan grasped the opportunity.

"Now," he said, turning his chair towards Alison, "what do you really think?" Her eyes crinkled with an amused look that surprised him, and she asked quite loudly, so that their host could certainly hear, "What sort of opinion do you want? I don't know England at all well, but I do know Hong Kong."

"Just a general picture will do. I'm utterly unbiased."

"Well, first of all, Chinese are cuter to look at than Africans. Then this isn't an international seaport and there aren't any millionaires I know of. Then Nairobi hasn't been here since 1840, and there aren't over two million people in it. I'm told there are 35,000 Europeans, three times as many Asians. Four million natives. Tiny, really. Although my father says there are now, since 1950, another 30,000 soldiers, police and civil servants. The climate is different and so is the flora and fauna." She paused and smiled. "Am I doing all right?" Jonathan, a trifle stunned by the precision of the catalogue, sucked at his empty pipe and nodded. "And you personally?"

"I like the animals in the park and I like the emptiness and the atmosphere. Pioneering, white hunters, Happy Valley and all that. For a girl it's the same thing in that there's a shortage of us in both places. I do rather miss the Navy, though," she added, with an impish grin.

"And the Mau-Mau?"

"Unless you live out on a farm you don't notice it. Much. We had burglars all the time in Kowloon and here the natives aren't as ingenious. As long as you aren't afraid of them, like the silly people who are always grumbling about how stupid natives are."

She paused on the implication and again Jonathan noticed the steadiness of her look. He was beginning to see why Tom had asked her to lunch. "And the social life?" he enquired, thinking that he may as well finish the interrogation, although he really wanted to know more about her, herself.

"Easy. Torr's isn't the Peninsula Hotel, and there are only about three more main hotels here, and the Golden Horn is

71

hardly Maxim's. It's over a fish shop." she added in explanation. "But," she went on, "I love country-come-to town atmosphere. I like the way people walk about draped with guns and stetsons amongst all the office workers. The way you get an even more weird mixture of faces and races in the streets than anywhere in the East. I'm used to the Colonial Office people and the real settlers, the ones who live here permanently, I mean, are real people you know."

"You sound as though you like the place."

"I like it better than I liked India, and I remember England as cold and wet and dark. Perhaps that isn't fair, but then you probably classify me as a bushwhacker, and have to make allowances for ignorance."

How wrong can one be, Jonathan wondered. Obviously it was going to be tricky to judge by appearance where people didn't fall into the neat categories of Ireland. Before he could continue his questions Tom came back, and asked if he and Tim would like to see the farm.

As the young soldiers stood up they reminded Bill Lerrick sharply of his second son Colin. Colin had been their age when he had last seen him and he had been just as they were, crisp and lithe in khaki drill. Colin had been killed in Burma, leading East African troops against the Japs, and it wasn't often he thought about it now. But here it was all over again, except that some of the men Colin had lead were in the forest now, and would be shooting at these two young men.

He ought to go down to the husking machine and see Samson, but his leg was hurting him more than usual. He had been listening intently to the opinion of these young people so that he felt tired, and the curry was heavy in his stomach. As they left him alone on the verandah, for the girl had been taken by Wambai to lie down for a while in his wife's room, he pondered over the state of the country. Was it really nonsense, he thought, to blame the government for this mess? Was it their fault that they hadn't put enough district officers in the reserves? And for the ten thousandth time he asked himself if they, having sold him Crown land, weren't responsible for what happened. At the back of his mind he always recollected at such times the interview he had had that day in London with the insurance company when he had asked to insure against locusts. Their price had been 40 per cent of the crop and he had refused.

Then, since he was in the City he asked them if they would invest in an irrigation scheme on the Tana river. He handed them the plan of the scheme and next day he saw two of the directors. Before they gave him their answer he told them what had happened when the Sultan of Zanzibar had asked Mackinnon, who had developed the British India Company, to develop East Africa in 1876. "Nothing," he told them. "Foreign Office refused."

They had scarcely heard of it, or Gordon's part in it, and when he had emphasised that the government now backed investment and that there was as yet no real industry, they had shown him that their confidence was minimal. Finally, when they refused the irrigation scheme and refused to put any money into the country at all he had lost his temper.

"You won't invest," he told them, "because you expect trouble. And trouble there will be simply because there isn't any work for the surplus native population. We need dams and power stations and light industries, and all we have is subsistence farming and plantations. Mackinnon had to take on the risk himself later. You could have had Tanganyika, but government dithered. Karl Peters walked in. Result, German East Africa. You refuse the risk and every day more natives drift out of the reserves to find work that isn't there."

But they had just looked at him in his odd suit, as though he was speaking in very poor taste. He had changed his insurance company, exchanging one set of hard eyes for another.

Back in Kenya, he had campaigned for a place to train mechanics, but the government had no money to spare. They had money to send a few natives to universities it seemed, but meanwhile he couldn't afford to send his children, and he went on de-carbonising his own car and overhauling his own tractors. He often wondered what it cost them now to run this so-called Emergency that was nothing, he thought, but a primitive demand for work.

Looking at his watch, he realised that his wife had been

73

issuing the rations for an hour and he would have to go down now with the pay. Poor girl, he thought, living out here with a rough old ignoramus like me. How she had taken to the two pink cheeked Rooineks. He smiled wistfully as he limped through the garden gate and out onto the soil he had sweated into for twenty-six years. And the old doubt prickled. Was it all for nothing?

Gillian trod on the brake, sending gravel spattering onto the steps of the verandah. It had been hot at the races and she had had several gins in the bar afterwards. She was feeling exalted and determined to enjoy the evening. "Go and ask Tom to borrow some clothes," she told Sammy and ran up the steps. She went to her room to wash and found Alison Lindbern sitting in front of her mirror, combing her hair. She liked Alison, perhaps because despite being quiet and what she always thought of as "ladylike", she never gossiped and never seemed discontented with anything or anybody.

They talked and laughed for a few minutes after Alison explained she had been having a siesta and had just woken up. Gillian went to look for a dress, which she thought was in a cupboard in Colin's old room. There was a very good-looking young man in khaki, sprawled asleep on the bed, the bush jacket with the badges of an Irish regiment hung on a chair. He lay on his back, his face white, slightly flushed, with smooth fair hair, almost the colour of her own. His mouth was set in an expression of peaceful amusement, which touched her oddly. His eyes were tightly closed and she found herself wondering what colour they would be. He looked rather sweet lying there. Perhaps he was drunk? No, of course he was a pom and they were too stuffy to get drunk in the afternoon. He would be one of Tom's wet young men who went blundering around the Aberdares in hob-nailed boots frightening the game, and being terrified of the snakes and the lions that never went near the mountains. And if she woke him up he'd say, "Oh dear," and "Oh my goodness, I say, I am most fraightfully sorry." She laughed aloud and opened the cupboard door noisily.

Hunting for the dress she looked over her shoulder at him. He really was appealing in a funny way. Not tough and hard and tanned like Sammy. Then she found the dress and still he was asleep and she looked at him finally from the doorway. Why on earth, she thought crossly, do we need these clumsy poms who don't speak a word of Swahili to sort out our problems? They give the mun... the Africans all the wrong ideas about Europeans too. Shut up, she told herself. Damn, I am so tired of all this Colonial versus the English stuff. Or is it that I am tired of or am I just... She shut the door gently, wondering what it was exactly that she was disturbed about.

Jonathan had heard the girl dimly when she opened the door, but he had decided not to stir. Bit embarrassing to be found conked out on somebody's bed. As soon as the door shut he got up, feeling hung over. The sun still poured through the windows, and he could hear far off noises of voices, and outside the window birds chirruping. It was the altitude, they said.

In a chair on the verandah a stocky, sunburnt man in shorts and a shirt was sitting reading a paper. He surveyed Jonathan quizzically and asked without moving, "Hullo there. Seen Tom?"

"No."

"Oh, Sam Webb." He lurched out of his chair and proffered his hand. Jonathan sat down too, and noted the wings pinned to Sam's shirt.

"Are you in the air force?," he asked, and as soon as he said it, it occurred to him that he hadn't heard if Kenya had one, but Rhodesia had.

"Kay Pee Arr Airwing," Sam said, still reading the paper.

"Sorry, what's that?" Sam's head came up. His mouth opened, then closed again.

"Police Airwing," he said, looking puzzled and running his fingers through his thick black hair, still looking at Jonathan. Jonathan looked away. Presumably this was Gillian's boyfriend, and a tough looking egg he was too. He heard somebody say that they were at the races. His face was burnt the colour of antique wood. Had he gone to the races dressed like that?

He was not to know that Sam, real name, Oliver Francis Graham Carton-Webb, although born in the colony, had no home of his own. Clothes were a problem, which didn't bother him, ever.

"You are from here?"

"Sure." Jonathan slowly extracted the information that his parents now lived in England, and his sister had a flat in Nairobi. That since he had left school he had lived in tents with all his belongings in a Ford Box-body. His father had left behind him three thousand acres of undeveloped land 200 miles from Nairobi on the eastern side of the Great Rift Valley, and it was still undeveloped with a few Marakwet and Nandi tribesmen running goats on it. Sam had only seen it twice and there was no building there. Now he lived mostly at the Kenya Police Airwing mess seventy miles north of Nairobi, at Thika near the Aberdare range.

He was twenty-five and had promised his sister Lalage to settle down to farming as soon as the Emergency was over. He doubted if he would keep this promise as he could always justifiably say that he must go on taking out wealthy Americans and Germans to hunt, in order to buy farm equipment. The life had suited him perfectly, as he was able to hunt for six months of the year and clear nearly £2000, spending the rest at the coast fishing. On £2000 you could live well. Or on trips to Somalia, Rhodesia, Portuguese East, the Congo and the Sudan, or just living in the bush somewhere shooting crocodiles for leather. Now and again he would be asked to put down vermin on a farm over-run with buffaloes, baboons, bush-pig or deer. From time to time he would stay on a farm for a month or two and help with cattle or machinery.

"It's a helluva responsibility to take on," he explained. "Crops and beasts, and a compound with a couple of hundred natives who expect to be fed and paid, can be a bloody bore." But farmer friends had been nagging him to do so and now Gillian's mother was hinting that unless he did so she would never approve of him. The trouble was that Wayne Rossiter had already written for a booking and he had told him he would be free to go on safari in six months. Wayne had been out three times before and paid him £1000 a month. Enough to buy a big four wheel drive. He had every specimen except a bongo, a situtunga and a really good rhino, and said that was all he wanted.

Tim Collins appeared on the verandah at this point.

"Tell us about this Rossiter," Tim said, as Sam helped himself to a beer.

"Always found Wayne a great buddy. Rich as hell. Never cheats. Always followed wounded game. Tips the boys handsomely for every head. Never made a fuss. Shares his Fortnum and Mason hampers with everyone. Even remembers to thank the cook."

A long speech for Sam, who relapsed into silence.

Suddenly he said to no one in particular, "Can't refuse a man like that. Specially as I've never met Wayne's new wife. Wayne says she beats all his 'exes'; Ava Gardner and Anita Ekberg, the lot. That must be something – ay?"

"Have they been here?" Tim enquired.

"Who? Ava, Anita? Oh, yes. On safari. Films, y'know. They hire folks like me to keep the wild beasts away. And kill a few for bait. And food and stuff."

"Sounds exciting." Tim said. After a silence and another beer, Sam said, "I have this farm plot Dad left here. Got to go and get some go-downs built and a cabin. Put fences up. Get the local kaffirs to put some rocks down on the track." With encouragement he sketched a plan on the back of a packet of Players Clipper. "Here's the bend in the river, and I can build a dam there. Plant tea. Dad wants two thousand acres. Get a contractor to plant a thousand to start. Takes fifteen years if the soil is O.K. Bushes should be ok then, if there isn't a drought, locusts or too many pests breaking in. My sister Lalage wants me to get on with it. Even while I'm still in the Forces. Wrote to Dad. Bullies me that girl." He laughed uproariously and swigged back his beer.

At half past six the sun had sunk behind the mountains and with it the all-pervading warmth. The air was left cool, dry and tingling, while rapidly the light failed. Tom Lerrick appeared and went off again to start the diesel generator. As Jeha and Wambai brought trays out to the verandah and the lights sputtered on, Gillian appeared on the verandah.

Tim and Jonathan stood up as they saw her approach and

Jonathan examined her with interest. Her long fair hair was sun-bleached almost white on the crown of her head and it swept her shoulders, left bare by an ice-blue cocktail dress. She was certainly arresting to look at. Her face, oval with a pointed chin, still had puppy fat clinging to the cheek-bones. She was almost as tall as her brother, taller, Jonathan noted with satisfaction, than Sam.

Tom mumbled. "This is my sister, Gillian," and they proffered hands.

"Hi," she said curtly.

"For heaven's sake go and get dressed," she told Sam. She helped herself to a drink and talked very fast and animatedly with Alison. You could see however that she was very conscious of the two subalterns to whom Tom was showing home-made Mau-Mau weapons. Jonathan caught over his shoulder such phrases as "... isn't quite the Ritz of course," and, "... but Nairobi is gay ... a helluva kilele..."

Sam re-appeared in a smart lightweight jacket that he swore he had left in the house. "Belong him me." He said. "Doesn't look it," Alison said. Gillian poured more drinks." I hear Sam told you he hoped you don't get lost in the forests."

"I did not."

"Don't you worry, me lad," Tim said firmly. "This place is a piece of cake. Ever been in a Malay jungle?" He told them a few stories about that Emergency. The look on Sam's face said that he might even like this tough pom who had survived Korea and Malaya.

Jane appeared and scrutinised her daughter carefully. An argument ensued as to whether they would stay for dinner or not. When Jeha was sent for, a lively exchange went on in Swahili, which Tom told them to ignore. They could stay if they wanted to. He had warned the cook, which Gillian never did. The invitation sounded so genuine that Jonathan could not help comparing it to the hint of annoyance or reluctance that would creep in, in similar circumstances back home, at such short notice. It was odd to see what a difference servants and no hangover from war-time rationing made to people's attitude to guests.

At eight Jeha went to tell Mr Lerrick that dinner was ready. He appeared without apology in pyjamas and dressing gown. Jonathan sat next to Gillian and she caught his look.

"Don't worry," she said loudly. "We all eat in our pyjamas as a rule," and her mother added, "But only you have lunch in yours, dear."

Back in camp, all was normal. Sentries pacing and fires still alight. Jonathan threw off his clothes, collapsed on his truckle bad and was asleep in seconds.

On Friday morning he was Orderly Officer and had to take first parade, and then walk around the troopers' dining room. "Any complaints?" he asked. No one took much notice. Then Trooper Kelly said, "I reckon that they quarry this porridge from a ruddy great hole somewhere out there, half way up Mount Kenya. 'Ave you tasted it, Sir?"

"No," Jonathan said, grabbing a spoon and scraping some into his mouth.

"Bloody delicious," he told Kelly. "Try putting salt on it. Not sugar." Somebody muttered. "Don't bother asking him anything on the grub."

The day went on with checking stores, maintaining vehicles, stripping and oiling weapons. In the afternoon they went to the firing range and had a competition, Blue against Red Troop. Blue Troop won and Seamus O'Malley was apologetic. For a Sandhurst man he was very unsure of himself.

"You shouldn't apologise, Seamus," Jonathan told him. "my lot need more practice, and probably their rifles need zeroing. Your lads are good."

Seamus followed him around like a faithful hound. "I reckon he fancies you, Sir," Flett whispered. "Shut your mouth," Jonathan hissed at him, "unless you want cookhouse fatigues for a week." Flett pretended to look scared, and was probably winking at his mates as he turned round.

He reported on the day to the adjutant's office and handed over the report book to the RSM. After tea he went for a ride. And after an early supper, he felt the travel weariness hit him. "It's the altitude," they told him. "We're over six thousand feet up here. You get used to it after a month or so."

It was 4 a.m. when they were turned out, bugles and whistles rending the night. Men stumbled out buttoning up, grabbing webbing and weapons. Marty Maguire ran in to the tent with his Webley and ammunition, Padgett sub-machine gun and spare clips, a torch, water bottle. Tim was already in his Land Rover. "Not your troop's turn, me boyo, but you need the experience." He laughed at Jonathan's grim expression.

They bumped and crashed over the rutted murram roads as Tim explained breathlessly in between the bigger bumps, "Greenjacket patrol outnumbered by a gang out on a farm not too far away. Anyway we … the nearest. Police too …on way."

They were met by a harassed major who said, "Sitrep. There's a gang now trapped between the farmhouse itself and my men at the forest edge. We need more firepower to move in on them. Farmer and family in a cellar. Too many cattle and horses about to storm all the buildings. Farm labour also hunkered down in their buildings."

"Right," Tim snapped. "Here's the plan. We advance in two wings. I take the right hand side of the buildings. Mr Fitzpatrick here and Sergeant Mac, go left. We might meet round the back, Make damn sure not to go blue-on-blue. Got it?"

Jonathan nearly asked, then bit back the words as he remembered – killing your own by mistake.

Wishing to sound fearless, but trembling all over he barked out loudly, "Follow me. No one fire until I say, fire." Mac muttered, "Noise."

A Kenya Police wagon roared up, and ten native policemen poured out, to be told by the major to get down in a line, rifles loaded.

There were then two muffled explosions. Screaming started, followed by shots and more screams and wild yells. It was not quite dark because the farm had a series of lights on towers and on the barn roofs.

"Grenades," Mac said and pressed on, tactfully giving Jonathan an accidental push in the back. They pushed on around the left hand side, well away from the buildings and out of the light. Then it happened. Three figures leaped up and ran for it back towards the police. Jonathan spun round and pointed his Padgett, squeezing the trigger hard. Nothing happened. By the time he got the safety catch off, Mac had dropped two. "Fire!" Jonathan yelled, too late. The third man was now target practice for the police.

After a lot of shouting and a few more shots Tim could be heard yelling, "Cease firing."

The major was back with his men and bodies were being dragged out and into the light. The farmer came out and shook hands with all. A large billy of tea was produced and Mac laced theirs with rum. "That's all I ever put in my water bottle," he said.

In the dawn light there was a pile of bodies. The head count was seventeen. There were three captured gang members, now being interrogated in a barn by the police. As they drove off, Jonathan noticed a tractor with a back hoe digging at the roadside. There was a pile of what looked like old clothes heaped by it. "Whassat?" he asked. Mac didn't look up.

"Burial party," he rasped. "Drive on."

Back at the camp they were all told to fall out and parade again at noon. Jonathan felt like another swig of rum, but he hadn't any and the mess was closed. It occurred to him that there was no sign of Blue Troop. He knew damn well that Tim had contrived to throw him into the deep end. He tossed and turned on his camp bed and eventually fell into a dreamhaunted and exhausted sleep.

CHAPTER EIGHT

LALAGE

"By Saint Mary, my lady
Your Mammy and your Daddy
Brought forth a goodly baby."

Skelton

On Saturday morning they had a bit of quiet, stripping and cleaning guns and equipment. Jonathan met more of the Commando and began putting more names to faces. Half his troop he noticed were at least ten years older than himself. When dressed to go out, most of them had two or three rows of medal ribbons. He got his head down for a nap when the lads went off to play football.

Sam had called the mess and asked Tim out for drinks and dinner. They met at a restaurant called the 'Lobster Pot' at ten o'clock and moved on to various places before midnight. Life here seemed to be one endless social circus.

Jonathan leant on the glass-topped bar and admired the scene in the "Croc." His head was churning with a hangover from so much travel, noise of the band and the confusion of his recent, violent impressions. Thank God, just now there was nothing else to do because Tim was dancing with Lalage and Sam with Gillian. He had a weird feeling he had seen Lalage somewhere before. Jet black, coiffed hair and her eyes, so brilliant white against the mascara. She had smiled at him as though she too, knew him. Tom had taken Alison away separately and there was no one at the bar he wanted to talk to. This pace of life was new for him. Nights at cadet school had been dull. Polishing boots and brass.

The Lobster Pot was dim inside, with tables on different levels and a tiny dance-floor. In one corner was a fish tank and a windmill complete with flowing water, although he was not sure if the water was supposed to be part of the mill or not.

The owner, Diggie Riddell, was a strikingly good-looking woman about 35, who knew all the locals. Lalage was clearly a pal of hers. "Her dad was a top white hunter," she said.

The people had been of all ages and types. He noticed several groups of Indians and others who were Greek or Middle Eastern. There was an atmosphere of hard drinking gaiety, with African waiters gliding about almost unseen in their dark kanzus. Padding silently on their bare and horny feet, they had the air of younger children slightly embarrassed by the goings on at an older children's party. Jonathan had watched them as they grinned shyly amongst the noise and laughter, and had wondered what stories they told, back in their villages, of the strangeness of the Mzungu's habits.

After dinner they had visited two similar places in the centre of town. They were both even smaller and darker, situated on the second floors of office buildings. More dancing than eating had been in progress in both, which went by raffish, outlandish names he had forgotten, the "Something Crocodile" and the "Equatorial Something Else". In both there were considerably more men than girls, In neither did Sam pay an entrance fee for them, explaining that if they wanted him to bring his hunting clients there, they had better not ask for it.

This earned him a reproachful look from his sister, and a jab in the ribs to go with it.

"This place is the Travellers Club," Tim said. "The height of Nairobi's sophistication."

"The décor," Jonathan said, "expresses the spirit of the colony, as far as I can see."

"Shut up and order a round," was Tim's reply.

He wandered off to do it.

Under the glass bar top was a python skin that stretched right along it to the end of the room as far as he could see. Against his knees he could feel the stiff hairy texture of zebra skin stretched as tight as a drum cover. Above and between the glinting rows of bottles were carved wooden masks and bizarre clay busts of tribesmen and women. Most of them were not of the now almost familiar Bantu face, with its thick, protruding lips, low forehead and squat nose, but of more picturesque Somali, Coastal Arab and Masai. These had small, compact mouths with thin symmetrical lips, long straight noses, with slightly flared nostrils and the eyes were often cruel slits below elaborate coiffures in which wire and beads were interwoven. The Masai, whose ear lobes dangled to their shoulders, loaded with heavy ornaments and thick leather thongs embroidered with blue and white beads, also wore on their skulls a wig of caked mud and sheep's fat. Beads of the same motif adorned this, the wig being garnished with wire, which in some examples was trained to a point in the centre of the forehead, suspending a larger bead in an effective manner.

"Reminds me," he said to the barman, "of portraits of seventeenth century Venetian courtesans." The Goan barman just looked. The female figures mostly included exuberant bosoms, their necks being encircled with copper wire of different thicknesses, necklaces of teeth, horn and stones.

The Masai women wore the same strings of blue and white beads. At the back of his mind Jonathan recollected something about this being characteristic of the Nile Valley. This puzzled him. Then he remembered Hullyer saying something about the Masai language being Nilo Hamitic. Not Bantu. Of the Nile.

He prised himself off the bar and looked round at the dancers. The floor was through a palisade of eight foot spears. Beyond it there was a roof garden, divided from the floor by more spears of a shorter variety with broader blades, some as broad as paddles, and a screen composed of garishly painted spears, knives, machêtes and cutting weapons in sheaths of crude design. There was something peculiar about the dancers apart from their clothes, that he could not identify for a moment. He listened to the band for a while and then it came to him. The dancers were enjoying the primitive rhythm and cavorted enthusiastically and energetically, grinning away like Mulcahy's Mare. There was something undeniably uninhibited about the surge of movement that was unfamiliar.

"What is it?" he had asked Tim, "the core of this lump of artificial Europe?"

"Shut up," Tim said. "How extraordinary it is," he said. "Basically the noises the band are making are a wailing, filtered version of the rhythms Africans would make around their village fires to dance and sing and throw themselves into an ecstasy of syncopated movement." Tim ignored him.

Jon looked at the band in their white coats and red fezes. Three of them sat, rocking their bodies forward and backwards, throwing their heads about and clapping their hands in a rhythm that was gleeful and remorseless. There was a pianist with a white face, burnt a coppery red that almost glowed in the light over his music, and a black drummer beside him, drumming with his eyes tight closed, and a tin whistle in his mouth.

The saxophonist swayed by the microphone and through the throbbing volume of sound he could hear from time to time a wild screaming whoop and then a piercing "tweet-tweet" from the African whistle that was a curiously effective counterpoint. The whole effect was mesmeric. Jonathan closed his eyes and leant back on the bar on his elbows.

"Bored?" said a sultry voice in his ear, and he opened his eyes to find Gillian Lerrick there, a quizzical, amused expression on her face. "No, no," he said, getting on to his feet. "Just thinking." She looked at him silently for a moment, and her expression of amusement faded, to be replaced by one of suspicion.

"About us?"

"About Africa and Africans," he said carelessly, and her expression told him that the remark displeased her, which did not surprise him. "Oh, Kenya's a livelier place than England when you get to know it," she said snappishly. "Come on, it's your round, you know, but I'll get it if you like." Irritated, he said, "I'm doing.it." And gave the hatchet-faced barman a note. They collected the glasses in silence and went over to the table where he sat down next to Lalage. She looked at him, smiling distantly. She had short, curling black hair, the same dense black as her brother's. She parted it in the middle, and had swept it up from her face. Her eyes glistened a vivid bluish-white in a Meissen doll face. He stared at the graceful moulding of her features, the dark irises and heavily defined eyebrows. She must keep her face out of the sun, as her arms and shoulders were quite tanned. She wore a tight black dress, with a silver chain round her neck and another round her waist with a big medallion on it that looked Arabic or Turkish. The small waist set off a beautiful, curvaceous figure. Impulsively he picked the medallion up from her lap to see whether the writing on it was identifiable. "Arabic?" he asked, It didn't look like Roman or Cyrillic script.

"Himyaritic," she said, their fingers touching as she reclaimed it. "Sam got it in the Hadhramaut," she explained. Jonathan was feeling too sleepy to continue the discussion.

"Shall we scrum down?" he invited. She smiled, showing perfect small teeth set very close together, and stood up. As he looked at her, a shock suddenly shook him awake. It felt like a jab in the region of his heart. She was just the most lovely woman he had ever seen. The smile pierced him. He could feel the stinging force of it. Something inside him touched his heart.

As they danced she snuggled close to him. This is one really gorgeous young man, she told herself. The tow-coloured hair above a dreamy pale face with that beautiful grin. When he was serious, the jawline was set firm. This soldier was different. So young, so naïve. But so bloody handsome. The floor was so crowded she let the crush push her closer. The medallion began to saw into him and Jonathan twisted it round so that it hung at her side.

"There you are now," he told her. "Sidearms."

"What?"

"Like a bayonet scabbard." She put up a finger to his lips. An African was singing abandonedly in a low bass, something that sounded like "Iza gazumba, zumba, iza gazumba, zumba...zay," and then on a higher, soaring note, "Hold him down, you Zulu warrior, hold him down you Zulu Chief, Chief, Chief."

"Mother Africa has us in her hand tonight," Jonathan commented dryly. She smiled happily without saying anything and they danced for some time in silence. There was a pause in the music. He felt that he had to say something. She seemed to be in a trance.

"Did you hear what Fats Waller said to the lady who asked him what rhythm was?" he asked. She shook her head so that her ivory earrings swung up into her hair, reminding him of the spearman guard at the Lerricks' house.

"He said, 'Ma'am yuh jes' has to ask, 'cos yuh jes' ain't got it."

She looked up at him and smiled sweetly, but he thought, maybe her heart isn't in it. After the dance he found himself edged out to the roof-garden, and he made no attempt to avoid it. On the way through the screen something very hard struck his hipbone and he turned to see what it was. A ginger-haired man in Kenya Regiment blues jostled beside him.

"Sorry," he said. "It's the ironmongery y'know." There was a large bulge in his side pocket.

"Do people usually wear shooting-irons in the evening?" he asked Lalage.

"Unless they can afford to pay a four thousand shilling fine for leaving them about," she said, edging back towards their table. But Jonathan felt that to calm himself he wanted to see the palm tree from the roof and went over to the edge. It was the wrong street and when he turned she was beside him. The music started again. "The band," he asked. "Kikuyu?" She looked at them. "Congo," she said. "Why?"

"I just didn't like the thought of shooting at them, that's all."

She looked at him with sudden pity. "I agree with you," she said sadly. "Let's dance."

"Where do you live?" she asked.

"Ireland."

She mouthed an "Oh."

"What about our Mau-Mau?" The noise of the band and the scent of her body had stunned him. He could not reply, just stared at her. She was older than Gillian, probably older than her brother, he thought. "Why does your brother call you 'Mua', and most other people 'Lala?'" She pulled her lower lip up and the corners of her mouth down before answering. "Papa, calls me

Mua, Hindi for mouse, because I was once very small, and Lala is supposed to be funny. It means "sleep," in Swahili. Kwenda Lala – go to sleep, go to bed. I am supposed to be bed-worthy, you see," she explained with a brittle smile which Jonathan found deeply appealing, the teeth so white and even against the tangerine lipstick and the café au lait complexion. It was a Kenya girls' thing, that light tanned skin, like very expensive silk.

He had really been very lucky. Kenya seemed to be a wonderful place and, next to Joanna, Tim Collins was the best friend he had. He looked at him now as he talked. He was very Anglo Irish; despite living in Ireland. The nose was straight, the mouth a little small, the chin firm and his brown hair brushed smoothly down on his unmistakable Celtic skull. His awards for gallantry in Korea and Malaya had not surprised Jonathan, who knew all about Tim's almost langorous sang froid.

Only that morning they had been watching a lorry tyre being changed, when one of the semi-circular keepers had sprung off. The metal hurtled through the air, past Tim's face, knocking his pipe out of his mouth. All he said was "Oh!" as he stooped to pick up his pipe. The white-faced driver rushed towards him, thinking he was hurt. Tim straightened his back and laughed. It was another of those incidents the men discussed later in the NAAFI, that endeared him even to the cynical and hardened regulars. But it was dangerous to have so little fear.

I wonder if he's interested in Lalage. He was the right age for her at 30. But he was forgetting. There was Julia. The delicious Julia, poring over her books still. The locals all seemed rather hearty and open air when you thought of it. Or was it that back home you were never so near to the rudiments of life?

Sam brought Gillian back to the table and went off to the bar for drinks. The waiters were very slow and your order tended to get a little confused in transit, so Gillian told him.

"Did you ever hear about the film star Webbs?" she asked animatedly, leaning forward over the table. Jonathan looked down at the side view of her cleavage as she twisted sideways. He could see where the colour of the skin lightened down there, and where the hair sloped down to touch the curve of her shoulder. It was only an inch or so away from his chin. She was Sam's girl. But then to hell with Sam. Her sudden friendliness was mostly brandy, he told himself, and he hadn't had a shave since leaving camp that afternoon after last parade.

He missed the beginning of the story, in which it appeared Lalage had had a small part as somebody's double.

"And he said to her, 'Well Ava...'"Sorry," Jonathan interrupted, who is "he?"

"Sammy, of course, do listen." Gillian's eyes widened as she stared at him He noticed how becoming the cheekbone formation would be in a few year's time when the childish plumpness fined down.

"What is he doing in this film outfit, then?"

"Well, he was really there to look after Lala's honour. He had only just left school and their parents were still out here. But he helped with the hunting. You know, they kill an elephant, say, miles away. Then they send the leading actor in a car to get to the carcass before the vultures get at it. They tie wires to its ears and trunk and drive the car or a jeep past it for dust. Then they pull the wires – last gasp. Hero rushes up with a damn great gun, collapses on carcase. 'Gee baby, that was real close.' You've seen 'em. Anyway, Sammy said to her this time,"'I'm disappointed in you, Ava, living in that hotel and flying out here every morning. We all miss you here in camp these long dark nights.' And she just looked at him showing those teeth and hunched one shoulder coy-like. Then she said, 'Sammy boy, ah guess ah jest wasn't cut out to be a Gurl Guide.'"

Sammy returned with the glasses and caught the end of the story.

"Hell," he said. "Not that one, man."

Jonathan was looking at Lalage. "She would make a most beautiful film star, too," he muttered, watching her grave profile as she listened to something Tim was asking.

"Who did she double for?" he asked Sam.

Sam smiled wickedly. "Aw," he said with a glance at his sister, "Most of it was walking into a pool at Buffalo Springs in the Eneffdee, in the raw, a hundred yards from the cameras."

"That's not fair, Sam," Gillian said heatedly. "But we better not go on with it. I've met three women who claimed to have been offered that part first, including that dreary wench who whizzes about town in an open pink Cadillac full of odd animals; and leaves it with the wireless full on outside my office. You know who," she added mischievously, catching Sam's eye.

"I heard," Tim said, "that Tom hunts with Hemingway when he is here. Is it true?"

"Sure," Sam said. "Gill, tell them about Denis and the letters."

"Oh yes," she said, "Sam was taking us down to Malindi last month, in a Piper Cruiser. There was a huge black cloud so we landed at Denis Zaphiro's place. He's Game Warden at Kajiado. He showed me a letter he had just got from Ernest, all about Robert Ruark. Denis always acts as his main hunter. He had asked Ernest what he thought about Ruark's book 'Something of Value.'"

"I'll spare your blushes," Sam said. "It was a fantastic letter saying that what the hell did Ruark know about Africa anyway? He said Ruark was telling everybody he had shot a record Kudu. Of course Ernest has the record for Greater Kudu. So, in the letter he went on asking Denis, 'Do you remember those Masai girls at Narok? And what about that Wakamba lass with the magnificent pudenda up at Isiolo? What the hell does this guy know about the real Africa?' And more like that. So Gill here folds the letter up and says Denis, you don't mind if I borrow this? Never seen Denis move so fast. He grabbed the letter and said 'Do you realise what these letters are going to be worth one day? My pension.' End of story."

"Wow," Tim said. "That is a story,"

"We must meet this Denis," Jonathan said, "and see his letters too." There was a silence.

"Hem is around now," Lalage said. "I met Patrick last week, his son, who is an apprentice hunter. I'll find out where old Papa is and let you know. Tom might know. Denis will certainly."

Jonathan excused himself to Sam and, avoiding Lalage's eye, asked Gillian to dance. It had occurred to him that Sam had noticed him staring at his sister. The tempo of the dancers had slowed off and the band was labouring with a Los Angeles interpretation of the noises that would be made by a lovesick African drummer. The crowd on the floor swayed sleepily, determinedly, crushing them close in its arms. In the smoke-blurred table lights he could see glimpses over Gillian's shoulder of shining faces looking like polished mahogany, of girls' faces eyes closed, dreamily lapped in the viscous pulse of the music that rose and fell, ebbing away into the night.

"Drums," he murmured, "African drums in Africa."

"Oh, do relax," she said. He looked over at Lalage. That is one beautiful girl. Soon she will marry and go out to some outback farm and drape jeans and a man's shirt on her fine bone formation, hide all the curves and burn her face leathery. Don't think. Live. He took Gillian back and swapped her for Lala.

He took care to swing out of her brother's line of sight. He took an nibble at her ear. She kissed his cheek quickly and said, "Careful. This is one very small town," and gave him a ravishing smile. People were dancing out on the roof garden and he piloted her out there, releasing the pressure of his arm around her waist as he did so, holding her far enough away to see her face. She was smiling and he smiled back and kissed the tip of her nose, which wasn't too difficult because the throb of the music was so slow they were barely moving. She looked at him coolly, then over his shoulder, then put her cheek against his. He leaned back against the wall and kissed her on the mouth. She put her face close to his again so that he couldn't see her expression.

"Do you think you will like it here?" he heard her say. He held her away from him to see her face. There was a queer imploring look in her eyes, almost of anxiety.

"I think so far it couldn't be better. How about asking me next week? Say here, for example, say next Saturday at about midnight?"

"Sammy will be here too."

"I thought he might stay up his mountain some time," he said, still smiling, but her eyes avoided his and when she looked up they swung away.

"Sometimes," she murmured vaguely, and her hand tightened on his arm.

"It isn't a bad place, is it?" she asked, her eyes focusing on his again.

"No. No it isn't." He didn't sound convincing because as he said it he was remembering what Gillian's father had said that afternoon. "I would like the chance you have to walk you about in the real Africa, but now I'm too old. This is the only really wild place left on earth. The only place with such a variety of game and trees and plants and this ..." His voice had tailed off as he waved out towards the horizon, to where the enormous sky came down all around them to meet the far off hills in a shimmering blaze of blue and brown. It was that huge embrace of earth and sky that had stamped the scene on Jonathan's mind. For a moment he had been afraid of it, afraid that he would be lost and helpless out there in it, leading men as green as himself, against natives who had reverted to savagery, whom the sun and the wilderness did not affect. And he did want to get shot either.

Back at their table, it was his turn to dance with Gillian. She leant forward again towards him. But he saw Sam give her a hard look. He sat there alone with a brandy.

Tim and Lalage emerged from the smoke-wreathed throng. Lalage made a wry face. "Home," she said, with a quizzical look at Gillian. Sam drained his glass and stood up, putting one arm around his sister. Lalage looked as though she had spent most of her time in the shade, in contrast to her brother, who looked almost as though he had been baked very slowly in a kiln and then very roughly glazed.

"A fine start to your military career, my boy," Tim said softly in his ear. Jonathan drew himself up with an alcohol thickened dignity, "I'll have you know, Captain Collins, that I am a soldier of some seven months' service." Tim growled, "Huh. Just watch it with the local talent. The competition is very fierce."

They filed down the steep stairs and down into the warm air outside. There was a garden just across the road and there was that faintly acrid smell he had first noticed coming from the airport. That already seemed an age ago. The girls were getting into a very low-slung open car, and Sam was already behind the wheel. Even in the ghastly light from the night-club doorway they were both strikingly good-looking. What was all that stuff Tim had said in his letter about girls being like uranium in this town – rare and expensive? Lalage. She probably had a hundred men after her. He had expected her to be tough and offhand like her brother. Gillian was much as he had thought, only prettier on closer examination.

"Come on," Tim was saying. "Polo parade in the morning."

"Oh no. Kipling is dead."

"No need to be flippant. Just wait. You'll be thankful for something to do soon enough." They passed a shop doorway where a wrinkled old African was lying, surrounded by a screen of cardboard and covered in sacks and a blanket.

"The Mau-Mau will get you," Jonathan told him, but the old man was asleep.

"Probably is one anyway," Tim said as he unlocked his car. "I think they blackmail the Indians into hiring them as watchmen."

"Clever," Jonathan said, and he was almost sure as they moved off that he saw the old man grinning at them from a chink in his barrier.

CHAPTER NINE

SUNDAY HORSES

"Brown is my Love, but graceful:
And each renowned whiteness,
Marcht with her lovely brown, loseth its brightness.
Fair is my love, but scornful:
Yet I have seen despised
Dainty white lilies and sad flowers well prized."

Anon.

The church was full when Jonathan arrived. It was too far from camp to march. So he had brought two three tonners full of the Catholic soldiers. People were standing at all three doors in the strong sunlight. There were many police among the African congregation. He felt very light-headed and the reflected glare from the white walls hurt his eyes. Squeezing through the crowd in a side door he found the sermon still in progress. A rich, fruity Irish brogue thundered from the pulpit, asking rhetorical questions and answering them with vivid illustration.

Jonathan knelt to pray, apologising for his lateness, and then stood again to contemplate Christ crucified, hanging dead, yet so vital and striking on a cross suspended over the altar. It has taken over nineteen hundred years for that event in Palestine to penetrate to Africa and now it was here, with them. He looked around curiously at the congregation. There was a majority of black faces, but not all of them were African. Almost half were Indian or Goan, and among the white faces were some unmistakably Slav, who must be Poles. Catholic, he thought, all-embracing. What a weird collection to be brought together by

God made man tortured to death so long ago. He remembered reading how the only Kikuyu who refused the Mau-Mau oath were the ardent Christians, and they had been tortured and killed. He looked back at the crucifix, thinking how hard it was to understand.

Joanna said "You Catholics are a smug bunch of obscurantists. All dogma and incense and all."

He said a prayer for her. The sermon had changed from avoiding violence to wife-beating, which it appeared was a local failing. "And thank You," he added, "for keeping me safe." Lalage's face came into his mind and he didn't know what to do about that.

The troopers all stayed in town after Mass. He walked over to the Norfolk Hotel where Seamus collected him. "It's a last twinge of the Raj, this polo lark," Seamus said. "I learned in Malaya. My folks lived there. Here they have a very rough tough team. But plenty of knock-abouts. You'll see."

Sam went to Sunday morning polo because he used to play before the Emergency, when he wasn't on safari, and so he met friends there. Gillian came occasionally because it was something to get out of bed for, and it could be pleasant sitting on the verandah in the morning sun, drinking gin and tonic in the open air. Tom had a couple of ponies which he used to send down to the ground on Saturday morning, but he never had time now, so she had given up her rare attempts at the slow chukkas.

She liked seeing the lines of ponies standing patiently while the Saises fumbled with their saddlery. The old Saises had been Kikuyu and being a hard-boiled lot were now all in detention or still in the Aberdares with gangs. The Kipsigis herdsmen who had replaced them were a feckless lot, always brewing Nubian gin with molasses and corn, and quite unable to exercise the ponies properly. Even so there seemed to be a good turn-out this morning.

The clubhouse stood between the two grounds, with a veranda running all around the second storey where the bar was. As Sam drove up she noticed with pleasure the police mounts neatly rigged out in dark blue leg bandages and saddle cloths, with their tails wrapped smartly in blue cloth. There was a group of ponies tended by British soldiers, looking strangely efficient amongst the proverbially scruffy Saises. She got out of the car and walked along looking critically at the ponies. Somehow Nairobi strings were never as good as those from the up-country farming areas, and tended to differ greatly in height and build.

It was a beautiful ground, with the Ngong hills over to the west. Her father said that the Nandi legend was that a giant had dragged his fingers over the hills, creating the four neat valleys. Mother's relative Denis Finch Hatton was buried up there. He had been Karen Blixen's lover. The Masai said that lions came and sat on his grave and roared. That was a bit thick, considering the number of lions Denis must have killed in his day.

A few players were cantering about one field, practising shots. She looked up at the club balcony; she could not tell yet who was there. Just a uniformity of white breeches and shirts and dusty brown boots. Sam hailed a friend but she could not make out his face under his polo topee. It was going to be fun if the two Irishmen were there. Sam was a little jealous of both of them, and she felt a stir of excitement, which gave her added pleasure. She left Sam talking and strolled over to the blackboard where the players' names were. A slim figure in long, tapering boots in old fashioned cavalry style was chalking the chukka numbers against the names. Down at the bottom of the list she noted were the two names, Collins and Fitzpatrick. The tall figure in the satiny boots turned round. His breeches were already stained with horses' sweat and his club shirt was darned and torn in several places, showing glimpses of sunburnt chest.

"Hullo, Gillian mah dear. Having a knock?" he drawled. She shook her head, her face creasing with amusement. It was "Boy" Hummel, a loveable Edwardian rascal, who, if all the stories were true, must be over a hundred. He looked at her appraisingly from his leathery, long-nosed face, the eyes hidden under the hooded eyelids and bushy, greying eyebrows. The devilish smile seamed his face, hiding the lighter age-lines on the drink and sun-pickled complexion. He wore a corset now over his breeches and his handicap was down from 6 to 4. Why weren't men like him any longer, she wondered, as the hand that never faltered on the rein, trigger, or woman's waist, came up to touch the silvery hair over the ear.

"Pity. We could do with a few hoss-women, what?" The voice dropped a little from the langorous drawl to a whisky-hoarse whisper.

"Got the most 'strodinary-ah-a foot soldjahs playing." His eyes narrowed as he parodied a pained expression. "You'll lick them into shape, won't you, Boy?" she said, joining in the game. His face twitched as he turned angularly to put down the chalk, muttering something that sounded like..."Fwitening." Then, "Come along," he said briskly,

"Just time to buy the prettiest gel in Africa her morning gin."

"Thank you. But don't you pinch my bottom as we go up the stairs."

She was glad he was here. To watch him play was an experience and to talk to him was fun. She knew that he exaggerated his air of vague cavalier eccentricity. He had in fact hunted lion with Fritz Schindelar from the back of a polo pony, and run away with several exotic women, but he was no fool. He had been present on the famous occasion in the Norfolk Hotel when a fellow hunter had got so cross with Fritz that he pulled a gun. Pointing it at the photograph behind the bar. Fritz holding a dying lion. The caption read, 'Dying in my arms.'

Boy had shouted, "Another word from you, Fritz, and you'll be dying in my arms." It was one of her favourite stories, and she could remember the photograph, although it was gone now.

Sam joined them at the bar and they went out on the balcony to watch the chukka in progress. "Something very stirring," Gillian said, "at the sight of eight ponies galloping wildly up and down. The crack of stick on ball."

"Not to mention the foul language," Boy said.

Hooves thudded out a furious tattoo as three ponies, riders heaving and sweating, locked together, went jostling past the balcony in a cloud of dust and headed off towards the goalposts. Boy Hummel grunted, "Very sporting, you know, of the Army, to come and play here." Sam looked at him and frowned.

"Well I *can't*, can I?"

"Oh Sam, don't be so kali," Gillian said. "They don't spend

all their time playing games, and they are stationed just near, so why shouldn't they?"

"Got to do something to pass the time I suppose." Sam growled. Boy Hummel said nothing and Gillian was thinking that perhaps it wasn't wise to defend the soldiers too warmly after last night. She had caught sight of that gorgeous Jonathan in khaki jodhpurs and thought it was very gallant of him to turn up at all. She remembered how tired she felt even without a late night, after she came back from England. It took some time before you lost that feeling of lethargy. That came with the altitude. Over six thousand feet above sea level. Jonathan must be feeling terrible, poor boy. God, he was a beaut.

Jonathan had scarcely ever felt worse. He had returned to camp after church to return Tim's car, only to find that there was no time for breakfast, since Tim insisted on going straight to the polo-grounds. Before going to church he had managed to swallow half a plateful of mulligatawny soup, which tasted as though most of its ingredients had been left over with the tradition, from the regiment's India days. The hollow, numbed feeling had returned, and when Tim flung him a pair of jodhpurs, only a twinge of nausea prevented him from flinging them back. "When do we do any soldiering?" he asked plaintively.

"Play hard. Fight hard." Tim said grimly.

On the way to the grounds he could not decide whether Tim's grave instructions were seriously intended or not. Advice on the rules of the game was interspersed with hints that a new subaltern's reputation hung on his Sunday morning performance.

"But I shall be away on patrols most Sundays, surely?" Jonathan had protested, only to be told, "So this morning make a good impression."

"I thought that you, the Colonel and Squadron Commander were reasonable men. I think you are pulling my leg."

"No. No. You've ridden ponies since you were knee high, laddie. We need to show the locals that we ain't just clod-hopping infantry."

"I'll try."

On arriving at the ground he was not cheered to notice the pace at which the first chukka was played. The sun-hardened earth looked uncommonly unlike the springy turf he was accustomed to ride on and he was given no time to reflect on that. Tim gave him a bunch of sticks and led him to a pit roofed with reeds and surrounded by chicken wire in which there was a wooden horse. Sitting on it, Jonathan tried to hit the ball which Tim threw in.

Jonathan having failed to hit it either forehand forward or backward, or backhand forward or backwards. Tim volunteered to demonstrate. Jonathan tried again with a longer stick and severely jarred his wrist. Tim eventually gave him another stick, lent him a hard hat, and it was time for the first slow chukka.

"This pony," Tim assured him, "is Minesweeper. Been playing polo for seven years. Past running away."

In the first mild scuffle Jonathan found that the wise old animal made no move that was not strictly necessary. Cantering along beside a girl who was apparently on the other side, Jonathan was taken unawares when the pony suddenly put out one front leg and pivoted around. The girl swung her stick backwards, hitting the ball behind her. The pony, hearing the noise and not seeing the ball in front of it, promptly gave up its forward motion, which would have been excess effort, and turned. Since Jonathan could not make out where the ball had gone, a dust cloud having obscured the rest of the players, he did not encourage the pony, which ambled into a walk. The opposition suddenly began galloping towards him, the ball shot past, and the pony turned again. Somebody shouted, "Go," and Jonathan remembered that as he was playing No.1, the others were supposed to feed him with the ball, and he was supposed to tap the ball through the goal mouth.

He found himself galloping along with the ball unaccountably travelling along beside him at approximately the same speed. He leaned over slightly and swung at it, but missed. Again the pony stopped and someone came up behind him in a flurry of creaking leather, panting breath and flapping reins, jostled past and hit the ball smartly underneath Jonathan's pony's legs. The pony at the time was in the process of turning, as presumably it had deduced, from the backward swing of the defender's stick, that to turn would be the most economical manoeuvre.

The game went on like that for what seemed a very long time, but was in fact only five minutes. When the ball again passed Jonathan, he lashed at it ferociously. It shot off at a slight angle, producing a scream from somebody and oaths from two others. Apparently he had not been facing quite in the right direction. He himself was not prepared to dispute this, as for one thing his throat was full of fine red dust and for another thing he was hardly capable of seeing at all.

About a minute later he found himself cantering slowly towards the opponents' goal. He was sure of this because a grim-looking woman shouted, "Your lot are going the other way." Looking down at himself he had ascertained that he was wearing a red bolero and she was wearing a blue one. Anyway there had been no females on his side as far as he could remember. Just as he had decided to turn, he heard a thunder of approaching hooves, and glancing round apprehensively he observed that someone had hit the ball in the direction that he was already going. There seemed no further point in turning, so he resumed his canter in the direction of the goal and waited for the ball to catch up with him.

Just then, above the sound of galloping, a voice shouted, "Get out of the bloody way, you." Nettled, Jonathan, who had just at that moment seen the ball passing a yard to his right, dug his heels in and lashed out at it, shouting at the same time, his throat somehow moistened by emotion.

"My ball, damn your eyes." He had to lean right out to reach it, hit it, but not squarely, missed the goal, and received the impact on his shoulder of the madman who presumably had just shouted. At that moment a bell started to ring, his pony stopped dead and he found himself wrenched free from his assailant, who he noted was on his own side.

Jonathan's shout had been clearly heard from the balcony. It was not every day that anyone shouted back at General Thynn, who had been an international in his day. Boy Hummel chuckled softly to himself. "That boy may not know the rules, but, by Jove, he must have shaken old Toby."

"He wasn't really in the way," Gillian said.

"Should have been moving," Sam commented.

"I'll buy him a drink after this chukka," Boy said, hitching his corset tighter. "Only I expect Toby will – while he's offering a spot of advice."

Still chuckling, he stumped down the steps to be hoisted onto his pony.

"You must go, go all the time," the peppery, dried-out little man on the great fat-rumped chestnut was saying to Jonathan between gasps.

"Yessir," said Jonathan, thinking he'd like to push him off his horse, whack him with his stick, thrust his helmet down hard over his ears and then ride all over him. Tim came trotting up behind him, a grin on his face which disappeared as he came level with the older man. Jonathan put his tongue out at him. "Come up to the bar," the mad old fellow commanded, and cantered away. "Who the hell's that?"

"Just a spare General, that's all. Retired, luckily for you. I think he is going to offer us a drink, which is sporting, after your effort." Jonathan patted his eccentric pony as he slid to the ground. It took no notice and began immediately to tear at the sparse grey grass.

"Effort," he panted, pulling off his topee and wiping away some of the sweat. He tried to produce a hollow laugh, but only a rasping squawk resulted. "Lead me to that bar, I need it."

After his second pink gin Jonathan felt restored, except for a heavy throb inside his head.

"I hear you've had a bit of action already," the General said. Jonathan nodded.

"Well done. G and T?" Then he resumed explaining about positional play and rights of way, but Jonathan was watching the prettier sight of Gillian standing against the sunlight out on the balcony. They had come up the other steps and hadn't exchanged greetings yet. At last the General had to go to another chukka and Jonathan thought that before he went home to die he might as well have another gin and mix with the locals. He was beginning to feel pleased with himself for having survived relatively undamaged, and had firmly refused Tim's offer of another "slow" chukka. Glass in hand he limped forward. "Jambo," he said in Gillian's ear. "Hi," she said, but someone dragged her away.

Back in camp Jonathan gulped down some curry and crept off to his tent. He threw himself on his bed, too tired to take off the jodhpurs, and woke at five o'clock with pins and needles in both legs, a head like a bag of scorpions and a tongue with the consistency of pumice stone. He dragged himself to a bath tent and wallowed in the reddish, luke warm water. Putting on civilian clothes helped his morale so much that he decided to have tea. He was greeted in the Officers mess by a facetious fellow subaltern, Sean Cosgrave, who grinned and asked, "Fit for tennis, old chap?" Obviously the story had got round, as Sean was Orderly Officer and hadn't left camp.

One of the mess waiters handed him a note from Tim. *"Am at tennis at Muthaiga Club. Please join me at 1800. Bring my Land Rover. Thanks."* He already said, "You'll start patrol this week. So get around while you can." Tim was popular wherever he went and no one could be a better guide. If he was only going to be in Africa for a year, the sooner he got to know people the better. On Monday would begin the real business of his being here. Payment for the ride. He was relieved to hear Sean say, "Don't worry. We don't get long tirades from politically-minded officials, or propaganda from half-baked axe-grinders. But there will be dreary briefings from Intelligence officers and bush warfare training. Also, Lerrick's lectures on the terrain. And on the Micks."

Feeling the better for tea he got into Tim's battered Land Rover. The sun was still strong and he lifted up his face and exulted in it. It might be a bit uncivilised living here, but for this glorious sunshine it was almost worth it. Or was it? Maybe after a few days in the bush it would be crippling. No, surely not any more than crawling about wet Wales or gallivanting about Salisbury Plain in a biting February wind. He shuddered momentarily at the memory of his two week's battle school, walking around Dartmoor's bogs in teeming December rain.

The pace here seemed quite fast. Sean said the Regiment had lost over twenty so far, of which four subalterns in a car crash, three in other accidents and twelve men in Mau-Mau clashes. Then the poor old C.O. No one told him until much later that four second lieutenants had also been killed in action since 1952.

As he drove out of the camp he could see Nairobi scattered out amongst the ravines, half concealed amongst clumps of trees, with the Ngong Hills beyond it marking the beginning of Masailand. There were a few wisps of cloud sailing over the hills, that were like the blue knuckles of some frozen giant. As he went round the roundabout a Chevrolet with three very fat Indian women and about twelve children in it came round the obstruction the wrong way, wrenching him back to reality. He resumed looking at the road, only glancing now and again at the weird mixture of architecture in the smart residential area. It varied at one end from great pink palaces, adorned with frilly wrought iron balustrading, like iced sugary cakes, where successful Indian grocers lived, to the curving white gables in Dutch Colonial style at the other.

The Muthaiga Club was surrounded, apart from a golf club and tennis courts, by flowerbeds full of magnificent blooms, and clumps of lissom bamboo stems. The vivid colours ached in the glaring sunlight, and Jonathan switched off the engine and sat looking at them. How odd it was, this plateau lifted high above the rest of steaming, humid, Africa. And odder still that in an hour it would be dark, and yet the chill that would descend never extinguished the brightness of the flowers. He climbed a trifle stiffly out of the car and look around.

There was no impression of mountain country. Just that faint strained feeling as the sun sank. That hint of rarefied air, he had noticed before. It was Europe transplanted, and in the process intensified, animated by the sun, almost exotic, yet without the sultry, stifling splendour of sea-level tropical places. But still these langorous blossoms survived the long, Highland nights when the clouds came down sometimes to ground level to envelop them. "Then it's almost like fog," Tim said. "Patrols lose their bearings and themselves, and start signalling for airdrops to find them." He looked up ruminatively at the embryo clouds. Long rains were not due for two months. There was a big one over in the west, floating with billowing majesty, thrust by some unfelt wind, or perhaps just moved by the air thrown upwards by the edges of the plateau by the earth's rotation. They were up so high on these uplands, it was perhaps excusable for the clouds to settle occasionally. He decided to forgive them that. There was still the sun. The sun that withered the grass as at Khartoum. That thinned it sadly on the polo ground, fed as it was for most of the year, only by a scanty dew that the parched ground had little time to absorb before the sun rose again and sucked up the moisture. Hence the dust, that fine, pervasive red dust, that seeped into a car and stuck to your skin and stained your clothes.

"Creepie-crawlies," Jonathan said half aloud as he went through the club porch. A trail of ants was pouring across the flagged entrance. Funny, but he didn't seem to mind them, or the other bugs. But then, they said, even the mosquitoes are rarely malarial up here.

The club inside had the look of a Roman atrium, a colonial one perhaps, but nevertheless classical Roman. It had been designed that way, with its ivory painted pillars and spaciousness. Through an archway from the main room he saw an open courtyard-cum-cloister, roofless and much bedecked in greenery, that smacked somehow of a veranda somewhere. In colonial Spain?

This then was where the old settlers had re-created their London clubs. This was where the pioneers had come to play in that lost Golden Age when Africa was in its naive state of simplicity, when any quirk of eccentricity had been admissible. Lalage had told him some of the stories last night.

"Our Lord Delamere. One night he and his party got sick of the old Victrola, poured kerosene into it and danced round it in the darkness as it burst into flames. They used to have rickshaw races from the Muthaiga, in the good old days. Everybody did as they pleased to relieve the monotony of seeing the same few familiar faces."

"I suppose," he said, "it must have been fun then. To leave stuffy Victorian England and come out here to Eldorado, Happy Valley."

"No comment," she replied.

There were a few groups of people sitting about after a late tea. Most seemed to be in their Sunday suitings. Some looked a little restricted and crumpled in them, with their deeply weather-beaten faces emerging from strained collars. The influence of the elegant matrons with strong, sunburnt faces, was forcefully displayed in the sumptuous flower arrangements in every corner. Huge sprays of wallflower, sweet-pea, snapdragon and hydrangea, blazing against tall, luxuriant stalks of arum lilies and scarlet gladioli. He went out to inspect the loggia, where strange vine-like plants wreathed around the pillars that supported the roofed ambulatory that surrounded the open space. Like some floral over-embellished monastery from days of King Arthur. Outside, a torpid river ought to flow past sleepy Camelot. There should be a soporific hum of over-fed bees, and the delicate rose thorns should scratch no one.

He was roused from his musing by a cry of "Oi there." Turning he saw Tim sitting in the far corner at an iron, green painted table, surrounded by white painted cane chairs. As he approached, he saw that Tim was with Lalage Webb and two other young men. Forsythia dripping from hanging wicker baskets brushed against his face, tickling him and helping to produce a smile as he approached.

"You look dopey," Tim said. "Had a good kip?"

He introduced the two others. One was in the Kenya Regiment, and the other whom Jonathan recognised, having known him at school. He was an ADC to somebody or other. The two were a perfect contrast, Roger the ADC being smooth and pink, sleek-haired with a voice adjusted to the rich, mouthful-of-plums tone he presumably affected amongst his boss's coterie. Bill was quite unabashedly a private in the Kenya Regiment, wore the customary shorts, displayed burly legs with ochre-coloured skin, and spoke in the slightly clipped tone, with a hint of South African sing-song that Jonathan had noticed was the local manner of speech.

Both were obviously trying to impress Lalage who was, he thought, looking magnificent in a dark suit with a white collar, setting off that intensely deep black hair. It was the first time he had seen her in daylight. As the conversation flowed round them he found himself sitting watching her. She was so beautiful in the brilliant light. Hair up. Gold necklace and bangles against the apricot-dusted skin. He went over to her chair, his heart thumping. She smiled fondly at him, he thought, but there were too many eyes on them both, and he backed off.

There was something taut and restless behind her movements and speech. Her eyes glittered, the dark irises flashing against the blue-tinged whites, and she moved her hands quickly and deftly in a way that made him think of a bird. She was like a magpie in her sharp mischievous chatter, or a jay, with that flash of blue at the black wing-tips as it twisted in nervous, febrile flight. She seemed quite different from the previous evening. He had found her so quiet, restrained, and here she was scintillating. He felt a sharp pang at the thought that somebody here had stimulated this lively mood, Maybe he had bored her. Because looking at her and listening to her now he realised that she was much more attractive than he had realised. He shook his head to clear it. It did not occur to him that he had been half asleep after that long flight. Was it only two days ago?

Standing in a doorway with a tray in his hand was a wrinkled old African in a white Kanzu that came down to his bare heels, a scarlet cummerbund and fez, and a gold-embroidered green monkey-jacket. He beckoned at this gaudy retainer, who came over with a slow dignified tread. "I signed that book on the way in," he said to Tim. "We are country or something members, aren't we?" Tim nodded and before Jonathan could say anything, said to the waiter, "Ingine vili-vili." (Another one, the same)

"Sorry, I forgot you hadn't got a drink. A long, cool, fruit juice is what you get," Tim told him. Everybody looked at Jonathan and a silence ensued.

"Beautiful place," he said to Bill, indicating to the creepers wreathed around the pillars, the tubs of oleander, poinsettia and spiked sansaveira-like cactus that surrounded them.

"Beautiful, but broke," Bill replied. "We haven't even got a swimming pool."

"It wasn't exactly broke when Pa was on the committee," Lalage said. "Can you see this place swarming with bright young things in bikinis and louts like you in swimming trunks?"

"It could do with a bit of life putting into it," Bill growled. Lalage looked tolerant. Not him anyway, Jonathan registered. But Tim's eyes kept moving to Lalage. He was quite obviously after her.

"Well, it's just what I need today," Jonathan said. "Cool and quiet."

"I wonder what the Africans would do with a place like this if they ever do kick us all out." Lalage said musingly. Bill's frown deepened to a scowl. Even Roger looked alarmed.

"Now look, Lala," Bill said, "You've got your folks in the U.K. but where'd I go to? What d'y' want to talk like that for, man?"

"You'd just go down to the Union," Lalage smiled. "But don't let's start an argument."

"The Union." Bill spat the words out. "Afrikaners. It'd kill me, you know that. Now, Lala" His voice was pleading. He leant towards her, his elbows planted one on each knee, his fists clenched. She just raised one perfect eyebrow. "We can't go, you know that. What's this country got besides farming? Nothing. Just a few second-rate minerals. Say we went and gave the Kyukes our land. In a few years they'd grab the Wakamba Reserve, then the Kipsigis, then down to the lake. They wouldn't dare to try to pinch any from the Masai. And would they farm it, or what?"

"And what do you want to do about it?" Lalage asked.

"I was in Desert Locust Control and when the Emergency is over I'll go into Soil Conservation or something like that. Our farm is too small for two of us. If we ever go, this place will get too crowded."

"Tell me," Jonathan said. "Surely the main problem is to employ the surplus population that isn't needed in agriculture."

"Exactly," Tim said, "But until there is a stable government, who will risk capital to provide work?"

"Nobody," Lalage said, "And a stable government means an African majority."

Bill glared at her. "In fifty years maybe," he ground out.

"No progress until then?" she asked mockingly. Then suddenly leaning forward, her face flushed she said, "It isn't really politics, it's just fear and snobbery. Fear of blacks in power and rising labour costs, and snobbery about our precious white clubs and hotels. That's what got us kicked out of India."

This outburst took even Jonathan by surprise. Bill put his glass down on the table, kicked his chair back, and, muttering under his breath, left them.

Lalage looked into her glass, smiled sweetly, and murmured "So immature." Turning to Jonathan, she asked, "Have you been to the Nairobi Game Park yet?" When he said he hadn't she gave him a long description of it and the times when she had seen various animals there. As she spoke it dawned on him that she would have quite a lot in common with Joanna. Both had an impish aggressiveness and minds with masculine traits. He was delighted to find that Lalage was so bright, a fact difficult to assess in any night-club at a first meeting.

Tim was talking to Roger about operations in the forest, or was he backing up, keeping Roger busy? He didn't want to leave Lalage and go back to camp for dinner, but maybe she was having dinner with Roger. Somebody must have brought her.

"Have you got a lift home?" he asked.

"I'm with Roger," she whispered. "Dinner at the Lindberns." Of course, he thought, the independent colonial female, and made a mental note to look round the second-hand car market. "I met Alison," he told her.

She smiled, "This place is just a family a couple of thousand strong. It's annoying at first until you get used to knowing everybody."

"In that case I won't make a date. Just see you when I see you."

"Yes," she said, and Jonathan thought that he didn't detect any particular warmth in the 'Yes.' Tim looked at him hard. "Got to go." he said.

On the way back to camp Tim asked with a wicked grin, "Quite a gal that. Eh? What do you think?" Jonathan was non-committal. He wasn't sure himself.

"I tried hard there." Tim commented. "She's a deep one. I think I may stick to the simpler girls like Gillian. She may be a settler's daughter, but she's lost her Native Reserve. Ha-ha. It's all right, it isn't mine. Local pioneer wit."

"I think you'll find that she's Sam's girl. Anyway, let's

change the subject," Jonathan said. "Is this trip to the Reserve on?"

"Yes. Don't know when yet. Got to send you and Blue Troop up-country as soon as I can. Then, one free day, I'll take you, at sparrow-fart to see dawn break in the Great Rift. You'll see plenty of forest dawns, but not that one."

"Somehow," Jonathan said, "Mondays and Africa don't mix." Damn, he thought. This is going to be tough. So few women and so many sex-starved locals, plus the troops. I haven't got a hope in hell.

PART TWO

SOLDIERING

CHAPTER TEN

RED TROOP

"Wars now is worse than walking horse
For like a hackney tied at rack,
Old soldier so, who wanteth force,
Must learn to bear a pedlar's pack
And trudge to so good market town
So from a knight to be a clown."

Thomas Churchyard
1520-1604

Jonathan had got to know some more of the lads in his troop by now. It wasn't his yet because Sean Cosgrave was handing it over to him. Cosgrave, a very large boisterous fellow, earned respect by being both competent and tough. He regarded Jonathan with amusement that bordered on patronage. He said that Jonathan was "as rustic as a local," by which he meant that Jonathan appeared to have most of the attributes of the "gentleman oblique officer," whereas he, Cosgrave, Liverpool Irish, was conscious of his accent and told everybody he was going into the car trade. Six foot five in his socks, he was clumsy and unpolished. But everybody liked him for his cheerfulness and wit anyway, and he would probably develop into one of those steely-eyed tycoons to be seen outside the Dorchester in Motor Show week, climbing into ninety horsepower limousines.

Red Troop were a tough lot, mostly regulars, some in their late thirties with campaign medals from 1940-45. Most were Irish or Scots. "This lark is a doddle," they told him, watching him carefully, when they thought he wasn't looking. He knew they would only judge him later. Tim, as adjutant, kept most of the national service men under the regular officers.

"They ain't got artillery. No worry about landmines and dive bombers. They're lousy shots. No snipers. Piece o' cake." Jonathan nodded and forced a cheery smile.

The Troop Sergeant, MacNamara, seemed devoid of personality. A dour Ulsterman, he never spoke except when addressed. Years ago, he told Jonathan, he had been a "monumental mason," in Aberdeen and Jonathan could believe him. The Corporal Noyk was that rare thing, an Irish Jew, born in India, where his father had been a Quartermaster. He and one Tosher Harris provided an endless cabaret, one interpreting the opinions of the ranks in pungent, obscene phrases, the other responding with an approximation of the official view in riper terms, enriched with the soldiering slang of British India. Some of these words such as "bundook," for rifle and "chai" for tea, Jonathan was told, corresponded with Swahili, having a common origin from Hindi.

There was a Flett fom the Faroes Islands, a Trehinnick who said his name was old Scots. Lots of Murphys, McEvoys, McDonalds, Campbells, McKeevers, McAuleys, Kellys, O'Briens, O'Malleys, O'Donovans, O'Reillys, O'Connors, Sheehans and several Kennedys.

From Tim's advice he knew that he must be able to recognise every one of them, very fast, in bad light, and as soon as possible,

There was also Chepkoin, a Kipsigi believed to have had a Kikuyu mother. He was the tracker, "attached," and was known to all as George. Dark green suited him, but his jungle hat did not, and whenever he could he sported in it, contrary to regulations, a shiny regimental badge. He was very keen, Cosgrave told him, and had once in an Emergency, tracked for three hours stark naked except for a vest, which, being white, he had discarded in the interests of camouflage. He said later, "When they wake me, I no find trouser. No need trouser, find Mau-Mau."

Recruits, arrived on the last ship, were attending various familiarisation courses. One was Tom Lerrick's lectures on tracking and the habits of Mau-Mau. This Jonathan found to be more like question time at the zoo. "The forest," he said, "is too cold for lion or snakes. Tigers stay mostly in India. Letting rip with a Bren at elephant, rhinoceros or buffalo is unwise. A rhino is a most unaccommodating creature, and buffalo are wily, mischievous beasts. They can be bloody dangerous. If you wound them, and meet them later, you'll be very, very sorry."

Jonathan was impressed by Tom's three rows of campaign ribbons, discovering that he had served with the Rhodesian troop of Long Range Desert Group and then with the Special Air Service in North Africa and Italy. He, like Sam, was in the Kenya Police Reserve, which, as well as Airwing, sported a Mounted Section, a Special Branch and numerous Striking Forces known by obscure symbol numbers. This seemed to be the most tactful way of using men familiar with the country outside cumbersome regimental formations.

On Monday after First Parade, they sent for Jonathan and O'Malley from the Operations office. Lerrick was there and a bunch of Intelligence officers and police. Pilots from the Airwing had seen more gangs moving south into the Aberdares. There were several large patrols already there, but the Divisonal Staff had asked for more men on the ground quickly.

At breakfast, Tim asked Jonathan to meet him outside. "Look, I'm sorry to rush you but I've had to send two more troops down to Naivasha.

There are four up at Longonot and Kinangop in the Aberdares. Some gangs have been driven out of the Lowlands and make for higher ground. So it's you and O'Malley for Mount Kenya. Marvellous scenery. You'll enjoy it."

"I'll be fine," Jonathan said, with a confident grin to hide his fear.

By lunchtime, they finished loading rations, water, ammunition, blankets. Then both Blue and Red Troop were moved by lorry up to Nyeri at the southern edge of Mount Kenya where more Mau-Mau gangs were reported. For the whole week they were on patrol in the forests around the mountain, and then climbing higher up the western slopes towards the summit. Day after day they trudged on through the forests, looking for Mau-Mau gangs or signs of their movements. Wary of ambush, they reached after two days "cloud forest," above two thousand metres and cold in February. Climbing higher they came to bamboo, with only narrow paths blasted through by elephant and buffalo. The trackers had to go first. They would smell danger. It was prime ambush country.

MacNamara said, "Let's get the hell out of here into the higher land, where it's open."

They climbed as fast as possible, and came out on another plateau with Hagena and St John's Wort trees. Then there was another treeline and, above 3000 metres, the land of giant lobelia, giant heather, giant groundsel. The men, by this time straining in the thin air, had to stop more often. "Look like bloddy great weird cabbages on sticks." Flett said.

Noyk, who had been there before, was the expert. "It's the result of altitude, bags of sunshine and water. Some of 'em are over a hundred years old."

They stopped to drink and fill water bottles from a stream and to gaze at the trees, until the trackers said there were too many buffalo around. They had been told not to spend too long at that level for fear of pulmonary oedema, or "water on the lungs." Then it began to drizzle and then pour, so they were glad to go downhill, quickly back through the bamboo.

Every evening they camped at one of the fortified bunkers built for the purpose. One was full of mules. Hundreds of them. Some cavalry colonel from the Dragoon Guards had decided that it was a better way to move stores, rations and ammunition than by lorry. No one had argued, so he had his mule train. He travelled in an old buggy he called "The Surrey with the Fringe on Top." His men called it "'Is Lordship's mobile knocking shop." But they had everything there from ice-cream to grenades.

On friday afternoon, footsore, and with their clothes torn to ribbons by Wait-a-Bit thorns, transport came. The men cheered when they saw the lorries. They returned to the main camp near Nairobi. "Week-end off," Tim said, and Jonathan passed on the good news to his troop.

"Providing, by five o'clock, all your weapons are all clean, bright and slightly oiled." No one felt much like going out that night. Too many blisters.

By the end of that hectic first week, he knew he had achieved something. He was less embarrassed than before when he asked the men what they thought of Africa. Apart from inferior beer, absence of public transport, few cinemas, no fish and chip shops or TV and a small NAAFI, sex was the main complaint.

"Bird situation is effin' wicked," Harris stated sourly. "I'm thinkin' of writing to me M.P. about it. Africa!" he snorted. "Leave these nigs and settlers to fight it out amongst themselves, I say. Have you talked to the trackers, Sir?"

"No." Anyway how could he? What would he talk to them about if he could?

"You 'ave a natter with 'em, Sir. They've got one wot speaks Swahili. I can translate a bit for you." Harris advised him, "They're all sorts and shades and they 'ate these Kikooyoo like poison. Always 'ave, they say. Then take the ruddy climate. It's bloody freezing up in that forest. Wot a liberty, sending us out 'ere on this caper! Ain't a proper war at all, it aint."

"Seen any of the reserves yet?" Tim asked at tea. Jonathan told him he hoped to go next day. "Take my tip, don't go near any I.O.s or educated Africans just before lunch. I did. They told me about the oath-taking ceremonies and showed me photographs of the Lari massacre. Have another sandwich. Yes, charming fellows these Mickey mice."

"What a silly name. Why call them that?"

"Ki-Settla, old boy. Surely you've heard the Lerricks call them that? It's so they can talk about them in front of the house boys."

"It's still stupid. The men don't seem to have much enthusiasm. I…"

"Let's talk about it outside, shall we?" Tim cut in.

Sitting on Tim's camp chair, he watched him cleaning his beloved pair of Holland and Holland twelve bore shot-guns.

"What exactly are we doing here?" Jonathan asked. Meaning, what are we dying for?

117

"Well, just lately we had to clear forty thousand of them out of slums around Nairobi. Not soldiers' work, but then we aren't fighting a war. We're aiding the Civil Powers. Why? Because we are better at it than policemen. Mau-Mau are just murderers. This isn't anything new. The Army has been doing this sort of thing for centuries, you know that. Your granddad was Indian army. It's just that with all this talk of freedom, things have got out of proportion. These people were savages. We stopped them killing, one tribe against the other, non-stop. Gave them drains, brass water taps, loony bins and a few schools. But they can't be made happy factory workers overnight. Track record shows they've been killing each other, big time, for centuries. Much like Europeans really."

"Oh, I know, I know," Jonathan said wearily. He lay back on the bed listening to the cicadas buzzing noisily outside the tent. It was a warm, whispering noise that seemed very much part of Africa, warm and dry and somehow dead.

"Do you, though? They tell me that disease, drought, tribal wars have kept the population here below three million. Which is amazing considering the size of the place. There's a big contrast here between rich and poor, I know," Tim went on. "Like that all over the East too, believe me, and is this any different from that, or from what goes on in South America, or even in Europe? Look at Italy or Spain or Portugal. Are they much better? They will just have to have patience here, and ..."

"And that's what they haven't got. They want the land now," Jonathan broke in.

"Exactly," Tim said, squinting up through a barrel. "Too bad, isn't it? They'll have to bloody well wait a bit longer." He put the shining barrel lovingly back in its red velvet-lined case. "Anyway, tomorrow I want you to see the Rift Valley and something of the so-called White Highlands, which is what most of the argie-bargie is about. It's north-west of here, Limuru, Naivasha direction. Your Mount Kenya area is off to the north, as you found out. Thika, Kinangop way."

"Don't I bloody know it."

Next morning, they left the camp while it was still dark and drove up long sloping hills out of town until the altimeter on the dashboard read nine thousand feet. The car slowed as they went round a hairpin bend, dropping a hundred feet or so. The road was clawed down into the side of a steep hill on the right, and there they stopped and got out. It was cold and from behind the hill came faraway, sad cries of cocks crowing.

"Look at that," Tim said. There was a pale purplish suffusion a very great distance away, far below them behind a range of hills that ran across their front. It grew quickly, and as the light spread, so the hills seemed to recede further and further away and thousands of feet below. But it wasn't like the sunrise seen from the aeroplane. It was more gradual and everything was more still and real. Then the sun flung itself over the hills and flooded the Great Rift with blinding light. The hills were the other lip of the huge fault from the one they were standing on. The floor of the valley was one huge dried-out-looking expanse as far as the eye could see in both directions, and already the chill in the air had gone and Jonathan could feel the heat of the sun on his face. There was a freshness and feeling of new life in the sudden daylight that was almost tangible. A huge silence and stillness seemed to dominate the vast sweep of visible sky and earth. Eerily, Jonathan felt, as though in all the enormity of the unchanging, unimaginably ancient African scene there should be some terrifying mind-swamping noise to accompany the sight that the eyes and imagination could hardly accept.

He took off his jacket for the pleasure of feeling the sun on his bare cool arms. Down in the valley there were wisps of a thin dew that evaporated into mist, curling off the ground as they watched, being sucked up into nothingness. He felt that he wanted to throw off all his clothes and swoop down into the valley. Then hover over it like the few birds they could see, circling, riding thermals. Probably vultures waiting for some animal to die, or some lion to leave its prey among the scorched dust and the flat-topped fever trees. Silently they got into the car and cruised down the hill to a shelf nearer the valley floor where a bluff bellied out to the left, hiding the valley to the south. To the north there was nothing but the endless bush with the stunted thorns and acacia, hard and sharp in the early light; little pools of bedraggled shade beneath the tattered, flat umbrellas of their branches. Far away there was a conical mountain rising from the flatness. "Longonot," Tim said, and the single, craggy word seemed to be all there was to say.

They turned the jeep and climbed back up the escarpment, past a large white noticeboard that read, "SIGHTSEERS ARE WARNED TO BEWARE OF ARMED TERRORISTS. THE FOREST IS A CLOSED AREA. NO PICNICKING OR LIGHTING OF FIRES."

He looked at Tim. He was smiling. Jonathan smiled back, but not because of the incongruous position of being a soldier sightseer, or the notion of picnicking, but because he was experiencing a sense of exultation that Tim would have thought ludicrous. He felt that he understood now just a little, the enormity of Africa, its seemingly pointless prodigality of desolate wilderness, and its harsh opposition to humanity. This thinking of Africa as savage, feral, a challenge not only to himself but to everyone he knew who lived in it, excited him. At the same time he smiled at himself for his intensity. "Such a contrast," he said, "between living on an over-populated little island where every square yard belongs to somebody, and just being here where space and openness gets inside the mind. This wild emptiness and distance. It's intoxicating."

"No need to get carried away," Tim said.

As they drove there was a fortified village dominated by an unstable-looking wooden tower, that guarded the cattle compounds and the round-thatched huts. The smoke of cooking fires rising in the morning air. "In those huts," Tim said, "are both common murderers and the future leaders of this country. See that ridge. The local Kikuyu rent yearly from the Masai. That's a bit weird, I think. Now. Pay attention. What you see here follows the Malaya plan. Isolate the villagers, so they can't feed the gangs. Fortify each village. Keep the terrorists away from sources of food information. Worked in Malaya. Might work here. Got it?"

They drove back in silence, up the steep road from the Rift Valley floor.

"Top o' the mornin'. Been shootin'?" Seamus O'Connor said at breakfast, poking at his kipper warily with the end of a fork.

Seamus was another one whose dad was a General. His mother, Tim said, owned more gold mines than you could shake a stick at. He wore a monocle without a string, which fascinated Jonathan, who watched it constantly for fear he might miss the moment when it fell off. "Um... Yes," he said vaguely. It might embarrass Tim if he said they had just been to watch a sunrise. "Get anything?" Surely he didn't need the thing if his eyesight was good enough to get into the Army? But it did suit him. "No. 'Fraid not."

"Hard luck," O'Connor said, looking straight ahead of him, his eyeglass discarded for the moment as he munched at his kipper.

The Reserves around Thika, with its fortified villages, were still dangerous. The atmosphere was tense, although the Temporary District Officer who showed them round carried no gun; everybody seemed either over-serious, or displaying a jaunty wartime sense of humour.

"Ask for names at all times," Tim had told him. So he jogged the elbow of the police sergeant, and asked. "Thomson, Sir."

"And the D.O.?" he whispered.

"'Enry Grattan–Bellew. Sir 'Enry to the likes of us." Jonathan gaped. The D.O. looked about nineteen. And back in God's Own Country, Grattan-Bellew was a name to conjure with.

Cosgrave said that it looked a lot better now that agriculture was more organised and the straggling cultivators brought in to live in the fortified villages. But it was overcrowded even so, and the goats and cattle were mostly puny and forlorn-looking. When Jonathan mentioned this, Henry the D.O. stopped at a village and produced an English-speaking headman. This man wore the blue jersey and belt as affected by the tribal police, with a khaki topee complete with a brass badge, the Lion of Kenya. While the D.O. inspected the fort Jonathan strolled around the village with the headman questioning him.

"They are suspicious and ignorant people here, Bwana," he said. "We have taught them to use manure and rotate their crops, but when they can get cash for them they grow the same things all the time. They can see the money, but they do not see the earth is tired."

"You need more land. Is that not true?" Jonathan asked him.

"Yes, Bwana, it is true."

"Do the other tribes also need more land?"

"Don't know, Bwana."

They passed a group of wizened old men sitting in a circle under a gum tree talking, their knees poking up around their ears as they squatted, baring their pointed teeth and squinting through their rheumy smoke-reddened old eyes. Some of them smoked and most of them carried snuff horns from which they took a vile-looking mixture of black tobacco and rock soda, snuffled it up their flat nostrils and spat wisely onto the hot red earth.

"What do they think about Mau-Mau?" Jonathan asked.

"Now they are pleased, Bwana, because the young men who would not listen to them have been sent to prison or have come back here humbled, to work. But, it was old men like these who helped to start it. They are always talking of ways to get land and cattle. They have nothing else to do."

They went for a beer to Fort Hall, the administrative centre of Kikuyuland, and Cosgrave tried to discuss trade with Thomson, who was a farmer's son and wasn't directly much interested in the future of the Reserves.

"No," he said, "You won't make a fortune as an import agent in Nairobi after this nonsense is over, because we are hoofing the Hindis out of the Reserves and it's all going to be controlled."

"Don't tell me," Cosgrave laughed, "You mean no one is going to flog them umbrellas and hoes and rubber goods?"

"Maybe to Kyuke traders, wholesale, yes. You won't sell them that sort of rubber goods, anyway. Kids are like cattle to them, they want to see numbers and to hell with the economics of it. They're hopeless, man, I tell you. And you want to give them a vote, eh?" He laughed a dry humourless laugh and called for the Goan who owned the bar to serve more beer. That he should be an Asian in this place seemed odd to Jonathan. Africans, they told him, were not shopkeepers.

The bar was the only one outside the club, and it was full of young men in khaki and camouflaged smocks. An air of intense camaraderie prevailed. People came up to Thomson, slapped him on the back and called him "Tembo". Everybody seemed to know everybody else, but no one was very anxious to talk to the two Commando officers.

"You'd understand that, begorrah," Seamus said. "You are only here for a year. They are in this for life. Only natural they don't feel no great enthusiasm for us. Visitors, sent by Whitehall. We don't have to live in twos and threes in mud and wattle shanties scattered all over the reserve. Where's Henry gone, by the way?" he asked Thomson.

"Horses," was the reply. He's got several up here. He rides about with Digby Tatham Warter, the colonel who commands the Mounted Section."

"Not the one who was at Arnhem?"

"That's the one. Used to carry an umbrella everywhere. Said he never remembered the password. Not too many Germans use umbrellas."

Jonathan was very impressed. Tatham Warter was highly decorated, and one of the heroes of the battle for the bridge at Arnhem.

He must have several DSOs if not a VC," he said to Cosgrave, who smiled indulgently and replied "Oh, at least."

After that he was glad to get back to camp and walk about talking to his men. On morning parade there were just lines of identical uniforms. Now they were cleaning their rifles and stripping down the Brens and Sten guns; oiling them and re-assembling. McNamara and Flett and Noyk strode about supervising. After the brooding threat of danger out in the reserves, he took a little comfort from the comparative friendliness of his troop.

When the men went to tea at four o'clock he went over to the horse lines and begged a hack from the corporal in charge.

"Only supposed to keep round the camp area, Sir," he said. "If you meets a gang and gets chopped, I'll get put on a charge."

"Let 'em catch me," Jonathan said over his shoulder, as he cantered off.

He galloped along the edge of a wood and through some

scattered maize and bananas until he was brought up short by a road. Crossing a concrete storm drain he noticed a flat water meadow on his left stretching away between mealie patches on one side and a coffee plantation on the other. He went down into the meadow that was really rough vlei and let the horse go until it was winded. There were more mealies at the end of the vlei and he threaded his way through them towards a house he could see in the middle distance.

In the middle of the mealies he suddenly came on a cluster of huts, their round thatched roofs straggling almost to the ground, and smoke filtering sluggishly through them. Naked children played about, their bodies streaked with the red dust. He got off the horse saying "Jambo, jambo" to the children, who clung to their mother's grimy dress, sucking at sticks and gazing at him with big white eyes from their pitifully comic, bald, black heads. He walked over to another hut and looked inside, while the horse strained at the bridle and tried to back away. There were no windows to the huts and all there was to see were heaps of rags and a few tins, boxes and old cooking pots. The roof inside dripped with gummy soot from the smoke and there was a stench, acrid and piercing, that he supposed was a combination of African sweat and stale smoke.

He turned away thoughtfully with a wave at the children and walked the horse towards the house. He was stopped by a wire fence, but coming to a track he rode along it. Turning a corner he saw in front of him nothing but coffee and he estimated that the road was to his right, so he went off the track down a ride through the coffee trees. At the end of the ride was a fence surrounding a big long bungalow and to get out he had to skirt the fence, since there was no break in the orderly rows of coffee. A man shouted at him from inside the wire, so he broke into a canter downhill towards a track he could see. After a few minutes the track emerged on a road that was really only a wider track. Among a group of nameboards at one track junction he saw the name "LERRICK" and on impulse he went up towards their house. But when he came to the gate the sentry refused to open it. Jonathan gestured and jamboed and smiled, but the African was adamant. Eventually he consented to send a young boy who was with him with a message, "Kwa Bwana Lellick."

Jonathan felt rather foolish when Tom appeared, stern faced, walking down the drive, followed by several urchins in khaki shirts that hung grubbily below their knees in place of trousers. He hadn't meant to visit anybody.

"Oh hello," he said, warmly enough. "Sorry about this, but I've got to do it; it's something you'll be told about anyway in the next few days, so come and see. But don't tell a soul, will you? I mean that." One of the urchins, the biggest, with a crop of enormous bow-fronted teeth took his horse's bridle and danced away with it chattering to the others in their weird language that seemed to be composed entirely of shrill liquid syllables and ululations without any noticeable consonants.

He lead Jonathan round to the side of the house where a new compound had been put up around an existing store room. He unlocked the gate and locked it after him. Inside Jonathan saw what looked like a group of Africans in the King's African Rifles. Tom went into the store room where there were beds and a chained rifle rack, and boxes piled along the walls. He opened one of the boxes and took out a pack made out of some animal's skin, and a shapeless jacket made of another skin.

"Out there is my private army," Tom said, "And this is our equipment. Those chaps include two Kikuyu, one of them an ex-terrorist turned Queen's evidence. He has volunteered to show us a few hides, for which I admire him, because even without helping us he half believes that having broken his oath, it will kill him."

"But what's the point?" Jonathan asked. "You dress up in skins and look like Mau-Mau, but if you meet a gang in broad daylight, they won't believe you're an African with your face, blackened or not. And what if I meet you? I will fire the minute I see men dressed like that."

"We shall see you first, or hear you, I'm afraid. Two of those chaps out there are Wa'Ndrobo. Okiek tribe, hunter-gatherers. Never worn uniform or anything like it until today. They are out and out bushmen, and they lived in this part of Africa before the Kikuyu came here. I got these two off the fringes of a farm on the Mau Escarpment. They still hunt for a living, but just at the moment they are willing to fight because a gang killed some of their people recently. I've got two big Nandi policemen and a couple of the toughest NCOs the K.A.R. could provide. We'll operate at night mostly so my face don't matter. Information we are after. Gang movements and numbers. But if we can get near any of the leaders then we will. I use the system I learnt from David Stirling in the desert with the S.A.S. A few skilled men behind the lines, can achieve far more than normal infantry. Sorry, Jonathan, but that is how it is. This is the way to clear this mess up. The Army can keep them moving and do sweeps to clear areas, but this is the way to clean the gangs up, you'll see."

"And if you walk into one of our ambushes one night?"

"We shall be killed. One or two of us anyway. As we will if we walk into a bus one night down in Nairobi." He put his hand out on Jonathan's shoulder. "Come on, man, let's get you away from here. Gillian came in just now."

So that is what we are, Jonathan thought. We act like beaters on a grouse shoot, driving the game while the locals, who know the forest trails, do the business. Thanks.

"Why are there so many natives over there, with no fences? No lookout towers, no…"

Tom interrupted him. "Don't need them around here. They're not Kikuyu. Kipsigis, Guluo. Brought in to replace Kikuyu. This area is between your camp and my shamba. Take a brave Mau-Mau to show himself round here."

As they passed through the compound the corporal stood up and saluted. He had a face like something from an Egyptian tomb, oval and coppery in colour, with almond-shaped eyes and a mouth like a knife slit. A cruel, un-African face, yet as he put his hat on Jonathan saw that his head was covered with the characteristic fuzz. Tom, following his look, said, "That's Ali, a Somali crossed with something from up on the Sudan border. They have some of the most Allah-forsaken country you will ever see in a part of the world that is only rocks, flies and sand." As they walked towards the house. Jonathan said, "It seems odd to me that some villages are surrounded with wire. Watchtowers and all."

"Lieutenant. This is Africa. Takes time to understand our

tribal systems. Worry not. Now let's go and have some chai."

He bounded up the verandah steps in front of Jonathan. As they entered the house, the harsh sunlight and heat dropped behind them like a wave. He walks as though he was always in a hurry, Jonathan thought, swinging from the hip. He must have calf muscles like spring steel. Following him, it occurred to him that Tom assumed he had really come to call on his sister. No use explaining that he hadn't.

She was sitting with her mother and a middle-aged man in an oil-stained tweed jacket and tattered flannel trousers. She sent Gillian to tell Wambai to bring more tea. "I can't think why we don't fit bells in this room," she said as Gillian went out.

"Tom," his mother said. "The Game Department rang. Apparently Bwana Mrefu up at Nyeri has had his fences trampled again. He said he was going out shooting in his headlights tonight if something wasn't done. He's got buffalo trouble as well."

"Oh, damn him. As if we hadn't got enough trouble, the bloody fool. Well, I'll take my boys with me and sort him out. He's probably got Micks on the farm as well, but as long as they don't trample his bloody fences it's all right."

The man in the remains of a tweed jacket had been introduced as John Gore. "At least I haven't got that trouble," he said, "But I was just telling your mother that they took thirty of my labour away for screening yesterday. I have to go out patrolling two or three times a week, the wife's got jaundice and one of the kids had just broken his arm. All I need now is locusts and I'll be ready to go somewhere else."

"Don't be depressing, John," Jane Lerrick said, "You'll give Mr Fitzpatrick here the idea that we came here for fun or something."

"Oh I couldn't leave Africa," Gore said. "But I'll have to go and work for someone at this rate. Well, I must go now. Excuse me, won't you?" As he heaved himself out of his chair, his revolver in its polished leather case slapped against his thigh with a hollow sound and as he began to walk it was obvious that he had an artificial leg. Gillian came in as he left, with Wambai carrying a tray.

"He really took on some odds, that old boy," Tom said in a low voice. "He only started six years ago and his trees have only just started to bear. If he doesn't get a crop this year he's finished." Wambai lowered the tray, the silver on it contrasting with her sagging bosom and her shining ebony face. Theirs was a savage beauty there under the ebony skin.

Gillian was wearing a tan dress that was just darker than the colour of her arms. The sun-bleached hair contrasted with her skin; she wore her hair razor-cut against the out-springing curl, so that it stood out from the curve of her neck. It was a wheaten colour, but closer to the skull it seemed darker. Looking at her in profile he realised that in her facial structure, in the sweep of her jawline and set of her nose and brow she was more than just pretty. The eyebrows folded back in a high wing away from the eyes, and the hair was lighter than the skin behind it. What a marvellous colouring she had, with those eyes that were almost violet and the skin that was café au lait, a smooth, creamy café au lait. How much did Tim know about her? What was there behind the lovely face? Jane Lerrick asked him questions about Ireland while he, tried not to stare at the daughter.

He told Jane, "People in Ireland are not very concerned about what happened in Kenya, any more than what happened in Algeria, Rhodesia or South Africa. After all," he added, "most of them wouldn't be able to locate any of them if shown a blank map of Africa."

"There are a lot of Irish farmers here," she said, "Sheep and wheat, mostly. Up past Nakuru. Ewart Grogan built the railway from here up to Londiani to get timber out. He's Irish. Eighty this year. Still working. Mr Big Business."

"Is that 'Cape-to Cairo' Grogan?"

"That's the one. We see him often. But this is coffee country. You'll see."

Tom Lerrick, who had been reading a newspaper, stood up, asked where his shooting hat was and said that he must go up to Nyeri before it got dark. "Look after Jonathan, will you?" he asked Gillian, "He's got a horse outside."

"Thank you, dear," she replied, "I didn't think he wore jodhpurs for scootering." But Tom threw his bush hat at her, and she turned to Jonathan. "What did you come over on a horse for?"

"Gillian!" her mother said.

"Well, I meant, the Army always hare about in jeeps, don't they? You never see any of our precious policemen in anything but a car, in or on."

"I'm just old-fashioned," Jonathan said. "Besides, I don't own a jeep or a car."

"Let's go and see it," she said, leaping up.

"If you see your father, tell him to come inside," her mother said, and added, "Gillian, have you still got a gun in your bag, because you leave it about all over the place." Gillian whirled round, an alarmed look on her face. "No, I haven't. Hey, don't say things like that. I forgot for a second, Sam took it to hand in. It was broken anyway."

Jonathan followed her out to the back verandah. The sun was much lower in the sky. He looked at his watch. It was nearly six o'clock and the horses had to be back, half an hour before curfew at seven. There wasn't much time. Don't mess about gawking, he told himself. This is infighting country. The scene on the verandah of the "Green Cockerel" or the "Golden Alligator" or whatever it was, flashed to his mind. She was Lalage's closest friend. So box clever, he told himself. Tipsy she might have been then, but there was none of the coy reticence of Knightsbridge there, be japers.

"Holler. Cheroge," she ordered, and without hesitation he hollered, only protesting afterwards, "I just gave it to one of them. Or isn't that a name?" Tim said.

She laughed. It was a good laugh. It sounded as though she had been physically tickled, and it was what his father called a "good, ripe, belly laugh."

"No," she said, "the Sais is called Cheroge, but they nearly all are Cheroges. When it comes to writing a pass or anything, Cheroge, son of Kamau is as easy to write as anything. On pay day they admit to other names, though."

A tough-looking man appeared leading a horse. He wore a torn white shirt and long patched shorts with puttees wound around his calves. His huge splayed feet bare. She spoke to him rapidly in Swahili and he grinned a slow grin. His teeth were filed in front and the two lower front ones were missing. He said something reluctantly.

"This one's not a Cheroge," she said. "He's a Kipsigis, a drunken old blighter too. Says he's called Arap Chepkoin. That's Kipsigis for Cheroge, although he doesn't agree." She looked critically at the horse. "That looks like Mrs Trumper's jumper. Hell doesn't that sound odd? It looks like it, though." She roared at her own joke. Beautiful teeth.

"It might well be," Jonathan said, feeling slightly outployed, "We get rations for so many nags and people seem to just send them along."

"Well let's send Chepkoin off to look for Pa. He stays out until dark unless you chunga him."

"I've got to get back soon," Jonathan said, feeling that that was a feeble start. "At least the horse has."

"Oh, stay for dinner. Arap Chepkoin can take the horse back."

"No, well, thank you, but I can't. He would be out after curfew, wouldn't he?"

"No, it's all right." She spoke to the Sais again and Jonathan resolved to learn Swahili. And again, to get some kind of car or a share in one; both immediately.

"But they won't let him into the camp." This was all very well, but wasn't she ordering everybody about just a little, and how was he going to get back to camp? The African hooked one bare, prehensile toe into the stirrup iron and swung into the saddle as Gillian said, "He'll stay there, he won't mind."

"I'd better ring the camp," Jonathan said, putting his hand into his pocket for a tip and finding no money at all. It occurred to him that he had to book out of the mess for dinner.

"I shouldn't bother," she said, as the horse trotted off. "He'll tell your saises."

"We don't have them. The soldiers look after them."

"Do they really?" she said vaguely. And a moment later as they walked away, "Poor Father, he was going to hand over to Tom and now all the managers have been called up."

Jonathan looked at her to counteract the feeling that was

growing that he should have stayed in camp and got on with Sir James Sleeman's "From Rifle to Camera." Perhaps it was normal to ask people to dinner here in jodhpurs at no notice, sending their transport away with a wave? Still it was stimulating, even if they did begin to refer to him in the mess as "Lover Boy Fitz." But trousers were a problem, if a tie wasn't.

"Glad you came over," he heard her say, breaking his chain, or rather jumble, of thought.

"I get so bored," she went on, punctuating each utterance by scuffling with one foot, then the other, in the dust, so that the tan suede was turning a rather pleasing auburn colour.

"Is the Army fun?" she said suddenly, pivoting on one foot with a quick skip, so that she was facing him. She seemed to be examining his hairline.

"I'm not really qualified to say, ...I..."

"How English," she laughed, doing another skip and throwing her head back.

"Irish actually, "Jonathan said firmly, "Only been soldiering for a few months; I can hardly judge. It is fun being an officer after being yelled at by sadistic drill sergeants. We spent six months marching up and down a parade ground, and learning how to fire a rifle. Something I learnt when I was ten. So I can't think of a better place to play soldiers in than Africa."

She half turned towards him with a frown. "You don't like having to fight Africans, do you?" But before he could reply, they had reached the verandah. She sat down with a flounce that distracted him and now, looking at her, he could see the mounds of her breasts pushing up from the top of her dress, which distracted him more.

"But," she went on as he sat down beside her, "it may sound rude but we don't really need soldiers from outside. Only police, really. But I'm not going to be dreary. I only asked really because working in an office isn't fun. At least not the one I'm in now. But Pa won't let me work *here*, and I have to do something. What are you going to do when you leave the Army?" The question took Jonathan by surprise as he had only been half listening as usual and most of his attention had strayed to contemplating her face and the fading colours of the garden.

"Do? I don't know. Farm with father maybe. I have a law degree. But I don't like the idea of being a solicitor."

"I've just had an idea."

"What. About what I should do?"

"No." Her eyes had become enormous. He saw in them what he thought of to himself as her 'verandah look'. Sure enough, a secretive smile had begun in the corners of her mouth. "No, about just now. Let's go out somewhere. I know lots of places. Let's find you clothes." She leapt up before Jonathan had time to display his empty pockets. After all he, could always take her to the Country Club and sign a chit. But this was getting embarrassing.

They passed Lerrick Senior in a corridor on their way to find clothes, and Gillian put her head round a door and told her mother that Jonathan was taking her out. "On his horse, dear?" Jonathan heard her say before Gillian shut the door. While struggling into a mixture of Sam Webb's and Tom's clothes he reflected that he might meet Tim or Lalage in the Country Club, which would faintly surprise both. He felt he could do with a little gin to smooth over the problems of the evening.

While Gillian changed, he phoned the mess and when he went to say goodbye to the Lerricks, he was offered the needed sundowner, and Jane told him, eyeing Sam's trousers, not to let Gillian stay out too late. But she said it so that he understood her real meaning. She was quite obviously aware of the real situation. This sort of thing had probably happened to Sam, and half Nairobi for all he knew.

She drove the MG very fast, skidding on the uncambered corners of the dirt roads, so that he promised himself to take the wheel and show her how a gearbox ought to be used on corners, on the return journey. "Hell, don't fret, Jong," she said in a mock South African twang. "I've got some shillingi. You might take me out again sometime."

Mario of the "Silver Bamboo" produced a table in a pool of darkness, the other side of the room from the band, and on the edge of the floor. It was only a restaurant, but the non-existence of an African branch of the Lord's Day Observance Society, and presumably a lesser competition for licences, plus the occupation of the police force with civil security, all had their effect on the atmosphere. There was a noisy party going on which Gillian said was a send off for someone called up into the Kenya Regiment.

Some people she knew called Dwent appeared, a quiet, pale-faced man, bespectacled and heavily jowled, with a dark haired vivacious wife who called Gillian 'Darling' and drank whiskies and sodas. There was the beginning of hardness in her face, he thought, under the vivid make-up, and she seemed to want to steer the conversation away from any subject connected with England. There was some indefinable tension between them and he found that he had little to say to Henry Dwent, who sat there watching his wife, and saying "Yum" and "Yam" when appealed to briefly for an opinion.

Jonathan was relieved when they decided to go to the bar whilst he danced with Gillian. "Locals?" he asked. She made a face. "He isn't. She was, but I fancy she'd settle for a little love nest near Brighton. Funny, really. She was brought up here on a farm up-country."

"What did you think of Brighton, or England, anyway?"

She paused and stared away into space for a moment before re-focusing.

"Terribly small and over-crowded. Everything was so complicated and organised. I mean you had to book everything months before and that sort of thing. No one asks you to stay. I mean here people come and stay with us for weeks. And there were white people doing jobs that Africans can do. That's what surprised me most. After those huge shops in London."

"Jobs?"

"Yes. Like drivers and porters and messengers. And there were terribly poor and decrepit people too. I always thought there wasn't anything like that in England. Not just poverty I mean, but... it's hard to explain," she frowned comically in concentration. Over her shoulder Jonathan was not happy to see the Dwents steering towards them..."I mean, me, I've always thought of blacks as manual workers. No...I mean, thought of labourers as being black; carpenters as being Sikhs, clerks and shopkeepers being Indian. Besides you always shout so much about the poor blacks and your Welfare state, that I didn't expect to see all those dirty little houses and poor tattered white people sitting on park benches. You ... Oh, hello, June."

"Got anything to eat yet, sweetie?"

As the Dwents sat down, June said, "Haven't you ever heard the story, about the Zulu cook who asked her Memsaab who mended the roads in England?"

"No," Gillian said, with a look at Henry Dwent. "Well, the Memsaab or whatever said white men did, and the cook flung her apron over her head and let out a great Ayeee of astonishment." No one smiled.

"She was trying to hide her amusement," Gillian said.

"Oh that's not the point. Well forget it." Jonathan felt like another drink. He offered the Dwents something, but Henry said he thought they might have a bottle, so Jonathan hastily took Gillian off to dance.

"Did you say she was born here?" he asked as they samba'ed rather inefficiently.

"Why?"

"Seems a bit po-faced, that's all."

"Do waggle your hips and relax a bit. Well I must say she's been very quiet since she married him. He's as dull as blazes. A typical sprig of our dear Administration. Nice fat pension waiting at home. Why should he care? She used to be one of Nairobi's jolliest. Can't understand it. You can be jolly in this place, you know. Not the variety you get in London but people are more human. I saw a bank manager do a strip-tease once when he thought the girl doing it was dull. You couldn't do a *thing* in London without the police arriving. Once they were taking some friends of ours away in a Black Maria and we shouted at them, so it stopped and took us along too. Still they are getting duller here nowadays. We got fined forty shillings last month for riding on top of a safari wagon. The judge asked me if it was Christmas and I said "No, Sir, it was just January." I think he thought it was silly. Poor old Phil Gredling got fined two hundred for throwing bus stop notices about. He said he didn't think anybody would notice at three in the morning, and he was only practising for tossing the caber."

They had finished their soup and the boy had just produced

Tilapia. Gillian was just explaining that they were lake fish and that you rarely got any other fish except at the coast; when all the lights went out. Candles were produced and Jonathan noticed that beside Henry Dwent's fork was a Biretta revolver. "What was all that about, the lights I mean?"

"Just the East African Power and Darkness Company, dear," Gillian said, and Henry Dwent chose to be nettled and launched a complex defence of officialdom.

"You'll notice, Jon, the subtle difference between the local bred and outsiders, like me. As regards attitude to everyday life. Seems to hinge on the fact that the locals consider that they have no support from officialdom. Settlers are committed to live in Africa. They tell us," Dwent went on, "that instead of investing in it, we and the Colonial Office smugly sitting in Great Smith Street haggle over every penny."

"Hang on a mo," Gillian broke in, "How about the primitive conditions up-country. Damn few domestic amenities. Constant battle against climate and green labour. Exasperating controls. Ask Dad. Do you appreciate the difficulties of entrusting expensive farm machinery and expensive cattle to illiterates with stone age habits?"

"Sound just like your dad," June said. Gillian ignored her "We have a school on the farm," Gillian said to Henry. "But this country can't have a university. You should provide them, or guarantee us security so that someone will risk the money." The band struck up a rhumba.

She stood up. "One of my favourites, Jonathan. Come along." He found himself jiggling around the floor, relieved to quit the argument.

He steered the conversation away by telling rather feeble stories such as the one about the Fellow of All Souls who asked him to tea, couldn't find the crumpets he had bought to toast on the electric fire. He sent for his Scout, who eventually located them under his pillow. They didn't seem to follow the joke.

"It's not that I don't care about Africa and all that, but Henry is so *preaching*, and I like to form my own opinions," she said, as the Dwents got up to dance.

Henry Dwent firmly refused to go on to a night-club and

135

June asked them to their house for coffee instead. "We'll go later," Gillian whispered.

"Where?"

"The Green Door. The band's *too* smoochy." She clung to his arm and Jonathan drove, finding the slithering wheels on the loose surface a little trying in the winding, unlit roads.

The Dwent's house was a bungalow, which was all it seemed to have in common with the Lerricks', apart from a skin-covered native drum, a few carvings on the mantelpiece and a slovenly looking houseboy in a grubby kanzu. June sent him away and they went into the kitchen, while Henry turned on a radiogram and picked up a book. The kitchen was modern in appearance but ill-equipped. June unlocked a storeroom and got out coffee and sugar while Gillian wandered about looking at things and munching a stick of celery she had found in the refrigerator. This was also fitted with a lock. Gillian poked her head inside the store.

"Far too small," June complained.

"Small?" Gillian said, removing the celery and lifting her eyebrows. "Hell, the mice in there must be hunchbacks. What lousy Hindi contractor did this?"

Jonathan exploded with laugher, but June only smiled fleetingly.

"It isn't a government bungalow," she said defensively.

"Never mind, dear," Gillian said between munches. "You don't have cockroaches dropping off the ceiling and young trees growing up through the floor."

"No. But we have ants crawling up through the so-called drains. I must come round and scrounge some of your coffee. This stuff is soapy."

"Do," Gillian trilled, picking up the tray and flouncing through the door into the bright, English-looking sitting room. Jonathan followed her, catching a catty look fading rapidly from June's face as she passed him. How healthy and vigorous they both were. Mustn't be too hard on the poor colonials.

Henry was sipping at a beer. Jonathan, thinking of the wine bottled in Italian Somaliland that he had just drunk, and of First Parade at 6 a.m., took a brandy although he was thirsty. Gillian and June swapped reminiscences of their schooldays over their coffee, and then became giggly over the brandy and more stories about what they called the "Heifer Boma." Henry yawningly discussed the second-hand car market and fiddled with the radiogram. Just before midnight Gillian got up to go. "Green Door, here we come," she said happily and outside she wanted to drive, and a scuffle resulted.

"No necking in suburbia," she said as she pushed him away. He let her go and she let him sit in the driving seat. But once he got there he asked her if she didn't want to go home. "I want to dance," she insisted, and leant her head on his shoulder. Jonathan was so weary he could hardly keep his eyes open. "Now I'm bored," he said. "Oh buck up, let's dance," she replied.

As soon as he could he dragged her outside. On the way to camp an argument sprung up. "Don't be so sarcastic," she told him, meaning his comments about the Dwents. "June is a funny creature but she hasn't had a very amusing life. Her father was killed during the war, in Somalia, and she's never been out of East Africa. Her father walked here from the Cape fifty years ago. Wait until you've done some walking around here, before you criticise."

"Sorry," Jonathan said, "but the Dwents bored me. I'll bring these clothes over tomorrow, and see your boy gets back."

"Yes, do. The boy will be all right. He'd better be." She stopped near the camp entrance and switched off the engine, but Jonathan got out. She held up her face to be kissed and Jonathan hesitated. "Are you really attracted?" she said, wistfully.

"M'm. Oh yes. But don't tell Sam. I like being driven about by girls in sports cars." He leant over and kissed her on the forehead, but she put out her hands to his face and pulled it down to hers.

"You're nice for a Rooinek," she told him, kissing him on the mouth enthusiastically. "You're a dreamy old thing, but I like you."

Then she started the engine with a roar, swung the car round in the road, let second gear in with a bang, and was off in a whirl of dust.

"Que sera, sera," Jonathan said to himself thoughtfully as

he walked towards the camp gate. And it never, ever occurred to him how much she really liked him, odd "Rooinek" that he was, lost and pale-faced in Africa. Not really entirely at home on this planet. Or, as his father said, "with a somewhat loose grip on reality."

Blimey, he thought as he marched through the gate, returning the smart salutes of the guard, Tim said women were in short supply. Where has Tim been since he got here? Knowing him, he'd been out on patrol or seeing that the men got the best there was available. Got to be careful not to get a reputation he told himself. He had always been shy with girls, having sisters much older than himself. School had been a Benedictine monastery and the Army had no women at all. Not in the cadet school, anyway. Here they seemed particularly forward. To the point of brazen.

CHAPTER ELEVEN

PATROL

"Baada ya kisa, mkasa. After a reason, an event.
Baada ya chanzo, kitando.After a beginning, action."

Swahili proverb

"Kifaru," whispered the old Wand'robo, as the dry twigs cracked behind a screen of bushes. The noise went on steadily as the patrol remained frozen, crouching where they were in the straggling bush. With a crash the rhinoceros emerged from the thicker bushes. The warning bird on its wrinkled grey back flew up with a screech, and with a flick of its horn the animal charged, massive, but quick on its feet, like a huge frightened cat, its short, stubby legs pounding the earth. It passed within three yards of Tom Lerrick and thundered off downhill, scattering branches and twigs in its trail. He handed the hunting rifle to the 'Ndrobo and took his Padgett back. He waved it over his head and the patrol set off again cautiously. There were a lot of fresh marks about where rhinos had been grubbing at the roots of bushes with their nose horns. The 'Ndrobo was making a soft hissing sound as he walked. Tom was too occupied with his thoughts to tell him to stop. Besides, the old man might well have some weird reason of his own for the hissing. They were a tribe which didn't make mistakes in the matter of bushcraft.

It was the fourth day and already he had confirmed one thing. The gangs were finding it more and more difficult to terrorise the Reserves. Driven out into the Aberdares it meant that only the hard-core were left. The part-timers in the Reserves and the European farms on its fringes were becoming cut off.

Then the Army had made sweeps through the Aberdare mountains and put cordons round likely areas. Ambushes and patrols kept the gangs moving. But now they were moving down from the high country into the Rift Valley where there was a good supply of European cattle and sheep, less police and only inexperienced and panicky farm guards.

He had reported a large gang by radio as moving in that direction. A spotter plane saw them just before dark on his second day out. An ambush laid ahead of it that night had split the gang up but caused few casualties in the darkness. Tom was sure that few had broken back his way and was following the spoor of the largest splinter gang, that was at least eight strong. This contact had proved not only his theory, but also that his type of patrol could be more useful than those which returned to a base every night, or every morning. This he had learned the hard way in North Africa and Italy. Four-man S.A.S. patrols were fast and flexible.

Now Tom had to show that he could obtain vital information by visiting labour lines as a Mau-Mau gang, and finally and most importantly, show that the use of ex-terrorists was justifiable, by enabling him to contact gangs. In addition there was the chance that Kathenge would be wherever the main gangs were moving. Tom considered that there would be small chance of coming across him, but it was his ambition. Kathenge had been gun-bearer to Karl Gottschmer, a farmer and hunter. He had murdered him personally during the first weeks of the Emergency. He was an expert shot, a first-class tracker, tireless on the move and gifted with more than his share of the Kikuyu forest cunning that centuries of harrying by the Masai had bred into them. Kamau, the ex-terrorist, had told Daniel, his Marakwet corporal that the only thing he was really afraid of was coming across Kathenge. On questioning him he said that he thought it was likely that either Kathenge or Dedan Kimathi would accompany any major gang move.

They had spent part of the previous night in a hide that had been used by gangs a few days before. Tom had laid out an ambush and normally would have stayed there longer, when one night produced no result. In the circumstances, following the direction of the gangs were taking was the obvious policy. They had used the hide to rehearse the system to be used in contacting a gang. To the astonishment of the two 'Ndrobo, they had surrounded the hide while Kamau said the Mau-Mau greeting, made the signs and approached, holding a conversation with imaginary terrorists. The two 'Ndrobo, both elderly men by African standards, being probably over forty, refused to have anything to do with Kamau or Kangi the other Kikuyu. M'kuna, who spoke for both of them, since his fellow tribesmen rarely spoke at all, said he didn't understand Kamau's Swahili, and the only reason he consented to carry a gun was, he insisted firmly, because he felt unsafe when Kangi carried one.

Kangi treated this as a joke and teased both M'kuna and his companion, who admitted to no name beyond the succinct title of "Mzee" – the Old Man, about their primitive habits such as their refusal even to wear sandals cut out of a car tyre. But Kangi was the patrol cook and Tom noticed that he was scrupulously fair with the division of food, and only amused himself by pretending to tempt the 'Ndrobo with things he knew they would never touch; Army biscuits, sardines and lumps of ration chocolate. Both M'kuna and Mzee carried food packs and Kangi would enquire at intervals whether they had been at the "Biscotti" or the "Samaki,"(Fish), or whether they would like to exchange packs with Kamau, who for the speedier redemption of his sins carried the heavy awkward wireless batteries.

The patrol had shaken out rather better than Tom had expected. He had given half to Daniel in the event of a split becoming necessary, and kept with him the two Kikuyu, M'kuna and one of the Nandi policemen, Kipkoin, armed with a Sten gun. Daniel's section was composed of Mzee, who carried only his spear, Cheragoi and another Nandi policemen, who carried the wireless and operated it, armed with an old Colt 45 with the serial number filed off. Lastly his fellow NCO from the King's African Rifles, a slim cat-footed man like himself, Ali Wainiri. Ali came from the Sudan border, and his long frizzy hair, now dyed black, had ginger streaks in it, indicating Somali blood. He had been the regiment welter-weight champion and liked to be addressed as Tchui (Leopard), a soubriquet which he justified by performing morning and night a series of exercises, watched by the 'Ndrobo with wide eyes. He would lash out with his fists, work his feet like pistons and snort fiercely through his nostrils. Mzee had been moved, so Daniel informed him, to make one of his rare utterances. "That man," he had said gravely, "has very bad spirit in belly."

They were a good team and got along together in the same way that soldiers did anywhere in the world. Minor friction was oiled with rough humour, made if anything more piquant by the tribal differences. The two K.A.R. men were nominally Mohammedans, Kangi and some of the Nandi were Christians and the rest were pagans, with the ancient myths, legends and superstitions of their tribes. None of them would cross the path of, or touch a harmless chameleon and all regarded the hyena and the python both as detestable creatures and with differing forms of supernatural dread. The Kikuyu traditionally put their dying old relatives out of the hut, to avoid having to burn it when somebody died inside it. This was a gift to the hyenas. As a result they had a complicated belief in the scavenger's spiritual association with their ancestors. Tom knew he would have difficulty in getting any of them to touch a corpse, even if it were one of themselves.

When they came upon the half-eaten remains of a bush-pig, Ali, to whom an animal which he had not seen die, its throat cut with a knife, was unclean, had chaffed at Mzee on the subject when they made camp that night. "Let us go, you and I," he said, "and take away that pig that my brother Tchui has killed. Then we will cook it and eat it." This brought so much laughter from the others that Daniel, already somewhat scandalised by the outrageous religious connotation of the joke, told them to keep quiet in a voice much harsher than he was wont to use.

The patrol moved fast. Tom had selected these eight from twenty candidates, eliminating the others by the simple process of walking them hard for a week and taking only those who kept up. It was a far cry from the very long walks across the North African desert from the jeeps of Long Range Desert Patrol to German and Italian airfields on the coast, but the principles were the same; surprise, speed and ruthlessness. For that matter they were the same as those used by Mau-Mau in their few successful raids on police posts and farms.

They were approaching the edge of the Rift Valley and the first few farms. As he walked, following Mkuna, whose head was bent to the spoor, he was going through in his mind a plan for operation should they come anywhere near a farm. The police in the area would have warned farmers by now and the watch towers should be manned, the stock penned in and the farm guards on the alert. It was not going to be easy to get information or to avoid being shot at, but then at night, not even M'kuna could follow the tracks of a gang, which was why they had not yet overhauled one. He would have to rely on silent movement alone; if fired on by farm guards he would have to hope that their aim was as erratic as usual. The only thing he could do was check with the local police that no ambushes were mounted in the area he reached at nightfall. That would not prevent him walking into a military ambush, but that was just one of the risks.

At the back of his mind he had a feeling that there was more than merely a tactical reason for the gangs to be on the move. There was something very deliberate about it. For them it was their last chance to frighten settlers into quitting. They had already failed to coerce the africans in the Reserves into being allies. He could only hope that all the Rift farms had reliable defences, and he looked forward eagerly to the wireless report at seven o'clock. Today he had been told at briefings, a "green branch" offer of surrender amnesty was to be made. Any terrorists who wanted to give themselves up were to come forward waving green branches. Pamphlets announcing this were to be dropped by air and distributed by patrols. Personally he thought that the result would be very small, but it would accelerate the break-up of demoralised and badly armed gangs.

He knew what the reaction would be amongst those Africans, Asians and Europeans who had lost relatives or property, but the idea itself had to come and he welcomed it as an experiment, even though it would allow murderers to escape retribution.

Just after sundown he halted and told Kangi to produce

food while the wireless was set up. Beyond the surrender announcement and a few of the usual stock thefts, slashings and minor affrays in the reserve, there was nothing. Tuning to the local police station he heard that one gang had been intercepted and rounded up about fifteen miles further on the floor of the valley itself. Intensive patrols were out, but it was not possible to bring more troops to the area. All farms had been alerted or visited by the police, and there had been no attacks beyond two cases of stock thefts.

It was unwise to approach a farm until the guards had had a chance to develop the usual sentry-going fatigue. He arranged for M'kuna, Kamau and Kipkoin, the Nandi policeman in his section, to be woken at two o'clock by the sentry, and with these he would approach the nearest farm. On the map this was marked with the tenant's name, Roberts, overprinted. If his reckonings were right, and he had been within five hundred yards of his reckoning every evening so far, he had only a mile to go.

He lay on his back listening to the endless chatter of the men. Daniel and Cheragoi were out as sentries, and the Wa'Ndrobo always talked amongst themselves in their own tongue. The other four spoke in Swahili; Kamau and Kangi being unable to understand the tribal tongues spoken by Ali and Daniel or Kipkoin and Cheragoi. They spoke of the curious mixture of subjects which partly de-tribalised natives discussed. It was, in their case, half soldiers talk and half the usual long meandering stories with which primitive people spent the dark hours after sundown every day telling each other, to fill the void. It was almost as strange as wondering about what eternity could be like, to think how it must be to sit every night of your life in a hut with nothing to think of but what happened today and perhaps one or two things that might happen tomorrow.

To understand Africans you had to try to understand that. To realise that people like M'kuna and Mzee not only could not and did not want to read, but that nothing that had ever been said or written had the slightest interest for them. Just a handful of legends and the bush lore their elders taught them. Like the Masai, they wanted nothing to do with civilisation. They didn't despise white people like the Masai did, but normally they would not work for them, or live in one place, use money or even cultivate. They had been in this part of Africa before the Bantu, and they were troglodytic cave-dwellers, rather than a proud and fierce pastoral people like the Nilotic Masai. And they had their secrets.

Tom put his head back, closing his eyes and opening them again. The dye on his face was beginning to irritate the lids, and he had forgotten to bring anything to treat sore eyes. It was unlike him. He got up and went to look in the medical box, which to save weight held only wound dressings and a snake bite outfit. There was nothing there so he cut a piece of fat off the carcass of the dik-dik that Mzee had trapped the night before. He wiped his eyes with the fat and squeezed them shut. Then he wiped them with the back of his hand. There were so many things you needed on this sort of trip. He was carrying seventy pounds himself. A Ford Box body was the answer. But if the Mau-Mau could move light, then he had to do the same. He went back to his pile of grass and rolled into his blanket.

There were stars out, but the moon wasn't full for three days. Three days. A full moon was the only real date in the bush. That was part of the hunch about the gangsters' migration. Two or three days before or after the full moon, or on the day itself. Tomorrow he must close the gap. And now he must stop thinking about it and sleep. He checked the safety catch of the Padgett and turned on his side.

Not since the war had he walked so much, and he could not deny that he had enjoyed it so far. It was almost as good as the days as a boy when he went out with his father, killing vermin: zebra, baboons, wild dogs, bush-pigs, hyena and sometimes buffalo. His father had never shot from a truck, although at times he had had to shoot from horseback. He could remember the lessons he had learnt, one by one, with a cuff over the ear to help the memory; the wrong sized ammunition; soft-nose instead of solids; the failure to see a snake; shooting at one, and ruining a stalk; badly skinned carcasses; and the cardinal sins of confusing a species or shooting a protected animal or bird. He smiled to himself as he remembered how like every second boy at school he had wanted to be a game warden. The war had solved that, and after it: the reorganising of the farm. Then just as he began to have more time on his hands, and had been able to do game control occasionally as a honorary warden, this savagery had begun. By the time it was finished his father would want to retire. He had promised his mother a year in England as soon as the raiding died down.

Then he would have no time at all, because in addition to running the farm and sitting on local committees, there was the question of the African's plantation he had started as an experiment, which was to be a reward for the loyalists. Coffee growing properly run, as a native co-operative on spare land, instead of the straggled trees planted far too close together, never pruned, mulched or sprayed, and the ripe beans just spread in the sun to dry, instead of being processed. Then there was Gillian to look after if she hadn't got married. And all these reasons for taking a good, long ground-level look at this part of Africa, were reasons why he wasn't going to let it become the misery it could become. Already it would be considered hardship by most standards. But there was even another reason wasn't there? There was Alison.

Had it been the champagne that bright afternoon at the Dwent's wedding up at Limuru? June Harrop had always been a hard-faced little bitch, but she had introduced him to Alison, and now she was married off, so why worry about her tongue and the stories she worked up from nothing? He had never got out of Alison what she had told her, but she had been hellish apprehensive that day. She had refused his invitation to give her a lift back to town, which had surprised him after all the poise and sophistication of her talk. But then Gillian had been a bridesmaid, so he had gone along to the party afterwards with her, and Alison had come with some Englishman, who said, "Actually, in actual fact," and frequently "Oh, I say," so it hadn't been difficult to outflank *him.*

She had told him then, "I've been told that you are a misogynist. But I have the strong impression that you are what I call the Rousseau-Hemingway type, and I can never manage those."

"Well, I took you for the clever bookish sort, with nothing else besides a prim air and a tendency to say wild things after the second gin." They both laughed and conspired to mock the rest of the party, and later to ignore it, so that even Gillian noticed. She asked him about his war days, and places up-country she wanted to see, and checked on the truth of various rumours and myths she had heard, so that he knew she considered him upright and serious.

And then next day he had put on a suit and driven downtown and taken her up to the Escarpment for lunch at the "Brown Trout." She didn't seem to have to go anywhere else that day, so they had stayed just talking and moved on to another hotel on the Kinangop for dinner. He had told her all sorts of things about himself in exchange for her account of Hong Kong, Australia and the U.S.A. He even told her about the misogynist part; about Deidre who was drowned going to Bombay in 1942, with forty other WRNS, all from settlers' families. She hadn't concealed her dislikes either, and wanted to know why it was that this and that, until he got bored and started telling her stories about eccentric residents and African customs. She sat in front of the log fire, completely relaxed, so that he could tell himself that this was what she was really like, without any attempt at any sort of front. He liked her frankness and the childlike curiosity beneath the intelligence; the way she swept the hair out of her eyes and then looked at him. Her voice that sounded as though it were being filtered through raw silk, the healthy smooth curves of her body and that amazing English complexion that not all the sun of India, Hong Kong, Sydney or San Francisco had ruined.

At first he couldn't understand that whenever he asked her, she was nearly always free. He could understand that she didn't like Gillian's set, but surely she was no intellectual. She had so many things to do, she explained, and asked him to dinner to see. Her mother died when she was a child and so, since she had left school she had kept house for her father.

"I grew up quickly," she explained, "and I meet more interesting people here than by going out with everybody who calls." Sensing his puzzlement she added that she liked to hear him talk.

147

"But you talk about things naturally, that to me are completely new. It's like watching a book talk, only I don't have to pick you up, just encourage you."

She had that gift of making everybody talk. She was a good listener. He liked that.

At the dinner party there was old Trenchard, nearly ninety now, who had helped his father find his first job in the country. Alison got him to tell about the occasion when he had found three dead lion on the Nairobi rubbish dump, and one empty cartridge packet.

"They had a serial number stamped on them," he explained, with a wicked smile at Tom, over his white goatee. "We traced the buyer to Tom's father. Tom here and his brother had shot them for a lark. They were vermin then, but even so Tom was only fifteen. He said he was holding the flashlight for his brother, but we matched the bruises on his shoulder with some more on his backside, all the same."

Tom turned over under his blanket, and looked at his watch. It was after nine. A shy, slow chuckle came from the group of Africans. He recognised M'kuna's and Mzee's laugh, like a couple of embarrassed children. It wasn't often Mzee laughed. "Funga meneno" (be quiet), he told them. They wouldn't sleep until they wanted to, but they wouldn't slow down the pace tomorrow either. Daniel was to track a mile forward and then lie up near the Roberts' farm. Would he be able to get all the dye off his face if he had to call on a farm in daylight he wondered? What would Alison be doing now? And Kathenge and Kimathi? He began to feel very tired of the whole business as the weariness in his body crept up from the aching soles of his feet and the blood began to distend the veins of his relaxed legs. His last thoughts were that he was beginning for the first time to feel his age, but he never thought of death as anything but very sudden and very final. He was not to know it until much later, but it was the sort of problem which would earn him more than a medal.

As he drifted off he thought he smelt something like wood smoke. He knew the men had bhang, but he watched them to see they didn't smoke it on patrol. Fires were forbidden. They would chew miraa too to kill the night pains. It was a weed like khat, a soporific.

At first light, Daniel came to him, holding Mzee. "What news?" he snapped in Swahili, but Daniel started to speak rapidly in Samburu. "Hold hard," he said, and gradually got some of the story. Mzee was a shaman. He could see the future, and he had dreamed that night. Daniel had found him asleep far from the rest of the men. "You smoked last night," Tom accused the old man. He carried his own mixture in a leather bag. And they had their firestick. They rubbed it between their palms, so that it heated and set fire to a bundle of kindling. In wet weather you could smell it. A mixture of bhang, a form of hemp, like marijuana, with ground-up roots, bits of animals intestines, insects, dried blood and God knows what else.

"Hapaaana," he said calmly and spat out a stream of words. "Go get Kangi" he told Daniel. Then Mzee spoke slower, with Daniel and Kangi to translate. Gradually, Tom got him to make sense. He had seen a lake in his dream. Three very evil men were there and some women. Daniel and Kangi knew he was a shaman. He knew things about them, about their lives, they said, that they had not told anybody. The shaman knew.

Tom knew the powers of a shaman. He knew that they had extra-sensory perception. As hunters they sometimes sensed danger long before anyone. They could smell water. Make fire from nothing. Track animals for days. See spoor invisible to others. For his men, Tom knew, Mzee was to be feared and what he said at such times was to be taken very seriously. Tom agreed. But which lake? Where?

That was that whiff of smoke, he recalled. The Mzee had a leather bag with bones, tobacco, and dried twists of plants, medicines whose uses and doses only Wandorobo people knew. He would have gone off to a cave or somewhere he knew and lit a tiny fire. The smoke would be inhaled, and the dreams would follow. Then their predictions. Often they were right. The next waterhole would be dry. The next elephant they met would have only one tusk. A leopard would spring out of a tree just before sunset. And Mzee had seen those things already. You laughed at a shaman at your peril.

CHAPTER TWELVE

RUTHAKA

"April is my mistress' face,
And July in her eyes has place;
Within her bosom is September,
But in her heart a cold December."

Anon.

Unwillingly, Gillian found that it was day. Sunlight, very bright, and no blinds. Molten metal, sluggishly heaving from side to side inside her head. Monday or Tuesday, Wednesday? No. Doesn't matter. "The Golden Horn?" No. Some club. First the choo. A little, conical hut, lit like a candle. The reeds crackling. People running about, laughing. Who the hell had lit it? That Irish chap with the angelic face declaiming in Latin or something. Then part of the roof flaming, with Ian and Henry up there, Africans passing up buckets. The smell afterwards and the D.C. and the police, very severe. Jonathan, spouting again. Lalage listening. He was dreamy. Those eyes, and the hair falling into them. The slow, slow, smile, quizzical and the long, long words. He and Lala. That Roger person, mad on animals, badgers, ferrets, foxes and queer ones like that. But anyway, what the hell. It was fun. Next time don't mix the damn booze. Stay on one sort. Mixing grape and grain, Tom says, very bad shauri. Yuk.

A knock on the door. Mother's voice. Hers, very far away. "Malaria, I think." The bottle of Nivaquin, quick. Mother looking round. Hell. One stocking on the floor, the other dangling from the top of the wardrobe. Dress in a heap with a shoe on top. A cool hand on her forehead. Another on her pulse. Frowns and a faint smile. Diagnosis.

"Father's Alka-Seltzer. Will you live? Shall I ring Walker?"

"Nooh, thank you."

Not after last Thursday. Father knew already. Unwise to let her know until there was another job. Walker, very cross, very blunt. No. Questions about Friday and Monday. And Tuesday? Lectures. Sanctions on Tom's car. Curfew at midnight.

The fizzing liquid slithering down her hot throat. Managing a smile. Response unpromising. Sitting up. "Walker is on safari." "Mm. Shake a leg for tiffin, darling. I'm going to town so you can give out rations for me. Pa's got the keys. And do put some clothes on for lunch." She picked up the dress, retrieved the stockings. As she turned to go. "I'll take Tom's car. And, Gillian, if this goes on I'll ask Pa to get you a second-hand one." Gillian covered her head again. A rattly little car. That would be punishment. She must cancel that lunch date and get a job but quick. Sleep first. Must have been nearly dawn when she got back.

"No. Not today. Tomorrow. Yes, that's right. Wednesday." Alison's voice sounded merry at the other end of the phone. Was it only Wednesday?

"Lunchtime. Where've you been?" Her father didn't look too concerned. Was he grinning?

"Nowhere."

"Got another job yet?"

"Not exactly,"

"Well, get one. Only thing to keep you out of mischief. God knows I can't. Try those people who market my coffee. Don't like wishing you on anybody, but better they should be plagued than anyone else. Here's your mother. Giving out the posho after lunch?"

Dutifully, "Yes."

Sitting in the store. Revolver on the table. Two farm guards handing out the posho meal after weighing it. Samson, the Neopara calling out the names: Wainiri, Susa, Cheroge Kaigi, Cheroge Watau, Daidi, Wambai, the old dried up women and the young wives, the totos with missionary-given Biblical names, Simons and Lukes, Daniels and Sauls. The white, ground maize

151

pouring into the leather bags; the twists of salt, sugar bags. The system that was a necessary weekly chore because they said, if you gave them a month's supply they would eat it all in five days and then not work for six with bellyache. Money and the allowance for meat and vegetables that used to be issued, were paid monthly to anyone who produced the headman's punched tickets for days worked. All so primitive and saddening to see the thumbs pressed on the ink pad and on the cash book, but what else could you do besides letting two or three hundred live on the farm and running a school? The tractor drivers got nearly three hundred shillings now, but the rest only sixty or seventy. Where were the government schools?

Gillian had once, aged 16, read some pamphlets about the value of labour, capital and profits and a lot of other things rather over her head. "Why don't we pay the best ones a hundred a week, Pa?" she asked. "Because I'd still need a hundred of them."

"Well?"

"Well what? That's forty-eight thousand a year. Pounds. Nearly a million shillings. What do you think I am, an oil company?"

"Well, why not just keep a few of the best, the hardest working?"

"I'd still need a hundred. And what do I do with the rest? Kick them back into the reserves to starve?"

After that, she had given up Progress, and went in for Religion for a month or so.

She walked up to the house with Samson, liking him because he was always dignified, although he made good jokes as well, and he was never sneaky like Jeha, fawning and telling tales. He wanted to know if she was going to help her father while Bwana Tom was away. "No," she said, adding with a smile, "You wouldn't like it, would you?" He considered this for a moment. "No" he said. "Our women wouldn't understand that you are blood of your father and your customs are different."

"Ayah," she said, "Ayah." In their eyes she was a toto, not a Memsaab.

"Mzuri, Memsaab," he said briskly and went off to find her father.

Next day she went down town, going to the coffee houses where she would meet girls she knew who had just got married and left a vacancy. Shorthand typists were always at a premium, even if they couldn't spell or take more than fifty words a minute. There were some Asian girls coming on the market, but they had a tendency to have a cousin who had a cousin who was in the bank, who had a cousin who was a clerk in your rival's firm. There were some Africans too, but not women, because like the Arabs they weren't fond of educating their womenfolk. She was just going to drive out to see June Dwent when she remembered about lunch at Alison Lindbern's house.

Funny that she should like Alison, who was so withdrawn. Quiet, calm as a Madonna, and then when she spoke, the bite in the words, the dry humour. She never went out with a crowd yet she seemed to know a lot of people after being here only a few months. English, yes. But different English. Tom asked her to find out her age and she was twenty three and dear Tom, he seemed to think that was very young. He's a goner. Never been like it before. Sitting about with a faraway look, drumming with his fingers, jumping up when you caught his eye. Please God let it happen. Let her fall for him too, because he wouldn't make a good bush bachelor, leaning on the bars, jawing away, waiting for the vultures. So odd to think of him with kids. No. Maybe not. He'd be good with them like animals, like the bushbaby and the young oribi he had brought her, and that young caracal, and yes, the Tommy gazelle that the leopard took the year the Gredlings had locusts. Must be good at the Lindberns. Good thing I put a white suit on. Of course I remembered this morning. All this job nonsense made me forget why I was wearing it. Mustn't get tight. But there is something inside that makes me want to. Even Sammy got cross about it. But it's partly Sammy that causes it.

And Jonathan was shocked. He looked so disapproving. So like the English. Irish. Whatever. Even refused to dance and outside in the car he wouldn't even neck. Then Sam had started to be uppity about Jonathan, though how he got the habari (news) on that from Nyeri was a mystery. What an odd bod Jonathan was. He just didn't care what he said, and he said the

153

oddest things, half to himself, or as if he were trying out the sound. What was it he said to Lalage? "You are a sunbird in a cinnamon tree. A hummingbird singing, humming in a baobab tree. Euphorbia. Isn't that a good round word? Not a bit prickly though, like cactus."

He rambled on, quite un-subalternlike. Think of Sammy saying things like that? But they wouldn't get on at all. All that stuff about the natives as though he could know anything about it. As though Arap Chepkoin didn't enjoy having a night out in the camp and coming back with all the latest habari, his stomach full of Army chakula. Hell's bells (she must have got that from Jonathan), how could he possibly know anything about it? Still he was sweet and it was fun to make Sammy mad. Serve him right.

Alison's father's house was one of the older government houses near the Country Club. He was something high up in government finance. It was white, two-storeyed with open balconies on both sides of the first floor and Cape-Dutch gables at both ends. To Gillian's surprise the only other woman there was Lalage. There were two men besides Alison's father, both of whom she had seen somewhere before. The one sitting on her right was somebody's ADC called Roger, and the other, Roderick, seemed to have something to do with Alison's father in his department. They began by discussing the Surrender Offer to the terrorists, which Gillian said she thought was silly, because it gave a free pardon to known murderers, and how, she asked, would the loyal Africans react to that?"

"Anyway," she added, before anyone could reply, "what are they going to do with those who surrendered? What about the Kikuyu chiefs, for instance, the one at Lari who had two hundred of his people butchered by Mau-Mau in one night? He would hardly welcome back surrendered terrorists who were recognised by survivors as having taken part in that raid."

But she could see that nobody agreed and after a few minutes she tried to change the subject, but it was as if they had met there to discuss such things. She said very little after that, and as soon as the meal was over Alison's father and Roderick said they had to get back to their offices. Roger and Lalage stayed on after coffee, and he sat next to her on a sofa while

Alison talked to Lalage.

He was very English; smooth fair hair, a city suit, signet ring and that careless, offhand drawl, the words pronounced with lots of long-drawn out vowels. He was very correct and she found him very dull, although he was obviously interested and putting on the fascination with the big digging stick. Bored, she tried to hear what Lalage was saying about the Capricorn Society people, and their multi-racial views, but Roger was droning on about cars.

"I envy you people," she told Roger. "You can park anywhere you like and the traffic police don't come up and chalk mark your tyres to the ground to prove how long you've been there." He rose to the bait, and she found that she had an argument on her hands. Very soon it seemed as though a little squashing would be necessary. The phrase, "you settlers" had never appealed to her. Opening her eyes wide at him she said in her silkiest, kitten voice, "Of course, it's not that I'm jealous or anything. It must be awfully hard to get a job like yours. All those exams and things. Dedicated to the Service and all that. Long hours with no thanks from anyone."

The look in his eye was murderous. His lips compressed, and he snapped out, "Yes, we do get a lot of criticism from ignorant people." She smiled her most sexy smile, leaning towards him.

"Yes, but you do give the most heavenly parties, don't you. The expense. You must be terribly rich." She was ready to bubble on, but with a savage stab of his elbow he looked at his watch, looked straight through her, stood up and announced he had to go.

"What the hell did you say to him?" Lalage asked when Alison had taken him out of the room, "He looked as though he'd swallowed a mamba."

"Just pulled his leg a bit. Touchy little devil, wasn't he?" She laughed. Lalage looked at her thoughtfully and, walking over, sat on the arm of the sofa. Gillian, sensing a lecture coming, closed her eyes. She felt hot and she could feel the sherry thickening her head, so that she felt tired and sleepy. "Please, Lala, no lectures. I've got to go down town now and get a job," she added pitifully, pulling a face.

"Not going to lecture," Lalage said cheerfully. "Going to give you a job though. I talked to Sammy and he agreed."

"Did you now?" Gillian let out a loud "Oh," so that Alison, entering the room, looked at her, startled. "Is it a plot?"

"Yes," Alison said, making as though she were going to sit on the other arm of the sofa, but squatting on the floor at Gillian's feet instead.

"We want you to come and work with us at Ruthaka."

"Ruthaka? I didn't know you worked there. With Lala?"

"When I can, yes. Please come and help us, Gillian. You can go and do the same thing on your farm later on." There was a long silence. What was it Lalage did, Gillian was thinking? Something to do with Kikuyu women. She had passed the signboard lately which just said "Ruthaka School of Handicrafts." Lalage ran it with Angela de Gynne, that extraordinary female she shared her flat with.

"I hate to be mercenary," she said, "But would that pay me a thousand, four hundred shillings a month?"

"No," Lalage said gently. "It wouldn't pay you anything at all."

"Are you kidding? I've got a car to run. Expensive boy-fr...," she broke off and laughed unconvincingly. "Hell. Could I have a drink, Alison sweetie? No, maybe not. Just more coffee, very black ... please."

Lalage was looking at her hard. She felt extremely irritable, and any minute she was going to get cross. What sort of mad idea was this? What would everyone think if she joined these Capricorn multi-racial do-gooders or whatever they were. Silly. They were the same people who collected for Mau-Mau in London pubs, weren't they? The sort who wanted to kick her father out of Africa, and then spend their time having long pointless meetings, and sending forms to each other while the watu starved. She was damned if she was going to be roped into any of these housewives knitting circle jokes. Telling Micks that they hadn't really sinned. *Sinned.* As for the women, they were the worst. The Kikuyu women went to the oath takings and egged them on. Took them food and slept with anyone, any tribe, any colour, with troops even, for two bullets. Ugh.

Alison handed her the coffee, and before she could speak, said, "Gillian, let me tell you. I've only been helping Lalage for a week or so, but I know it's what is needed. It isn't as impractical as it sounds. And it is independent from anyone else."

She paused and sat opposite Gillian on the floor, legs tucked underneath her.

"Apart from teaching them hygiene and knitting and getting them wool and reeds for basket making and so on, we are developing their pride as women. You know they need that. You know that some of the men treat them worse than their animals. You know how many have a baby a year until they have ten or more. We don't tell them not to carry water and firewood and cook, but we do tell them to let the men do their own digging and hoeing. We show them how to market the posho they grind, and how to sell the things they make."

Gillian tried to interrupt, but Alison held up her hand.

"If we don't help, it will all happen again, this murdering. We might even be able to stop them having a child every year, stop them killing twins, and all those things you can never din into them properly with their men around on the farm compound."

Where had she picked up all that, Gillian thought wildly? She knew about all the objections. She was damn clever. Damn quick on the uptake. Wasn't she too clever for Tom? Was he going to put up with all these crazy ideas that never came to anything, because the Kaffirs never listened, or if they did, the old men told them to get on with it and shut up?

"I don't know," she said slowly, sipping her coffee. "I'd have to think about it." She looked at Lalage. Dear old mixed-up Lala. Everybody said she was just helping Angela to smooth her conscience down a bit, and it needed some smoothing if the stories were half-true. Did she go to the Ruthaka place like that, in a tight skirt, bunched up now showing her long legs, and that close-fitting top that made the men look and look back quickly?

"Please don't go and get some damn silly job," Lalage said. "You don't need the money. Other women do, but you don't. You'll get married one day soon, and won't be able to help us.

Can't you give it a try?"

"Give what a try?" Gillian broke in crossly. "You go on about it as though it were a secret or something. Can't you explain?"

"No, just come and see. If you'll come we'll pay for your petrol, but if you've got the Lerrick guts you'll want to start the same thing going in your area, and you won't need ..."

"Hey. Have you been talking to my folks about this?"

"No," Lalage said, "Of course not. Now look, Gill, are you going to come with us or not? It's our last chance to do something you know, we ..."

"Damnitall," Gillian burst out "I didn't start the blasted Mau-Mau. It isn't our sort who cause the trouble and you know it. It's the bad farmers, the drunks and remittance men and Greeks trying to cut their sisal production costs." Dammit, she thought, I forgot. Lala's Ma is Greek.

"Anyway," she finished lamely, "we always treat our watu properly."

"I know, I know." Lalage said wearily. "We understand them. We don't exploit them. We don't have to. But we have to pay for the ones who do, for lousy farmers and the bullying little Memsaabs from England and other places who scream at them because they're scared of all natives. We are the only people who can do it because we can speak their language. But there aren't many of us."

"And what about the Hindu women?" Gillian broke in. "Five of them to one of us, remember. Got any fat subscriptions from Nairobi's grocery brigade? I bet you have." But Lalage was being very, very patient. She just took a deep breath. "The Muslims did contribute, yes."

"Oh they're all right. They're settlers. Not just grabbing and sending it all back home like the rest of them."

"We aren't political or racist, darling. Do we have to discuss that?"

Ten minutes later Gillian was on her way to Ruthaka in Lalage's car. It was all very well. Quite a good idea. Possibly better than typing for some stooge in an office. But what would the gang say?

CHAPTER THIRTEEN

AIR DROP

"The essence of operations in a guerrilla war
is that they should be unpredictable.
A base is a hive. NOT a nest."

Major John Woodhouse
22nd SAS Regiment
Malaya 1956

In the dream Joanna stood there watching, her arms folded, mandarin-like, in a glossy fur coat, her hair splayed wildly over the collar. Tim was there, inexplicably in morning dress, while a man with a khaki hat on the back of his head fixed a car wheel. Behind them there was someone on the steps who was a merged combination of Lalage and an older woman. Then the wheel exploded and flew past Tim's head. He laughed, the older woman, who suddenly became his mother, screamed, and a fur-coated arm clutched his, but the girl had Gillian Lerrick's face.

Jonathan woke to find Corporal Flett shaking his arm. He felt heavy, still tired and not clear as to where he was. He took the tea, put the dixie down and shook himself. He scratched his scalp hard with his fingernails and took long, deep breaths. The air was cold, and a shaft of brilliant light came through a small square opening high up in the wall opposite.

"How do you feel, Sir?," the corporal asked, with a wry, knowing crease running across the seams of his old soldier's face. "Average," Jonathan said, testing his feet gingerly. "Average to bloody awful. Any news of Captain Collins yet?"

"HQ said he hadn't arrived by five, but it's half past and the

159

S'arnts on the blower now. The airdrop's due at six, so I woke you." Jonathan was wondering whether he had brought a comb. "Um. Oh yes. Yes, that'll be a help."

"Tell every wog for miles that we're here, it will."

"Well, they all know where the place is. They only built it two months ago, but they must have made a helluva noise cutting trees down. I'll be out in five minutes."

Fort Jericho was eight thousand feet up in the Aberdare Mountains, an earth and log construction like an American frontier post in the Bad Injun era. The day before, Jonathan's patrol had been moving over the unforested, open area on the upper slopes of the mountain, just after the bamboo's level. They moved slowly with the trackers out on the flanks, being very careful not to get to far in front of the other section. They were supposed to have tracker dogs too, but they had been taken off somewhere else.

The first thing they had known was a shot and a scream from the right flank. All flung themselves flat. "Fire," both Tim and Jonathan had shouted and a ragged volley had gone off, with just enough delay to allow the trackers to fall flat. Tim had run forward and, seeing a muzzle flash, had flung a grenade. This had dispersed the gang, who fled into the cover of clumps of leleshwa bushes a hundred yards in front of them. There was one automatic amongst the weapons firing at them, and this had hit two men. One of them, Kelly, he thought, a bullet in the face, fell just behind Jonathan, who spun round as the man screamed. Half his head was gone but he still screamed. Jonathan stood paralysed, retching. Mac came running up

"You're hit, Sir," and put his hand up to Jonathan's face, which came away bloodied.

"Sit," he barked, and as Jonathan crouched, snatched his Webley revolver from his holster. As Jonathan put his hand up to his face, saw the blood, and nearly vomited. Then he heard the shot.

"…died instantly," he heard Mac grunt. He took out a rag from his pocket. "Lean back," he snapped, and Jonathan did as he was told. Mac was rubbing away at his neck, looking puzzled. "I'm fine," Jonathan protested.

"You're right. 'Tis Kelly's blood on you." He ran off towards the other man down. Noyk and Flett came up. They quickly undid Kelly's pack, and unwrapped his cape. Then they rolled the body in the cape and used the dead man's belt and webbing to strap it up. They wanted to hide the sight from the younger soldiers.

Jonathan went over to where Mac was kneeling over the other man down. He was shoving a field dressing under his shirt. It was McEvoy, who, running out to one flank to set up the Bren, had been hit in the chest. He was wheezing and groaning, the blood from his lungs that bright, bubbling red. Jonathan helped Mac hold him while they got the morphine syringe ready. Mac and Taffy got him on to a stretcher. Jonathan got out his binoculars and tried to spot where shots were coming from sporadically. "Fetch me the sniper rifle," he said, and Flett brought it. He adjusted the telescopic sight, and, after about 15 seconds, squeezed the trigger. They watched as a body thumped to the ground 200 yards away. They looked at one another as they crouched over McEvoy. He looked to be a goner. No one said anything, but all of them looked hard at their pink-cheeked officer. McEvoy died as they reached the fort three hours after sunset, at ten p.m.

On firing back at the ambushing Mau-mau, all their fire had ceased, but on moving forward again, the automatic weapon fired again from a clump two hundred yards back, hitting Tim Collins in the thigh and another soldier in the arm. Twenty minutes later it was almost dark, and all chances of tracking had to be abandoned. It had been a well directed ambush, obviously managed by an ex-soldier from the K.A.R. They had some good weapons and must have numbered thirty or so.

They had wirelessed for a tracker team with dogs, then carried the two casualties to the fort. Helicopters could not be used at that altitude, and anyway there were very few ever available. So Collins had started off in the dark with the other two wounded, to the nearest track. His wound had not touched bone and he could move the leg. He refused to be supported after they put a field dressing on and said that as long as he moved it would not stiffen. The track was roughly bulldozed up to the fort, but stopped three miles short. It was waterlogged from several streams crossing it. Collins had headed for the track nearest the main road six miles away down an escarpment, but although the track was being patrolled, nothing had been heard of the party since they left the fort at eleven p.m.

Why had he let him go? Jonathan asked himself. Surely Tim should have stayed.

"I'll get a relief patrol up, Jon. You and Mac get on up the fort and stay there. I have to get this leg seen to quick." Then he disappeared.

The only urgency now was one man with a shattered elbow and the sergeant could have taken him down with the stretcher party. Maybe the shock had upset Tim's normal judgement. And now he had certainly got lost. At least he had made Tim take an escort of two men, who could carry him if needed. What a bloody mess for such an experienced patrol. There were only eleven of them left now. He had sat up from three a.m. with the wireless. The tracker team had woken him at two and gone off with their African tracker. Orders were to stay put with sentries out on both flanks of the fort. There were supposed to be several large gangs on the move in the area.

Jonathan slept from sheer exhaustion. He woke well after dawn and went out into the compound. The sunlight stabbed at his eyes, almost blinding him. Sergeant MacNamara straightened up from the set, with a face Jonathan thought was actually a shade grimmer than usual. Mournfully he twisted his short red moustache. "Nothing," he said, avoiding Jonathan's eye. Even Tosher Harris was almost silent as he changed the battery. Only a murmur of obscenity growled sullenly from him. "This ruddy air drop is going to be a fair old pantomime, isn't it?"

Jonathan turned to the speaker, opened his mouth to tell him to shut up, closed it again, took a deep breath, remembering his battle-drill training, and said, "Get the men out, Corporal." He turned back to MacNamara.

"I want them all shaved, properly dressed, weapons clean and magazines full, Sergeant. Get those tribal police or whatever the hell they are, out too. They can help collect the air-drop canisters. Those who have been up signalling can go back and kip. Let's get this place cracking. The relief patrol will be up about three hours after first light."

MacNamara's face gathered itself up.

Harris started humming "I don't want to join the Army, I don't want to go to war," very softly, so that it could hardly be heard above the crackle of atmospherics. Jonathan looked at his watch. It was ten to seven. "Start performing," he said to Harris, who began chanting into the rubber mouthpiece, like some starstruck railway station announcer:

"Stardust Dog Zebra for Moth Three. Aybell, Baykerr, Charlee, Dorg; Aybell, Baykerr, Charlee, Dorg. Do you read me? Do you read me?"

Fool I am, Jonathan thought, watching the men scurrying about with mess tins of water, pulling their rifles through, loading clips from bandoliers. I should have got them out earlier, or else just checked their weapons and deployed them for the drop. But the rush would shake them out of their present mood at least. The six Africans left behind by the fort garrison were stumbling blearily into line, chivvied by a fat little ebony-coloured corporal. They were wearing floppy jungle-green hats, tunics and canvas boots. The hats drooped over their faces giving them the sad-farcical appearance of ersatz Pierrots. They seemed to handle their rifles confidently and their expressions were alert and one or two either amused or very eager.

"Corporal," he shouted. The African pivoted from his men. "Effendi," he barked. Corporal Flett appeared from a doorway at the double. "Mzuri," Jonathan said to the African. "Tell them to deploy on that side," he said to Flett, pointing, "And explain what to look for. What are we supposed to be getting?" Flett's eyebrows flickered. He had a trick of jerking his head sideways when he didn't understand.

"How many canisters, I mean!" Jonathan added. "Dunno Sir. If it's a Harvard, two. Maybe only one if it's a Piper."

"OK Tell 'em that, and that they should try to recover them damn sharpish," Flett told them and their corporal doubled them to the gate.

"What will we get?" Jonathan asked. Flett produced a greasy blue notebook. "Well, Sir. We asked for rations, ammo,

163

field dressings and morphia?" "Well, Morphine then. Two or three canisters would do it. But we'll probably only get one. Hard tack, Verey lights, paludrines and salad dressing most likely." Jonathan interrupted.

"Verey lights. Who's got the pistol? Quick, get it."

"Sar'nt Mac. Right, Sir."

The men were ready. Jonathan inspected them. Mainly that their weapons were clean and that they had ammunition. "We'll be relieved some time this morning." He heard somebody mutter, "With a bit of luck, mate." He pretended he hadn't heard. He tried to sound as cheerful as he could with the thought behind him that they would be carrying two corpses, and that somewhere nearby there were probably the remains of half a dozen more. African bodies, not his problem. Then he sent six of them back to try to sleep and the rest to watch for canisters. As they went he remembered Tim's story about the air strike briefing he had attended before a bombing run on Mount Kenya. The air crews had been issued with loaded pistols and instructions in the event of crashing to avoid being captured alive. The order had been received with hilarity, Tim said.

The wireless emitted a louder crackling. Harris looked up and shook his head. Another problem was when to fire the Verey. Tim would have known, he was always sure. He would never be captured alive. He didn't believe in a God. Like Joanna. She said, "God is only for the weak." Lalage seemed to have the same attitude. How hard women could be. But a crisis, like this sort of war, seemed to bring the hardened to a belief. All those stories about the German and British paratroopers praying together over a dead comrade in the middle of a battle. But Tim had been in a real war. In Korea, a tougher emergency than this one. And another in Malaya. And now he was in another sort of semi-war. His hardness was real, based on a belief in himself that was utter and complete.

To take his mind off it he thought about the last few days. Lalage. She seemed to him to be hard too and a touch bitter. Maybe it was just being an African. Or anyway a Kenya-born.

"I would never marry," Lalage had said, that night when he last saw her, "a man who hadn't slept with a lot of women." The statement had repulsed him. "Why?" he asked, feeling schoolboyish but at the same time, sad for her.

"Because then I would be sure of keeping him," was her reply; it made him want to cry out in pity for her, and then just afterwards, to shake her. But like the boy he was, fast becoming a man, he had only been able to say "Oh," and change the subject.

"She's here," Harris said.

"What? Oh yes. Let's hear." He took the earphones. "Mm. OK. Tell the pilot I'm going to fire a Verey, to show him which side of the fort to make the drop."

"What colour, Sir?" Swearing, Jonathan fumbled the gun open to look. "Green."

Harris transmitted the message. "OK, Sir." Jonathan stretched his arm vertically over his head and pulled the trigger. It was like that moment of exultation, only once before, on Dartmoor, when as a cadet platoon commander he had seen his attack work perfectly as planned, and had for the first time fired a Verey. He felt now only a dull weariness. Why hadn't he gone out with Cosgrave as they had intended?

Harris' transmission was drowned by a thunderous crackling, and looking up Jonathan saw the little blue plane banking steeply then sweeping down on their white marker strips. It swept over low and he could see the pilot looking out and waving as the plane disappeared beyond the trees. All the men who were off duty were out watching. It had been pointless letting them go off duty. It occurred to him that they should be covering the canister party. But MacNamara had left one of the Bren gunners on guard, without being told.

The plane was coming back, higher this time. Two canisters came out, the parachutes streaming behind as the static line tugged them into the slipstream. Then they both blossomed, crackling and suddenly like great white flowers, floated down. The plane tilted its wings, flattened out and roared over the fort. As the roar died, Jonathan was astounded to hear the noise of firing. "Get your rifles," he yelled, running to the gate. He was just in time to see a figure crash through the line of bushes in a clearing where the marker strips were. One of the parachutes was blowing along the ground, but no one was running for it. What the blazes could have gone wrong, now?

"Sergeant," he bellowed, and from a bush about a hundred yards away he heard a "Sah," shouted rather shrilly, and sharply cut off. Had they all gone mad? Why was no one firing back?

A parachute had hit a bush and collapsed. Then he saw Corporal Flett emerge from a bush near it. He pounced on the container, then sat down and howled with laughter.

"Corporal," Jonathan screamed, as angry as he ever remembered being. "What the bloody hell is going on?" He looked round him as a man behind him laughed nervously. "Lie down," he barked.

"It's all right, Sir. Only buffalo. The plane stampeded them. They went across the D.Z. going straight for the sergeant and Flett. They had to fire to distract them." All around, sheepish faces were emerging from bushes, some of them scratched and bleeding. "I'll just go and get t'other container." Flett went off at a trot into the trees. "Go and get the blasted container," Jonathan said to a man behind him, and turned back to the fort. Harris was standing up waving the microphone. "They've found them Sir. A patrol's found the Captain. They're all right." He laughed and did a little caper at the end of the flex. "Good," was all Jonathan could say. He wanted to sit down very badly. His knees were going to buckle.

"Check it? Course you checks it. 'Cos it falls out of the bleeding sky, you don't suppose the Q.M. is in bleeding 'eaven, do yer?" Flett chewed his pencil as he watched the unpacking. "Got everything?" Jonathan asked, after Flett had been working for another ten minutes, frowningly writing everything down in the blue notebook. Flett made a non-committal noise. He rarely admitted to anything being right where it had any remote connection with the Army. "Yerss and no. If you like your sossidges square, Sir. No bumph again. Effin' biskits all barstad well broken. Tins and tins of flamin' raspberry jam. From Orsttrylier. Marvellous, ain't it? This 'ere place crawlin' with froot and they send there for this muck. If we was in Greenland they'd send yer tinned blubber and penguin steak."

He was acting, filling in the time before they had to take up the poles with the two stiff bodies slung between them in blankets like two sagging carcasses of proud wild beasts, shot down as vermin. For nothing ever surprised Flett. Not "blacks running berserk," or eighteen year old national servicemen asking for a NAAFI break in the middle of a patrol. Having checked and distributed the stores and organised cooking, he sat round the cookers to entertain those who could not sleep.

"Blacks? This lot ain't nothin. No worse than them gibberin' Hindoos. Riots they was always havin'. Not as bad as the Soodarn, or the Ay-rabs in North Africa. The worst was them there Sinigorlees wot the Frogs 'ad on Madagascar. A proper lot of 'Erberts they was. That time we took where was it? Diego Swares. Straight out of them bleedin' assault boats and straight up the hill behind the town. Bayonets it was and stinkin' 'ot at midnight. Them Sinigorlees, they bit lads' fingers orf they did. An took chunks out of their calves like ruddy gorillas…"

Jonathan was completely drained. His hands trembled when he took a slug of water. He knew that the men were watching him from time to time, and he kept his face rigid, except to laugh at Flett's prattle. The men loved it. Pure Kipling, but even though it tickled him to listen; he was too tired and relieved to stay awake.

"…six fausand gibberin' Malgashes…"

Marty Maguire's voice, "a pack of dirty lousers. Small wonder ye didn't see it over there beyant the trees. I'll give ye an unmerciful skelp in a minnut."

Jonathan fell asleep, slumping back where he sat. The sergeant pushed Jonathan's pack under his head and put his hat on the side of his face exposed to the sun. Sure that he was asleep now, he slipped the Webley back into the innocent officer's holster.

CHAPTER FOURTEEN

A PSEUDO GANG

"A commander can make men do almost impossible things
by showing his men that he can do them first."

General Sir Michael Rose
"Fighting for Peace," 1998

The light in the watchtower had not moved for ten minutes. The
beam was focused on the cattle boma and the sentry there,
probably asleep by now. It was just after three a.m. with no noise
except the steady throbbing of the diesel generator from the
Roberts' farm buildings. He groped in his memory for the last
time he had seen the Roberts. At the races? In some shop or at
the Kenya Farmers Depot in Nakuru?

A hyena howled, the unearthly scream turning into a
chattering cackle of laughter. Kipkoin shivered beside him.
"Mzuri?" Tom asked him. "Ndio." Kipkoin said, between set
teeth. The 'Drobo didn't mind but Kamau and Kipkoin were as
frightened as any African at night, with a deep, atavistic fear of
darkness and spirits. The hyena that ate their dead embodied the
spirits of their ancestors, yet if it dropped dung near a hut, the
hut must be burnt. How could anyone ever understand the
complexity of the African? He smiled to himself in the darkness
and started to creep forward to cut the wire of the labour lines.

Long before he reached the wire he could smell habitation
with senses sharpened by the days in the bush. No wonder
Mkuna, and Mzee, after a lifetime in the bush, could hear and
smell things which he could not. They wriggled through the wire
and crawled to the largest of the huts. At the corner of it was a

168

sentry with a spear stuck in the ground between his knees, his head leaning back on the wall. Kipkoin inched forward and held the man in a strangler's grasp while Tom and Kamau forced the door. The torch showed three men and two women asleep. Africans slept very deeply, a fact Tom was counting on. Kamau shook one gently. When fully awake he got this man to wake the others. Kipkoin brought the sentry, teeth chattering, into the hut and stood with Mkuna, pointing his Sten at the occupants.

"We are Mau-Mau," Kamau told them. "We shall go away now. Prepare food and we will return to eat it." The sweating black faces were paralysed with fear. One woman in the corner, making frantic efforts to conceal her baby, let out a moan of terror when the infant began to cry. Tom could not help her himself. "We will not harm you," he told her in Kikuyu. But Kamau was interrogating the headman, his panga turning in his hand in the glimmering light of the oil lamp, so that the blade caught it and glinted. He asked them where and when they had taken oaths, how many, and how many gangs they had fed, and when. "If you betray Mau-Mau, the oath will kill you," he repeated, so that Tom made a mental note to tell Kamau to leave that out in future. Kamau questioned each shivering face in turn. "…had they maimed any cattle? Did they like their Bwana? How many Kikuyu were there on the farm? When had they last seen a gang?" They had given some mealies to a gang, they said, only that day. Tom moved over and questioned them further. There seemed no doubt about it. Silently they left, running to the wire and out across the cultivated fields, back into the forest, to sleep. Tom scattered pepper behind them to put off tracker dogs, should they be betrayed. He had not understood all Kamau had said, or all the replies, and before they slept he questioned Kamau, and then Kipkoin, who understood Kikuyu well.

At first light next morning, with face washed, looking strange in dirty jungle boots, shorts and a shirt, Tom Lerrick walked up to the gate in the wire fence of the Roberts' farm. His face, washed and reddish, was enough to give him entrance, and the sentry called a boy to take him to the house. The Memsaab was with the cattle, the boy explained, taking him behind the house. The Bwana was away.

169

"Hodi," he called. "Police."

"I didn't hear your truck," the woman said, coming out of the dairy, wiping her hands on her corduroy trousers. She looked at his clothes and then at his face. "I'm combat police, on foot," he told her. Her face softened a little. "Good for you," she said, "I'm sick of these two-year-wonder contract boys flashing about in cars while I'm busy. What's the trouble now? Don't say they came this way? Chris, my husband was called out last night to the Phillips' fire. Weren't you there?"

"No, we are following a gang. I don't want to alarm you, but they visited your lines last night. We saw them leaving and followed up." Her hand came up to her mouth, then she felt tremblingly in her pockets for cigarettes.

"Oh, God. No. Are you sure?" She turned away to light her cigarette and then remembered to offer him one.

"Let's go and sit down," he said hating to see how upset she was, knowing that he had to use these methods to avoid worse. "I'll make coffee," she said, and he asked to use the phone. Ringing the nearest police post he told them to come and screen the labour, leaving a message that he recommended all Kikuyu be removed from the farm. Going into the kitchen he told Mrs Roberts that her labour were not to be trusted unless they reported a gang in the next hour, and even then, that they obviously could not be relied on.

"Your watchtower guard must have been asleep," he told her, "And all your sentries. What time did your husband go?"

"Just after four." Tom bit his lip. He had been very lucky. He had heard a car as they were crossing the farm, and had assumed that it was a police patrol. The noise must have woken the sentry in the watchtower and others too.

After coffee they walked around the compound and Tom 'discovered' the hole in the wire. "Listen," he said, "Frighten them. Tell them there were four men, and that the police captured them and they are in prison. Sack your headman and get rid of all Kikuyu."

"But we did," she said. "They took them all. We got Guluo but it was hopeless. We're a dairy farm and they were dirty and lazy and pulled the old trick of burying gourds in the ground in the milking sheds and stealing half the milk. You can only get Kikuyu round here. The Kipsigis are snapped up by every farm, and most of them are quite happy farming in their own reserve anyway."

"It's got to be done. It won't last long now. Have you a siren?"

"No."

"Well, get one, and time clocks for the guards to punch. And that wire is too thin and needs tins and rattles tying to it. Tie a few crow-scarers to it outside and you'll find the first toto who lets one off will keep the others away."

"God," she said, dazedly. "Just think. The gang you saw burnt the Phillips' farm."

"How far is it?"

"Two miles."

"No. Your gang left here at four."

She gasped, her face contorting for a moment before she spoke.

"Just as Chris left. I... I..."

"Look, don't worry. We'll get that gang and the police will send three men up here. You'll be OK. Let's see you fire that revolver."

"Now?"

"Yes. Fire at that box over there." After three shots he took the gun from her, and showed her how to hold the revolver.

"Imagine you are just pointing your finger. Like this. Hold it in the centre of your body, elbow close to your side. Not that it matters. Just the noise is always enough."

He gave it back to her and she emptied it, but he filled it for her from his pouch and made her fire it again. All the labour not working had gathered round and Gwen Roberts felt confident of her gun for the first time since she had unwillingly handled it.

"Tell me about the fire."

"I don't know much," she said. "Just what Chris said when he rang me back. The labour lines were fired and some cattle trapped in their boma were suffocated. It's only a small thatched house, so that may have gone too. They have three kids and his mother is staying with them.

171

"The kids were going down to Tanganyika with mine, to old Mrs Phillips' place, but I don't know what will happen now. It's hell living here now. What's gone wrong with these people? I... I can't describe how it is with all this on your nerves. Worse than the London Blitz, and I know, because I drove an ambulance then. But what have we done to deserve it? They begged Chris to come here, to develop the land, to give employment. What has gone wrong with them? Why all this land-hunger talk? This land has never been farmed. Not ever. The humus was a foot thick in parts. I just don't understand. Africa was so beautiful once."

She stopped and Tom handed her back her re-loaded gun. She looked at it with loathing, tossed the hair out of her eyes and tried to smile as she tucked it in the holster.

"Thank you. Haven't you any opinions?"

"Well, I must get going quickly. It's no use having opinions just now. All the mistakes have been made. We let everybody accuse us of running a colony for our own profit and amusement, and then we let things like this happen. We run the place on easy-going lines, without severity because fair's fair, or some other daft cricketing term. Then we are surprised when this starts. They're more careful of the Europeans' interests in Portuguese or Belgian or French Africa. But what's the use. We're too soft and slapdash that's all. You're not Kenya born, I take it?"

"New Zealand. That's why I can't understand. The people here are just the same as Kiwis, and we never had trouble like this with the Maoris. Didn't have to kill them all off like they did in America, eh?" She looked at him with a thin, tired smile. "Still, I'm sticking. Just let them try to shift me."

"Goodbye," Tom said. He was to remember the passionate emphasis of her last sentence in the next few days. She stood on the step and watched him go, a small, plump figure with her hair blowing about her face that was freckled like a trout's belly.

He picked Mkuna, Kamau and Kipkoin up at the ford and they went off at a jog trot after Mkuna and the rest of the patrol who had been tracking since first light. They passed near the Philips' farm and saw several groups working in the cultivated lands. The patrol had all put on olive green tunics and hats to pass through the farming area. Their packs looked odd, and they had wrapped their ponchos round them to hide the rough skins. There would be a gang somewhere quite close. The gang that fired the Phillips' farm at four a.m. could only have moved six to eight miles before daylight. Probably, he thought, bitterly, they were sleeping now in the labour-lines of another farm. After twenty minutes they found Daniel's section waiting. The tracks lead straight to the Phillips' farm, but already a tractor had been driven, probably purposely, up and down the tracks where the footprints mingled with those of the farm labourers. Daniel, under orders not to approach another police or army patrol, had halted, but sent Mzee forward to pick up the point where the tracks left the farm. Ali Wainiri had gone with him to lend him an air of authority in case they met a patrol.

Ten minutes later Mkuna had located Mzee, who had picked up the spoor of the gang's exit. They followed all together, going as fast as they could go, due west down to the floor of the Rift Valley. Where on earth was the gang headed? Would they risk day moves? Why were they heading across a farming area? Why had they burnt a farm without attacking it? The questions seethed in his mind as with his eyes he looked for a likely lying-up place. He had checked the men's weapons and warned them to be ready.

The tracks started to veer towards a clump of trees with some broken ground, uncleared bush, ahead of them. Tom swung his hand to left and right, and the patrol fanned out in an arrow-head formation, with himself just behind Mkuna. Kamau was on his right, Kipkoin on the left. Kangi behind and to Kamau's right, with Mzee and Ali behind him. Daniel brought up the rear with Cheragoi and Kipkoin in front of him.

They entered the line of trees without incident. They were spaced out without much cover, but Mkuna lost the trail on the springy ground. They walked straight through the wood and on the other side he and Mzee hunted up and down like a pair of keen spaniels. Tom took deep breaths to steady his breathing. It was like the first time he had been out for buffalo in the thick riverine belt on the Tana river. With the knowledge that around

173

any kink in the elephant tracks they might come face to face with a ton of snorting bone and muscle, horns lowered, with half a second and a few yards to fire to kill. Mzee found the tracks and they pushed on through the scrub, tensed and sweating.

They heard the arrow fall before they saw it. It had been fired vertically in the air, and others swished down after it. A ragged volley came from a clump to the right. The patrol ran forward, fanning out. Tom ran, blinking to keep the sweat out of his eyes. Another volley and he saw a figure in a dirty raincoat running away from him. He fired a short burst from the Padgett, stopped and put the gun to his shoulder and fired a longer burst. At the same time there were two screams and he saw two figures dodging around a tree. Ali ran in front of him to his right, flung himself down and took aim with his rifle. As he fired, a bullet whistled past Tom's head and he flung himself down at the side of an anthill. Just as he fired again, one of the two running men dropped.

"Stop here," he shouted in Kikuyu to Daniel. "Pick up the wounded and report contact on the wireless." Mkuna, Mzee and Kamau would stay with him as arranged while he went forward with Ali and the two policemen.

He had been changing his magazine as he shouted. There was a smell of burnt oil and cordite in the air, and from somewhere there came a steady moaning. He was relieved to see his three men stand up as he ran forward. The bush was becoming thicker, and ahead on a slight rise was a dense belt of trees. The next few minutes would give them the only shooting they were going to get unless the trees were only a very thin belt. He saw a figure diving into them as he fought his way round a bush, and blazed off at it, but it was out of range and he was panting heavily now. He reached the trees a few minutes later, cursing silently to find that it was an extensive indigenous belt of rainforest. He emptied his magazine into it in fury. He would have to call in at Gil-Gil to collect more ammunition anyway. Ali pushed his way through the scrub towards him, a broad grin on his cat-like face. "Well done," Tom told him, still breathing hard with the effort of running. "Into forest?" Ali asked eagerly.

"No good. Army come now." Tom told him. Ali's face

registered intense disappointment. He looked longingly into the trees.

Daniel had collected two dead Mau-Mau and two wounded, one of whom was dying. Tom picked up the wireless microphone to ask for a police truck and a European with a camera to record the dead terrorists in case any were on the known Wanted list. He had just begun to transmit when there was a loud "Ayeee." He dropped flat and told the operator he was speaking to, to wait. Daniel ran off to see what it was. "Bwana," he shouted, "Bwana come quickly."

Tom ran over to the spot where Daniel stood with Kipkoin. What he saw lying on the ground brought him to an abrupt halt. He blocked off his nostrils as he fought down the impulse to vomit. "Turn it over," he said to Daniel, hardly recognising his own voice as he spoke. With his foot Daniel reluctantly moved the bloody corpse. The head stayed where it was on the ground, attached to the body only by a few shreds of purple skin. The blood, where it had not sunk into the earth, steamed in the sun. Ants were already crawling over the body. It had been slashed to pieces by a dozen or more pangas and knives. Tom looked up at the sky. There were no vultures, and any that had been waiting would have been frightened away by the shooting.

This must be the result of some sort of Mau-Mau execution, which they had interrupted. He wrenched the body away from where it lay, gripping the rough skin tunic. There was a shred of blood-soaked paper under it, which he picked up. Daniel handed him another. It was the surrender pamphlet, the "Green Branch" offer of amnesty. There was no need to look further. They turned away, Tom retching slightly as he went. He had been thinking of food before the incident. Now the thought made his entrails jerk inside him.

Back in camp, Jonathan, after seeing to the wounded, was surprised to find the orders were to take a long weekend. He slept from 5 p.m. but woke at 9 p.m. thinking that this was no way to spend free time, and he had to go to the hospital to see Tim some time. He managed to get the keys of Tim's Land Rover from a sleepy corporal in the guardroom. As he roared out of camp towards Nairobi, he realised that he had no plan of action, except a longing to see Lalage again. He stopped and looked into his pocketbook. One thing he was not sleepy about was noting addresses and phone numbers. He wanted to see if Lalage was at home, but she told him not to call without a warning, as Sam might well be there The Lerricks' number he had. Couldn't turn up there at this time uninvited. No one else, except who was L.G – Webb? It suddenly dawned on him. Lala. She would be out by now, but he could leave a note and then "creep around the bars," as Grainne claimed he usually did when he had no plans.

But when he rang the bell, marked de Gynne/Webb, it was Lalage who opened the door. Wet hair done up in a towel, she seemed quite pleased to see him.

"Sorry. Been up-country. No phone boxes."

"No," she said, rubbing her hair, "not beyond Rumuruti. Have a drink while I get the dryer," and she vanished. He took a large whisky and she re-appeared in minutes in a dress which looked to him to be probably a going-out-at-night-number.

"Meant to stay in for once," she yelled from under the dryer. "Have you eaten?"

"No, he said. "Not hungry. But can take you out. Got Tim's car. He got shot slightly. Be OK soon."

"Oh God. Is he bad? Where?"

"Upper thigh. In the muscle. Won't worry him."

"Very sorry. Shouldn't we go and see him?" She wandered to the drinks tray and poured herself a stiff vodka tonic.

"Tomorrow. Won't let us in now," There was an uneasy silence. She looked at him hard. "You look exhausted. You can stay here, you know. Angela is away as usual. Zanzibar I think. Have another drink. I can do you an omelette." To her amazement he began to shake as he poured himself another drink, both hands trembling, pretending to need ice to disguise it. She went to the kitchen to let him recover, and brought back an ice bucket and fussed over his drink.

"Tell me more about it. If you like." He didn't answer. After a while he said, "Lala, have you seen a lot of deads?" She didn't answer, studying his drawn, so boyish face

"I... I never saw any before I came here. Seen... er... rather a few lately." His voice trembled as he said, "Not nice." She walked over to him, grabbed his arm.

"Come over here," She plonked him down on the sofa, and took his head in her arms. He shuddered, his face turned away. She stroked his hair. After a while, she lifted his face up to hers. His cheeks were wet. She gathered him into her arms and kissed him passionately. He couldn't speak, and she knew better than to say anything. After a while she released him, and they sat there just looking at each other. He got up, grabbed his whiskey and downed it. "Thank you," he managed to get out before he choked up again.

Suddenly, she became very managerial. "Bed for you, me boyo. You're jiggered. Off you go." She pushed him into a bedroom, and threw him pyjamas.

"Sam's, in case you wondered. Come on. You've been over-doing it." He came out of the shower. "Nice clean soldier boy," she teased.

"Stay with me," he pleaded.

"Later," she said, tucking him in. "Another drink?" He nodded and closed his eyes.

Opening them he murmured, "Lala," but she had gone. She returned with a three finger whisky.

"Lala."

"Yes?"

"Got a long weekend."

"Sleep, my little soldier. Just sleep."

He woke sometime in the middle of the night. He had dreamed of buffalo charging. Of falling down cliffs. Of the whoosh and crackle of small arms fire. Thump and blast of grenades. The half-face twitching, screaming. Marty yelling "Gerraway outa that."

Blood pumping out from under the field dressings. He put out his hand. She was there beside him, sleeping, and her hair in a dense halo all around her head. He reached out to touch it. She stirred and then woke up, stretching. "Supposed to be sleeping," she murmured gently.

"Lala. Why are you here?"

177

"Damn silly question. You need mothering, and besides I..."

"What?"

"I'm in love with you, stupid." She hid her head in her pillow. He took her in his arms. She could tell that he didn't know what to do next, so she wriggled underneath him and showed him.

CHAPTER FIFTEEN

BIBIS – THE WOMEN

"The best form of welfare is training."

Field Marshall Rommel

"It's all so easy once you make a determined start," Alison said, looking round the roomful of shaven-headed bibis in their flowered print dresses and head scarves. "They're all avid for education of any sort, so it isn't like trying to reform girl prostitutes or drug addicts in Hong Kong. No lure of rice or religion to bring them in, but the room is always full whenever I come." Gillian stared at her.

Alison mused. These colonial English women aren't inclined to idealism or woolly thought. She had never realised before the difference it made to grow up in Africa as Gillian, Lalage and Angela had, giving orders from the age of ten, witnessing the fundamental processes of life, birth, copulation and death from the age when they could toddle round a farm. The language they used at time still shocked her but they didn't realise that women in Europe didn't express themselves quite so forcibly. It was different from the refined circles of Hong Kong and Delhi, the convents in Penang and Washington. Living in Africa where a woman had to know how to change a wheel, stitch a scalp and deal with rowdy drunks, as well as to be able to run a house without gas or electricity, or drains or any public services; these things put a patina of hardness on them. But it was a tough, bustling, energetic hardness, and not a sour, cynical shell.

"Tell me about Angela de Gynne," Gillian asked Alison. "Tough lady. She used to go on six-month safaris with her husband into the bush. She shot at least a dozen elephants, and ran a farm during the war. Lost one husband on D-Day, and the next one was killed by a buffalo. Divorced number three, who drank. She hasn't bothered to sign up Number Four. Don't see him much. She paints, and she's a keen and fairly successful racing and rally driver. She has got backing now, for this place from WHO. And several other charities, I think."

"Who?"

"World Health Organisation. The UN."

"Oh."

"Gill," Alison said, "tell me about Lalage."

"Clever girl. Her Pa was one of the first successful coffee planters. Her mother doesn't like to live here. They live in France, I think. She's not too well."

"But Lalage herself?"

"Another tough cookie. Like her brother. Don't be deceived by the fluffy dresses. She's moody, but no fool. Reads a lot of books. Lots of men after her. Had a boyfriend here but he left. Went to Europe somewhere about six months ago. The army men are after her too."

"Sam looks so different."

"Yes. His mother was South African. They got divorced and he then married Lala's mother."

It was Angela's ability to charm that had won Gillian over. She had not been at all enthusiastic, apparently thinking that Nairobi's young fast set would mock her. Angela had guessed this at once and challenged her with it

"Oh no," Gillian said, "I'm not afraid of that."

"Balls," Angela responded firmly, "And you aren't sure of young Sammy. I'll have a talk with that young man." And talk she did, just then on the spot, ringing the airfield at Nyeri and telling Sam that Gillian was going to work for her. And that had been that. You couldn't resist Angela. She swept things out of her way with a jaunty energy, her great actress's eyes flashing from her wonderful broad browed slavonic face. Russian by birth and rich by marriage, so that when she had swamped your objections, she would buy you a gin, or several, and then sweep you off in her Mercedes. So fast that any remaining protest would be silenced.

Combined with Lalage's stern, non-sectarian realism and intensity, they made up a force that bulldozed clean through the red tape and the shocked opinions. She had talked WHO into buying equipment and she was negotiating with UNICEF for trainers, and funds.

Typically, she had agreed with the local UN office to help the ILO, the International Labour Organisation, to "investigate the carvings racket," as they put it.

She started by questioning the hawkers who hung round the hotels selling carvings. Found out from where they were supplied, they had then contravened several regulations by driving through the barrier into the Machakos Reserve and interrogating shifty native carvings dealers.

The dealers paid a few shillings, and sometimes less than a shilling, to the carvers, collected hundreds of items in sacks and sold them in the towns to other dealers. Some of these were exported to Europe and America where they fetched prices from five to twenty times what the carvers received.

The native dealers made two or three hundred per cent, and the exporters another two or three hundred. Traders were excluded from the reserve to prevent this, and the native dealers evasively gave false box numbers and muttered about missionaries when asked where they sold. Angela had blasted their network apart and set up several co-operatives at legal trading points and up-country hotels, effectively cutting off the racketeers' supply, at least for a time. Some of the women who came to the Ruthaka school brought carvings with them and some were sold at the roadside and at another point on the main road in Limuru where Angela owned a store and a petrol station. The profits from this helped to finance the school, bought materials, wool, knitting needles, thread, furniture and enough food for the cookery classes.

Gillian, diffident at first, had interpreted for Alison, who took a class in hygiene and domestic science. She was inclined to be impatient, as was to be expected, because the standard of comprehension, mostly due to language problems amongst the bibis and the unmarried nditos, was appallingly low. Babies, which were brought to Ruthaka in amazing profusion, bored her stiff, she said. But Angela, who supervised the administrations of medicine and had arranged for half a dozen doctors to call, each once a day for an hour, soon persuaded her to "show she wasn't afraid of blood and guts," as she persuasively put it. Anyone who brought a baby or a child had to stay for the morning or the afternoon to be taught something useful and by sitting with the hard core of industrious, chattering, giggling basket weavers, knitters or sewing-machine operators, they were indoctrinated. Those who had just come for a pill either didn't come again or started to come regularly, so that there were always crowds around all four sides of the building and the other buildings that were going up under Angela's supervision.

Lalage was the only one who was there most of the time with her air of dogged, almost feverish pre-occupation, that made Alison wonder what sort of compulsion drove her on, day after day. Gillian worked on the family farm most mornings, typing for her father and doing other jobs that Tom's absence made necessary. She herself had to run the house for her father and be back in time for his meals when he was not eating out. Angela bustled around from her dress shop in town to her Limuru store and back to Ruthaka. She brought a rush of new life into the workroom with her explosive laughter and her voice stimulated everyone, black and white, into activity, whereas it was the signal for a stream of new requests from those waiting round the door.

The men and boys Angela sent packing if they would not help with building, and the others she chaffed into some semblance of a queue in front of her desk on the stoep. Often there would be a policeman or a district officer or a visitor from a rehabilitation centre or a prison officer waiting to see her. But these often had to take there turn behind a couple of bibis with wailing children slung on their backs.

"Look around," she would tell them, with a wave of her hand. "Have a good look. Talk to them if you like. I'll be with you in a minute," and she would turn to her desk, firing off questions in a mixture of Kikuyu and Swahili that made the natives giggle, as it was meant to do.

"They'll catch on eventually," she would say when the visitors had gone. "A bit dim, the poor dears. Centuries of neglect. Just got to show them how to do it and that you don't need much to do it with. Another year or two and they'll catch on. They still think I'm doing it for profit or to show off or annoy them or something. Of course I've got a big advantage, I know. I don't have to account for public money. We're free and like Doctor Schweitzer bless him, we don't try to convert them to anything."

Then in her serious moments she would talk of the future and of the work that there would be re-educating Mau-Mau. "What we need really is a couple of woman doctors or a few native ones. I know of a couple of African doctors in England, both with nice fat London practices. If only I could get the blighters out here and get someone to pay them, or make enough to pay them myself."

The problem, Alison could see, boiled down to lack of money in every field; clinics, schools, hospitals road building, dams, soil preservation, housing, administration. She had never realised before how much it all needed. How few taxpayers there were and why the shops and the hotels weren't as big and prosperous as Hong Kong or Penang. It depressed her at times, especially when the eternal comment was made.

"Yes dear, but it's only a drop in the ocean, that Ruthaka thing." And then there were the others who said, "Of course we have a school and a dispensary on our farm, but it will take a century to educate them all properly and they'll get the vote and kick us out long before that."

But Angela would point out that the government, like all colonial administrations, was trying to keep the costs down. "You know," she told Alison, "the Governor once told me that he wasn't going to build hospitals while the District Chiefs' Councils had shares in Britain in City development bonds. Damned muddled thinking, that. Not the Governor's. He's fine. It's the Colonial Office, who are still recruiting district officers, as though the Empire will last forever."

Both Gillian and Lalage at times took the attitude that they knew theirs was only a small amateur effort.

"But what the hell," Gillian said, "I suppose it's better than typing for some twerp with his dirty vest showing through his horrible nylon shirt." And Lalage said it made her feel less helpless when she saw the crippled ones crawling about the streets and the dirty and feckless ones hanging about the Indian stores. But she said this with an earnestness that was patently genuine, her eyes unfocused and for a moment she had stared ahead of her while Alison wondered what went on inside the small, neat skull with its helmet of ebony black hair.

She looked over at her now, wrestling with a sewing machine that a bibi had entangled in a mass of flowery material. Her face was expressionless as she bent over the machine. It was not often that she smiled, and then the smile transformed her face, melting each feature, so that framed in the dark hair it radiated an intensity of happiness. But when angry, only her lips compressed and the shadow of a frown appeared as she fought with the anger below the surface. She separated the material from the needle at last and the bibi broke into a torrent of thanks. Lalage nodded, as briskly she returned the piece to its right place.

Alison strolled over to where Gillian was talking to a group of four mothers. Her face was mobile, expressing every shift of emphasis and opinion. She turned as Alison approached, her face breaking into an easy grin. "Y'know, I reckon they must think it's dead comical for an ndito like me to know so much about kids. Or care. Anything wrong?"

"No. I just wanted you when you've finished to come over and explain sterilisation for me in Swahili." Gillian's face wrinkled comically.

"No," Alison added, "Not that sort. Bottles and stuff like that."

"Tricky. There aren't the words, y'know. Two or three words for washing of different sorts. Have to work in boil. Boil/wash. Something like that. Be with you in a minute."

She waved carelessly. That was Gillian. Easy-going but co-operative. Thoughtless. But when she accepted your reasoning she piled into the problem with gusto. Since Angela had asked her not to wear trousers and explained why, she had turned up looking tidier ever since.

Today she was wearing a white dairy coat over her dress and tied her hair in a chignon. Angela had, as always, handled her skilfully. White women she had said were different enough for the bibis to understand, and trousers didn't help. The idea was to get the native women to stand up to their men. Did she get the idea? Gillian had grinned helplessly. Yes, she got it. Angela didn't like women working in trousers. Fair enough.

"Now," Gillian said briskly, coming over to the corner where the sink was. "Let's wise you up on these washing words. They ought to know a bit about it already. The D.O.s are always at them about boiling drinking water because of the bilharzia. Imagine having tape worms inside you. Ugh."

Lalage overheard her and laughed. "Tell you what," she said, "After all this killing business, it's going to take a lot of re-education to put them all straight."

"Re-education, my arse," was the comment. "Serikali (Government) never got around to educating most of them in the first place."

CHAPTER SIXTEEN

THE RACES

"Hey nonny no!
Men are fools that wish to die!
Is't not fine to dance and sing
When the bells of death do sing?"

Anon.

"Kwaheri Stakes," the announcer said. His magnified voice sounded thin in the wide, warm openness of the scene. Jonathan leant back on the bar, drained his gin and tonic, and walked out to ask Hullyer what the system was for this last race. He halted with the sun on his bare head and took a long gin-restricted breath, exhaling the mixture of fumes and dry, dusty air with satisfaction.

What a crazy sort of war it was? Tim in the local hospital, he at the local races.

"Take a forty-eight," Cormac said. "We'll do a sweep back about Tuesday."

But Lalage had gone off somewhere, saying, "Get yourself up to Nakuru Races. Sam will take me. See you." And she was gone, blowing kisses.

Somebody said the whole Commando was out ambushing. Somebody else said that some gangs were moving up here to Naivasha in the Rift valley. One I.O. said the gang that hit them was fifty strong. A local in the bar said that Kimathi, Mathenge, a character called Mekanika and another called Alphonse something, were all knocking about in that area allocated to the Commando. Jonathan didn't know. All he knew was that

McEvoy and Kelly were dead and he wasn't too sure what they had died to prove.

"The right not to be murdered." Was it Tom Lerrick who said that? Did it matter anyway, as long as men made guns and pointed them at each other, who started it and what they proved? Wouldn't they go on somewhere else, a decade or two later, squabbling over the same things? Wasn't all this a repetition of other revolts against the status quo. As in Ireland. In the Balkans. In South Africa. Nationalism gone berserk, with a primitive latter day Industrial Revolution thrown in, with a dash of the Matabele Wars?

"Come on," Hullyer said, "you're getting broody." Taking him by the arm. "Going to buy a horse."

Don't want a blasted horse, Jonathan said to himself. Aloud he said, "What sort of horse?"

"Share in a syndicate. All the winning horses can run in the last race Kwaheri – Goodbye. You buy a name and if it wins you share the stake total with the owner."

"That girl will win," Jonathan said dully. He had wanted to stand there out in the sun, just letting his mind tick over in neutral. He was missing Lalage already, he knew, and was sulking.

"Which one?"

"The one who's been winning all day. She can't ride them all." Jonathan had backed her three times and won. He had felt sorry for her because he had met a Rooinek in the bar who said she looked as though she had just won first prize in the cow-drenching competition. She had a face like boot leather, a flat chest and male mannerisms. The bar was packed with people bidding for the names. Jonathan gave Hullyer a note to bet on the girl's horse and said he wanted a pee and went outside.

The course was on a slope, overlooking the Rift. You could see fifty miles into the distance, and he stood there just looking at the enormity of it. Over on the right there was a valley with dark green umbrella-topped trees strewn thickly all over it with a farm here and there by a cleared patch. On the left there was a shoulder of the Rift wall and the valley stretching off to the north. Straight ahead was a huge open plain with a road running across from left to right. Just over the road, that was a livid ribbon on the landscape, were two shallow lakes that stretched like great mirage-puddles into the level bush around them. A pink flush in the far corner of one lake was a flock of half a million flamingos. A narrower ribbon ran past them, leading to some habitation that the eye could not see, somewhere out in the far, flat emptiness that ached endlessly in the shimmering heat.

One day he would go there and look at the flamingos rising from the water and walk up to the funny little conical hills that pushed themselves up from the valley floor, wartlike in the rust-coloured desolation. Perhaps elephants went there when it was cooler, stumped down to the lake and soused themselves with the water while the flamingos just stood about on one leg and pretended not to notice. If they didn't then they should, because elephants would look magnificent against the background, and it was their sort of scale.

Suddenly it didn't matter so much about the cow-drenching girl with the tough face, and McEvoy and Kelly and those Kithenge, Mathenge people, and Tim lying there pretending it didn't hurt. The gin didn't help, because he suddenly realised not even gin could take away the fact that he was in Africa. That Africa was big, merciless and raw, a place of extremes, and that the petty orderliness of Europe held no dominion. And therefore he said to himself firmly, as the babble behind him indicated that the horses had been drawn, now that girl could get on with her winning, there was no use at all moping about a little blood because there would always be blood flowing in Africa, because it was that kind of place.

Out there in the bush the cats went out at sunset not to walk on the tiles, their bellies full of milk, as in tidy old Dublin, but with bellies rumbling for live flesh. And when they had killed, the hyenas and wild dogs finished off the smaller pieces. Followed neatly, if you like, by the vultures and the marabou storks and then very, very neatly by the ants. Until very shortly indeed there remained only the clean white bones and presumably a few million microbes of some sort, that didn't matter anyway, because the sun would soon bake the bones dry.

Suddenly he felt a lot better and not morbid at all and he

kicked his mind out of neutral into a gear that would take him back into the current problems of living.

Hullyer met him and gave him four tickets he had bought at the Tote, because the Nairobi bookies hadn't thought it worth their while to come to Nakuru to these races. Perhaps they knew about the girl too.

"Don't let me keep you away from the fillies," Hullyer said, "And don't hang about. Get on with it. This is in-fighting country. They expect it."

Jonathan laughed and wished he could tell him about it, but he was keeping his own counsel and in the circumstances there was precious little else he could do.

"I think you know them?" Hullyer said, "the Lerrick lass and the Webb lass? They drove up from Nairobi this morning and collected Lala's brother half-way, at the Naivasha air strip. I had a drink in the hotel with Sam just before lunch; they had all swept in together and started discussing some sudden increase in terrorist activity in the area. Said Captain Collins got shot. He's got the hots for the Webb lass. They all seemed to know you. Asked if you were around. So I thought I'd tell you," he added archly.

This cheered him up immensely. It was a bit embarrassing to have Sammy around. Lalage was still burning in his mind. What an extraordinary woman she was. He wandered out towards the parade ring, and there she was. He waved at her, but she did not see him, surrounded by men as she was. He supposed they were all the lot she had grown up with. They all seemed to worship her. Too late he wrenched himself away from Hullyer. How to do this with Sam around?

The opportunity had been lost, for when they returned to the course for the last race she was escorted by two or three more bronzed, muscular, locals and Jonathan just didn't feel sufficiently inspired to do battle. There had been a fight recently between locals and some British soldiers. She would detach herself as soon as decently possible, surely?

He walked down to the rail of the paddock to watch the start. The Africans in the shilling paddock were all lively jostle and animation, high screech and flashes of those terrific mouthfuls of brilliantly white teeth. From the stable boys, they had a shrewd idea about most of the races and hordes of them came away from the queues marked "Pay-Out," at the end of each race, grinning delightedly. They were so childlike you could hardly believe what savagery there could be below the shining brown purple skins. What power the oaths must have, to drive them back into the forests, roaming with the carnivores, living in caves, forever moving? Or was it at first just the boredom of the townships? The endless dull, hot days in the shanties, with no dances or drums, no spear and shield, no ceremony, nothing to break the monotony?

Hullyer came over. Jonathan said, "The races must be great for the locals."

"What ya mean?"

"Well, with the gambling, excitement, the meetings must be for them, something like the old days."

"Hell, no. The tribes are all mixed now, and the old allegiances melted down in the township settlements, with the chiefs, headmen, elders and witch-doctors replaced by white bwanas, Gujerati traders, Sikh craftsmen, Muslim businessmen. Locals who have learned to read and write pick up gambling damn quick, and good luck to 'em."

"But, it must seem very strange and confusing to see the world changing with no one to explain it. Maybe the Masai are the wisest, to keep aloof from all the changes, stay in the bush with their cattle, free from a money economy. No need to work for a brown or a white or a black man."

Hullyer stared at him, then grinned. "Don't fret yong. Hakuna matata. Let it all hang out."

The girl in the blue and white racing silks lead from the start. The course went out in an oval on the perfectly flat course, so that the horses were visible all the way. There were only four starters and the race was four furlongs down the nearer side of the oval. She came in amongst tremendous excitement, the winner by six lengths. Jonathan found himself in the Tote queue not far behind a noisy trio consisting of Lalage and two men, one of whom, in a flat green hat, was either very tight, or not quite right in the head. The other was attempting to match his vivacity, and was producing an equal amount of hilarious noise. Lalage herself, elegant in a deep-blue dress with a white silk scarf over her hair, in a nun-like coif, seemed subdued. He could not see her face, but he realised that she wasn't teasing him. She could not afford to suddenly ditch friends of a lifetime.

Knowing that, he was still hurt. "Fix bayonets," he muttered to himself and pressed forward to launch an attack. The opportunity came when she stood aside to let the green-hatted one, who answered to the name of Hamish, to collect her winnings. He raised the hat he had borrowed with the other clothes, from the doctor's mess at the hospital.

"Having fun, Ma'am?" he enquired solemnly, and was rewarded with a delighted smile. Then a flicker of the lids in the direction of Hamish.

"Mary won again. What more can you ask?" But her voice wasn't confident. She seemed almost shy, distant. "See you later" she whispered, groped for his hand and squeezed it. He couldn't think of anything to say. She turned her head half away. A wisp of hair blew from under the coif across her cheek. The line of the bone, he thought. Like the sweep of the horn of a gazelle. He wanted to lean forward and kiss her. "Come on, Lala," a voice bellowed.

"What are you doing this evening?" he asked quickly.

"Going to the club darling, like everyone else. See you there." She turned to look at him, their eyes locked. Then she turned away, looking for her escorts. It was almost a shock. Until now he had not realised how closely the young white people stuck together. Friends for years and years. He was an interloper. An Uitlander. And there was Sam guarding her, too.

"Club? Which one?"

"Nakuru, silly. Hamish and Henry will talk to Sammy all night about aeroplanes and get screechers."

"Sounds fun." He smiled and she smiled back quickly "Gotta go – darling…" The last word was muted.

He would have to go and see when she could be prised away. When her escort had drunk their winnings it might not be too difficult. They had collected now and came away with their money, talking noisily. Lalage waved and went with them.

A voice behind him said gruffly, "He wants to keep that hat on, or his ears'll fall apart." Jonathan turned gratefully to see a bluff, brick-red face under a mud-coloured Stetson, looking grimly after Hamish.

"Come and have a drink after this." Hullyer smiled a wry, shut-away smile, showing Jonathan his hand with its meagre winnings.

"Got to get back," Jonathan said. "Look after yourself." He walked away past the bar, so full of unknown faces and one face he could not bear to see.

He didn't know why but he suddenly felt an attack of that loneliness which soldiers expressed by the pithy phrase "Fed up, fucked and far from home." All those black faces with whom he could not communicate, and then, on top of that, the white faces with which he had so little in common, who recognised at once from his accent and his pale face that he was not one of them. I am missing the joviality of the Curragh, of James Fitzpatrick, and all the Dannys and Jimmys and Seamuses. Sean O'Malley and his shillelagh and leprechaun wit. Tim's brothers, his own sisters and all the others whose way of life and childhood experiences had something in common with mine.

Tim looked much better and was laughing about something with the man in the next bed as Jonathan entered the ward. He felt better just to look at him lying there, still contriving to look military somehow, even in bed. Tim introduced him to the man, a subaltern in the Dorsets, who explained that he had been bitten by a tracker dog in a very awkward place. "Intact but slightly chewed," he said. They had had news of a gang contact which had probably been the same gang that ambushed their patrol. Tim gave advice on the "return match." A return sweep was due to start back to the Aberdares on Monday and they discussed the chances of avenging the ambush.

"How's Gillian and Tom. And Lalage?" Tim enquired.

"At the races with Sam. No sign of Tom."

"Webb is a rude young man," Tim commented. "A sharp kick in the arse would improve his manners."

They turned to talk of other subjects, and Jonathan, sensing that they felt him to be very lucky to be able to walk about at all, tried to be funny, but failed. He left the ward feeling much heartened. Lalage had mentioned the club. The alternative was to borrow a book from one of the doctors and eat in the temporary mess there, alone. "Shut up," he told himself. "She can't dump everybody for a two-bit soldier, and look a ninny in front of all her chums. And how close to Lalage had Tim been?"

Gillian enjoyed driving Sam's Dodge, a 1950 model. The blurb in the American handbook stated, apart from the fact that it was "longer, lower and wider than ever before," the stimulating trope, that in it you "rode high, wide, and handsome." If you had to hammer over the corrugations at speed then it was the machine to do it. A grateful client had sent it to Sammy as a tip for a two-month safari. Apart from an awkward occasion when parked outside the flat during the long rains. The automatic window winder button had jammed, and the car had filled with water, but it had given little trouble since.

Angela told her "Go. Get out of Nairobi. Get some air." She had been working hard and did feel lethargic, but a trip to the coast and the stimulus of sea-level air would have been better. The races were all very well but the horsy crowd were more over-sexed than most and there would be the usual hints from the brasher, younger ones and maybe the usual flight to the protection of one of the older ones. All the same, they were a more open lot than the townies and she shouldn't sneer at them. At least they were doing a hard job and she knew how hard it could be and how lonely; even without the Mau-Mau.

Sammy had been on the airstrip tinkering with his Cessna. In the car on the way there Gillian asked Lalage about this and that. Sam dozed in the back and Lalage sat up front. The chat turned to men. "Give me the Kenya boys every time," Gillian said. "Hey, have you seen those two who came to lunch?"

"Who?" Lalage said, looking in the mirror to see if Sam was asleep. Gillian chatted on. "Right over my head," she said. "That Jonathan chap." She imitated his accent and the phrases he used. "My dear" and "Mah dear girl," and "Quite preposterous, old thing."

193

"I can see him," she said, "In his bowler and umbrella, with a stiff white collar and his regimental tie." But Sam was not asleep.

"But you like the daft pom, 'cos he's good looking. Same as you took to Tim whatsit." Sammy growled. "A long drinka water, like most of 'em."

"Rubbish," Lalage said, knowing it was hopeless to try to draw such nice distinctions for Gillian who had left her English school at seventeen. She had no real idea about what made the local lads so different from the European educated. She changed the subject, and climbed over into the back.

Gillian wanted to drive faster, so Lalage sat in the back with Sam and talked about his flying and about giving it up now that he had finished the two years in the KPA.

"You know we've lost three this year," he said. "Bill Rutherford crashed near Rumuruti. Charlie Bell near Mount Kenya and now Jimmy Barlow."

"Why?"

"Looking for lost patrols. Dropping supplies in lousy weather. Running into cloud. Then into hills. Jimmy hit a vulture or an eagle. Smashed his windscreen. These Piper Cruisers are not too strong. I 've had enough."

"Oh good. So now you can start the farm going." But she knew it was really the itch to be hunting again, to be out on safari miles away from anywhere without clocks or newspapers or appointments or people. "Better than killing time in the Concrete Forest."

"Yup. You're right girl. But …"

"But what?"

"Not the best time to start."

"Ain't no tourists for you to take out walloping game."

Sometime she must have a talk about Gillian with him, because she wanted him to go to Europe at least once before he got married, and now that their parents had gone there permanently, it would be a good opportunity to persuade him. But he had already planned, as much as he ever did, to spend his K.P.A. gratuity on equipment for the farm.

"I wanna go off on a spree first, man."

For Sammy a spree was a box-body truck, two drums of petrol, rifles and as few game licences as possible. Sammy tired quickly of discussing his future and began telling jokes and the latest funny story from the Nyeri area which concerned something about an Indian storekeeper and a man who asked him for "a dozen scruples," which the Indian had looked for earnestly amongst his stock. "Screws I am having. Nuts, bolts also. Scruples I am not having." The wit had capped this by saying as he left the duka every day, "Kwaheri old cock," which he had explained was the latest saying amongst the "European type fellows," with the alleged result that the duka-wallah had said it to the local D.O.'s wife.

Lalage tired of listening. Sam went on, saying," I met an American in the Norfolk last week." He said, "It's not so much the black faces I mind, but the fact that the white faces are so damn foreign as well. God dammit," he said, "they don't know what a waffle-iron is for and I never get around to discussing the ball games."

Jonathan had reminded her sharply of Andrew at first and that had been painful. But he was different, and just now he was in shock, although he didn't seem to know it. Normally there was that fey casualness about him that relaxed her. She liked the way he didn't seem to accept everything just as it was. He was gentle and unassuming and there were no prickles to him. He was just a bit hard hit by Africa, and its bloodiness. And suddenly getting shot at and all that shit.

It had been comforting that time in the Nakuru Club when she had flared up at Bill Gredling and he hadn't minded. So that time up at Fort Hall when he had got tight again, really tight that time, she hadn't minded either and then they had talked about books and he had recited poetry to her. First time in Africa since her father had read aloud to her. He hadn't been so military then. Telling her how much he liked the flowers and the Kikuyu children squabbling stark naked in the dust.

"You are my sort," Jonathan said. "Oh," she replied. "Thank you master. So the rest of us are country bumpkins, all stiffly buttoned up, in our Sunday suits, are we?"

Anyway they had talked and laughed and argued nonsensically and he hadn't let Sammy see how strong was their mutual attraction. There would be time enough later. If there was going to be a later. She tried to tell him that here in this tiny social group, you had to be very careful of the wicked tongues. "And with Sam. Boy he uses fists first and brains later."

"Maybe it's daft to expect you to stay here, " she said. "Why should you? We made the mess and you have to sort it out for us."

She was not sure if he had been sent here against his will. Not wanting to ask that, she kept asking him what he thought about Africa.

"I always wanted to see the place where Saint Exupery met Le Petit Prince and where the Elephant Child came from."

"What?"

"And the background to the best of Hemingway's stories."

So comforting to think about him. How sharply he brought Europe back. How long ago it all seemed, the ship and the strange languages and the cool, moist air. He reminded her of those long, low valleys in France. And the lush green fields all broken up and intersected with hedges and clumps of trees and small stone buildings. The way the ground tilted, swept up and down, with many folds and the way everything seemed to be on a miniature scale, so that hills that seemed to be a long way off were really quite near. And little rows of houses everywhere. But he was different from the calm, orderliness of England, so tamed and restrained.

"I'm a revolting Mick," he explained. "Tim and I are soldiers in the tradition of the Wild Geese." Then he explained about those Irish soldiers shipped off from Limerick two centuries ago. "They ended up fighting for the Catholic Kings. There are still Irish names, from those soldiers, in Madrid, Paris, and Vienna. And statues of Irish generals."

"What's it got to do with geese?"

"The ones who didn't get away in 1691 were sent out in crates marked 'Wild Geese', so they say."

That was Irish, for sure. Dreamy boyish charm. Casual relationship with life's problems? And those long words he used.

Anyway, it was there, whatever it was and it was fascinating among all the local the rawness and the naivety. It was what poor Sammy lacked. A little of the veneer that he didn't even despise because he was unaware of its existence. Maybe that was why Americans liked Sam, because he was raw and tanned and gauche and blunt, like something out of Hemingway. That was part of what they came to Africa for wasn't it, to meet bush babies like him?

After the races, and drinks in the Nakuru Club, somebody had the idea not to return to Nairobi. So they all booked in at Thompson Falls, an old Highlands hotel way up in the foothills of the Aberdares. So cold there at night, you needed fires in every room.

They went down to the bar and Lalage saw with a start, there he was, talking to John Hullyer, terribly shy and muttering something about being here by accident. Gillian gave him a wicked grin but he seemed to be embarrassed all the same. He didn't know *her* very well, that was clear. But then although Sammy had been talking to him, to Hamish and Hullyer about the dreary Micks, he had hardly glanced at her. She realised he was acting innocent, so that Sam didn't smell a rat, as he put it. Over tea, with the Dayrells, Hamish and Ian Burns had tried to push Jonathan away.

The thought of an evening squired by Hamish and Ian was so dreadful that she said to Jonathan, quietly, so they couldn't hear her "I have to be careful. Sammy is such a drag."

She looked embarrassed. He just blushed.

"I understand," he said, from the side of his mouth, so that only she heard it, "I had no idea the competition was this fierce." Hamish and Ian were glowering at him. In between beers he heard them mention "the bloody Brits," and "Fuckin' pongo officers."

"Do not take the bait," Tim had told him. "They are looking for a fight. There have been quite a few, and I don't want any of my officers involved. Got it?" So he ignored them and pretended to be dead interested in what Sam was saying.

"These people are a bloody bore," she whispered to him. Then much louder, "Which may be unfair, but that is Africa.

Anyway. I'm going up to get the dust off,"

Hamish and Ian looked at her and just grinned. They turned their back on Jonathan as she left the bar. She saw that out of the corner of her eye. Sam was going to find out very soon.

She lay in her bath wallowing. It would be interesting when Sam did notice. About her and her lovely Roinek. He would be incandescent with rage. She shivered. Was it anticipation of the cold air outside the bath, or something else? She liked this hotel with the piles of firewood outside every room and the coolness of the highlands contrasting with the cosiness of the cedar fires. It was more like Europe than any other part of the country, with its cold night winds and the long rainy seasons. She pulled out the plug with her toe and jumped out into the towel. You are getting more cheerful, she said to herself. Or is it the altitude up here which gives you that light-headed feeling that nothing much matters anyhow? Oh God, my beautiful soldier. How I long for you.

When she went downstairs, Jonathan and a doctor who came with him from the hospital, were still in the hotel bar drinking with Sammy, Hullyer and Gillian. There had been a drunk in the bar when they arrived, who rapidly got worse, staggered against the doctor and muttered savagely, "Blurry policeman. Bugger off."

The doctor, Bill Temple, merely shrugged his shoulders, but the drunk, a middle-aged man in shirt sleeves, fixed him with an unsteady eye which wavered between Bill and Jonathan, and went on talking at them.

"Don' wan' you. Go home. No use with Africans. Cost me money ... all the time. Go home. Go home." Two men who knew him handed their guns to Sammy to look after and bundled him outside and shoved him into his boxbody truck. Bill was very angry. "I come out here and spend my time stitching up stinking Mau-Maus and Blimps like that. They take you for Contract Police. Sheer snobbery and stupidity."

"Take no notice," Sammy said. "he was drunk."

"In vino veritas," Bill replied. "he doesn't like me because he hadn't seen me and Jon here, around the place for the last twenty years that's all."

"They have a hard time out on the farms you know. They get like that," Lalage told him, and Bill changed the subject because he was obviously attracted to her too and Sam was keeping Lalage firmly in his corner.

She was looking almost out of place in the rough wooden bar. She wore a cocktail dress that was tight round the hips and flared out from a band just above her knees, with a lot of ruffling petticoats under it. The necklace she wore was in the same pattern Jonathan remembered her saying was Himyaritic, from the Hadramaut, East Yemen. Beaten silver, lighter than the colour of her skin. Because, although Gillian had a deeper tan, when Jonathan put his hand near Lalage's arm, he could see how pale his skin really was.

Another man hailed Sammy loudly from the door, and came over, his Padgett swinging from a rawhide sling, to pump his hand. Sam knew him. Jan van der Costhuizen. He was a wiry, whippety fellow, with half an inch of beard and a camouflaged jacket that smelt of sweat and smoke. He spoke in a curious clipped sing song like a Welshman trying to imitate a Glaswegian, and most of his utterance were prefaced by …"Christ man." and ended with an interrogative "Aye?" He wore a bullet belt to support two home made holsters. A crudely carved ivory pistol butt stuck out from one, and a knife with a deerhorn handle from the other. The bullet cases were polished and the loops at one side of the belt were empty. He had sharp, pale blue eyes set in his wind-cured, kipper coloured face.

"The bastards hamstrung Kobus' dry herd last week man. Took two away and slashed the rest. Twenty-seven of 'em man. This bloody Imperialist Government, I'm telling you ay, it don't know what it's doing." He addressed Jonathan as "Yong."

"Down in the Union man, we had a riot a few years ago ay? In Durban. Anyone out on the streets after seven, man, gets shot. Kaffir, coloured, Hindi or white man. They shot a few and it was over. And Madagascar ay? You ever heard o' that?"

He nudged Jonathan, who was not flattered to be recognised as a Roinek.

"They killed thousands there man, a year or two ago. Bloody Huovas planned a massacre. But they kept the damned newspapers out. All over, in a coupla days. This lot…" He made

199

a noise as though he was going to spit.

"Well let's go and eat," Lalage said, ignoring him completely. "I'm hungry."

Jonathan found himself opposite her with Gillian beside him. There seemed to be some sort of a tiff going on between Sam and Gillian because she flirted steadily throughout the meal with Jonathan. Bill Temple thought he was making good progress with Lalage.

The local Sports Club was only half a mile away, but everybody took their cars. It was a wooden building, really just a golf club with the usual verandas, and the biggest bar cleared for dancing to an RAF band.

Jonathan tactfully danced with Gillian. She told him about war time in the forties, when they ran the trucks on kerosene, and stuffed the old tyres with straw to keep trucks running. It was then they first saw soldiers treating Africans as equals. He concealed his irritation, as she went on.

"They all think we live like the old Gilgil set, pre-war, don't they?" she challenged. "We're all on Remittance, living it up in big white Gin-Palaces built out in the sticks, playing polo, sniffing coke, and swapping partners. 'The Happy Valley Crowd' – that's us. 'A place in the sun for shady people.' Ha- Ha. "

He laughed and only interrupted when she brought up the old chestnut about the way the troops had no responsibility for the African and cheerfully slept in the same tent as the trackers. "Well they don't care. They're soldiers, and so are the trackers, so why fuss? That's how they see it. Why be so sensitive?"

As they went to the bar she said. "I know. We exploit them don't we. We underpay them, beat them, and live like…like your aristocrats and fat businessmen."

"Oh dry up Gillian." Lalage appeared beside them, and out of the corner of his eye, he saw Hamish hovering. He was quite drunk now, staring at Lalage. "What a ribcage," he blurted out, and Ian Burns dug him savagely in the ribs.

"Here's old whatsisname," he said quickly to Lalage, "Let's dance." As Hullyer said, it was in-fighting country, and Bill would be back in a moment. Hamish poked his head over Gillian's shoulder, a glass in his ham fist, held tenderly, like some rare moth.

"Ho," he said, fatuously. Gillian turned without enthusiasm and smiled bleakly, her eyes searching in the crowd for something. Hamish opened his mouth to say something but he was too slow because Gillian ducked away and Lalage looked over her shoulder as Jonathan hustled her away, and told him to stay there. "You dance badly," she said and clung to him, so that they shuffled in a desultory way on the darkened floor, her hair brushing Jonathan's cheek. Neither of them spoke for a while.

"And keep your eyes off Gillian. She's Sam's," she said with a big grin.

What was it she said? You are the clean-cut, blue-eyes type that women always... Rubbish of course. "I'm not good looking Lala, or very attractive. Just young."

"Let's sit down," Lalage said in a neutral tone. She found a corner and tucked her feet up under her, sitting on a step. Their eyes met. "Some time, you need to tell me more about you than I know now." she said.

Jonathan winced at the phrase. He had told her about the farm at home, his sisters, university, and Army days. Both his sisters had fled the farm, and married into cities. Grainne to a London money broker. Fiona to a city vet. Ireland he told her was more like Kenya than anything in England. Both were farming communities. Neither best organised.

"My parents," she said, "had been among the first half dozen white people in the colony. Father had gone down to the Union of South Africa, had sold his share in the mine there and come back to Kenya. Without Sam's mother. She refused to leave South Africa. Father was disappointed with the lack of progress here since he left. Then in 1930 he met Mother. Just after I was born they returned to Europe. But they came back to work with Ewart Grogan just before the war. He built Torr's Hotel. But father was a sisal expert, and managed his sisal farms. I grew up here during the war. After it they sent me to a school in Switzerland and then to London. Sammy didn't want to go. He had finished his schooling with relations of his mother. In the "Union," as they all called South Africa. Came back to Kenya. He has never left Africa in his life. And doesn't want to either."

"My dear parents will ask me about you, and I hardly know you really," she explained.There was a silence then during which Jonathan looked at her hard. She was quite staggeringly beautiful. And she was talking parents already, to his amazement. She had, in contrast to Gillian, a seriousness in her, under the glitz, that was something Africa did to you.

She gazed at him, thinking. "Don't let me down because you sound so real and your eyes melt something inside me and you look like a lost little boy one minute and the next like the kin of those who should rule this earth She found his hand on hers and she squeezed and looking down, her eyes met his again and they both smiled and both wondered if the other had guessed something.

"You're a rum sort of subaltern," she said, smiling happily. "Rum sort of campaign," he countered. She took a gold cigarette case out of her bag and offered him one. He shook his head, wondering, not for the first time, if the Carton-Webbs were very rich. Gillian had said that this school she worked at paid her nothing. Lalage lit her cigarette.

"You don't smoke," she said, musingly. "Live here and you will."

"Only a pipe," he said.

"A drink?" and this time she nodded.

Gillian was by the bar, and while Hamish brayed at her, her eyes flickered round the room, but there was no sign of Sammy. The doctor was dancing with a chilly looking blonde, a look of concentration on his face.

"I drink too much of this," Jonathan said, putting the gin down.

"Ugh," she said, "How you can drink it in the evening. Everyone drinks whisky or brandy."

"Gin and brandy make me randy. Whisky and beer make me queer." He looked at her.

"Is that right?"

"I don't know. Try brandy. But why do you drink so much gin?"

"To stop me thinking too much."

"What about?" she asked.

"Things ... Such as ... tomorrow. What's ... what's going to happen here. What's going to happen to you all, tribesmen, farmers, dukawallahs and the Arabs and everyone."

He paused. She looked quizzically at him. "Go on."

"No," he said. "It would only be boring. I can't stay here, that's all. Sexy place as it is."

"Sex?" She grinned. Her eyebrows lifted so that the eyes widened lustrously and he had an impulse to kiss her, there and then and the hell with Sam.

"Don't you dare to tell me that you can't stay here."

"I'm joking. But this stupid colour-bar nonsense. No natives in the hotels? Look at the French. They breed in with them and have lots of lovely chocolate and tan efforts as "heureuses consequences." There are more coloured people in the world than white anyway, and we haven't run it so cleverly."

"Ah." Lalage broke in. "Two half truths. We haven't real colour-bar here. We mix in cinemas and buses, post-offices, shops. You should see the Union. A line down the centre of the pavement, Native one side, White the other. Then go to Madagascar. You've got lots of half breeds, métisses, octaroons, the lot, but you've still got a colour problem. We don't do too badly here. The Indians are a bolster, and there's no Bible banging about it, as with Afrikaners." She frowned. "The whole thing's a bloody bore. Let's go for a walk."

The night sky was a hard, deep, almost blue colour, and the air was colder and drier than on the Aberdares. The chorus of cicadas and frogs was there as ever, in the background. He walked with his arm around her, and she clung to him for warmth. The stars were clear, picked out on the cloudless dark, brilliantly. The Southern Cross and the other stars Tom had pointed out. The Ram, the Bull and the Heavenly Twins. The Man who carries the Watering Pot. The Fish with the Glittering Tails.

All dimmed momentarily by an enormous flicker of heat lightning springing from behind the Aberdare mountains. It seemed a long time ago, and almost in a different world, that he had been up there, lying where he had flung himself on the long grass. Pack pressing on his back through the soaked shirt.

Feeling the rifle kick, as he fired for the first time in his life with the intention of killing another human being. The first casualties. The death screams, he could still hear. Now the memory revived with the peculiar tangy scent that seeped up from the ground when the sun was down. Vegetation withered in the day's heat, mixed with a green smell that would always be for him, Africa under the open sky.

They crossed a road, stony, rutted and uneven, and walked on to the golf course.

"Senti kumi for your thoughts," Lalage murmured. "Ten cents."

"Smells." He said, "That unromantic one now."

"The Boiling Potato tree. Come over here. Can you smell it?

"Come here, there's a bush of Yesterday, Today and Tomorrow. Better?" There was a row of them by some steps. A sweet, tangy perfume in the night air. The bushes were like miniatures of what the Army called 'Bushy topped trees,' to distinguish them from Coniferous, and Poplar which formed the second and third class accorded official, military existence.

The bushes' surface was covered with tiny blossoms, exuding the perfume. Jonathan leant his head forward to it and Lalage leaned with him. Their heads met in the foliage, and as they drew away the moon slipped out from behind the dark shape of the mountains, a new moon, cradling Venus. It shone on her hair, touching the silver earstuds she wore. He bent and kissed the line of her jaw and she smiled at him, a smile quiet, enquiring, her lips quivering slightly. "Will you kiss me like that when you find out how African I am?" She asked in a half whisper, and he put both arms round her to kiss her again, but she put her face against his shoulder. "Will you?" she urged, her voice low and firm. Jonathan squeezed his arms tighter round her body.

"Lalage. I don't give a damn how African you are. I want you. So do shut up about it and let me kiss you." She flung her head back then and spoke rapidly a stream of Swahili. "What," he said, then kissed her on the mouth. She breathed quickly and one hand caressed the back of his neck. Jonathan felt a terrible tenderness for her creeping into him. He released her.

"I'm a damn silly fool you know. Did you know that? And I don't deserve you."

"You shut up, roinek," she said, kissing his left ear. "I'm cold. Let's go in now. You can come and bring me more firewood to room seven,"

"Good idea," he said, "Let us go, we pretty pair, hand in hand and all that sort of rot."

"Steady."

"It was Carlotta wasn't it?" Gillian said. "I can smell her. Why her? I suppose she collects bods like you … Why did you come if … Oh Sammy, what's wrong?" Sammy just pushed out one foot and worked the clutch of the stationary car up and down. Then he yawned and Gillian could smell the whisky from where she sat. He had been asleep when she found him, and now she was trying hard not to cry. It had started at the races, or was it before that? Usually it was so easy. You just flirted with some other man and he came round. This was dangerous. Women like Carlotta were hateful. She wouldn't just sleep with him, but tell everybody as well. She opened the door violently and stepped out. Sammy stirred.

"Where'y going?" his voice was very slurred and she felt like hitting him. "To the hotel."

"Can't walk. Gangs." He sat up and inhaled deeply. "Don't," he said urgently. She breathed a great sigh. It might be all right. "Stay here," she said, "I'll go and see if the others want to come." This is getting bad she told herself. This strain is telling on all the men.

In the Clubhouse Lalage was bunnyhugging Jonathan. who said he'd walk. Carlotta had a grip on the doctor. Gillian went back to the car and drove to the hotel. There was a guard huddled in a great coat in front of a storm lamp. Two others were sleeping. Sammy joked with them in Kikuyu. They took two lanterns and walked along the planked verandah. Sammy stumbled over a pile of firewood outside the door and swore viciously. Gillian winced. Was he drunk? Drunken. Not funny when it was him. Maybe he wasn't too bad. He'd driven the car hadn't he and he could walk? He stopped at a door and looked at his key. It was the wrong one. He didn't say anything, just moved on. He was like that when he drank: silent. This was the right door. They stood in the pool of light thrown by the two lamps. His eyes avoided hers and his nose twitched once, flexing his upper lip in a sort of silent sniff. She knew the mannerism so well. Before getting on to a restive horse; when somebody was mad at him; before speaking harshly to someone. The day he had to shoot his Ridgeback dog that Christmas at Langata.

It meant "All right damn you, I'm going to do it." His face looked strained now, the lips set. The features were small like Lalage's but carved, wooden, instead of her polished marble. He cleared his throat but didn't say anything. It was cold and a shiver ran through her body. She dropped her forehead on to his shoulder.

"Are we going up to your farm tomorrow?" she asked.

"Farm?"

She stood up straight. "Well you are going to work on it aren't you Sammy?"

"Yes, yes." He sounded tired. "Let's go to bed now." His voice wasn't slurred any more. She leant forward and kissed him on the cheek, and he smiled and put an arm round her shoulder. "Sorry Gill," he muttered and she kissed the other cheek, but he turned and fumbled with the key. "Remind me to have words with that Pom who's chasing Lala."

He was a bastard to treat her like that, Sam thought. She was a good kid and it was her right to fool with other men if she wanted to. It did no harm and she was only a kid. Like a white mare in a field of bay stallions and he was proud of her.

"Goodnight," she said, and he replied between set teeth, wrenching the door open.

If he wasn't damn careful she'd drop him. She wanted some sense out of him and she wasn't getting any. But the life of flying small planes over endless bush just got you. Scared all the time, on edge and not admitting it. Teddy gone, and Bill. Then Jimmy and Charlie in one week. All for nothing in this phony damned war that the munts started because they were so bloody bored there wasn't anything else to do. But *They* wouldn't let the Masai in to butcher the Kikuyu. And no, they couldn't drop napalm either. Bloody roineks.

He kicked off his shoes and threw the rest of the logs he had filched from outside somebody's door, on to the fire. No, napalm was for the Chinese or the Koreans, but not for the precious munts because of the Labour Party and the English newspapers. It wasn't a war, just a tribal squabble, like Africa had for thousands of years. But you had to fight for the right not to be slashed, your ears and genitals cut off, your eyes prised out for use in another oath taking, that's all. Fight to keep your cattle from being hamstrung, or have their teats cut off.

He was sick of it. Sick of the whole bloody thing that had changed every African he knew, so that there was a queer look even in Hatari's eyes. The old devil heard things in the bazaar of course, from the taxi-boys and the Hindis, and daren't ask about them. He said once about the K.A.R. in Burma that the Wa-Africa were well off compared with the Hindis he saw during the war. "Shenzi kabisa," he said, "hrufu sana, hapana centi." Very wild, very smelly, no money." African eye view of Asia.

Carlotta. Sexy old bitch. Why the hell did she stay married to Hans anyway? He was off somewhere all the time, even when not playing soldiers. The farm belonged to her. Crazy the way she glued herself to you. Rubbing her pelvis into your crotch. Why did she do it like that? With everybody? Well it wouldn't last much longer. She was getting flabby. But what could you do when they were like that and you had been stewing up in that flying greenhouse all the week? There was a noise somewhere. Nerves now. Gun? At the door. He hadn't locked the door. Foot near the lamp, gun in hand. "What?" Gillian's voice, "Sammy," Something he didn't hear. Hide the gun.

"Come in."

"My fire's out. Can you light it please. It's terribly cold in there."

"Have this one. Swap."

"Can I?"

"What the hell." He followed her into her room. Clothes all

over the place. He hadn't brought any except a small pack with a razor. She was collecting them all up. "Don't fuss girl. We'll change back in the morning. Leave 'em." There was a click as something fell out of her hand. He bent to pick it up but she snatched at it. What the devil? He slung his pack on the bed. Idea. Any Rum left? Maybe light the fire. Good to have a fire and a roof. She was going. Goodnight. Goodnight. That wood outside that door. Go and get it. Can't sleep now after the rum. Another swig. Feel like a party. He came back with an armful of wood and threw it on the embers, sprinkling them with dregs of rum and blowing up a flame. Better here than in bed.

That nurse at Nanuyki. Told Tom not to sleep on the floor. He said he couldn't sleep in a hospital bed. They burnt his clothes. He'd been in the forest a month. She didn't understand. English. Said he smelled worse than a hyena.

More scratching. Forgot to lock the door again. Let 'em come. Must have dropped off. He turned round to look at the door, but it was shut. There was the noise of a key turning. The lamp had gone out, only the fire cast a wavering light. Hair prickling, fear in the belly suddenly, the bowels loose. He jerked to his feet, turning towards the gun on the bed. As he turned the light flickered brighter on the ceiling. The connecting door by the wardrobe was open, and dazed, sprawled on the bed, clutching the gun, he saw Gillian standing there in the doorway with the firelight behind her outlining her body through the thin stuff of her night-dress.

"Whassamatter?" he asked hoarsely. She advanced towards him slowly, as though she were walking on eggshells. She didn't answer, so Sammy went on quickly, "What's the idea? How did you open that door? What goes on?"

"You were making noises and I …"

"Noises."

"Yeee-es. Sort of growling. I thought your door would be locked. I found this key in here. Oh, Sammy, I couldn't sleep. I'm cold. Then that sound." She huddled down on the floor between the bed and the fire, her arms wrapped round her breasts, her eyes wide and luminous in the glimmering firelight.

Sammy went over to her and picked her up wordlessly. He went back through the door and put her down on her own bed and tucked her in. She put her hand out and touched his face.

"I must have been asleep," Sammy said. "Just a minute." He went out and locked his own door to the verandah.

"Now what's the matter?" he asked as gently as he could, sitting on her bed.

"I don't know. Just, I can't sleep and I was worried I s'pose." She sounded unhappy, but you couldn't think any sense at this time of day. Did she want him to sleep with her? Was that it? Well he wasn't going to because … because of several things. Mainly that he didn't hold with sleeping with the girl you might marry one day. Anyway he didn't feel like it. He felt muzzy and his eyelids had developed fur linings.

"Let's talk about it in the morning," he said.

"Don't go Sammy. I want to say something."

"Yes." It was going to be the ruddy marriage question again. Women. Always trying to tie you, fool with you, flirt with someone else to make you jealous. Then floods of tears.

"Sammy. You don't really like Carlotta do you?" The voice tremulous and uncertain, her head bowed. "I mean … Oh hell, well she's just sex isn't she. And if it wasn't for the Emergency we could have …" Sammy put his head down on hers.

"Sweetie I know what you mean and I'm sorry. But I can't take this stuff, you know that. When I get free and build a house I'm going to trot up and ask your Dad for you, and by that time you won't want me probably so …" A great sob sounded and he stopped and looked at her, pulling her chin up. Her cheeks were wet, her eyes closed. He kissed her on her cheek, and her arms went round his neck, her body heaving against him. "Oh Sammy I want you now, now."

He took the arms from round his neck." I won't see Carlotta any more. And remember what you said. You weren't going to be a bitch like the rest of them. They say …"

But he couldn't think of what he was going to say and there was a long silence during which she closed her eyes and turned over away from him, her shoulders still shaking periodically. He rolled over on to her, moving his hands over her body, naked now, warm and trembling. "Please," she murmured urgently. "Please just let us do it now and ..." He stopped her with a passionate kiss.

"No" he said finally. "I'm drunk. No good. Wouldn't work."

She began to cry. He picked her up, wrapped in a sheet and took her to her bed. He hurled more wood on the fire and wobbled back to his own room.

As he got back into his own bed it occurred to him that Lalage was in the next room. Tomorrow was going to be a sticky day. He took a swig at the rum, shook the bottle, forgetting it was empty, and kicking off his clothes, fell on to the bed. He was instantly deep in sleep.

Jonathan did what he was told. He picked up firewood and took it to room seven.

He was sure that Sam was in number eight. He checked the locks on all the doors.

"No giggling," he commanded, diving into Lalage's bed.

"Funny sounds from next door actually," Lalage said, "But never mind. Let's get on with it, quietly."

"And with huge enthusiasm," Jonathan said. This night he would not have the terrors. The demons of the forest would not close in on him as the mist settled. She wrapped herself around him. He needed love to restore his battered spirit. To chase away the horror. The memory of that blood spattered half-face, the brain sac pumping obscenely. He hadn't looked after Mac had fired. Pretended he hadn't noticed. He knew exactly what Mac had done with his Webley that he had grabbed. To save him from the obscenity of it.

He slept only fitfully. Woke in the early hours. For a moment he thought he was back in the Aberdares. Opening his eyes, he was thrilled to find he was under a roof. The fire was out, and it was cold. He pushed logs on to it, and watched them ignite, flickering in the darkness. Crawling back to the bed, she stirred, and reached out for him. "Do you really love me?

210

Really?" he asked.

"Try me," she said and he grabbed her and showed her exactly how much.

"And," he said, panting, "I want you to tell all the world. Not hide it any more." There was no answer. At dawn Lalage woke and crept back to her room. Jonathan snored on.

CHAPTER SEVENTEEN

SAMMY WEBB

"One rule for survival in war – when someone is out to kill you,
you had better get him first, or at least keep out of his way –
otherwise you will not be thinking about the problem very much
longer."

General Sir Peter de la Billière
22ⁿᵈ SAS "Looking for Trouble."

They were climbing through heavy undergrowth up to the cave.
He knew that inside there would be nothing but scraps of animal
hide and a pile of rotting meat at the far end. Then Bill picked up
the skeleton, still clad in the sodden skins, and threw it at him.
He turned and it hit him in the back. In the few seconds it took
him to grope to full consciousness, he had the sensation of lying
in a dew-soaked poncho, cold and wet to the touch, and even
when he woke he couldn't remember where he was.

He opened his eyes slowly, blinking and there was that gut
feeling that there was someone else nearby. He twisted round in
the bed and sat up sharply. Gillian was sitting in the chair, her
head bent, peeling varnish off her fingernails. "Good morning,"
she said coolly, without smiling. Her face looked very pale
without lipstick. She looked almost ill, and there were two red
marks on one cheek near her ear. "You'd better hop it," she said,
"before Lalage comes in here." Sammy, about to leap out of bed,
remembered that he had nothing on. He got out gingerly,
clutching a pillow to himself. Gillian looked up, her forehead
puckered, and then smiled faintly.

Sammy let out a loud "Shit," as his feet touched the cold

floor. The very slight impact jarred his head and he felt like lying down somewhere dark and peaceful where there were no problems, no aeroplanes, and no women. He sat on the bed and looked round at Gillian. She was sitting with one bare knee up near her head doing something to her feet. As he stood up he saw that she was painting her toenails. He made a noise that sounded like 'Huh,' and immediately wished he hadn't. She looked up, expressionless, took in the pillow and then said quietly, "Go ahead, I'm no prude,"

He opened his mouth to reply and then closing it, marched over to the dividing door, slamming it behind him. There were two tablets beside a glass of water on the bedside table. He was standing there looking at them when the door opened a little behind him and a hand pushed his clothes through on the floor. He was half way through the glass of water before it dawned on him that he had been sleeping in the same room as his clothes. He forgot how he came to change rooms. Let people think what the hell they liked. Lala would find Gillian in his room.

He wasn't going to try to think because he felt like an old wounded buffalo with a spent bullet in his neck must feel, on a hot morning when the waterhole has dried up. Who started it anyway? That bloody smoothie, wet dream of an Irishman playing at soldiers, who couldn't decide whether he was chasing his sister or his girlfriend. Who started all the room swapping business anyway? For two pins he'd push off in the car to Carlotta's place ... well maybe not. Just somewhere far away from everybody and everything except the odd Tommy Gazelle he could shoot and roast on a couple of flat stones. That, when you thought about it, was one of the good things about Africans. They never tried to make conversation. They could just sit there and give the fire a poke now and then. When they wanted to talk they made another fire and sat round that and talked amongst each other. Left the Mzungu alone.

He looked at his watch, surprised to find it already after nine. As he shuffled out to the bathhouse he thought, one thing is clear at least. I want to get out of this uniform stunt and start building up a farm and knocking a piece of Africa into shape. I do not want to get married, yet. I am twenty five and haven't

213

done a thing except fly a very small aeroplane round in circles, and shot a few large animals, mostly with quite small horns or tusks. And he told himself as he winced from the noise the bath taps made. I am damned well going to go and work off some steam walloping into some more; as many as the Game Department will allow and a few more they'll never see. And I don't care whether it's a couple of fat Krauts from Dusseldorf or a big loud Joe from Texas, but they'd better be rich, because someone is going to have to pay for a whole lot of farm equipment.

Jonathan was explaining to Lalage that John Hullyer had asked him up to his farm. Lalage had artfully knocked on his door and loudly asked him to breakfast in the hotel dining room, He was digging heartily into a large half moon of Paw-paw as she spoke. "We'll ring him up and all go in my car. We must get Sammy up on our plot up there. He was supposed to have started on it four years ago and he hasn't done a thing to it yet. If we can only get him there it would help. It's not far from the Hullyer's place."

At the end of breakfast Sammy came in, very pink eyed and glum. "Hi," he said, and pulled his chair up viciously. Lalage didn't speak to him beyond saying "Good morning darling." Jonathan watched Sammy ladle a huge, spoon shaped piece of Paw-paw into his mouth and close his eyes. His Adam's apple swelled as it slithered, soothingly, down his gullet. He ate fast, pouring quantities of steaming coffee into himself and then sat back, shook his head, blinked and announced that he felt better. "Very glad to hear it dear," Lalage said icily.

"Oh shut up Lala." Sammy said. Lalage's eyes narrowed and she spoke slowly holding back each word, letting it drop carefully. "Don't you be so damned rude young man." Sam looked around him woodenly, "Ok, ok." he said diffidently.

"Well apologise," Lalage demanded and to Jonathan's astonishment Sammy did.

"And would you mind ..." she continued, but at that moment Gillian appeared, greeted Lalage and Jonathan nervously, nodded curtly at Sammy who made a noise as he picked his teeth with a match, then resumed looking round the room. Lalage sent him off to pay the bill and get the bags put in the car, and turning to Gillian said, "What the hell has he been drinking?"

"Rum," she said, through a mouthful of toast.

"And do you mind me asking but what was all the noise about last night." Gillian flushed slightly and mumbled, "I thought you'd hear. My fire went out so we swapped rooms and Sammy kept coming back for things."

"Things?"

"Well he left this rum first, and then his gun, and then he insisted on collecting firewood from all over the place and dumping it on the fire so I had to throw him out in the end."

"A likely tale," Lalage grinned. "Well just you come and tell me if he gets uppity again and I'll fix him. He had the cheek yesterday to say he was going to sell my car and buy a tractor. Apart from the fact that he gave me that car, I have a half share in that farm, and any more of his nonsense and I'll sell."

Gillian didn't reply, but went on miserably chewing at her toast with a hangdog expression on her face which made Jonathan feel a bit embarrassed, as well as guilty. Her lipstick was smeared and her dress didn't seem to fit. There were two livid spots on her face and she looked as though she had spent the night wondering whether the ceiling was going to fall.

In the car a brisk argument developed about who should drive. Eventually Jonathan sat in the front and Lalage drove. "A ghastly American gave this thing to our hero here, or rather he sent him a tractor with six crates of spares, probably all rejects from his horrible factory in Pittsburgh or wherever, and I swapped them for this beauty. Last year's Dodge."

"He was ok, that boy," Sammy said from the back of the car. "He shot a good leopard and stayed out three months to get his elephant. Didn't have fresh lettuce flown out from Nairobi every day either."

"Well maybe I'm biased," Lalage said. "I never saw him away from his imported whisky for long enough. The only client you ever had who was human was Bobo Whatsit, in spite of his name, and his dollars."

"Howard," Sammy said and relapsed into a gloomy silence.

Jonathan was seeing the three in a new light this morning. First it was plain that Sammy was a bit scared of his sister. It wasn't the small fluffy creature jabbing a spiteful hatpin into the unresponding hulk, but neat little whiplashes, as and when required. Gillian seemed cowed and stripped of her usual bounce. Sammy's hangover was making him childish as well as boorish. He looked much older than his sister.

This morning she was all clear-eyed, flashing lustrously, magnificent, as few people were, when angry. Whereas Sammy was like a rough, dried-out old bear that had been recently taken out of a damp attic. Beside her he was coarse-featured and clumsy although normally his rather squat face looked harmoniously balanced and he moved springily enough. Gillian was showing the effects of her night out. It surprised him that he felt a twinge of anger that was near to jealousy when Lalage had quizzed her about the creeping about. If Gillian had been sleeping with Sammy it seemed to him a pity and a waste of a very good-looking girl. But he reflected, judging by the lack of harmony and content this morning, it seemed unlikely. Glancing in the mirror he could see the two sitting as far apart as they could get, Gillian with her eyes shut and Sammy looking out the window with a scowl on his rumpled face. These locals all had known each other since they were toddlers.

After half an hour's driving through open country, climbing all the time, the road became a switchback, plunging into a steep valley timbered with great green cedar trees, cutting out the sun. Towards the bottom there was a light mist and the plume of red dust that rose behind their car had dropped. Climbing up the other side, they emerged again into the harsh, white sunlight, and a noticeboard with a crude globe and the single word "Equator."

"Is it?" Jonathan asked and Lalage said it was.

"I need a pee," Sammy said and when they reached the summit, Lalage stopped. The country was open grassland, thin, tall grass of a greyish colour. Hills rose and fell bleakly and enormously, like some stretch of primeval moorland. It seemed that you could tell merely by looking that the land had never been used or even walked upon. Here and there trees straggled, but apart from them and the odd giraffe and zebra there was no sign of life.

The animals looked incongruous there, as much so as if they had been on Dartmoor or the Limerick mountains. It did not look like Africa at all. The sun hidden behind heavy cloud.

Squaring his shoulders ostentatiously, Sammy set out to walk away from the car. "Don't get lost sweetie," Lalage jeered, leaning one elbow out of the car window, and Sammy turned round, put his tongue out and for the first time that day, grinned. "Thank God for that," Lalage said. "When he's in a mood he's sheer hell. You and I must have a nice girlish chat when we can get rid of the men," she said, turning round to Gillian, who smiled faintly behind her sunglasses.

Sammy came back and insisted on driving. He drove very fast, throwing the heavy car, lurching from one side of the road to the other to avoid potholes. Overtaking another car in a dense whirl of dust he put his lights on and kept his hand on the horn. The road was badly rutted. "Higher rainfall," Lalage explained. "It rains much more up here. That's why you can grow tea, but the rain ruins the roads. They always seem to decide to scrape it with those grader things just as it gets really wet, and it pulls all the stones up."

"The theory," Sammy said, "is that the rain leaches out the silicates, whatever the hell they are, from the murram, and forms ironstone. A bod from PWD (Public Works Department) told me. But the blackcotton soil is so spongy that the rain gets underneath the murram they dump on top. I got stuck in blackcotton for a month once down near Garissa. I'll never enjoy eating guinea fowl again."

The country started to look like Wicklow or the South Downs in England, without any hedges or barns or houses, but with the windbreaks planted in orderly lines along the hillcrests. Side-tracks began to appear with painted boards giving the farmers' names. The one with 'HULLYER' on it was clean, painted white and the lettering was professionally done, "Maji ya Mbovu. J.D.W. Hullyer Ltd," it said.

"Meaning?" Jonathan asked.

217

"Buffalo water, oddly enough," Lalage said. "Probably meant to be ambiguous. Some local joke perhaps. An Admiral up here put up a sign, "Admirals End," and the bod on the next farm put one up on his gate. "Mid-shipman's Bottom.""

"Not much Buffalo dirt about old John," Sammy said. "He's knocked a fair few over in his day. They used to trample half his maize every year. He must have flattened hundreds of 'em. And ate 'em. Used to say – 'Buffalo balls for breakfast, nothing like it.'"

"Steady…" Lalage said.

The farm was a low, grey building, roofed with cedar shingles and built into the lee of a hill. The track lead up behind it and over the roof the land dropped away and went on dropping so that the earth seemed to be tilted downwards and the horizon was somewhere in a haze of distance, thousands of feet below. The track swept round in front of the house alongside a paddock with a dozen or so horses, and a herd of cattle in it. In one corner there was the now familiar shape of the watchtower and behind the tower, the neat lines of conical huts surrounded by a stockade.

Getting out of the car, they saw a woman walking down the lawn towards them with three or four children. The lawn was a vivid green with flowerbeds set all around it full of roses in a profusion of bloom. In one corner there was a 'rustic' garden hut, and in the centre a stone Sundial.

For a moment Jonathan felt a distinct pang of something approaching homesickness. "Just look at those roses," Lalage said, "and that lawn."

"Marvellous for mid March," Jonathan said.

Mid-March, he told himself. Cedars and roses and hard, brilliant sunshine that the colours miraculously survived without being bleached and withered into nothing.

"Seasons are a bit odd here," he said, but nobody took any notice.

He wondered at the lack of variety. In this seasonless climate there would be no delicate crocus knifing up through the thawed loam, no clouds of bluebells in the woods, no white mist

218

of blossom on the hawthorn and in every hedgebottom. There could be no gentle beginning, no subtlety of light or shade, no still, long evenings, full of far off noises; no feeling of luxury in the rare summer days of super-abundant sunshine. And there would be no autumn, no gradual slope away down the sky of the sun, or ripening day by day of apple, plum and cherry. The leaves would never turn golden brown, coppery or ochreous yellow and float one by one down from the trees. Meanwhile the scenery here was magnificent. Sub-tropical, alpine, luxurious.

"Hello," Carol Hullyer said delightedly, looking from face to face. "Ages since I've seen you all," and Jonathan somehow felt however warm her voice, she could never really include him; never welcome him fully as one of the tribe, with their lives bound up with the enormous dilemma that was Africa.

But then she walked up to him. "I've heard a lot about you from John," she was saying to him, and he was smiling and saying 'Yes' and wondering where John was at gin-time on a parching Sunday morning.

The children had found a live, black stream of safari ants in the grass. Suddenly one of them shrieked, and without any hurry Carol went over to them.

"How many times have I told you not to play with ants, Frank?" There were five children, and he thought John had said three. The boy was dancing round shaking his hand and one of the girls was crying. All dressed in denim overalls, their chests bare and brown, were shrieking at the tops of their voices. The boy came up and displayed a small bird he had rescued from the ants. The children chanted "Poor little sunbird. Poor little sunbird. We found it. We found it."

Carol took the bird from them and Sammy examined it, while the children went back to sabotaging the column of ants. Carol went over and grabbed the smallest two.

"Not all mine by the way," she said to Gillian and Lalage, "Two of them belong to the Phillips from Ndaraka. Their farm was burnt down by the Micks last week and I'm looking after them while Joe and Sally build a couple of rondavels, and a stockade."

"Phillips?" Jonathan asked. "I seem to have heard that name, apart from the news of the attack."

"Joe's mother, Tania was on the same flight from Europe with you and John wasn't she?" Carol said. "John mentioned that you had met her."

"Oh. The old lady from Tanganyika."

"That was her. A very gallant old lady. Sally took her back home and I hope they stay down there, both of them, for a while. We're very lucky up here. Not Kikuyu country and no trouble at all. The local tribes are Samburu, related to the Masai, and some Turkhana. No love for Kikuyu, who never venture so far north, and never will."

The eldest girl had taken Jonathan by the hand as they went up to the house. "My Daddy's gone to see some sheeps. The Fisis nyonga'd them." (Hyenas killed them).

"Oh," said Jonathan, stumped. Carol turned round smiling. "It wasn't fisis Janey, it was dogs. We thought it was hyenas," she said to Jonathan. "They killed seven last night."

"Nasty old dogs," Jane said.

"Lose a lot that way up here?" Sammy asked.

"No. John goes out with the Headman and shoots them. The watu let them breed and they escape and go wild. There aren't any lion or leopard up here to keep them down."

"There won't be any Kaffir dogs on my place." Sammy said grimly.

"Oh, if it isn't pie-dogs it's something else," Carol said. "We lost thirty in a night last year. They were standing along a fence that was struck by lightning."

"But dogs can be controlled," Sam said, and Lalage looked at him hard as though to say. You big lout, a pie-dog isn't necessarily a "Kaffir," dog, and anyway belt up.

As they entered the house the sun's heat was shut off, replaced by a coolness and shade that felt almost chill. The low roof hung wide over the windows and kept the sun in its long hours vertically overhead, from soaking the house with heat.

"I've got a pussy-cat," Jane told Jonathan, tugging his hand again.

"Show me," Jonathan said. "I've lost it," Jane told him

sadly. Lalage said in his ear. "My oh my, what a fascination you have for females at first sight."

"Sure. They get wise slowly." He was looking around, comparing this house with the Lerricks and the Dwents. Here everything had been tacked on as it was needed and inside it was like a farmhouse anywhere except there was no fussiness or consciousness of neighbourly opinion. There were extensions to be seen from both sides of the bay window of the central room, and the furniture was scattered comfortably around the fire. It was extraordinary to think of it now, but it must be cold and misty so high up here, morning and night. There were log baskets each side of the fire. Books, cushions, toys and papers were scattered about everywhere, and at one end of the room a native in a white kanzu was picking things up and chiding the children in Swahili.

A small boy, a replica of John Hullyer came rushing up shouting, "I know where Janey's cat is. It's under the floor. And," he added importantly, "It's got kittens. I heard 'em." Jane loosened her hold, let out a shriek and ran after the boy shouting, "Andrew, Andrew, show me."

Carol said something to the native, and he went out to re-appear a moment later with another, who had almost European features, fine-drawn lips and coppery skin. His hair however was characteristically short and woolly, and Jonathan watched and listened in amazement as Carol spoke to him in English. He began to collect up the children and take them outside, chiding them in a high-pitched voice, speaking basic English with an intonation very obviously copied from Carol Hullyer. It was the first African Jonathan had heard speaking English, in Africa, and somehow it was as strange as if a Chinese in Dublin started speaking French or German to you.

It was strange too, to sit inside, out of the sun while Sam and Gillian drank fruit juice and he and Lalage and Carol drank the ritual gin and tonic and made the jokes about the others' livers. But this house didn't run to fancy garden seats and sunshades and it didn't even have the traditional verandas. It was good, solid split cedar set on grey stone. No architect had ever had a hand in it, and since ground space was no problem there

221

was no point in having more than one storey. The plasterboard ceiling was sagging here and there, but it looked like a home, and there was no attempt to make it look like either a Cotswold cottage, stockbroker version, or to turn it into a gallery of African curiosities. There was not a head or a horn to be seen, which Jonathan thought remarkable until he reflected that the kids would have made short work of them on the low walls.

John Hullyer didn't appear, so they started lunch after Carol had gone out to see about the children. The pieces of English silver on the table and in the houseboy's hands were a nice contrast of barbaric and civilised as they glittered in the reflected sun. The food had the familiar tang of food cooked a few hours from its living source. The butter was salty, the vegetables had a sharp flavour, the bread was coarse-grained and full of tiny pieces of husk. Everything had a tang of earthiness and freshness about it.

The conversation flowed around Jonathan in a maze of names and places that meant nothing to him. His thoughts went home. His father would be sitting with his tankard in front of him, roaring with laughter in his Sunday-go-to-meeting clothes, while his mother sat and watched the people listening and murmured, "Oh Mark," whenever his comments became too frank, or were interspersed with too many round oaths. Birds would be chirruping outside and the bleat of the first lambs, mingling with the clangour of bells hanging in the still air. Or would the rain be pelting down, gusting against the windows under a grey, lowering sky? He caught Lalage's eye, and immediately she steered the conversation away from what the Hurrons up at Mau Summit had said to the Walkers from Ngoleita about young Charlie's horse.

"Were the whole darned lot of you born here?" Jonathan asked and there was a chorus of "Yes," happily and confidently.

"How high up are you here?"

"Nine thousand feet,"

"Strewth. It must get cold at night."

"Yes. Sometimes we get hailstones instead of rain. There are photos somewhere of the fields all white with it."

"We must seem a horribly cliquey little lot to you, don't

222

we?" Carol said, and put like that, Jon was reluctant to say, "Yes, you do." So he said nothing.

"We don't often get visitors now the war is over. At least," she went on hurriedly, "the proper war I mean. And we don't get soldiers up here so we aren't used to them at all, so you must excuse us. Last time I went to England we met some people from here and got into a huddle in London. It is rather silly, but people in England think we've got two heads and are the modern equivalent of slave-traders."

"You look quite normal, someone said to me, and another woman refused to shake hands with me because she had read something in the papers about people in South Africa and of course Kenya is in South Africa isn't it?"

Jonathan looked round the table. They were waiting for his comments, for some polite reassurance, knowing that he was part of a huge and powerful force, ruled by the same Government that controlled them ultimately. But to them he was surely a smooth, educated young man with no real interest in their future, and no amount of familiarity with farming life could overrule that, could it?

"Maybe the trouble is that being a settler here isn't the same as it is for other colonials. Canadians and Australians are in a different position. There just aren't enough of you here yet." It was not convincing and he knew it.

"There never will be now," Carol said glumly. "The idea originally was to fill this up with Europe's overspill." She waved in the direction of the bay window, where beyond a small wooded hill the land fell away with its horizon in the sky. "But they sent all the POWs - the war prisoners,- mostly Italian, back after the war. The Italian who made this table told me his whole family of nine slept in the same bed, but they wouldn't let him stay here or bring them out."

"We're Settlers anyway," Gillian said fiercely. "The Government got the land by treaty and sold it to us. Why did they ever sell it to us? Who else is going to develop it?"

"Poor sods... er – blokes like me." Sam said. "I read a book once about Kenya. Seems we live a romantic, free life walloping kaffirs and when we're sober we go out shooting all the time

223

with millionaires, who just love you to spend the day in bed with their wives while they prowl about on their own looking for *Lions*. Ha-ha. I only know a few millionaires. Either they aren't married, or they leave wives at home. Usually,"

He laughed uproariously at his own joke, and kicked a lurking cat which scurried from under the table with an outraged screech. Jonathan couldn't help laughing too, because anyone less romantic than Sammy Webb he never hoped to meet.

"But you have taken people shooting haven't you?" Jonathan asked quietly, feeling his eyes drawn to Lalage who had turned down the corners of her mouth.

"Hunting, we call it. Can you tell me a quicker way of paying for your truck, rifles, food, or your wages, seed, fencing, fuel, machinery and every other damn thing? Lots of people try it, but you have to do it illegally at first and you can't even start nowadays. One little vulture, hovering over your kill, and the Game scout comes running and the Ranger has you in Court. The Micks have stopped all that for the time being. I worked for a bloke for a year for nothing, getting experience, but we only did two safaris. He had a degree in arthopology is it? The rest of the time we collected specimens for zoos. His brother ran a farm he had a share in. Miserable devil he was. Didn't smoke or drink, laughed about once a week and ..."

"Who asked for your life story laddie?" Lalage interrupted, "We were talking about normal people, not the tourist industry."

"Who is normal out here?" Sam retorted.

"I think most of you are," Jonathan said. "It's the country that isn't. The thing that surprised me most wasn't you or the blacks, but the way the place is organised."

"What 'cha mean?" Sam asked sharply.

"Well, it's a farming country, but the Europeans seem to leave all the commerce to the Indians."

"Why not?" Sam said.

"Quarter of a million. Five for every European." Gillian said.

"Don't you cuss our nice duka-wallahs?" Carol said. We owe them Lord knows how much, and they carried us through the Depression."

"We were talking about Settlers weren't we?" Sam said,

adding "Bloody racists we are."

"Settler isn't a good word you know," Jonathan said, and enjoyed seeing Sam's head come up like a startled horse. "It smacks of someone settling where he shouldn't be. You should use another word or hire an advertising agency in London to plaster the country with signs: "Settlers are nice. Settlers are human. Settlers are ordinary. Settlers are Good For You." Sam frowned into his beer.

"It's a stupid term," Lalage said. "Snobbery really. Distinguishes us from the Administration - civil servants and commercials."

To Jonathan's relief, John Hullyer appeared, sweat stained and dusty, full of gusto, dismissing the dead sheep with a wry face. He kissed his wife and shouted "Kaufi."

"He's looking after the children dear."

"Must show off me butler to the Quality."

"He isn't your butler. He's my nanny and he's busy. Here's Mturi."

Sam stayed with him while he ate, discussing crops and stock while Jonathan went down to the other end of the room with the womenfolk.

It was curious to be treated as an ignoramus on country topics, but he had become used to well meant digs at "all that book-Larnin'" from visiting farmers at home. At one stage he had been determined to shock them all by farming himself, but his father was against it and he hadn't enough capital to set himself up. He was supposed to decide what he was going to do with his life while he was in the Army. A law degree meant years of being a solicitor's clerk or a junior in a barristers' chambers. As long as it didn't involve wearing a bowler hat, or any other uniform, he had few ideas.

Lalage asked questions about the area on Sam's behalf, and Gillian sat silent and reflective as she had been all day, avoiding Jonathan's eye. When John Hullyer had finished eating, they sat talking while he smoked a pipe, during which time Mturi came in twice to announce that there were 'shauris' to settle. 'Bado kidogo" (In a while), he replied to both and Mturi nodded solemnly and withdrew.

They went for a short walk round the farm buildings, and while Carol talked to Jonathan, Lalage manoeuvred Gillian out of earshot of the others. They met them later by the mill that ground up maize every week for the farm labourers, and by that time they seemed to have had their talk, and both to be the better for it.

When they left, the children were let out to watch them go, and amidst the babel, the houseboys and cook appeared from the kitchen and stood, grinning hugely, watching the excitement. "Let me know when you start," Hullyer said to Sam, "and come over any time.

"You too," he said to Jonathan, "Come and spend a few days, a week, a month." He looked Jonathan in the eye and meant it, making him feel profoundly ashamed about his thoughts on the subject of welcomes. Just before they drove off there was a commotion amongst the Africans and the children, and Jane came yelling from between their legs, her head down, and her hands clasped together over something. She rushed up to the car and held her hands through the window. "Look," she said breathlessly. The bundle of fur in her hands stirred very slightly. "That's sweet," Jonathan said. "You are a lucky girl."

Her mother lifted her off the running board. "Put that cat back at once Janey."

Lalage let in the clutch and waved.

"They certainly get down to reproducing themselves hereabouts," Sam commented. "Something in the air I reckon. Hope it doesn't hit me."

"You'll be lucky," Lalage said, and Jonathan was remembering a last beery Oxford morning. To all enquirers as to his future he had replied, "Going to the country to do some serious breeding." To think such callow wit was not yet a year ago.

Lalage stopped the car on the thin grass where the river curved round in a loop. "That's where my hut goes," Sam said, leaping out. A group of wild looking natives had assembled already, and stood, mostly on one leg, chattering and pointing.

"No wonder the grass is so thin," Sam said. "Look at all those goats. Look at that cow. No bigger than one of Hullyer's sheep. These blasted squatters'll have to wake their ideas up."

Lalage lit a cigarette, flicked the lighter shut, and dropped it in her bag. "Let's go and listen to Bwana Mkubwa," she said.

"Who are they?" Jonathan asked, pointing at the Africans.

"Squatters. Not proper ones though. Up here they are pastoral and most of them move about without cultivating. Real squatters live on a farm, graze their stock in the forest and work when and if they feel like it. With luck Sam will get them to build him a hut or two, and when the news spreads he'll have a labour force."

Sam was talking to an African who stood out a few paces from the rest. They were of a different build to any Jonathan had seen. Tall and slim, their skins were lighter and they wore necklaces and armbands of beads. One or two had ivory plugs dangling from their lower lips, but these were of a shorter, thicker build. Most of them had their hair twisted into a coiffure, and the women wore ornaments which dangled on their foreheads. The man talking to Sam had a long knife in a red leather scabbard in his belt, and several coloured plumes bobbed on top of his head. "What do they live on now?" Jonathan asked.

"This lot?" Lalage said vaguely, looking around thoughtfully, "Oh, they're Marakwet, Samburu, Rendille, some Turks."

"Turks?"

"Sorry. Turkana. The ones with the lip-plugs. They all herd cattle and they all seem to live on very little, as they don't eat meat very often. Blood and milk mostly. The blood is rich in vitamins and proteins. Except the Turkana they are all poor cousins of the Masai. No, maybe not the Marakwet. None of them would have dared to come this far south if we didn't keep the Masai south of the Rift Valley."

"Why are they all together? I mean the tribes don't all muck in do they?"

"There must be a duka near here, or a load of Nubian gin. If they cultivate at all they mix a bit. But just a minute, I want to listen to the shauri."

A ripple of laughter went through the knot of Africans. Nostrils flared, ear ornaments jingled. One or two were doubled

227

up with mirth, and collapsed on the ground. There was no attempt to restrain themselves, Jonathan had noticed. He paused to watch a great plump Bibi clad in a little more than a tiny leather apron and a blanket, giving suck to her squalling child. In her ears she had cords, threaded through Five and Ten Cent pieces, that reached almost to her shoulders. The lobes of her ears were stretched about four inches. Lalage had slithered back into the seat of the car.

"What are they saying?" he asked her.

"They told him that there was a leopard here, so Sam said it was his leopard, the spirit of his grandfather, and it would eat their goats if they didn't graze them somewhere else."

"Is that what they were laughing at?"

"No, they believed that." They laughed when Sam said he'd killed nearly all the Mau-Mau, and when he'd killed them all he would come and live here."

"Do they understand that you own this land?"

"They know about it, but they don't care. They don't give a damn for anything, and they don't want anything much except space to roam. They think we are fools, who plant crops and stay in one place. But they humour us, and the less wild ones will work for Sam off and on. He'll build a dam so they can water their stock when the river dries up. These tribes are like the Boers. When we move in, they trek away. And like the Masai, they think that to work for anyone is ignoble, and to sell stock reduces your status. Only the Veterinary people can really help them."

"And will Sam?"

"Sammy can handle Africans. He is one. Like me. Not many people want to risk opening up a farm nowadays, but Pa's plan was to run a farm, for the short term and plant tea on the rest. It can take about ten years to get tea bushes to yield. The tea companies from Assam, India and Ceylon are buying land here, and it grows successfully a few miles from here. If Sam sticks it, it could pay off, but the tea wouldn't pay for maybe fifteen years and that's a lot of money to have idle that long."

It was hot in the car, even with all the windows open. Sam was talking to the Africans with Gillian standing behind him, the sun glinting on her corn yellow hair.

"Can you see those two living out here?" Jonathan said, half to himself. "Let's go and look at the river." Lalage nodded, got out and from the boot produced a blue straw hat with a wide wheel brim. "Keep an eye on the car," she shouted to Sam, as they walked towards the river.

"It certainly wouldn't suit me," she said, "The pioneering or the dullness of living here, breeding. But now Sam is twenty-five he will have his mother's money, and he can put it in here or waste it."

There were traces of fish scales on the banks where they were sitting. Jonathan pointed them out and was told that the natives speared them. Possibly this was what they had been doing when they saw or heard the car.

"Luckily for Sam, Pa married her under Roman-Dutch law, so her money becomes Sam's and she left it to him anyway."

"I thought your mother was alive. You spoke of her." Jonathan said, puzzled.

"Mine is. Pa divorced Sam's to marry mine. That's why he's two years older than me, and in case you wondered his mother was South African."

That cleared up some of the mystery. He looked again at her nose and her hair. It explained the differences between her temperament and Sam's, apart from the dissimilar looks. She intercepted his glance with a queer defensive smile. "The hat?" she asked.

"The hat?"

"Saving my complexion. Mother is Greek you see. You know Greeks aren't very popular here. They're supposed to be a cut above the Indians that's all. And my great grandmother was Indian. A lot of Greeks own plantations in Tanganyika, mostly in sisal. You know the joke. Oh, ... maybe not. There was a man you see, looking for the manager of a farm, and he saw a white man down at the bottom of a vlei, so he said to an African, "Iko Mzungu? – Is that a European? 'Hapana', the Africa said – 'No'.

"Wahindi?," he asked. (An Indian). – Hapana. "Well," the man said, "it's not an African"

"Hapana," the African said, "Iko Greeki tu," – "it's only a

229

Greek."

Jonathan was mildly shocked. To what absurd lengths did racism go. "Silly," he commented. "Bloody silly."

"Yes," she said, "but very telling."

There was a silence which Jonathan broke to ask, "Is that what makes you a little bitter Lalage?" She looked at him startled. "No. Am I as bitter as that? I…"

"I'm sorry. I shouldn't have said it."

"No. You're right. I can seem to be a little bitter. But it isn't that. That was Andrew, and I haven't told you much about him either. He …" She lowered her head.

"You don't have to you know," he said, the pity for her soaking into him with the sunlight, so that he longed just to take her in his arms and comfort her. But apart from Sam and Gillian, he knew already that you didn't demonstrate affection with Africans around. Curiously you never saw an African showing affection in public to a woman either, but maybe there was a different reason.

"You may as well hear," she said, tearing a stick to pieces and throwing the bits one after the other into the river. "We met in London, and he was supposed to come out and settle and marry me. His father wanted him to start an Import/Export business in Nairobi, to link up with his London business. After he had been here a few months, he got malaria badly and there wasn't enough oxygen for his asthma. When Mau-Mau started his nerves went all a-jangle and he managed to get some weird skin disease and his Mum flew out. I refused to leave and there we were. I was very fond of him really, but in the end it was just pity I think. But his Mum, Oh my God, she was terrible. The fuss. Boil everything you can't spray. One ant on the floor and down went a bottle of Jeyes. One cockroach in the kitchen and out went all the food. It's the flat Angela and I have now, and she says she can still smell the Jeyes."

He put his hand out, half to stop her and half because her voice had been rising to a pitch far higher than her usual, quiet, gravelly tone. She laughed, a dry, joyless laugh.

"Some other time I'll tell you the rest," she said, more calmly. "Let's go and see if Big Bwana has made any progress with building his thingira (native hut)."

Sam was down to discussing how much he would pay for getting a living hut and a kitchen built.

"I say ten men, three days, hundred shillings bad, two hundred not so bad, three hundred for good enough," he told Lalage.

"Mm. Three days is optimistic. Three weeks perhaps."

"No. I mean three days work. I told them they can cut timber across the river if they burn the stumps out. I think the next full moon. Tonight is the full moon isn't it?"

"All right," he said turning to the Africans, "Mwezi moja. Na-rudi ku-ona. Mzuri." (In one month I shall return to look. Good.) The shauri was over, and they climbed back into the car.

As they went off he said. "If they screw it up, I'll still have the timber, and just start again."

"Huh." Was Lalage's comment.

CHAPTER EIGHTEEN

DEATH OF KAMAU

"Msasi kagopi miiba."
(A hunter is not afraid of thorns)

Swahili proverb

With half his mind Tom Lerrick was listening, above the sound of a waterfall and his own footsteps in the undergrowth. The rest he allowed to grapple with the problem of what exactly could be going on in the area. The sun was in his eyes, coming through the leaves, half blinding him.

He had crossed the Rift Valley, through the farming area and picked up tracks on the other side. They had picked up two straggling terrorists, one of whom had got himself slashed in the brawl. Not much information had been forthcoming from the other, who appeared to be mentally deficient and certainly knew no more than that his leader's name was Cherenge, and there was to be a meeting a day after the full moon.

They had turned him into the nearest police boma, collected rations, wireless batteries and ammunition, and gone on. The tracks had been found by some trees on the far side of the Rift escarpment, together with signs of a night's camp. They led south, up through a bamboo forest and out on to the Masai plain, where they circled. Tom had attempted to approach a gang the night before, but the sentry had refused to let Kamau pass. He knew there were other gangs near, he said, but "General Aloysius" had given orders not to let anyone visit. There were thirty in the gang and Aloysius was away, the sentry said.

There had been no hope of a successful attack and to attack

blindly would have broken up whatever was brewing. He had alerted the police and several tracker teams were out, troops were moving in, and two spotter planes on patrol. Time was very limited. Soon it would be too dangerous to move as the gangs concentrated. At least he had been able to get this information, and with luck there should be a big haul in a few days. The long rains were due now.

The problem was, where were they headed? These tracks lead back east to the floor of the Rift, and then across it, back to where the Aberdares began. Somewhere a place had been appointed for a meeting. So much was now obvious. Beyond the scattered farms on the Rift floor there was little to attack. On the Masai plain there was only the empty waterless bush that stretched down west to Lake Victoria and Tanganyika. Any body of men would soon starve there, and the Africans in the area would mostly be Masai, to whom a Kikuyu was second best sport to a lion for blooding the spear of a young Moran. Here they were beyond reasonable striking distance of the main farming area, and with the rains coming on it would not be comfortable. The Police said that stock thefts in the Rift had only increased slightly, which was not surprising, as the area was largely dry, consisting of great open areas of sheep pasture and ranches that carried one beast to five acres.

The going was downhill now, back to the floor of the Rift and not so exhausting in the cover of the wooded escarpment. The terrain was a violent contrast to the parched bush and scorched, sandy wadis of Masailand. A waterfall crashed heavily from somewhere behind a screen of heavily creepered cedars. There were springs that flowed down into the lakes in the Rift Valley. Clouds, sailing over the Aberdares, threw their contents down on this sloping edge of the Rift. To the north was the Mau Escarpment Forest, Mau Narok and then the main tea-growing area of Kericho, where it rains practically the whole year round for a few hours every day.

The two Wa'Ndrobo were in front tracking, and Daniel stopped them every half-hour while Tom looked at the map. The waterfall was not marked. It probably went underground or had been dry when the map was made. The Wandorobo were squatting with Daniel, and Mkuna was chattering animatedly. Even Mzee was paying attention, his old turtle's head cocked to one side, nodding away.

"What do they say?" he asked Daniel, moving over to the three.

"Mkuna say now gangs go to lake. One other gang join them here and tracks go that way." Tom looked round him. He hadn't noticed, but now he saw that there were tracks joining at the spot, which was why Mkuna had stopped. The other tracks came up from the Rift. Now they must slow up a little in case other gangs joined up with the main party. He took a deep breath and looked at the lake on the map. Lake Longeita ran east-west along the line of the Rift Valley. It was about twelve miles long and two wide; shallow and surrounded by papyrus swamp. The other lakes in the valley were extinct volcanoes, circular in shape, and very deep. They were three miles from Longeita now, and if the gangs were going to cross the valley it would be best to descend now. Their direction meant they would have to pass along the side of the lake. This would really be something. The first thing to do was to wireless for the spotter planes to keep off, and get the dog-tracker teams in, with a big ambush at the far end of the lake.

He would need support to act, forming the backstop himself and troops would have to go up on the plateau of Masailand in case they broke away from the lake. That was if they believed him, because the spotter planes had seen very little.

While he waited for Cheragoi to contact base he told Daniel to have a weapons check. He propped a mirror up and examined his face to see if his sweat had thinned the dye anywhere. If they met up with a gang now he would have time to ask where the meeting place was and perhaps find out if Dedan Kimathi, or Stanley Muthenge were with Kathenge and Aloysius, as seemed possible. These two were the last of the six leading Mau-Mau generals. The migration had no conceivable tactical reason, so it must be for a very high powered conference. Muthenge hadn't been heard of for months. Was this where he had his headquarters? A bird screamed raucously in a tree overhead. He clutched wildly for his Padgett. Steady, he thought, steady. He was getting over tense. He repeated the hunting formula he used for calming his nerves just before the kill. You are ready for any emergency, especially the unexpected, and you can shoot fast and straight. There is nothing difficult about it. Relax. Think of something funny.

That time when Gillian's ice-cream bill at the Malindi duka came to thirty shillings in a week. "But Bwana," the Arab said, "she didn't eat them all. She brought her young cheetah, two bush-babies and a parakeet. They all sit round eating ice-cream on the floor."

He smiled, but the bad feeling came back into his stomach all the same. Only a little of the tension was gone, but it would be all right. "Kamau," he said, and spoke to him in Kikuyu, to get the feel of it.

"Ask me the questions. Good. Then if they put hand to a gun, don't forget, drop flat with me. Don't run. The others behind us won't wait to fire."

Mkuna came up and held out his foot. There was a split in his heel an inch deep and suppurating. The skin was like horn, splaying out where it met the ground in a series of symmetrical cracks. What a time to produce this. Yet he didn't limp in the least. He poured iodine into the crack, and scraped it with a match. Mkuna did not even blink and did not thank him either, because he was not in the habit of being helped or given anything and politeness was as alien to him as an atom bomb.

Tom understood, but then there was never any trouble with the country natives. It was the city boys who went to the cinema who were the trouble. They had acquired a knowledge of the world where money was needed, and there were white folks and Asian shops. If only they had patience like Mkuna. If only more of them could stay out of the cities until there was work for them, and do something they understood. If only we could drain Longeita and irrigate. If only, if only. Cheragoi had contacted Base.

The Wa'Ndrobo could smell the water. Their nostrils kept twitching when they stopped. Tom always watched the trackers intently as they came up to a kill. There was a lot that could be learned. Their eyes did not see *more*, but they saw quicker, and

235

they had an inexplicable sense of intuition to supplement their lack of skill in speech and thought. It was not altogether surprising when their daily food depended on it, and they didn't waste any energy developing the ability to read, write or plan beyond tomorrow. Just a hand on a pile of dung was enough to tell how long ago the animal had passed, and a glance at the tracks enough to say how old and what sex. And Mzee had his dreamtime lore. That inexplicable power to see the future, which the shamans had.

Mkuna started to scramble away from the tracks to the left. He turned round and beckoned. Tom followed unquestioningly. They pushed their way through some scrub and climbed up on a small knoll. There below he could see the lake, turquoise, the sun casting the shadows of clouds on its surface. He dragged his eyes away from it, searching for gaps in the papyrus reeds. There were rocks here and there with open spaces where nothing grew. He turned to see the men bunched up behind him, trying to see the lake. He hissed at Daniel to spread them out and keep watch on the track they had just left.

Mkuna didn't want to move. After five minutes Tom grew restless, but Mkuna sat peacefully watching. At his side Mzee stoically cut and dug at his toenails with the point of his panga. Tom passed the time wondering whether the ambush troops would be on their way yet. They were not high enough up to see the main road up to Molo and Mau Summit, so he would not see the trucks unless they were fool enough to drive right down to the far end of the Lake. That was if they hadn't said, "Well it's only that fanatic Lerrick. Send a patrol to look, some time."

The clouds were building up, so that the blobs of shade on the water were coalescing. The timing for this meeting would have something to do with the start of the rains, besides the fact that the full moon was today. But what? He took out a piece of dried meat and started to chew it thoughtfully. Freed of his pack, his tattered shirt and skin jacket began to give off a smell of sweat and smoke and dirt as the sun and air got to his skin. God, what would I give for a cool shower. It hadn't been too bad at first. Just like one of the old foot safaris. But then you had time to wash, and you carried big tins or a canvas bag to cool water. It made you realise how soft you lived and how hard the Mau-Mau must live, those of them who didn't live in caves. The strip of biltong was making that tooth ache again. He asked Mkuna if he had seen anything, but he hadn't and the toothache was still there.

He hadn't felt so rough since the time they walked all night back from the Tobruk raid to the L.R.D.G. trucks and found they'd gone from the luggah where they hid. The next rendezvous was sixty, miles back towards Cairo and there was another fifty miles to go. Nearly all the water had gone and their boots were cracked. They slogged on for another ten hours without food or water. And they had to wait there to walk at night. So it was not only hot like this as they lay up, trying to sleep during the day. On a cupful of water and a few biscuits they made it. And all Paddy Maine said when they did get there was, "Where the hell have you been? Oh. Well, you've been long enough getting here."

At least in those days you didn't have to dye the roots of your beard every morning and trim it short and straggling like a Kikuyu's. Or cut your hair down to the scalp to keep it from showing under the hat. Nor did you have to smell like a Kikuyu. But, come to think of it, Mkuna was right. They were too close now for the gangs to pass this side of the lake and …

Ali Wainiri appeared, nostrils flared, his eyes dilated. He took a breath before he spoke, spitting the words out venomously, "Come, Bwana. Mau-Mau, down on track."

Tom crammed his hat on and snatched his Padgett up. "Stay here," he snapped to Mkuna. "If you see men, count them. If you hear shooting, hide." He stumbled down to the main track after Ali. Daniel was lying down with his hand on Kamau's arm. Kangi knelt behind them with his gun pointing at Kamau's back. The men did not trust Kamau, since no one had yet known a captured Mau-Mau to help the security forces.

"Cover us," Tom said to Daniel, "You, Ali and Cheragoi. Go about ten yards back out of sight and listen." He kept Kangi with him to stand behind Kamau, and Kipkoin who looked most like a Kikuyu, with his ears only pierced and the lobes not stretched and looped over the top as with most of his tribe.

237

Kamau gave the Mau-Mau cry of recognition. There was an answering cry and a scurrying sound as six terrorists leapt off the track and into the undergrowth. A surly voice snarled out, "Whose men?"

"Say we are going to meet Aloysius," Tom whispered, and Kamau spoke. "When?" the voice said. "At the full moon," Tom whispered. Kamau translated.

The bushes parted and six men appeared, all but one bare-headed, with their hair twisted into clumsy spirals like horns. They wore filthy skins except for the leader who had a bush jacket that had once been faded white. All of them were armed, two with revolvers, the leader with a rifle and the other three with what looked like home made guns patterned on the Lee-Enfield, with gas-pipe for barrels. Every muzzle pointed at them, and their eyes focused on the automatic in Tom's hands. Kamau had a Sten slung on his shoulder on a hide strap, the magazine for which was in Kangi's pocket. "Is General Stalin with you?" Kamau asked, for that was the name of his last leader. The men shook their heads.

"I am Kamau, son of Mutuyu. This is General Mathias," he said, indicating Tom.

"I am Cherenge," their leader snarled. His face was a greyish colour, his eyes sunken into his head, his wide, flat nose twisted sideways on his face. There was a recent scar on his forehead. Tom caught a glimpse out of the corner of his right eye of something on the track moving. He turned his head as slowly as he could and turned back to meet Cherenge's stare. There were at least another half dozen on the track, some of them women.

"We came by the burning of a farm yonder," Kamau said. "Was that your work?" One of the men at Cherenge's side opened his mouth to speak and then closed it. Cherenge's sullen face lit with bestial interest.

"You had killing?" Kamau prompted.

"What of it?" Cherenge sneered. His rifle was a sporting type, probably .375 calibre. Tom wondered how much ammunition he had. "You have food?" Cherenge said. Kamau hesitated. Tom's lips compressed. "No," Kamau said, and Tom wriggled his toes with relief.

Cherenge moved forward towards them. Tom gripped Kamau's arm and his other hand felt for the trigger guard. "Let us get off the track and sit," Cherenge said. "How many men have you?"

"Thirty," Tom said. Cherenge said something very fast, which Tom did not catch. He backed away and when Cherenge sat down, he sat. One of Cherenge's men went away and another stood by the main track with his back to them. One of the men sitting looked as though at least one of his parents had been Masai. He fingered the revolver. The bluing had worn off it and the bare metal glinted where the sun caught it. The man flicked it open, spilled the bullets out and lovingly re-loaded.

"So," Cherenge said, and looked first at Tom, then at Kangi and Kamau, then at Kipkoin. For an insane second Tom thought of introducing them. He wanted badly to know the names of Cherenge's men.

"And how many men are with you?" Kamau asked.

"Let him speak if he is your leader," Cherenge said savagely, pointing to Tom.

"I will speak when I know you," Tom said, keeping his face half covered with the brim of his hat. Couldn't go far wrong there. It was nearly a Kikuyu proverb his father often quoted. Cherenge hoicked and spat. A woman appeared carrying a gourd, which was snatched out of her hands by Cherenge. As he drank Tom thought what would happen if they fired and there were more of them? If this was a sample of their arms it was all right, but somewhere with the gangs, there were three Bren guns adrift, plus a dozen or so Stens and there was no reason why Cherenge should not have acquired one or two of them. He might also be waiting for more of his gang to arrive. And if they fired what would the others do down by the lake? He leant forward to keep his eyes in the shade. They were really too light for an African's. But there would be no suspicion once it was clear that they were not a K.A.R. patrol. Mau-Mau had not yet encountered a pseudo-gang. That also implied that no Mau-Mau must survive this meeting if they came to fighting.

"You came by Kikipiri?" Cherenge asked suddenly. Tom nodded.

"You saw no one?" Tom shook his head.

"We were told Muthenge or Kimathi would be here at the lake," Kamau said eagerly. The terrorists all looked up. One handed the gourd to Kamau. Tom suppressed a wince. These men would almost certainly have syphilis and he did not relish drinking from the bowl.

"Silence," he said to Kamau. Evidently there was no news of the top brass.

"You had fighting?" he said half tauntingly to Cherenge. If the main questions failed Kamau was supposed to talk to the subordinates. In his state of tension he had forgotten, so it must be done for him. The ruse seemed to work since one of the henchmen answered with a surly "No." Another said, "We had no killing. Many have taken no oath in this part. They will ..."

He was interrupted by Cherenge who had been chewing a mealie cob that one of the women gave him. "We burnt the hut of a white man," he said, turning to the speaker.

"But there was no killing?" Kamau asked quickly. Cherenge leapt to his feet trembling and cursing. "We have killed many," he shouted in an almost hysterical voice. "I, Cherenge have killed, and I will return to kill that white man and his woman."

"Will Kathenge send us back there?" one of the squatting gangsters enquired. "I think we shall not see again that shamba."

Cherenge swung the butt of his rifle at the man's head. It was the one with Masai features who had spoken. His face twisted with fury he leapt to his feet and faced Cherenge. Tom nudged Kangi with his elbow and slid his hand down the butt of the Padgett so that he held it with his fingers around the trigger guard. The two men stood cursing each other as the others scrambled to their feet. Suddenly Cherenge looked wildly around him, hitched his rifle into his armpit and pulled back the bolt. Kangi's bullet hit him before he had time to get finger to trigger.

Tom leapt backwards with a shout, "O koha-ha" and as he did so two of the terrorists turned towards him. The Padgett jumped in his hands, a swathe of bullets thudding into the three men in front of him, slicing their bellies open like some terrible

240

knife. Then he dropped flat on his face. There was a scream as he did so and he heard the whistle of lead over his head coming from Daniel, Ali and Cheragoi behind. Kamau was writhing and kicking beside him. Ignoring him, he crawled under a bush on his right. Screams were coming from the women on the other side of the track. Then he caught a sight of Daniel, kneeling on one knee firing steadily, single shots, with his Sten tucked into his shoulder. He crawled nearer and called his name. "Get the Sten off Kamau," he shouted in Swahili. But a few seconds later he saw Kangi already holding it, stepping over the bodies of two terrorists.

He wondered for a second which of them had shot Kamau. Still, if he had not dropped, as planned, it was his own fault. None of them went near him as they crossed the track. He switched the Padgett to single shot and dived into the bush. Thank God there was no need to give orders. The bush was dense and there was no sign of others of the gang and he knew from experience how little use it would be to follow up. They were all too tired for one thing.

Walking back to collect the dropped weapons he wondered what the reaction would be, first on base and second on the terrorists' meeting. Cheragoi had already tuned in the wireless and Mkuna had collected the weapons. He went over to Kamau. He was dead. A bullet had hit the back of his head, and there was not much left of his face. He had been of little use, but he had been willing. Nothing had yet been proved as to the real usefulness of ex-terrorists. Then a wave of anger swept through him. He had come to respect Kamau, who in his way risked more than any of them. Surely they could have avoided hitting him? But that was the way it was. The Kikuyu had damned themselves for many years to come. There was no point in thinking about it too much. There would be enough questions as to his death later on.

He went over to the body of the man with the Masai features, and turned over in his mind the pictures in the files of leading terrorists. Kmara Ole Longosa, the bastard of a Kikuyu woman, whom the Masai had contemptuously returned to the Kikuyu as unfit for the company of warriors? The ex-milk roundsman and taxi driver, believed to be operating around Narok? Was that why Cherenge had gone in that circle up on to the plateau? Musing he went to get the old Kodak out of his pack. As he passed, Cheragoi said, "Bwana, tiare." Base. Yes he had forgotten about base. His toothache had started again. There were so many things to remember, and then, so many things which had best be forgotten. He slumped down by the set and squeezed his face in his hands before taking the microphone.

"Hello," he said irritably, "hello," thinking momentarily that it was a telephone. He closed his eyes, shook his head and remembered the day at Ringway after the first parachute jump. With the lifting of the tension he had gone to sleep over a cup of NAAFI tea.

"Keyway Four Two Six Able. Contact made with gang today. Oh nine hundred. Figures Six Terrorists killed. Casualties, Figures One. Returning Baker Dog Two from Map reference..."

The operator acknowledged and Tom closed down.

CHAPTER NINETEEN

NAIVASHA

"We are the little white boys,
The little white boys in green-O
And if we catch a Kenya man, a naughty man,
A Mau-Mau man, we'll feckin' kill the bastards, an'
They'll never more be seen-O.
For we're the little white laddy-Os in green-O,
For white is white and black is black and off-white is a Hindi,
And down in the forest if anything stirs, don't we make a shindi."

Anon.

The noise in the back of the truck levelled out into a semblance of a song, with most voices singing the same words. They had climbed three quarters of the way back up the Escarpment when the orders came to climb down again. The men were in a mood of mocking ribaldry: This was repeated with variations. Some more raucous versions made no sense. They sang to keep their spirits up. They knew the trackers didn't understand the words.

As they turned off the main road and down a rutted farm track they passed a field kitchen, and there were shouts of "Starvin',' mate. Stop the flamin' bus, Feckin jammy cooks," and more ripe obscenity. Jonathan felt hungry too, but he was following two trucks in front, which did not stop. He could see only as far as the dust in front of him, so that when the noise of mortar and rifle fire crashed and crackled through the dust curtain, there was a fresh uproar in the back. They started singing their favourite, drowning the noise of firing weapons with the frenzy of their bawling.

"From the slopes of Kipipiri to the lip of Longonot

Every sheep and goat and Gombi, we'll shoot the bloody lot.

Unless the farmers will co-operate-

Unless the farmers will comply-

And fence 'em in.

And fence 'em in.

And fence the barsteds in."

It went on for a dozen verses to the tune of *"All Things Bright and Beautiful."* The reference was mainly to farmers whose stock was slashed by gangs. When they rang the police, a patrol would be sent. There was a special verse about the native tracker who turned out stark naked, because he said there wasn't time to dress and the Bwana, he knew, was particularly "kali" (sharp).

When they debussed, as the Army pedantically calls the process of getting out of a lorry, they found themselves on the fringe of a swamp into which a dozen mortar platoons were pouring their two inch mortar bombs with gusto.

"Wot they got 'ere, then? Bloody Kikooyoo Navy?" asked Corporal Flett, who had succeeded Tosh Harris, suffering from in-growing toenail, as platoon joker. There were several new Chalkies and Lofties and Smilers since the last patrol. Jonathan had already identified amongst the new intake, Jumbo McKeever: who carried packs and rifles for anyone who asked. And Uncle Bun O'Malley, a huge avuncular prize-fighter of a man who said he was nineteen and could have been thirty. Flett, now known as Larfin' Boy and another contrapuntal wit known as Smiler. Jonathan himself was known as Prof, and the Sergeant as Guts and Gaiters. Corporal Noyk reckoned, he said, that he had them "sorted", but there appeared to be some argument as to who carried the Bren ammunition box. Jonathan caught sight of Cosgrave's platoon doubling from the truck behind.

"Pick the damned thing up," he shouted. Jumbo picked it up. "By the right, DOUBLE march." He usually left the shouting to MacNamara and Noyk but he wasn't having Cosgrave double past him, even if he didn't know where he was going either. When they were just about puffed, somebody noticed a group of

Africans in jungle green standing with two policemen. Among them was Chepkoin, their tracker. Jonathan halted, and Chepkoin greeted his platoon with an ivory grin of his bow-fronted teeth, and a shrill "Ayee."

"Can we have him?" Jonathan shouted to the policemen, who were Europeans.

"What sector?" they asked.

"K," Jonathan said on inspiration and Chepkoin came running over. He was wearing his steel-rimmed spectacles, which was not a good sign since he normally only wore them when drunk, but at least he might know what was going on.

When they had gone another couple of hundred yards they were stopped and told to deploy beyond the next troop. As always Jonathan had the feeling that he had come in the middle of the reel and missed something vital. Chepkoin set off like a bloodhound, leading the way towards the fringes of reeds along the lakeside, while from all around the lake came the crumping of mortars and rattle of rifle fire. A spotter plane zoomed over them and from the water came the sound of a couple of marine engines. What sort of a joke was this, Jonathan thought, feeling the effect of his week-end of late nights? But Chepkoin seemed to know and forged on in the wake of the troop in front.

Sam Webb watched the green lorry swing in through the gate in the stockade and stop in a swirl of dust. The cab door burst open and a black in a dirty skin jacket jumped out. Sam gulped and dropped his hand to his hip, standing up and knocking over his camp chair. The man in skins was undoing the tail-flap of the lorry and before Sam could take breath to shout, a swarm of whooping black ruffians poured out. Sam dived inside the tent and grabbed the Sten that lay on the table. He was just about to fling himself flat at the mouth of the tent when he noticed the truck driver in neat KAR. khaki drill and bush hat, strolling unconcerned around the front of the truck. A couple of African police had run over to the group debouching from it, and were shaking their hands and chattering shrilly.

The apparition in the rough-sewn skins and torn bush hat turned towards him.

"Hullo Sammy," it said, in fairly cultured tones, and there was a flash of close set teeth.

"Wait till you see my haircut." Tom swept his hat off, and displayed his head, like an old frayed toothbrush that had been used for dubbining boots.

"My God," Sam uttered finally, and repeated it aghast. "My God. You don't look human, man. What in hell have you been doing?"

"Can you get my blokes out of the way quick and cleaned up? I don't want anyone outside here to see us in this rig. Then I want the I.O. on duty. Before I forget, here's a roll of film, and don't let any of your coppers out of camp, will you?"

Sam stood there, just staring.

Tom went over to the lorry cab and took out a filthy mackintosh, a skin pack and a Padgett and then went back to his men, who were standing in file with their mouths shut. He spoke to them and they dismissed.

"What are you doing here anyway?" Tom asked.

"My kite's grounded," Sam said, "So they roped me in here. If you want the IO, I'm it. T'others are all out snooping. Question is, what do I put you down as?"

"Force S-One. Call-sign Keyway. Didn't they tell you?" Sam turned to the tent and thumbed his way through a signal code book. At the other end of the open-sided tent a couple of wireless operators were taking down messages.

"Yes," he said, "They told me something about... Oh, that's you, is it? I wondered who the hell it could be. Mzuri kabisa (very good). Well, you got the bastards into a corner whoever they are. Even the pommies are excited. All rushing about in small circles. We've just had a meeting. I asked for napalm and they all looked as though I'd suggested putting lead in the ball or using four stumps. R.A.F. could fly it in in twenty-four hours.

"Not on, old boy' they said. 'No more will the pilots' balls be.' I said, 'if they come down in that swamp.' They told me to quenda (go), so I reckon that's Sam's war over. Or whatever it was. Now let's have your report. No detail will escape sleuthing Sam, never fear. Hell, you stink, man. What about a bafu?"

"Thank you," Tom said, looking up from his map.

"NGANGA," Sam roared and there was a "Sah" offstage. "Tanganesa maji moto kwa bafu." "(Make hot water bath)," he said to the orderly.

"Now I'll get my little book. You give me their names and addresses and I'll go and round 'em up." He went to a chop-box on the floor and took out a bottle of whiskey. Tom had never heard him so garrulous. He was taking the loss of his plane very hard evidently.

"I was going to ask you to get hold of a dentist," Tom said, "but a drop of that would be very welcome."

Sam poured him half a tumbler and hid the bottle again. He took up what Tom had written, read it and shot to his feet. "Kathenge," he said, "and Aloysius Muriathi." He tipped back his head and sat down with a faraway look in his eye. In the distance there were muffled bangs and a white smoke cloud floated over the lake.

"Muriathi," Sam repeated. "That devil. They said that Kimathi and Mathenge might be there. You know they got two this morning?"

"No?"

"Apparently there's some big meeting going on with the two top witch-doctors and the Chief Justice and all. So there'll be a lot of the gang leaders. A kite saw at least fifty of them. Three tracker teams went down and the Micks went into the swamp at the north end of the lake. They're trying to cordon off now. But Muriathi. Goddam. He did the Leghorn raid, blast his evil black soul."

"David?" Tom asked gently. He had been Sam's biggest buddy.

Sam nodded, his face set. "I didn't understand what blood lust meant until that morning I went up there, to the Leghorn farm." After a minute he said slowly. "Tom?"

Tom stopped writing. "Yes."

"You know where they are, don't you?"

"The gangs. No. What do you mean?"

"Remember the year when the lake level fell two feet just after the war?" Tom shook his head. "Well, the Whittakers' farm, as it was then. They were growing lucerne right down into the

247

water. There was a tongue of land that stood right out. Well, I reckon the reeds have piled up and broadened that since then. That's where they'll be. They've probably got a shelter dug, or slit trenches out there. People underestimate some of those chaps. The ex-Army ones can be dead crafty. We bombed one gang last year and the pommies went in to look for them. They didn't find a one. Next day they got one and he told them. An ex-KAR sergeant they had with them had told them the Jap drill. Stay in the holes where the bombs fell and hide. All that mortaring's a waste of time. Most of 'em go off under water anyway. I've got an idea, boy. Listen."

Tom swilled the whisky round his tooth. That was a lot better. He listened to Sam's plan and knew there was something in it. An orderly came with a sheaf of messages and Sam went off to talk to the wireless operators. Tom went off to look for his bath. He hungered for it as keenly as he had ever hungered for any physical comfort. If he didn't have it quick, the Interrogation teams would be back, and he had a lot of talking to do. He went over to where his men were splashing about and saw that there was food for them, and then he went over to find Nganga and his own warm water and soap and a clean towel.

He lay in the water, feeling the comfort soaking into his bones. It was better than the aftermath of any three day trek after a wounded elephant that he could remember. He relaxed and listened with satisfaction to the thumps and bangs in the distance. If I wasn't so deathly tired, he told himself, I'd sing. This is going to save us a whole lot of trouble if we can keep that lot in the area and just pound them to pieces for the next week. Then, the worst will nearly be over. Nearly three years of it will be finished and we can all get back to living some sort of sensible lives. His mind strayed to thoughts of Alison, but the contrast between the image of her placid gentleness and the business of the moment made his lips tighten. There was a lot to do first. He tensed himself and heaved out of the tin bath. Nganga was ready with towels and some spare clothing. In five minutes he was back in the Control tent.

Sam was sitting there with three other men, and got up when he saw him.

"I've laid on a fang butcher for you," he said, coming out of the tent. Then in a lower voice he said, "Can you make tomorrow morning? They've got all sorts of fancy ideas in there, loudspeakers and sky-shouter kit, bulldozers and beaters, parachute flares and all the other taka-taka (junk). I've got to go off now. They've just got a wounded one they can't move; I want to talk to him. They've got Brens and more than one Sten in there, Tom, and we've got captured documents half sorted now. They've been using the lake as an HQ for months. Well, they haven't been standing about in the water, eh? See you, boy." He patted Tom on the back and ran over to a Land Rover. Tom went into the tent and sat down for de-briefing.

"Blimey," O'Malley said, "Much more uv this an' Mrs O'Malley's little boy'll be web-footed."

They were wading chest deep in the papyrus with the reeds waving fifteen to twenty feet above them. The bottom was slimy and glutinous. "Cor," McKeever said, "Don't this stuff pong?" "Shurrup," Flett hissed.

The mortars had stopped firing and the cordon was being closed. Only five terrorists had been seen and three accounted for. The rest were somewhere in the reeds and replying to fire with bursts of automatic as well as single shots. The sun beat down on the muddied water and intensified the nauseous smell. The water was thick with leeches and there were hippopotamuses about, although most of them had fled to other parts of the lake. There were lake flies too, which stung, and after two hours wading they came up against great sodden areas of floating reeds and a boat came and rescued them.

Back on the lake fringes amongst the reeds, listening posts were set up and swathes cut for the Brens to enfilade in case of a breakout. Sergeant MacNamara and Noyk went round showing the younger soldiers how to burn the leeches off with cigarette ends. The mortars opened up again and as it grew dark they fired flares which cast an eerie light over the water, shimmering down, swinging from their parachutes, to fall into the water with a hiss.

During the night it began to rain, gently at first and towards dawn the drops slowed up, got bigger and then began to teem down with unbelievable abandon. It was not like rain so much as a frenzied emptying of gigantic celestial reservoirs. The cloud ceiling appeared to be only a few hundred feet about them, and sleep became impossible. Dawn came very slowly, the sun-leaden sky, blue-black and lowering. It was unlike as it could be to the glittering jauntiness of Upland dawns, when the sun came up so briskly that it caught the whole world asleep, and the animals as they slunk to water had that air of half-awake surprise about them.

Lorries came round with food and insulated canisters and the cooks jeered cheerfully at the troop and asked them how many pythons and crocodiles they had seen, telling them that they were bound to be trodden on by hippo if not savaged by leopard or bitten by snakes. "There's a partickerly narsty one rahnd 'ere," one of the hash-slingers confided gloatingly, "wot sits up on 'is 'ind legs and spits at yer. Spiff--like that." He clicked his greasy fingers dramatically. "Dead in ten seconds." He stabbed at a sausage and went on serving in exaggerated gloom. MacNamara frowned at him but said nothing.

"As a matter of fact," Jonathan said to the cook, "I happen to know that the leader of this lot in the swamp is the Mau-Mau's ambush expert. I expect they are getting very short of food by now." There was a faint ripple of laughter at this, and it served to start the chaff flying.

"I reckon," Flett said, "That the bleeders wot don't starve 'll either be drowned in this 'ere rain, or, if not, at least the buggers 'll be deaf for the rest of their puff. Cor wot an effin' racket."

The mortars had started again at first light, and in the intervals a loudspeaker blared in Kikuyu at the terrorists to surrender or be killed.

"You put your hat on and keep quiet," Noyk said, "There's a lot of woodpeckers round 'ere, lad."

"Oh Corp, ain't you a giggle?" McKeever said as he went off to relieve one of the Bren-gunners.

"Quiet," Jonathan roared, and the nattering stopped.

Gradually the rain eased off and the sun turned the swamp into a steam bath. Squads of Kikuyu beaters appeared, brought from the reserves, and cut down areas of reeds. But it was as Corcoran, the brigade major said, a gnat bite in the vast area and it seemed as pointless as the apparently aimless mortaring. The area where the gang could be was being reduced slowly however, and the cordon pickets came closer together during the morning. Jonathan came across teams of men building bamboo rafts and talked to a policeman who said that they would be there for a week at least.

Vultures fluttered down from the escarpment looming to the south and perched in the stunted trees that grew on the lake edge. The blast from the mortars ruffled their feathers as they sat unwinking, waiting. People were taking pot shots at them when no one was looking, but even this failed to budge them from their optimism.

Suddenly the firing stopped and Jonathan's team were sent in for another wading trip into the lake. It was very hot and quiet in the tall reeds. There were eddies of warm wind that stirred the feathery tops of the papyrus, whispering them together. There was the monotonous squelch of their jungle boots in the mud, but otherwise the stillness was pierced only by occasional shrill bird noises and the whistling snort of a surfacing hippo. Then there was a burst of fire behind them, which went on irregularly for some minutes. They stopped and Kennedy whispered, "Dead loss, this lark. If the bleeders came in a-purpose, they wouldn't a-stopped. If they did we'd never find 'em. This lot goes on for bloody miles."

"Bear up lads. Soon be over," Jonathan whispered before telling Kennedy quietly to shut his mouth.

Then the rain began again. There was a gust of colder air and it fell in stifling sheets with a steady hissing sound, rapidly growing to a lashing crescendo, millions of spears lancing into the water, stirring it to a bubbling, boiling turbulence. Visibility was cut to a few feet. A twinge of panic caught at Jonathan. He set his teeth and dragged his compass out, thinking as they plodded back that he had a sight too much imagination ever to make a proper soldier.

They had been soaked through their thin drill jackets in under a minute, and the sky was blanked out with huge low clouds. With the semi-darkness and the streaming rain, Jonathan tried as he glanced at his compass to think of something cheerful. Lalage. He was altogether sure that she was happy just now, a very cheerful thought. What an unhappy little soul she could be. In contrast, to Gillian's gay vivacity and fecklessness. She seemed to be getting on well with Webb at the moment. Lalage, so lovely, so African. Somehow it turned him up as Flett would say, to be dragged into her past. He must try to make her forget it. What could he do to stay here? Farm? What else? There was a chattering noise. He stopped. Looked up. Looked around. It was a bird of some sort, a heron type, fishing.

"Concentrate!" he snarled at himself.

They began to rise out of the water until it was only knee deep, with the occasional hippo holes that submerged you arse over tip, so you wondered if the wretched gun would ever fire if it was needed in a hurry. At last there was dry land and they walked back to the shelters feeling that at least it could be no worse than that.

"Brew up," Jonathan ordered. The men chaffed. "Bugger me old boots, mine's fulla mud."

"Send for the rum issue."

"Send for an ambulance."

"Send for me old Mum, I'm fair fucked, mate."

"Cor wot a bleedin' war."

In the early morning mists, the next day, the boat nosed silently through the reeds, with only the bird noises and the whizz and chirrup of early morning cicadas presaging the heat. It was one of those clear-washed rainy season mornings. Out on the lake a thin wind was blowing the night water-mist away, and rippling the surface, lapping it against the boat with tiny slaps that sounded deafening in the silence of the morning.

They were twenty-four hours late, because there had been an attempt at a breakout the previous dawn, and even Tom found boats difficult to borrow. Now even the loud hailers were quiet, and this was the last chance, because there would be too many beaters about later who were coming down from the reserve that day. Soon somebody would hear about it and forbid them to go.

The boat was low in the water with the four men bent down, their heads level with the gunwales. Tom was in the bows and Sam steering with the outboard motor propeller shaft, while the two askaris paddled. It was just like the Tana river, Sam thought, hunting crocs, at the end of a night floating downstream. Which were worst, crocs or Micks? He thought of David Leghorn's murder and winced. Crocs at least hid their victims, ramming them under the bank to putrefy. What would the reaction be to coming face to face with Muriathi? He knew the face well from the photographs. But he would have a beard now, more scars and maybe one of those hats they made of skins to look like British officers' peaked caps. Anger suffused his whole body, so that he trembled. That was the trouble, you didn't feel angry with even a croc or a rogue tembo with musth trickling down from his tusk pouches. He gripped the Sten harder. Stupid little gun it was, but it would do. His Padgett had got rusty.

They were now jammed completely in a floating mattress of reed stems. There would be a few islands before they reached the strip. Tom looked back at him and he turned his mind fully onto the problem of where to go and how. Sam whispered to the askaris and slithered over the side, clutching the grease filled Sten. It might not fire but the Luger in his shoulder holster would. He half swam, half groped his way onto the floating island, crawled up onto it and disappeared. Three minutes later he re-appeared and slid back into the water, climbing back to the boat with the help of Tom's hand and his own bare toes. He pointed out to the left and the askaris backed the boat and thrust it up a narrow channel of water by dragging at the reeds on either side.

This time, after disappearing for slightly longer, he came back and signed for Tom to follow. The askaris turned the boat round and grasped their Stens.

If he is good at anything, this is it, Tom thought, watching Sam wriggling along in front of him on his elbows and knees, his whole body dyed black, and only ragged shorts, the Luger holster and a skin hat on him. But I don't like the feel of this gun. I miss the weight and grip of the big Gibbs .562 elephant stopper.

I shouldn't have started to smoke because now I need a cigarette badly although they make me feel dizzy early in the morning, Sam thought. Nicotine for nerves. Christ, will I ever be any good again? He could feel his heart beating against the damp, springy surface of the reeds. Wayne Rossiter coming out soon, and maybe Van Zy, or Bobo Thyringer. What would Bobo say if he saw his hand shake? Not much. He was paying for results, and if it wasn't good, he wouldn't say anything then either, just go and not come back. Relax. Just relax and listen.

They wouldn't be cooking, so there'd be no scent of fire. Rain bugs flittered across his face, and lake flies stung his exposed flesh. He drew himself up from the hips to see round a thick clump and there was a sudden splash to the right. I must be getting blind, he told himself angrily as he watched the slimy yellow green shape writhe away in the water. Nyoka-ya-maji – water-python. No wonder they scared the locals silly. He looked round to see how close Tom was and made a wry face. Had he noticed the way he jumped?

Wonder how quick the Micks were, after two years in the bush? Their eyes would be quick, but on the barrel, the fraction before your hand and eye came together, steady after the jump of your start? Not too good after the mortar bombs, and the days and nights sodden with drink, or women, or blood.

It was about here. You couldn't blame the pommies. Like using a sledge hammer for mice. How many would have swum out already and got through the pickets? Last night in the flare lights there was a movement or two that wasn't hippo or vultures. They might be right down in hippo holes, all jabbering away like mad baboons. A hippo blew out water with a sudden roar like an angry dog-baboon. Over to the left. No joke if they came over here. What was it Tom's father called them? "Most unaccommodatin' beasts." Or was that rhino? Have to work over to the left. Arms getting cramped. He stopped and stretched them and wriggled his fingers and inspected the Sten. Useless things, but the right size for this job. He was plucking a few slivers of dead reed out of the bolt mechanism when he distinctly heard what sounded like a woman's voice say, in Kikuyu, "It isn't here."

He froze, and then turned very slowly to see if Tom had heard. He was wiping his hands very carefully on his hat, and he smiled and nodded his head. Keep cool, Sam thought, cool.

He sat up on his haunches, searching for a crevice in the thick stems, moving only his eyes. He wanted to get up and tear the foliage apart, but it was like that time when he had only the light Mannlicher with a telescopic sight. Although he could see the rhino through the screen of dry bush, every time he put the gun up the sights brought the twigs closer together and blotted out the view. Like a nightmare, a paralysis, with Nganga gone off at an angle with the double .475 Express.

The wind was eddying across from left to right. He wrenched himself into infinitely slow movement, listening above the rustle. Suddenly an enormous cloud overhead was illuminated on one side by the invisible sun. A bird flapped and just then a low voice said something he could not catch. It was a man's voice, turned away from him, rumbling like a grazing elephant's belly. Instinctively he held up his cheek and watched the feathery papyrus tops for the direction of the wind. Then he started to edge forward. He stopped and could hear Tom coming up very softly behind. A bug stung him with particular viciousness on the back of the neck, and he closed his eyes for a mini-second with the pain.

When he opened them he could see a dark shape that seemed to be somebody standing upright. Or was it a small black-barked tree? He pushed his face through a clump, pulled his knees up under him and inched further forward. A tree. Then a shape moved just behind it, and taking long slow breaths he ceased looking down to see where he was putting each foot, and pushed forward with the Sten tucked into his right shoulder, and the left hand free. Tom came up on his left as he had signed for him to do, and they both moved forward.

The woman screamed when she saw him, although afterwards Sam wondered why, because she must have had far worse shocks, and the gang had made very little noise up to then. Her nerves, raw with tension, must have snapped at seeing Sam's blazing eyes, and the fact that at close quarters he could be nothing but European.

The man flung himself backwards and fumbled in his tunic. Sam lunged at him, bringing the Sten down with a thump on the side of his head and then head down, landed with his knees in the man's belly. The gun fell out on the ground, a revolver, the worn finish glinting in the sun. Sam put his foot on it, crouched, and looked round. Tom had bowled the woman over and she lay on her face whimpering. Both Africans were plastered in mud. He had no time to look at the man's face. There was a noise of someone else approaching. The noise stopped and a shot rang out. The lead whistled past Sam's head and he flung himself flat and fired a single shot, squeezing the trigger gently without snatching, and there was another scream. They could hear the noise of the outboard motor as the askaris started up.

"Take these back," Tom said in his ear, "I'll take a look."

"To hell," Sam said. "My shauri." Handing the revolver to Tom, he crawled forward obliquely to the left of where he could hear a moaning noise. There were two figures running on all fours, and with a searing stab of savage joy he pressed the automatic fire button and pulled the trigger. Nothing happened, and he dropped the gun and whipped out the Luger, but in the instant the figure on the ground moved and distracted him. He was just about to riddle the body on the ground when with a shock he saw that it was another woman.

"Don't move," he rapped out in Kikuyu. The woman blinked, her eyes turning upwards so that only the whites showed. Every nerve in his body quivered and he felt his stomach heave as he pushed her over onto her face. She smelt like a dead hyena and her skin tunic was twisted up showing her thighs. The first bullet had hit her low in the base of the spine. He stood up and raced forward, stooping to pick up the Sten. Tom's voice shouted out for him, and he shook the Sten, banged the magazine with his fist and it fired. He emptied it in the direction he had seen the two figures run, and then turned, retching, and stumbled back to where he could hear the outboard engine revving. Firing began before he reached the boat, but he made no attempt beyond a cursory look behind him to evade it. Reaching the boat he threw himself over Tom's shoulder and the askaris, sitting on the two prisoners, pushed off. The mortars began pounding as they chugged across the sunlit water, and Sam sat in the bottom of the boat, staring at the stunned face of the bearded terrorist.

The paraffin lamps in the hotel hissed with the tremulous persistence that in the tropics, takes the place of the cat purring before the flickering coal fire. Sam had just been explaining to those assembled around the bar that in his opinion most of the lake gang had already gone, and that he was going too.

"What are you going to do now?" Tom asked, but Sam didn't hear.

"Uniform?" I said, "What the hell for? Dress up for a lot of brass hatted Poona wallahs to come and say 'Jolly good show actually.' Uniform!" he banged his glass down on the bar and roared with joyous laughter, throwing his head back and enjoying the full savour of being able to make noise freely. The others laughed with him and asked him for more details. It was Sam's day and most of them knew that Tom, if he talked at all, would not give the story the flavour that Sam would. They bought them both drinks and Sam paid in entertainment.

"His eyes didn't look like the bad ones," he was saying. "The blast must have shaken the wits out of him. I didn't think it was anyone much until that hood thing of his fell off in the boat. Then I looked, thinking that if it was him, I'd like a little chat before they took him away. But Tom here said no, and the boys came and gave him food and he talked the usual crap about only having a gun for self-defence and the two women were his wives since long. To think I would have been scared of meeting that sod in the dark. Oh the big bad Kathenge. And there he is, just a dazed, mixed-up kid with about forty murders to his name."

But they weren't interested in his opinions, they wanted the facts, and Tom wandered off to talk to a local D.O. about arrangements for patrols further away from the lake.

He went back to the bar and Sam was talking about farming. "Try everything," he said, "Sheep, cattle, wheat, maize, pythrethrum, tea. Got a few shenzis knocking me up a hut or two."

"No hunting?" somebody said. Sam looked dubious. "Will it pick up?" he said guardedly. "The Yanks have read all the books and the papers will make this shauri sound like Korea, Algeria and the Spanish Civil War instead of a lot of lousy Kyukes trying to put it over all the other tribes. Then there's the Game Department trying to put a stopper on it."

He noticed Tom back at the bar and changed the subject.

The barman leant over and told Tom he was wanted outside. Tom picked up his gunbelt and went out. He heard Sam saying, "Bloody native poachers kill five thousand elephant and year and the Game Department have got a bod on a control contract knocking off five hundred at fifty shillingi per head right now."

There was a girl standing on the wooden verandah, the light from the windows shining on her hair.

"Tom," she said in a low voice, and came towards him. He stood fast, wondering, watching the smooth swing of her walk and the crisp lines of her tailored dress. It wasn't possible, he thought, as he recognised her and smelt the fresh, girlish perfume of her that drove through him like a knife slash.

Her face had a half-happy, half-fearful look on it, and he fumbled with the clip on his belt for something to do while he stood there feeling stupid. "Alison. What are you doing here?"

"We heard on the wireless at lunchtime. We were all so worried. Gillian's got fever, so I said I'd come. Are you all right?"

He was so touched that he could not speak. He had telephoned his father yesterday, and Gillian was used to him being away. She put out a hand to his arm and he took her arm and led her to the empty lounge.

"How did you get here?" he asked, and she told him that she had rung her father from Ruthaka and Lalage had lent her car and sent Ian Gredling with her.

"Is he out in the car? We'd better have him in. I…"

Tom turned and looked at her. Her mouth was trembling and she was looking at him with a curious strained look. He put out both arms and she moved into them with a soft cry of "Oh Tom," and he felt as awkward as he had ever felt as her smooth cheek rubbed against his roughened, red-raw skin.

"My knees," she said, *with* a catch in her breath that was

almost a sob."I must sit down." Fool, he told himself. Clumsy oaf. He knelt at the side of the chair and she took his head in her hands and put her face in his hair, that was garishly en brosse and stiff with dye.

"I'm sorry to be silly," she said. "But you've been away so long, and Gillian didn't know anything. You've got some grey hairs, you know."

This isn't possible, he told himself. Women just aren't like this to me. He felt filthy as though he would leave marks on her clothes and face. She should go away and give him time to feel human again. He had been too long with Daniel and Mkuna and Ali Wainiri and all this just didn't happen any more. He had been thinking like an African for too long. Like a bush African, of essentials only, and now he had this lump swelling in his throat so that he felt like a schoolboy.

"It's good to see you," he said, choking the "sweetie" off just in time. "I can't say how, … how good it is to see you." She kissed him on the forehead and smiled, cupping his face, and he put his arms round her shoulders. Her arms went round his neck and their lips met and he felt a peace flow down inside him that hurt almost as pain.

After a while she said, "We'd better see about Ian."

"Bring him into the…" He was going to say "bar", but he realised in time that that was no place for him or her now.

"Where are you going to stay?" She told him that Ian knew some people he had rung up. They went out arm in arm, like old people supporting each other, and Tom thanked Ian for coming and they got into the car and drove away from the lake, Tom asking about Gillian's malaria and she asking him why somebody else couldn't go into the forest and let him stay safe in Kiambu.

They told Sam to get cleaned up as the press was coming but he said he didn't feel like cleaning anything and he had not a thing to say to any pressmen or presswomen.

So they said, 'well there's a General coming too. He wants to meet you.' And Sam said 'thanks and all but he didn't want to trouble anyone, and he hadn't got a plane to fly so he'd just take leave and go home to his shamba.'

259

Anyway the General came, very distinguished and fit-looking with glittering eyes. He was a very famous General, called Templer, who had been in charge in Malaya when the communist terrorists were at their worst. His eyes blazed from a tanned grim face that radiated power and strong will. He knew everybody's name and called Sam "Sam" and asked him questions. Even Sam seemed impressed.

Sam's eyes went to the A.D.C. behind the General, who was a pale-faced young one, with a highly polished belt. On one shoulder he had gold coloured rope ending in a pointed thingy like Sam's Rhodesian Aunt Milly had on the end of her curtain pulls. Then there was a very tall major with red tabs and a red band around his blue cap, which had gold "scrambled eggs," on its brim. These all fascinated Sam, who wasn't listening to the General, and they had to prompt him. "Tell the General how you knew where they were."

"Ah," Sam said, "That's easy. When I was a toto (little), we used to come down here shooting fisi and kifaru (hyena and rhino) and stuff. And we had a boat."

Someone translated, as the general had little Swahili. Sam went on. "In the dry season when the water was low you saw these islands. You can't see them now after the rains, but you can in January."

"Tell the General," the A.D.C. drawled in a voice which irritated Sam with its sheer fruitiness, "something…some ah – details." After that Sam wouldn't speak at all, and just looked at his hands and pretended he needed to go for a pee. Then he made a big effort and saluted the General and muttering to himself in Kikuyu, he shambled off. As he went he took a sidelong glance at the General, who had a quiet grin on his face as he pretended to nod at his A.D.C.

Sam only got ten yards when a photographer ambushed him. He was an old buddy from Rhodesia, so Sam agreed to be led back to the General. Someone produced Kathenge, quite surly by now, half way through his de-briefing, gave him a tin of bully beef and a jack-knife and made him stand next to Sam for the photograph. Sam hated it, but years later he was glad to have it all on record.

CHAPTER TWENTY

PLANNING AHEAD

"There's no time to plant bombs.
Let's just drive along and shoot up whatever we see."

Colonel David Stirling
(Founder Special Air Service.) North Africa
Wadi Tamit. Cyrenaica. December 1941

Timothy Collins sat outside his tent, having discharged himself from hospital and hiding all signs of bandages. He knocked his pipe out fiercely and refilled it from his tobacco pouch with the neat, methodical movements characteristic of him. The thigh wound caused him to limp quite badly. He needed his shillelagh now.

Jonathan sat cross-legged on the grass, fiddling with the wings of a flying ant. The rains brought them out, clustering in thousands around any lamp, shedding their wings and metamorphosing into sausage-shaped insects which Africans baked and ate.

"Sometimes, I think you're retarded," Tim said, watching him.

"Cheer up, Tim," Jonathan grinned "Did you hear about Seamus O'Malley's troop?"

"Not officially. What's that ass done now?"

"Well, the M.O. said that as Naivasha is full of leeches, men operating in the water should wear condoms, to stop them crawling up their penises. So Seamus said he wouldn't, and as he is a fervent R.C. he wouldn't order his men to wear them either."

Tim laughed. "What happened?"

"Well the R.S.M. told him that if he or any of his chaps got anything up their plumbing, they would be put on a charge for self-inflicted wounds."

Tim laughed. "Bloody silly of course. As though a condom would stay on when your cock is underwater." He added. "I hear that Sammy got General China."

"Well, he and Tom, I think. Sam thinks we are all a pack of left-footed clod-hoppers, blundering about."

"Cheeky sod," Tim cut in. "He needs a good thump round the ear, that one."

"Oh he's all right," Jon said, knowing how angry Tim got if anyone made any sort of criticism of his beloved Irish Rifles. It meant as much to him as his parents, his home and Ireland itself.

But the lake operation had been mostly a failure. There was a rumour that the mortar shells they had fired were due to be dumped soon anyway, which lessened the waste, but not the feeling of failure. Jonathan had been infected more than he had realised with the sense of belonging in some way to the future of this beautiful country. Constant patrolling, week after week, was not yet becoming tiresome. There was so much to see.

Sammy had departed for his shamba, and he and Tim were taking Gillian and Lalage to a cinema. "The bioscope," they called it. Tim's continued interest in Lalage surprised Jonathan, but on commenting tactfully Tim had merely said, "She's very decorative, isn't she?" Meaning Gillian. "And rather involved with Sammy Webb, I thought."

"You ought to know," Tim said tersely and without malice.

The evening went fairly well because the film was about Africa and the girls seemed to know most of the people in the film and quite a few of the animals, which amused them hugely. Tim supported Gillian's request to be taken to the Golden Horn, although he was still limping.

"I expect," she said to Jonathan, after a few brandies, "It's nice for you to see some dim, dissipated faces after all those red, stupid, bit-between-the-teeth ones up-country."

Perhaps, Jonathan thought, she understands us better than we think.

Someone in a dinner jacket twice asked Gillian to dance,

and the second time Tim stood up and told him so firmly and quietly to go away, which, without any argument, the civilian did. "And that," Lalage said, "is the form."

The atmosphere of gaiety was as intense as ever, reinforced by a strip-tease dancer who had blown in from Cairo, and somehow got past Immigration. Jonathan was not entirely happy, since he could not forget that his troop were waiting for him, still sore and angry and all determined to avenge the deaths of their two mates as soon as possible. Later in the evening they went to Lalage's flat and Tim took Gillian home in his Land Rover, leaving Jonathan to borrow Lalage's car.

"You're bored," she accused, smiling a sad, eye-wrinkling smile that pierced him. He smoothed her hair and took her in his arms and cuddled her, kissing her wet, soft mouth and the vivid black-and-white eyes, thinking at the same time that perhaps he was already blotting out the memories of Andrew.

"You know," he said slowly, "We are all like oysters really, with a shell of indifference and cynicism we turn to the world, to keep off the clumsy fools who poke their sharp sticks into anything they see unprotected."

"M'm," she bit his ear gently. "Not terribly original dear, but it's nice to have someone to talk to all the same. You are going to stay with us now. For ever."

"I was thinking about oysters. Some people grow the shell all over or get so stuck to the rock…"

"That's limpets."

"Shush. You know the sort with shell all over, and then there are the two halves of the oyster. When they cling together no one can hurt them."

"Except each other."

"Except each other. Funny how some oysters one knows seem to be always hurting each other."

"I'm tired of oysters," Lalage said. "Can't I be something else?"

"A bear," he said. "You could be a bear. My huggable, tropical bear."

Lalage sighed soulfully.

On the way back to camp in the car he thought, hell and holy jumping mackerel, how did she get so hurt? He saw again the lines on her cheek as she spoke, where the trickles of sweat runnelled the face powder. Jesus, the things people go through. First in fact, and then over and over again, lifting the guilt a little by confessing, like a hand caught in a moving gearwheel, watching and then not being able to stop, feeling it being smashed to pulp.

Back in Nairobi on Sunday, and feeling hypocritical, he prayed for her next morning, together with the souls of Kelly and McEvoy, and all the Mau-Mau in the forests and those that would die. Perhaps it was too cosy and smug, he thought, to be able to forgive and pray for them, but at least it was better than just hating. And no one would know.

Outside after Mass, the sun blazed down on empty streets and he walked about a little looking at the buildings, at the wedding-cake Parliament, all chocolate blocks and syrupy twirls, beside the old stone church that lay empty and surrounded by tall grass. There were the old railway bungalows on stilts, with red tin roofs beside the big six storey barrack blocks of the Administration. It didn't matter it seemed, what you built, because there was still enough empty space and trees and swarming bougainvillea, to make it all look new, experimental and slightly gawky like a young girl imitating her married sisters.

In between two big new company offices, pillared on stilts in weird Corbusier-cum-Jacobsen, tropical-Scandinavian style, all cantilevered concrete and plate glass and gleaming tiles, was a squat little Vedic temple, crouching like a trapped mouse between the two six-storey blocks. It must be fun to be an architect here, he thought, looking at an office block that sprouted up alone among a line of red tin roofs shaped like some massive outdoor cathedral organ in white concrete. It seemed that some architects must have let it all hang out.

He got in the car and drove past some of the new office blocks. A group of Africans were squatting, playing some game on one of the vacant plots that gaped muddily between the blocks like great raw gaps in rows of shining teeth. He drove

264

down towards the river that was still lined on both sides with drained swamp, covered with an eruption of maize stalks and vegetable patches. Here, a few hundred yards from the statue of the Pioneer Peer, was this sluggish stream that looked as though it harboured unfiltered sewage, bilharzia, anopheles mosquitoes, dead animals and a corpse or two. No doubt the authorities saw to it that no such things occurred, but one could see that once, not very long ago, they had.

"Let's not be oysters." He smiled. Here was Europe and on the other bank Asia, with Africans no different from the Stone Age, walking in between. Not just white and black, but the exiles of half a dozen European cultures and how many Asiatic, mingling with natives who had now slowed their own progress. They had cleared how many? Forty thousand Kikuyu out of Nairobi in April.

He went back to the main avenue where the jacaranda trees grew in the middle of the road and at both sides of it, with another road and pavement before the buildings began. It went straight up the hill to the big pink boxes which were the flats where Lalage lived, and then was lost in the trees again. He cruised along slowly, went round two roundabouts and there in the middle of an expanse of grass was a group of wooden huts surrounded by barbed wire. One could believe that the hyenas came out of the game park to forage at night in the dustbins, and one could imagine the lioness that was shot just there, the week before, slinking along in the dark, lost and perplexed in the empty streets.

And this was where he would live with Lala? But no. This was the city. The Concrete Forest, she called it. They would live out in the Highlands.

The flats were unique as buildings and as massed living quarters in the City. They stood out brassily on a hillside among the smoky gum-trees and red earth and concrete roads, their square massivity mocked by the stilt fronted garages beneath them, and by their colour. The same icing-sugar pink favoured by the rich Indians to set off their wedding-cake houses, with their roofs like the sunshine decks of river boats, with wrought iron instead of railings. Pink was in keeping with the fussy messiness of the grocers' palaces, but why it had been chosen for six storey flats for 'Europeans Only' could only be ascribed to the contractor's malice. It was "Late marzipan period", Lalage said.

When he rang the bell he heard a voice after a minute or two say, "Good God, what an hour to pay social calls," and after another pause the door opened to reveal a woman in khaki slacks and a rather too large yellow jersey. Her hair was wound round her head in smooth, flat bands away from her broad forehead, and the look of outraged propriety had not swamped the enquiring openness of the wide, lustrous eyes. He hardly recognised her.

"Who the hell are you?" she asked, with engaging forthrightness.

"Jonathan. Lalage wanted her car back."

"Oh, it's you. Sorry. Never told me," she said, standing back to let him enter. "I'm Angela. You remember? Had breakfast? No. I'll just wake Lalage. Again."

"Awake?" Angela enquired, flinging open a bedroom door.

"For morning in the bowl of night has flung the stone which puts the stars to flight," said Jonathan, feeling extraordinarily pleased at his recherché and probably incomprehensible joke.

"Eh?" Angela gave him a hard, curious look as he passed her. He never made out why most people didn't follow his jokes.

This was the Angela of the many husbands, Lalage had said. She kept losing them one way and another. Some died, or got killed. Others disappeared. She looked well on it. She was also very rich, apparently. Not surprising, really.

Lalage was lying back in a bed pushed against the far wall. Her face just perceptively darker than the ivory of her pillows. He went over to her, feeling unaccountably shy and kissed her forehead. She smelt of sleep, flesh and soap, a sweet, fresh smell that mingled with the morning air that had not yet had time to smell of dust, ripe fruit and the deep, rich smell that was an amalgam of all those, of Africa, and the sweat of dark-skinned bodies.

"I like your early-in-the-morning face," he told her.

"Thank you," she said, "and thank Helen and Elizabeth too."

"Who?"

"Rubinstein and Arden, I mean." He sat down on the edge of the bed. Her hands lay by her sides, childlike, outside the sheets. He looked at her hair, massed around her head, giving her an appearance of frailty and softness. There was no facade now at all. She was several years younger, a rebellious child, her eyes glinting with wickedness. She lay there smiling at him

He looked away to the low table where there was an array of miniature animals; a white lion in soap stone; a wooden warthog, its stump of a tail erect; a woebegone giraffe; an ostrich with feathers straggling from its rump; and several obese, sad-looking dogs.

Her eyes followed his. "My frustration beasts," she explained, and suddenly he felt a melting pity for her, that she could not be so natural always, and instead, put on a brittle layer of protection with her make-up.

Her hands rose up and joined behind his neck and he leant forward and held her to him, the soft mounds of her breasts warm through his shirt. It was like holding some delicate wounded creature, knowing that mere touch was of no avail, and the sensation of comfort illusory. Her arms and back felt smoother and softer than any other thing he had ever felt, and at the same time he thought perhaps it has been a long time since she had been held by a lover. A real lover. Not just the sex thing.

"Sorry you're going away today," she said softly after a while and he released her and thought the same. There was also the slight guilty feeling that the men up in the Rift had no such comforts, and that the ghosts of the two dead men still went unplacated. Stupid, he told himself, but it was there with the mess discussions about the lack of women and transport and the other things that helped with morale.

It was priggish and hypocritical too, to think of Uncle Padraig who handed him the old Sam Browne, which he had last worn in Burma, with the words about "looking after the men." But wasn't it really something else, a deeper reason? Wasn't it that this girl was a part of Africa as surely as he was not?

Impulsively he asked, "Don't you miss your father and mother at all?" She smiled her knowing, social smile that ended the mood and the moment, and shook her head slowly.

"Let's be crazy," she said in a louder voice. "Angela's having some people to lunch. Let's make love. She knows about us. No problems. Then let's go out somewhere and forget about everything. I'll get up quick and help and then we'll go. You go and ask Angela if she wants any booze or anything. I don't suppose so because they're the sort of dreary do-gooders who don't."

"What has she asked them for?" Jonathan asked, puzzled.

"Mainly to show them that she isn't mad and her Ruthaka idea is better than talk. They're the type who'll pay a few hundred pounds to fly down to Rhodesia to a do-gooder conference, but as for paying their boys more or building them decent houses, that's different. No one else does, so they can't. But we don't have boys here, so we can't talk really. Now hop in."

Afterwards she let out a whoop of joy. "Ahyeee!"

"Now I'm hungry, my love," she added as she leaned forward to kiss him again. "Off you go, get dressed and chat up Angela. Oh, hell, I forgot. I have to collect some UN people from the airport for Angela."

It rained as they drove off to the airport at lunchtime, and halfway there, the end of the exhaust pipe fell off and lay in the wet road, hissing. The people Lalage half-expected to arrive didn't come and they went off to a hotel outside the city for lunch. The day passed in laughing and talking, eating and playing Russian Billiards with another couple Lalage knew. He was a contract policeman, and she his fiancée.

"I like this," he said, "because back home on Sunday in 'licensed premises', you can't. But you can play Shove Halfpenny, Liar-dice or draughts. Anyway, it's nice to feel debauched," he added.

Jonathan rang the mess to tell Sean Cosgrave, who was giving him a lift up to the Rift camp, where he was. He came to the hotel and stood polishing his eye-glass and saying, "My word," and sipping champagne. Until some people came in and took him off to the bar. After lunch they saw him swept away by a very young brunette in white lace.

"She's new," Lalage said. "On the way back from the Ladies, I heard her say to Sean."

"My dear I'm just a poor, lost charity child, isn't it dreadful?"

"She looks about sixteen," Jonathan said.

"Huh. Could be fifteen. Your chum had better watch it."

Sean came up to them in the coffee lounge. "Who's your girlfriend?" Lalage teased.

"Don't ask," he said with a wicked grin. "Come along, Lieutenant Fitz. We gotta go."

He sat in the back of Sean's old Mercedes. He paid his batman to drive him, and an African to help the batman. As they cruised along, they had an argument about Kenya people.

"A charming place without the settlers and those nasty policemen," he said, and Jonathan turned to look at his horsey face with the Norman nose, deep-set langorous eyes and the girlish cupid's bow lips, and saw that he was serious.

"Sean, isn't that a little unoriginal for you?"

"Oh, I know," he said, flicking ash fastidiously from his Sackville Street tropical suit. "The pioneers may have been well bred, but these uncouth slobs nowadays, my goodness, you only have to look at the amenities they are content to have. The pioneers built the club and there it stops. Beyond a couple of little night-spots where mercifully the poor illumination conceals their wallpaper. And those frightening complexions."

"But the racecourse is good, even if the horses aren't all thoroughbreds. The hospitality of the up-country farmers is exceptional, even though they can't at the moment offer game-shooting as a diversion."

"Bloody bores," Sean grunted.

"You can't expect angels in any colony, Sean. Surely they are as high a standard as in Malaya, and we made better masters than most Europeans, didn't we?"

The sleepy eyes swivelled enquiringly. Jonathan felt embarrassed for a moment, and Sean shook his head. "He can't hear," he said, in a low voice, and above the noise of the road, the batman driver probably couldn't.

"I don't think we understand Afrikaners," Jonathan said,

thinking of all those like Sammy who were not Afrikaners but shared many of their beliefs. "The real ones aren't Europeans at all. Far more African. And do you know that the local natives prefer working for a Boer who takes his coat off and works beside them than our languid, polo stick-swinging sort?"

Sean made a sceptical noise. "No. They are very short-sighted here." He glanced out of the window at the great shadow of the valley on their left. The car was nosing down the steep, and rather dangerous Escarpment road to the floor of the Rift.

"It's very beautiful and all that, but too raw for my taste. There are some charmers about. That girl you brought, and that precocious little thing we met. She was bursting to be off to London. Gaol bait of course. My word."

Jonathan listened with interest. He had wondered how Sean got on with her.

"Deirdre. Quite a good family, but bored stiff here of course. Just been to the States so you can't blame her. She's staying with some coffee baron cousins. I must say it just shows you when you have to take an interest in gaol bait, and here's me trying to be madly interested in the opposite sex to ward off the rumours that I'm queer. But what can one do? There aren't even any brothels and if a girl starts up in the trade, they're so afraid of shaming our white skin before the natives that they deport them. No wonder all the young farm louts are so aggressively randy and the popsies get married at seventeen in self-defence."

"Seems to me," Jonathan said, "that no one has decided what to do with this place. The settlers want to have a majority in Legco..."

"What's that?"

"Legislative Council. Mostly civil servants with a few settler members, one Indian and one nominal native. But the lads in Whitehall refuse to let the settlers spend any money, or get enough votes to do anything much. But since India got independence, all these colonies want it too. It will come here, sooner rather than later."

"Not my bag, old boy. Not going to be here much longer. You thinking of staying?"

Jonathan started, and grunted vaguely. It was getting

270

obvious that he and Lalage were an item. But she refused so far to even visit the camp. Later, she could scarcely refuse to attend the chemin-de-fer evenings in the mess, or the desperate appeals to be a partner at Nairobi parties. Or could she? Looking around the upholstery of the Mercedes he resolved again to make enquiries for a second hand car.

Within a radius of twenty miles from Lake Longeita, two sorts of forward planning were taking place. Both were anguished in different degrees, and both were intensified by the knowledge of the distances that would separate the parties, and of the difficulties of making arrangements in a country of poor communications and sudden, violent changes in weather, circumstances and mood.

"Why does it have to be you?" Alison asked Tom, not for the first time, voicing what had been unsaid all evening. Outside she felt the vast, flat openness of Africa oppressing her, and she hated the dried-up expanses of eye-aching wilderness that were to swallow up Tom Lerrick again. She felt helpless looking at so much emptiness and deadness, and she was glad when the sun went down, blood-red in a haze of cloud behind the hills, and left only its long purple spears, probing up into the huge rain clouds above the lake. At first, she had been impressed by the sight. Now it was somehow threatening. The clouds towered up higher in the sky, looming black and dense as the heat receded and the sky trailed grey streamers of rain far out beyond the hills where the sun had not yet sunk. The dying light, reflected from the sky threw great moving shadows on the surface of the lake, touching the water, already ruffled by the evening breeze, with quick-moving streaks of red and orange. The breeze shook the heads of the papyrus rushes and the light caught the lake birds as they circled and came in to settle on the water. Thousands of flamingos made a huge pinkish stain around the lake edges.

Tom stood behind her at the hotel window. "It frightens me," she said. "I've never seen anything so primitive and ... " She hesitated, afraid of using the wrong words and hurting him, because she was always conscious of his fierce, jealous pride of all things African.

She looked out and up to the great black towers and bastions of cloud that filled the whole western sky now. A thin sickle moon suffused the flat vlei with a pale, hazed radiance picking out the shadows of rock outcrops, clumps of bushes and giant ant-hills eroded into tapering cones of red clay.

"It looks as though Man had never touched it. As though God meant it only as a place for wild things," she murmured. Tom put one arm on her shoulders and stood looking out beside here. "He meant it for us all right," he said. "There's a Somali saying that God made their land on that last day of Creation, and he was in such a hurry he forgot the water. Every time I go up to the Northern Frontier I think of that. One day I'll show you."

She nodded and her fingers curled round his elbow, her arm round his waist, pulling herself into his reassuring bulk. "Coming through the Red Sea on the ship," she mused, "round Cape Guardafui, you wonder how many human beings can bear to live there. Just rocks and hot sand and dust blowing."

"Yes," he said cheerfully, "Here the rain makes plenty kilele.(noise) But it does rain here, at least. And when you know it well, it's not such a wild unfriendly place at all."

"Oh look." Alison clutched him tighter. Far out at the edge of the sky the sun had thrown up a last reflection on the distant clouds, staining them a deep mauve that faded almost at once into darkness again.

"I'll take you on safari soon." he said. "Up in the N.F.D. That's the place for dawns and sunsets. No Mau-Mau either. I've been promising myself a trip there for a long time. Maybe on the way down to the coast at Christmas."

Only Babs and Peregrine would have had wine with curry after those cocktails out on the lawn in the blazing heat. That sensational view over Lake Naivasha. Where there was a lot of noise these days as soldiers chased Mau-Mau into the lake and lost them. And only Babs would have thrown two kikois on the huge Turkish bed and left them to their fate with a gay laugh. They were both relics from the Happy Valley days of the Delameres, Denis Finch Hatton, Joss Errol, Bror and Karen Blixen.

Certainly it was too humid so close to the lake to wear anything else and Babs had a wonderful collection of the bright striped fabrics in Indian cottons and Chinese silks. The one she had on was Chinese, a pale turquoise with broad silver stripes woven into it, with a hem that was three inches of weft unpicked from the weave. Sammy had one of the Indian ones in a mixture of reds, from a dusty pink to a deep purple, in a pattern of intricate squares that crossed and re-crossed each other.

Gillian kneaded the smooth pad of relaxed muscle that sloped away under his arm to the centre of his back. Even in sleep his chest was like a well-filled basket, the frame work distended by the contents. The whole of Sammy's chest was covered with this elastic layer that when you pinched in between finger and thumb, snapped back, pulled by the tautness with which it was stretched across the frame. The top of his back across the shoulders was stippled and rough under the coppery tan, with the remains of a boyhood's heat rashes and sores, insect bites and endless doses of sunburn. His skin was almost like the coat of a young country-bred pony, marked white on the dark sheen with tick-bites, like white freckles. And she knew about most of the scars too. The one on the jaw was the fall from the water-tower, the long one, a raised purple weal on the right shoulder from where Karioki's son slashed him with a panga when they were both about twelve.

He was dead now, Kamau, son of Karioki, killed by his own people up on the reserve while stealing food for his gang. Then the jagged one on the hip was from the time the Land Rover turned over on the coast road: the stitches over his left eye were the same shauri. There were so many round his wrists and forearms that she could only remember the one from the time the baby croc fastened on to him that day at Lake Baringo. Not really very romantic. Tom had made him stand still while he opened the creature's jaws and put it back in the water.

Sammy she could tame in time, though the fierceness and wildness in him was appealing: an explosiveness that fascinated her. Already, since he had been flying he no longer got into fist fights or drank so much. He still got bored very easily, but he wasn't to blame too much for that, and the cures were simple enough. He wouldn't stay long up on the farm by himself anyway. He'd get some old Afrikaner to run it and spend his time off shooting. All the Bobos, Jo-jos, Hanks and Butches would be back soon now the Mau-Mau were getting less dangerous and the hunters would be free to hold their clients' hands again. But that way you had to avoid being fined for overshooting your licence. If you had it suspended, then you hung around the bars trying to get a job as someone's assistant hunter or camp manager. Finally you sold your plot and in no time you had nothing. Sammy needed a woman to keep him steady.

There would be a row with Pa and another with Ma, and another with Tom and lots of advice from everybody, but then it was a bit late for that. Maybe it was the wine at lunch, or the closeness and heat of the day. Maybe it was just the atmosphere of this house with its white walls and airy oriental columns built round the pool and fountain in the centre. There was something very pagan and relaxing about the whole place. You expected to meet someone in a toga around every corner. Or Roman lovers spread-eagled on a couch in a painted alcove with their bare feet dangling over the green and white floor tiles.

She leant over and rubbed her hand on his chest, feeling the sleek black hair, caressing the curly tufts that sprouted around the flat male nipples. He opened one eye and smiled, and was fully awake at once. He rolled over and felt for his watch on the floor, then rolled back, avoiding her eye and grabbing her gently by the hair pushed her back and kissed her.

"Just a minute," Gillian protested, struggling free. "We've got a few things to arrange, haven't we? This sort of thing may be a habit with you, but ..."

"Don't fret, honey," Sam interrupted. "The sooner we can arrange it the better. I need a good strong wanawouki (woman) up there anyway to look after my thingira. I'll have them start a hut for you right now."

She lifted one hand to cuff him, but he caught her wrist and she was not quite quick enough with the other hand so had to kick him instead. They rolled about struggling and ended up with Sam pinioning her to the bed. "Sammy, how many goats will I be worth to my poor father when you have finished with me?"

"Nary a one," he answered cheerfully, "He'll have to make me a handsome present for me to take you off his hands. When do I see him." "You'd better come down on Wednesday. I'll invent a party I met you at in town this weekend. Lala will back me up. You'd better get the banns organised and all that so we can race round together that evening and put them up, and fix a date for about six weeks if I can talk the parents into it."

"Suits me fine," he said, lifting up her chin. "But you better make it two months. Give me time to build the odd bedroom or two. Ay?"

"No, Sam. Come on, boy. I've got two hours driving to do and I don't want Pa asking me where I've been." Meekly, he let her go. I think I can handle him she thought. It won't be too easy, but I can break him in slow, and I don't want him too tame anyhow. He's just like a cub without a mother, really. Just mother him a bit and he goes all woozy; not being used to it.

Whatever he got from Carlotta and her ilk, they didn't mother him for sure. Just screwed him, I suppose. There was that queer tender look in his eye that went with the twitch of the nostril, that was the nearest he got to showing emotion. She had pierced that armour. He would never be the same again with her now because he had let her see the little boy hiding behind the thrust-out jaw and the set lips. It was the same little boy who for as long as she could remember had been putting frogs and grass snakes down her back and pulling her hair.

He was sitting in the window embrasure looking out of the window. She went over and pulled both his ears. There was an odd, puzzled expression on his face when he turned, that was part admiration, part something else that instinct told her was going to be good.

"It's going to rain like hell," he said, with an unfamiliar catch in his voice. "It's going to be a long rainy season up there waiting." She bent over his shoulder and kissed him hard on the mouth.

"You're going to be busy, my boy. I want a big store as well as a proper kitchen, and a stove and boiler for hot water and at least three rooms with a big fireplace in every one."

"Hey, steady on, girl. I haven't even got drinking water piped in yet."

"What do you use, then?"

"Boil stuff from the river."

"Well, better get some piping put in. What about a dam?" He groaned.

"In the middle of the rains? My oath, woman, you don't want much."

"You'll find out," she said hugging him. "I'm going to be a difficult girl to please. Now let's go and see if Babs and Perry are back. And you can hop it while I get dressed." Obediently he went, turning at the door to blow her a kiss. I wonder, she thought, as he shut the door, how long it was since he did that?

She watched from the window as he went across the lawn to join their hosts. They were lounging by the swimming pool, sipping drinks as though the world was still a peaceful, untroubled place. Their butler came out to the tinkling of a bell. A rifle was propped against the sunshade. Perry had been a hunter pre-war. Then, with Tom and David Stirling in North Africa, had been captured twice and both times escaped. Not a man to waste ammunition. Well, she sighed, one day soon, we shan't need to carry guns all day and all night.

CHAPTER TWENTY ONE

ALISTAIR

"The idle life I lead
Is like a pleasant sleep,
Wherein I rest and heed
The dreams that by me sweep."

Herrick

Red Troop was re-allocated a patrol area in the high country that sloped out in a broad offshoot of the Great Rift, up through thick rain forest to the Masai Plain. There were wide expanses of newly opened farming country between the forest and the plain, and the only road grew so muddy and rutted that farmers were dragging their cars up to their farms with tractors. Forty-eight hour foot patrols were ordered, but, despite the incessant rain, Jonathan was so fascinated by the high altitude country, a mile and a half above sea level on the Equator, that he occasionally stayed out, camping at a farm for a double period. But he was tiring of the tension and the constant state of apprehension.

A sawmill and a farm were burnt down by Mau-Mau one morning while the patrol was sleeping in a barn. The tracker came running in to say there was a gang in a wood near the farm. By the time Jonathan had deployed the troop around the wood, five local farmers, the policeman and district officer had arrived and crashed into the trees firing like maniacs and throwing hand grenades they had begged from the soldiers. Jonathan saw one farmer armed with a sawn-off shotgun and a Luger go plunging into the trees shouting in Swahili, and a few minutes later the same man came running out holding one arm that was bleeding, throw down his weapons and shout at a soldier to lend him a Sten.

Someone said he was the one whose farm had been burnt. Only three Mau-Mau emerged from the wood alive. About twenty bodies were recovered. The incident, the noise and the sudden savagery left Jonathan disturbed. Not as shocked as before. He was accustomed to the violence. Three of the farmers went off afterwards without even saying good morning, and the atmosphere saddened him.

Apart from that there were two other curious incidents which enlivened the long hours plodding in the streaming rain.

The first occurred one day far out where the last farm and American missionaries houses ended and the real bush began. For once it was not raining, although the clouds were gathering as usual to the west over Lake Victoria and to the south over the vast Serengeti Plain.

They had left the forest fringe that morning with cloud looming, black and imminent over the Mau-Mau Escarpment. As they left the shelter of the tall, liana-clad podocarpus and the thick cypress-like trees, the cloud burst and the rain crashed down, as though the sky had split a few feet overhead, and let fall a solid mass of dark, condensing water, extending upwards to an unknown height, as vast and unimaginable as the sea.

It stopped as suddenly and they had met the usual groups of natives, their ragged clothes emanating a damp, acrid smell of fire smoke and sweat as they stood to have their passes checked. The sun blazed down spasmodically, making the sodden earth steam, and drawing a scent from it of deep, peppery green richness.

They were sitting down waiting to go back to a farm for the night when a tall lithe figure carrying a spear sauntered out from behind a bush a hundred yards away. Flett shouted at him and he dropped immediately on all fours. Then seeing the soldiers he walked arrogantly towards them holding his spear in one extended hand tucked closely into his side. Wiping the sweat from under his sodden bush hat, Jonathan studied the man.

"Better 'ave that prodder off 'im Sir." Flett warned, and moved towards the man.

"Wait," Jonathan said, "Get Chepkoin." But when the tracker came and spoke in Swahili he elicited no response at all and looked thoroughly frightened.

The stranger stood with a disinterested and haughty expression on his face while Jonathan stared at him. He was over six feet tall of slim build, and wore nothing over his coppery skin except a dull red cloth hanging from one shoulder and a thong around his hips, with a brown leather pouch like an over-ripe fig hanging at one side. Over one shoulder he carried a folded blanket. His face had high, prominent cheek bones, narrowed eyes, a long thin nose and a thin-lipped mouth compressed in contempt. His hair was caked in red mud and primped up like a wig with furrows running from back to front coming to a point in the centre of his high forehead. There were beads and copper wire round his neck, some circling it and some hanging down like a dowager's pearls. On both wrists and around his left bicep were strips of leather worked with brilliant blue and white beads. The spear protruded a foot above his head. The blade was about three feet long and brightly polished. The haft had a bound hand-grip and the metal above and below the grip was perfectly round and symmetrical for a hand's length, then tapered down to a blunt butt.

"Can't you speak any Masai?" Jonathan asked Chepkoin who grinned unhappily and said a few halting words to the man who answered in a high, rapid stream of words without looking at any of them. After a few exchanges Chepkoin reported that the man's manyatta (home) was near the Hill of Lions in the Serengeti.

"Damned helpful," Jonathan commented. "Ask if he saw any Mau-Mau and tell him he must come with us and give us his spear to carry."

But the man had lost interest completely and refused to answer any more. Jonathan was tempted to tell the Masai to clear off, but the area was a closed one and he had no business in it, and no papers. Also, several of the local terrorists dressed like Masai and a gang had recently murdered two water engineers from a civilian firm.

"I'll have a go," MacNamara said. "Come on, you nice

bloody savage, or I'll give ye an unmerciful skelp," he said soothingly and grasped the spear.

The Masai grunted and stepped back, wrenching it free and clutching it to him, the muscles in his arm tensed. Hating to do it, and feeling his helplessness in the face of primitive dignity, Jonathan said, "I'm going to fire one round. When he jumps, grab."

He cocked the Webley, without drawing it, and fired through the holster into the ground. Flett leapt forward and grabbed the spear from the Masai's uplifted hand. MacNamara threw himself at him and two of the men pinioned his arms. He still showed no fear, but wrestled fiercely, his teeth bared and a look of elemental hatred in his rolling eyes.

Jonathan wished more than ever that he had let him go. Probably the man would never forget this insult. What did he know or care of the Emergency Regulations? And, for that matter, what did bureaucracy care? What would they know of Rousseau's Noble Savage? He kicked himself all the way down to the police post where the Masai was questioned by an interpreter.

"Quite right to bring him in, old boy," the Inspector said, while the prisoner stood erect and as aloof as an ancient Egyptian god. The Inspector was a Sikh, and very regimental in smart khakis ironed to knife edges. He spoke with a cut glass accent.

"Sam Singh," he said. "In case you wondered. Yes, Balliol."

The Masai's name was Kura Ole Olgaraini and his manyatta was in or near a place called Ol Karok in Tanganyika, and he had come to visit his brother and said he was lost.

"A likely story," Sam Singh sniffed. "Masai moran don't get lost. Tell him that," he said, waving his cigarette at the interpreter. "It might cheer the miserable blighter up." The interpreter told him, but there was no flicker of an expression on the Masai's face.

"He's a bit too damn cool, this one," he told Jonathan. "Some of these chaps have Kikuyu relations and they aren't so damn simple as they look. How has he kept his hairdo so nice and dry? He's been sleeping in huts here and there. It always amazes me how the Micks get their messages passed on, and it won't hurt to put this one in the cooler."

"Lock him up?" Jonathan said dubiously. It seemed to him that to question him and attempt to reduce such a magnificent creature into a caged, dumb animal was as pointless as feeding a leopard on milk. To lock him up would be a terrible experience for him.

"Just until his messages get stale. Teach him to wander about without a pass. Cheeky sod, anyway. He must know some Swahili, or how does he buy the snuff in that bag? Says he doesn't know quite where his brother lives." He paused and looked at the man, inhaled his cigarette deeply and sighed.

"Brother," he exclaimed with heavy irony. "Ndugu," he spoke to the man in Swahili.

"Who is my brother?" he asked. Like Pontius Pilate. "Everyone in the bloody tribe is their ndugu. These warrior moran types can sleep with lots of women. They're riddled with syphilis too. Brother. They don't know who the hell in their brother and who isn't. But," he added gently, "I suppose it's rather touching, really."

Jonathan felt that it was sad rather than touching and he was sorry about the whole business. He got up to go, telling himself it was sentimental to have an irrational pity on anyone who was likely to be helping to arrange an ambush or raid a farm. The inspector screwed back the top of his pen, picked up his papers and motioned to the two police askaris who gripped the prisoner's arm and lead him to the door.

"Tell him," the inspector called out, "that we'll let him have his spear back. Later."

He turned to Jonathan. "You can't help admiring them for walking about in the bush with only those things." But Jonathan was watching the man who had turned at the door to give him a look of piercing hatred. The Inspector chuckled and dug him in the ribs.

"Doesn't like you much, that chap," he said.

The second incident took place later in the same week, and he always thought of it afterwards as one of the oddest encounters he experienced in Africa.

281

They had been in no hurry that particular day since it was the end of the week and transport was coming to meet them on the next day. They had been diverted however from the direction of the road by Chepkoin's discovery of a recent camp site, with fire ashes still warm.

Since the incident in the wood the troop considered itself as having evened the score on behalf of their casualties, and there was no great enthusiasm to follow up. So when Chepkoin lost the spoor in the rain-soaked ground, they turned willingly back towards the road. At seven o'clock, as the sky turned blue-black and a deep, woolly dusk descended on them, they were still going downhill through the forest fringes.

When they emerged into open fields the night was pitch-black without a trace of a star. At the first farm building they came to, a farm-guard armed with a panga, seeing them, let out a piercing screech and an arrow whistled past Jonathan's ear before he or anyone else could shout. Then he and Chepkoin both shouted together, "Rafiki" and "Askari," and walked over into the light of a fire to be seen.

At this moment a European voice said "Ah, soldjahs. Er, do come in, won't you?" Jonathan saw a tall, stooping young man standing at the corner of a shed. He explained that he had twenty-two men with him and would like to use the phone to confirm his position, and possibly sleep the night in a barn. The European ushered all of them into a large kitchen and produced a crate of beer, taking Jonathan with him to the phone. First he had phoned someone himself, about which store sheds could be used. Someone Jonathan supposed, from his tone, to be a partner. He certainly did not look like a farmer except in dress, but Jonathan presumed he was one of the cheque book variety, although he looked very young even for that.

He introduced himself as Alistair and asked Jonathan to join him for dinner. He went out with him to arrange for the men to use a stove in a shed outside, lending them Dietz and hurricane lamps and generally being more helpful even than the average local settler. In the end he overdid it slightly, fussing round with unnecessary advice and oddments to supplement the men's rations. Eventually he took Jonathan into the main living room and gave him a drink, by which time Jonathan's tongue was feeling shrivelled.

After the drink Jon began to notice that the room was unusual for a farmhouse. The ornaments and pictures would have done credit to a junior Oxford don. Looking at him closer in the better light, that was what Alistair resembled, apart from the khaki trousers and possibly the suede chukka boots and open neck. His face was heavily freckled, with a high forehead, a large nose, humorous grey eyes behind rimless glasses, and a mouth that grimaced oddly as he drawled out the words in a lazy, deep Oxonian accent.

As he went out again to see his cook, Jonathan looked around him, intrigued. The room was panelled in some local, polished wood, and most of the paintings were propped on shelves, their white frames and light sunny colours pleasantly relieving the darkness of the wood. They were mostly oil paintings by talented amateurs, predominantly Mediterranean scenes, with much sea, sky and blinding white groups of buildings. Among them were scattered two types of weirdly assorted objets d'art. Mostly Victorian; an ostrich egg mounted on a stand surmounting a gunmetal clock, an epèrgne, the glass flute held in filigreed silver, a brace of hand-embroidered fire-screens and a saddle shabrach embroidered in gold wire on dark blue velvet, two glass domes containing stuffed birds and wax-fruit, and a display of elaborate custard-cups, fruit and sweet bowls and moustache cups. Then native woodcarvings, busts and wall masks in ebony and a light-grained, waxed mavuli wood. On a table, books in new dust jackets piled among old copies of the airmail "Times," and magazines, including "Encounter" and the New Statesman."

In the bookcase Jonathan noticed among other recherché works, "The Unquiet Grave", "The White Goddess", and Talmon's "Totalitarian Democracy". Was he a young don spending the long vacation with his farmer parents? But surely in April it was too early for that? Apprehensively he sat down again contemplating the possibility of enduring an evening in heavy political and philosophical discussion. After months of soldiers' company and language he felt more like a good night's sleep. He did look forward however to discovering more about his host.

Alistair bustled in and began more or less talking to himself on the subject of wine. "Not much choice, in fact," he concluded. "Not a bad little claret even if, er-um, well I always distrust even numbers after '45, '47, '49 and '51 were all such good years weren't they?"

Without waiting for the reply he scurried off again to return to fill Jonathan's glass and turn on a radiogram. The record turned out to be a series of seventeenth century songs accompanied by a spinet or a harpsichord, and Alistair provided a spasmodic commentary.

"A roundelay," he explained, "A poem. Donne, you know," and sat back taking ecstatic puffs from his pipe. "Good stuff, this Restoration work," he told his guest. "Purcell and those chaps. This one's by Phillip Trevor. He was a page at Charlie Two's court. And this one's a typical Ground. The theme recurrent in the base." The record ended with a minuet and a duet, "Man was made for woman," at which Alistair snorted as he turned the instrument off,

"Hah, was he indeed?" O God, Jonathan thought. One of those.

"Now tell me about yourself over dinner," he invited, adding, "Once I start you won't hear anything else all evening. The only snag up here. No audience. Except a tape-recorder of course. An excellent cure, that." He chuckled and rang a bell on the table that stood at one end of the room away from the fire.

To his amazement it was the best dinner Jonathan had eaten since leaving London. Iced melon was followed by enormous globe artichokes in butter, with a stronger flavour than any he had ever tasted. The vegetables and meat had an earthy farm taste and, instead of the eternal fruit salad, a soufflé appeared.

"Used to work on a ship, that cook," Alistair said. "I suspect he's wanted for some abominable crime, and that's why he works up-country."

Not greatly to his surprise he found Alistair to be a Christchurch man who had emigrated to get away from the welfare state, and had spent some time in India, South Africa and Rhodesia before settling in Kenya. When Jonathan asked him his profession he smiled resignedly and said, "Commerce."

"You mean you're a trader?" Alistair shook his head, subjected the cork from the wine bottle to a careful scrutiny, and replied, "No. Merely the wage slave, selling, against considerable opposition and at outrageous prices, various commodities essential to the farming community."

Then he changed the subject, pressing Jonathan for details of his army life.

"You know," he said wistfully, "It must be rather quaint to be a soldier in a colony like this. I mean, the Army being a society within a society, and society here being like a honeycomb, you are one more utterly separate cell. People like myself are cells too."

He paused, offered Jonathan a cigar, lit one himself and made his way over to an easy chair, after ringing the bell for coffee.

He went on. "It's an interesting subject, Comparative Imperialism. You could write a thesis on it and submit yourself to All Souls to become a Fellow when you go back."

Jonathan replied, "I can't think for the life of me, why you don't do exactly that."

Perhaps he was wanted for some "abominable crime", or hadn't paid his taxes or his bookmakers before he left England?

Jonathan shifted uncomfortably in his chair. "Do they make the natives comfortable here?" he asked, as pleasantly as he could.

"Of course not," Alistair said. "Where are we supposed to find the money? This farmhouse I rent, for example. This was the manager's house, but they can't afford one now. They employ over a hundred male natives who do the work of ten competent English farm labourers, and, counting repairs to mistreated machinery, at twice the cost. It's the same in business. A lot of the managerial staff out here wouldn't keep a job as ledger clerks in London. It's a glorious muddle, with third rate administrative misfits like myself making it far worse."

He laughed so much that he had to take his misted glasses off and wipe them.

"I'm not quite clear as to why you think it's any better than the other two systems," Jonathan said.

"Oh, the people, the gentry you see. The dear, old muddly English gentry. There's nothing else here except farming really, no mines or manufacturing to speak of."

"Seems to me," Jonathan said, "There is no long long term policy. When independence comes, a lot of these farmers will quit, won't they?"

"Dead right," Alistair said. "Ten out of ten."

He stopped to wave to the houseboy to bring glasses, and poured out some brandy. Jonathan excused himself both to have a pee and see if Sergeant MacNamara or the men had any complaints. Alistair had told him to ask the NCOs in for a drink, but he knew that they would be bored stiff listening to the conversation, so between them they compromised by giving them half a bottle of whisky to finish round the stove in the kitchen.

When he got back, Alistair showed him where he could sleep.

Jonathan asked, "Why, in view of the idyllic picture you just painted of Kenya, is there a revolt here, and not in Rhodesia or South Africa?"

"Good question," Alistair said, just like his tutor, Jonathan thought. "The quick answer is because no one expected it here. They let back into the country Moscow-trained agitators like Jomo Kenyatta, and let them organise unmolested. They wouldn't get away with it anywhere else, certainly not in French, Belgian or Portuguese territory. Then you have to remember that Mau-Mau only affects one tribe and is basically a reversion to savagery, and a rejection of missionaries, caused by sheer boredom. All that stuff about land starvation is cock. They want employment, I agree, but you talk to captured terrorists and see how much they talk about land. They want to be left alone to live in their own tribal way. Kenyatta is a clever chap. He has a firm policy. When he comes out of prison he'll be a hero."

"But what brought you here?" Jon asked.

Alistair saw what he was fencing at straight away. "Plain economics, old chap. A higher salary, plus cost of living allowances, instead of pigging it in a tiny flat in London. As for the rest, I find the climate here agreeable and the scenery not unlike Greece or Spain. Where you have poverty you at least have beauty. Anyway the sort of beauty that lies in the wilderness. I tried other places, but this is the most beautiful and the people nicest."

"But aren't you rather compelled to behave like an ostrich to live here as you do?" Jonathan enquired dubiously.

Alistair smiled. "Believe me," he said with emphasis, "It saddens me much less to live here than it did to live elsewhere in Africa, and considerably less than if I lived in, say, Notting Hill Gate. I can't change anything much myself, and its no good shouting, 'White Man Go Home' at me, because I don't own any land and a black government tomorrow wouldn't affect me. It's the difference you see, between the humanist approach on the one hand and the two extremes, sentimental and economic on the other. I hope I'm a humanist."

His cigar had gone out, and as he attempted to re-light it with a taper from the log fire, Jonathan noticed that he was tipsy. His perception must be getting blunt, too.

"I don't follow you," he said, "What great difference is there between the sentimental or the economic view of the situation here, and your own?"

The cigar glowed again. Alistair poured himself another brandy after Jonathan had shaken his head. This time his hand was quite steady.

He stood up, stretched and threw another log on the fire.

"Surely there is something positive for everyone to do?" Jonathan said, thinking of Ruthaka and Tom Lerrick's co-operative coffee farm. Alistair looked down at him sharply.

"You mean the commercials? The expense sheet and free car wallahs like me?" he said fiercely. "The answer is no, not being bloody politicians. Nothing beyond trying to get our labour paid more." He kicked the pile of logs in front of the fire.

"I pay a boy aged ten to chop those. Ten bob a month. Otherwise he'd just be herding for his parents for nothing. His grandmother, the oldest Wa'Ndrobo hag you ever saw, collects kindling for another ten. In all I employ four totally unnecessary menials, to help the other two, and salve my conscience."

Alistair paused in the filling of his glass, blinked and continued.

"Don't despair," he said bitterly. "As the old Kuwaiti Arab said to Freya Stark, about 1920. 'No Ma'am, we're not quite civilised here yet. We don't make our own poison gas'."

He went over to the radiogram and put on an Eartha Kitt record. The deep purple tones quavered and throbbed plangently around the room, smothering the air with its sad, longing sentiment and acrid wit. Jonathan sat, trying to think whether the choice was meant to convey anything to him, but Alistair remained slumped in the armchair with his legs slung negligently one over the other and his eyes shut.

When the record ended, he stirred and said "Bedtime. I'm going duck shooting in Karamoja tomorrow. My office thinks I'm going to Kisumu, so I'd better get away before they ring."

"You must come round to our camp and have a meal some time," Jonathan said. Alistair closed his eyes sleepily and breathed "Thank you." As he led Jonathan to his room he gripped his arm and said dreamily, "I once visited a factory in the Midlands. A noisier, hotter, smellier and dirtier place I never hope to see again. Most of the workers were black. Bantus, like these. Mostly from the West Indies, no doubt."

He yawned cavernously. "I wonder if they were really any better off after they'd paid for their rent, rates, coal, gas, electricity, food, clothes and bus fares. Eight hours of torture every day. I wonder."

Jonathan didn't reply.

"Goodnight," Alistair said. As he went off down the passage Jonathan heard him saying aloud to himself, "I wonder. I wonder."

PART THREE

END OF MISSION

CHAPTER TWENTY TWO

WINDING DOWN

"Jog on, jog on, the footpath way,
And merrily hent the stile-a;
A merry heart goes all the day,
Your sad tires in a mile-a."

Shakespeare

Early next morning Jonathan's troop reached the road where transport was waiting to take them back to camp. Alistair never visited the mess. Later Jonathan found that he had the reputation of being a misogynist and hermit, who never mixed with the local farming community or came to any of the country clubs. Or the Saturday afternoon and Sunday morning polo games.

Months later, after Jonathan acquired a 1939 Chevrolet, with a thirsty V-8 engine, in order to visit Lalage in Nairobi, he went up the winding, rocky, rutted track to Alistair's house one evening to find him at a typewriter, morosely playing back verse to himself from a tape-recorder. They talked about miscegenation, psychology and ballet, but Alistair remained lethargic and detached, and Jonathan, tiring of his company left early. He never saw him again except on one occasion months later down at the coast, on a long weekend, when he passed him one evening at sundown, walking in the surf chanting to himself in what to Jonathan sounded uncommonly like Greek. He caught the words "borboros" and "temenos." Alistair did not recognise him and he felt there would be little point in interrupting his declamations, which evidently carried him away. "Poppy or snow," somebody said.

But, as Alistair said, Mau-Mau seemed to be on the wane. As the months of patrolling went by, there was less and less contact or ambushes. The farm labour who previously supported them and on occasion joined them, no longer did so. Many surrendered under the terms of the "Green Branch" agreement and a deputation went into the forest to discuss the ending of the uprising with the remaining "Generals". Gradually the slashing and hamstringing of stock ceased to be commonplace and few farms were raided. In two and a half years less than thirty civilians had been murdered by Mau-Mau, although nearly 300 Police and troops had been killed in action. So they were told at Army briefings.

So far, over twelve thousand Africans were known to have been murdered by Mau-Mau, and nearly all of these were Kikuyu. Nearly six hundred native police, soldiers and home guards had been killed, between 1950 and 1954. Twenty-five thousand Africans joined the Administrative Home Guard. Of twenty-five shousand "activists," the polite government word for terrorists, about eight thousand Mau-Mau were killed. Eighty-five thousand Kikuyu were in detention camps awaiting the long process of distinguishing the hard core who had taken the more advanced and complicatedly bestial oaths, from those who had joined merely for excitement. Or had helped in some way, or merely been identified by the white hooded collaborators, as having taken one or more oaths.

Jonathan, increasingly exhausted by endless patrols, began to spend weekends with Sam Webb and Lalage on his neglected farm. Talk swung more often to 'after the Emergency.' "Makes you smile," Sam said, as they walked around his weed overgrown coffee bushes. "They really made their point, our Kikuyu brothers. Now the Brits are sending out more experts than ever. Met one yesterday. Straight out of Cirencester. Told me he gets a bonus if he stays for his whole two-year contract."

"Problem is," Lalage explained, "they have to let them out of the detention camps now, back to the reserves where the chiefs don't need them. But as yet no one dares take Kikuyu houseboys and cooks back inside the house."

"Puzzles me," Jonathan said, "why you all look down on

the Lake tribes and don't employ them."

"We don't look down honey. It's not that. The Kikuyu are tough, hardy folk, whereas down around the lake they have a lousy humid climate and malaria, bilharzia and trachoma."

"I do love it when you talk so technical," Jonathan said, and Lalage let go of his hand and picked up a stone.

"Watch it, soldier. We memsaabs aren't quite civilised." No answer to that, Jonathan thought, and took the stone away.

"Well, I can leave beasts out at night again now," Sam said, "and I think I will be able to harvest vegetables next year."

They took him one rainy day up on to the Mau Escarpment where there was a group of European pioneers living in mud and dagga shacks, with their machinery, tarpaulin covered, parked outside with their trucks. They were tilling virgin land, some of it for tea, but with a plan they were shown, with contour terracing against erosion and channels for storm water and irrigation in the long dry season. "Looks good to me," Jonathan said, but he did wonder why they were still all Europeans. He had expected some Kikuyu among them, but he only saw a few labourers and drivers.

"Yields here," Sam said, "about a quarter by weight of European. Not much humus. Sun sterilises the soil. Rains wash the topsoil off. You can tell it ain't much good, because if it was, someone would have worked it earlier."

The view from the Escarpment was a bit like Cumberland or the Dublin mountains. Bare and windswept, no cottages, hedges, walls, sheep pens and winding lanes. There didn't seem much difference to farming here or in Europe. And a damned sight less rain to cope with here. Sun, he could live with that.

"Don't get much game up here, either," Sam explained. "Something to do with vertical sunlight, being on the Equator. Damn cold at night. Look, over there."

Jonathan squinted. In the middle distance, there were groups of zebra, giraffe and some kind of gazelle, Thompson's or Grant's, but they were a long way down in the valley, where the grass was thicker.

Sam hadn't begun a real house. He had built a cowshed, a

barn and stables. He had slept in a hammock in a tree or when it rained, in a mud hut with an elegant reed thatch roof. He would start to build with stone soon. "Bedrooms for all, with running water, I hope. This is base camp," he explained.

"Don't tell that to Gillian," his sister warned.

"What does that mean, young lady?"

"It means, buster, that girls like a man who lives in some place and not just a guy who come and hangs up his hat and leaves his junk around and then goes. Get it into the skull, darling."

"You Kenyans," Jonathan told them, "are a funny lot."

"Watcha mean?" Sam demanded.

"You are, well, more like Americans, mad about guns and hunting and slaughtering the natives." Sam looked quite pleased. "Nothing wrong with that," he grinned.

Jonathan went down to Nairobi on his precious "forty-eights" as often as he could, and earned another rebuke from Tim Collins as a result. By now, Tim knew that Lalage was serious about Jon, although he would never in a million years let any jealousy show. One day they went down together with a much-bandaged Cosgrave. The latter had thrown a grenade which, hitting the branch of a tree, had rebounded and exploded near him.

"A typical, fatuous Cosgrave thing to do," Tim commented. "He says he threw it at a terrorist, but from what his sergeant said, or didn't say, I gather he was just making a bang to impress the men."

"Neither of you," Tim said, before Cosgrave arrived that day, "seem to appreciate what we have to put up with having national service clowns like you with us."

Jonathan said nothing, feeling guilty because he was wangling his third "forty-eight" that month and he knew that Tim had heard about a terrorist at whom Jonathan had taken first shot on a patrol the week before, and missed. He found later that he had been using a rifle whose battle-sights were marked. " Do not use."

In the event he did not have to wait until Cosgrave had gone. He got drunk at dinner on his dining-out night, and in his speech he said that the Army was reviving useless traditions and snobbery which had been cut out during The War, and that he was glad to see that the men accepted officers who had no use for old fashioned class consciousness. He went on to say that he thought he was as good as anyone in the regiment, that he had earned his place at UCD, Dublin. And that he hoped one day to have the pleasure of selling them all an expensive car, or something.

"You see," Tim said afterwards, "he got a commission just to prove that he was as good as us, and for the money, of course. The men knew that and they could hardly love him for it. But what I'll never forgive him for was for agreeing with some local in a bar, that it was solely due to the stuffy priggishness of the average ex-officer-cum-settler that Mau-Mau had ever started."

"He said to me once," Jonathan said, 'Youse are stuck-up sissies all right, playing polo and not going with black women.'"

Nairobi was buzzing with the news of Gillian Lerrick's engagement to Sam Webb.

Lalage was enthusiastic about it, rather to Jonathan's surprise.

"They'd both get into trouble on their own sooner or later, and it will curtail Sam's jaunts into the bush a bit," she said in explanation. Sam asked them all up to see the progress on the plot. It was arranged that Lalage should drive up with Gillian and collect Jonathan in two week's time. Now the rains were over, the days were going faster and faster. Soon he would have been out for a year and in six months he could leave the army for good.

Lalage. Outwardly she was a bright, chic young woman, and they were happy together, but there was always that shadow. That one day he would leave, and she would certainly stay. Several times she told him how much she would like to spend a morning in Oxford Street, or a week of theatre-going in the West End.

"Well, why not? Now the Emergency is ending, you deserve it," Jonathan would say and she would smile sweetly and promise to spend six months in England. She didn't get on too well with her father, that he knew. There was friction too with her mother.

Questioning her gently one day, she flew at him saying, "Yes. Of course I'd like to live a nice easy life in England, but not now, not with all this here to battle with. What on earth could I do in England of any use? I'm an African."

One day in her flat, Tim had brought a tough, red-faced, husky girl who roared with laughter at everything. Tim talked to Lalage, while Jonathan watched, smiling to himself. He overheard Tim say to Angela, "I have an idea, if you don't mind me saying so, that your activities in that African school place… could be seen to have an ulterior motive."

"What the hell do you mean?" Angela snapped.

"Well, are you just teaching bibis pottery and weaving or…"

"You watch it, Captain. You have no idea how little the bloody stupid Administration have done to educate these people. They leave it mostly to missionary schools." She grabbed his arm and steered him off to a corner out of earshot.

Waiting for Lalage next day, he met Gillian in Torr's Hotel bar. She seemed radiant but with a new steadiness below the shilly-shally, a wise air of womanhood. She startled him by asking, "Jon. Are you looking around here?"

"What for?" he asked stupidly, but it was Sunday lunchtime and it was easier in the heat than thinking. A few months earlier she would have hacked his shin, but now she merely looked patient and said, "You don't seem to realise laddie, that you are the first thing in pants that Lalage's looked at twice in nearly two years. If you think *she* will abandon us here…well, think again."

He looked at her hard. Her bare shoulders were a magnificent tawny gold under the crisp, corn-coloured hair. He wondered how often she would wear that silly white straw hat up on the farm. There was a heat rash under her ear and for the first time he noticed that her neck was a bit too long. "I know that very well." he said, and she pursed her lips and looked away. Before he left with Lalage she came up to him again. "Africa does something to everybody," she said, with a radiant smile that didn't look forced. "They say you always come back in the end."

"She's right," Lalage said. "We need people like you. I must get you to meet Grogs, the chap who owns Torr's. He spent fifty years fighting the government for permits to open up forests and to let him build dams and expand farms. He's eighty now, and still slogs away creating thousands of jobs."

"You mean the Cape-to-Cairo Grogan?"

"The one and only."

"I would like to meet him."

"I'll fix it."

She did, and Jonathan listened to him, still lucied in his eighties, explaining how he had battled for twenty years to get the railway extended to the Nandi Forest to get the timber out. Now the railway was extended right up to Kampala, but in Whitehall they had dubbed it the 'Lunatic Line.'

"They accused me of wanting only a means of making money from timber. I had seven saw mills at one time. And now there are twelve thousand farms up there using the railway."

He showed his maps of the estate down at Taveta at only two thousand five hundred feet above sea level, where he had damned the river Ruvu and Lake Jipe. "They told me I could not grow anything at that altitude. Too low. No Europeans lived there. I cleared 30,000 acres and grew sisal, beans, cotton, citrus, linseed, maize, pineapples, avocado pears, paw-paw, black mint, lavender and asparagus. Eliminated the tsetse-fly. The Colonial Office have a lot to answer for."

"Wow," was all Jonathan could think of saying. Grogan smiled, his craggy, seamed face splitting with laughter as he sucked on a *Juliet y Romeo*. "I told them twenty years ago to educate the natives or there would be big trouble." He paused dramatically. "Now they've got it. And the joke is that at one time the Jews were interested in Taveta, as a new homeland. The Rothschilds came out to look at it. Some came and started fishponds. Then the London lot accused me of hogging the water, so I gave up in 1945 on my seventy-first birthday. Balls to the lot of 'em. I offered them a fifty-room house as an agricultural training college. But they refused."

"Why on earth?"

"Same people would not let locals grow coffee. It might

make some of them rich."

"Unbelievable."

"Stick around, lad," Grogan said. "You'll learn a lot."

CHAPTER TWENTY-THREE

PIONEERING

"Siku njema huonikana asubuhi."
A good day becomes evident in the morning.

Swahili proverb

Two days before he was due to visit Sam Webb's farm again, Jonathan ran into Tom Lerrick in the Thompson's Falls police post. He was thinner, and his face was almost gaunt, with the skin round his eyes wrinkled and black. He looked as though he should have gone to bed and be put to sleep for a week. He only managed a faint smile and when Jonathan told him that his sister and Lalage were coming up on Friday, he took scant interest. Jonathan piloted him into the nearest bar and persuaded him to have a whisky, but he refused a second.

"Look," Jonathan said, "why not ring up Alison and get her to come?" Tom shook his head wearily, his eyes unfocusing. Suddenly he put his elbows on the bar in front of him and let his head sink down between his shoulders. It was so unlike him that Jonathan felt almost embarrassed. After a moment or two, Tom raised his head, licked his lips and said in a hoarse, hesitant voice, "I don't want to see anyone just now, Jon, thanks. I..." He left the sentence unfinished and, picking up his Padgett, slid off the stool. Jonathan took hold of his wrist.

"I'm going to ring Lalage and ask her to bring Alison up here," he said firmly.

"You need a rest, badly. If you don't relax, you'll crack up." A spasm of anger passed over Tom's face, and then he slowly swung his leg back over the stool.

"I've never been so ... so bone weary," His voice rose in pitch, "So bloody well browned off with the blasted natives in this God-damned country. I'm sorry," he said.

"Whiski mbili," he snapped at the Indian barman. He looked Jonathan in the eyes briefly, and dropped his head again. Jonathan was beginning to think how he could contact a doctor without any fuss.

"I've lost half my ruddy patrol," Tom said, his chin propped on the bar," and...Oh hell. You'd better get me out of here soon, or I'll have to be carried."

They carried him to the doctor's house, and when he woke up he started to shout and tried to get out of the barred window. They gave him a sedative and he slept until Friday lunchtime, nearly forty-eight hours. When Lalage arrived at four, Jonathan was overjoyed to see that Alison had come too. Tom got into the car without a word, slumping into the back seat next to Alison, and when Gillian had disentangled herself from him they left them alone and went shopping because Gillian had a list Sam had sent her that included two camp beds and a tin bath.

"Better get some food, too," Lalage said, "or we'll be living off waterbuck steaks and tinned bangers. Doesn't Tom look terrible? Have you two been drinking?"

The doctor had said to behave as if nothing had happened, so he didn't tell them about Tom's collapse, or the things he had shouted out in his nightmares, or how he had wept uncontrollably when the askari came to the door and asked to see him. Jonathan would never forget the way the African said the words, although he didn't understand them.

He thought at the time that no actor could have looked so grave and solemn, heavy with grief as that simple African soldier.

"Ali Wainiri is dead," Tom had said to Jonathan and turned his face away.

As the African saluted and left the room, Tom's shoulders began to shake, and Jonathan left him and went to ask at the police post what had happened, but the Assistant Inspector there just shrugged his shoulders, and said brusquely, "Don't fret, yong. Just a patrol got bumped, that's all. Couple more munts less in the world for us to worry about."

Gillian chattered gaily about Sam's plans ... now got a tractor and plans to bring down some Boran cattle from the Nanyuki sales and cross them with a Hereford bull. "Borans," she said, "have a pigment in their skin that enables them to reflect light and so resist heat better. If they survive the trip from the Ethiopian border through the Northern Frontier District, they would probably resist most diseases."

Jonathan tried hard to follow it all, and look interested.

The last part of the road was rutted and pot-holed so much that Lalage had to drop down to bottom gear in places. There were a few culverts across the road but the drains at the side weren't deep enough and the soil underneath was soggy black-cotton. At last they came to a roughly daubed sign, 'J.C. Webb,' where they turned on to the farm track, and soon they passed a large water-filled crater with a yellow caterpillar-tracked tractor, perched drunkenly on its edge with deep ruts and large stones scattered round it.

"Looks as though he's been digging for diamonds," Lalage commented. "But at least he's had the sense to keep that thing off this track."

In the river elbow where the huts, were, Sam had built himself a stockade, and there were now four square huts: plus bathroom, kitchen and a beehive native hut, all reed-thatched. A young boy ran out of the stockade and swung the gates open, jabbering excitedly in Swahili. "Bwana Mkubwa is out looking at something," Lalage said as she skidded the car through the gap. An African in shorts, shirt and a red fez ran out and greeted them in a high-pitched stream of words, then turned to shout for the boy to help him untie the tin bath from on top of the pile in the boot.

They walked over to inspect progress on Sam's living quarters. Four of the huts were now connected by an open-sided, roofed corridor. One appeared to be where he slept and kept miscellaneous gear, the other, divided in two, where he sat in front of his fire, and did his paperwork. There were signs of more building between the house and the barn.

"I like your bridal chamber," Lalage said, sniffing the smell of sheep-dip, creosote, paint, oil and half-dried skins. "We'll change that, don't worry," Gillian said determinedly. "But where in hell are the women to sleep tonight? Sam must get some damn beds in here."

"Let's have a look at the rest of this luxurious little love nest," Lalage said, and they met Tom lugging the new camp beds, as they went down the covered passage.

"What's wrong with that place with the fire in it?" she enquired, and Jonathan with difficulty repressed a laugh at the comical expression on Alison's face as she peered round the door post.

"Tom," Lalage said, "for God's sake get that boy to tidy some of this junk out of the way. What's that hut over there next to the kitchen? Isn't it a store? He leaves every damned thing lying just where he last used it. Does he really want all these filthy boots and old clothes in his drawing room?"

She bustled about, piling things into everyone's arms. Poor Sam wouldn't be able to find anything for a week, Jonathan thought. He found himself going towards Sam's sleeping hut, walking beside Tom. Apart from tins and drums and cans of nasty smelling liquids, the hut was littered with boxes and crates; home made Mau-Mau weapons; a raw leopard skin stretched on a rough frame; a couple of Kongoni heads; three of Thompson's gazelle and two Grant's.

"Sammy seems to be living off the country," Jonathan observed.

"Contrary to the game laws," Tom said cheerfully. "But," he added, "It won't be long before they learn the range of his bang-stick and keep away. Let's move some of this junk into the store. I wonder how he can sleep with this stink in here."

Half the store turned out to be a rough stable with a battered jeep parked outside it. They sent the boy in the fez, who said he was called Titus, for a lamp, but the store was locked, so they left the paint and the heads outside it. When they came there before, they had to bring their own camp beds. Sam had said,"I'll let you two share one rondavel. But only hold hands, young lady." Lalage had put her tongue out at that.

"Sammy has certainly got on with it," Jonathan said admiringly. Two new rooms were nearly ready. The stable was lined with fencing posts. More were stacked outside with bales of wire, and through a gap in the rough door of the store could be seen cement bags and sacks of mealie meal.

"Glad to see he isn't feeding his watu off the country as well," Tom commented, pointing at the mealie bags. "He's had the whole Emergency to plan for it, and once you're in a place like this, the only thing to do to prevent yourself going nuts, is to work. Work like hell."

"How about Gillian? Will she be all right here?" Jonathan asked. Tom frowned.

"Yes," he said dubiously. "She hasn't chosen the ideal time for it, but I suppose Mother went through it and came out no worse. Our folk hadn't got the money Sam has behind him, either."

"How much will he need, roughly?"

"The Serikali don't let you start unless you own the land, with less than five thousand. That's sterling. Sam owns this, or his father does, but he won't get loans from land banks or his local agricultural committee unless he has some capital for wages and fuel and seed. He'll need ten thousand here, and that's without building a house. But its amazing what you can get in way of development grants for a dam, fences, and even stock, once they think you are trying. You get an advance on crops too, a guaranteed minimum return of eighty per cent." Jonathan raised his eyebrows. It sounded unusually lavish considering that African independence could not be too far away.

By the time Sammy arrived it was nearly dark. The sky was flushed amethyst with streaks of dusky pink, and it was already getting chilly. "Hodi," Sammy roared from the gate, and Titus came running with a lamp. The horse stamped and shied at the hissing light, and Sam swore roundly at him. He flung Titus the bridle and ran over to embrace Gillian, who threw herself at him and emerged rather mud-stained.

"What a horrible … " she began, but Sammy looked at them all and said delightedly, "Am I glad to see some white faces. Let me near that fire. Come on. Hell, it was nice of you all to come. How's things Tom? Hullo Alice girl you look fine." Alison murmured something. Sam nearly always called her Alice.

"Sorry I wasn't here when you arrived but I had to finish a shauri about a drain at the sheep-dip." He spat the words out with a rough snarl in his voice, using the same emphasis he used all day long giving orders in Swahili to green labour. He wore a rifle slung over his back across a filthy camouflaged smock, and his legs were encased in rawhide chaps, strapped over blue jeans. He moved with the rifle as though it were not there and he had forgotten about it. He hadn't shaved for a few days and his hair straggled out from under a dirty broad-brimmed felt hat. He seemed reluctant to relax when he got to the fire and moved about looking at them and asking questions.

Alison was watching him with an expression of near disbelief, her eyes moving from the rifle to his oil-soaked hands, down to his mud-caked calf boots, and back to the horn-handled knife in his belt. He exuded a smell of horse and creosote.

"For God's sake have a bath or something, Sammy," Lalage said, "and we'll see to food. I brought a hip-bath and its in your bedroom," she ended, with a glance at Gillian.

"Hell, don't worry, chakula's organised. And there's now running water in my bathroom, believe it or not. Proper bath too. Sit down and I'll open the bar first."

He went through the partition into the "office" and returned with a clutch of bottles. He then went to the door and let out a roar of "Tiriki." A thin voice answered "Ndio, Bwana" and a small boy arrived, complete with a too large trilby hat propped on his ears. Muttered instructions followed, and Sammy returned to pour drinks and stand there, legs astraddle, grinning at them delightedly.

"Feels grand to be a host," he said But Lalage and Gillian were already lost in a discussion of what needed to be done to make the place habitable, and they shooed him off to clean himself. When he returned he apologised for the lack of space. "All you girls will have to share my cot and…"

"What?" Lalage shrieked.

"I mean," he gasped, "You get the room with my big safari

bed and there are two of them in there."

"What?"

"Beds, I mean."

Jonathan said "Not a bad room at all for the inside of a hut." The walls were lined with the thin, straight kavirondo reeds normally used as matting. Behind them the walls were hard red mud between posts, with split cedar on the outside. Skins were pinned on the walls and floor, giving the whole room a pleasing, furry effect. The floor of stamped mud was covered with a closer woven type of matting, and there was no ceiling, just the beams under the thatch. Tom inspected a sketch map of the farm that showed the road as one boundary and the river as another, with forest on the other two sides. A dam site was marked, the fencing layout, a sheep dip, and a site for a stone house.

"So this is pioneering," Alison said to Jonathan, with a laugh that expressed her continued amazement. "I didn't think it could still be quite so rugged nowadays."

"I'm sure Sam wouldn't have it any other way," Jonathan said. Certainly she looked groomed for more civilised surroundings, with the sandy hair piled up in a chignon, and a tailored suit. Still, he thought, she looked as though she could stand a shower of rain. Her features were the sort that didn't strike you until you saw how well moulded and balanced they were. The sort of face that with a lot of make-up would look as though she were trying to act some part not entirely her character. And he liked her quiet, slightly husky voice that was musical without any over-emphasis, giving an impression of serenity. Again he noticed the way she turned her eyes slowly towards you, watching you quietly as you spoke.

Lalage sounded almost harsh beside her, but then that was the difference there was with a girl brought up outside a complicatedly civilised society. Lalage had learnt early how to handle most male jobs and run a house without electricity, gas or main drainage. Such things put a patina of hardness on you. You couldn't expect her to be placid, either. But nor did she belong to the school of tweeds and pearls and sensible shoes, and sure, she was a hundred per cent feminine under it all.

"I suppose if one got to understanding it all, one could be

very happy," Alison was saying. "Having the place bristling with animals, I mean. Then gradually one becomes like the Dayrells if you know them, over at Molo, so that at least when its raining you seem to be in Europe at some time long before the war."

Jonathan thought it was probably true. Old Dayrell was really a Huntingdonshire squire. His house might have been built in the Cotswolds, and he bred horses and labradors and kept pigs.

There was a scuffling and clinking at the door and Titus appeared in a kanzu and began laying a table aided by Tiriki, the shamba boy, who had made the concession of removing his hat. Sammy appeared in slacks, shirt and a sheepskin jacket and Jonathan went with him together with Lalage to the kitchen, while the others washed. The cook looked up from his stove and grinned, a huge, sweaty, feckless grin at them and chortled happily.

"He's an old safari mpishi (cook), aren't you, eh?" Sam dug him in the ribs. "Eh, Chepkoin, you old devil. Don't know how he'll take to a Memsaab, though. Hell's teeth. Never thought of that. He's bound to scarper." He lifted up pot lids for Lalage's inspection and she rolled up her sleeves to help, while Sam assured Chepkoin that she was part of his family, to his further delight.

"How do you get new cooks up here?" Jonathan asked.

"Bush telegraph." He sounded a little uncertain.

"How much do they ask for, here?" Jonathan asked casually, meaning how much less than the official Nairobi rate.

"Sixty and rations," Sam said. "Only this one gets safari rates, or in other words a bonus for a blow-out, as long as it's good."

Conversation at dinner turned to hunting and the prospects for revival of the tourist trade. Sam had had the tact not to serve game, and had slaughtered a sheep, but he didn't join in the discussion, until Alison asked him.

"I haven't done much," he said off-handedly, with a guilty look at Gillian. "I've taken out three or four bods. I tried to get a few regulars. I had one old timer, Wayne Rossiter, whose father went out hunting with my father, and then there's old Van Zyl who doesn't shoot any more, just takes photographs, and then there's Bobo, of course, and a few fat Germans who shout 'Hummel-Hummel Weidmans Heil,' and 'Wunderbar,' at everything."

"Which is the one with all the wives?" Gillian asked.

"Well, Wayne I suppose, but Bobo is really America's gift to women."

"As long as they pay," Lalage said. "Your clients, I mean," she added.

"Three safaris would get me started on a proper house," Sam mused, and caught his fiancée's eye over the table. Then they talked about Germans and got round to atom bombs and nuclear war. It seemed quite unreal and remote to discuss that, and as Sam said, "At least no one would bother to drop one near me. I always think that European politicians must be plumb crazy. Only five years ago, they tried to grow groundnuts in a desert, down in Tanganyika in the post war time. They could have asked Grogs, or even me, and saved millions." Having delivered himself of that he went off to bed.

Next morning, as they cleared up, Tom picked up an old spear-head and told Jonathan, "You know, although the Bantu in Central Africa never discovered the use of the wheel or animals to carry burdens, the use of metal had filtered down to them from Abyssinia, almost entirely in the form of weapons. One small clan of Kikuyu, who were shunned by the others as possessing evil powers, acquired the art of working iron, which they bought for ivory and slaves from Arab traders."

"Same as our tinkers in Ireland,"

"Oh."

"Yes, nobody likes them. They're nomads and they mend pots and pans and steal horses. But they don't kill people, like they do in this neck of the woods."

"Well, our tribes have been killing each other for centuries. But until recently, nobody knew. Or cared. I sometimes wonder why we bother to stop it. But the politicians in Europe seem to think it is essential."

"It gets them votes."

There was a silence. "Jonathan. How long have you been

patrolling now?"

"On and off, a year. I'm on patrol twenty six next week."

"Don't you get leave?"

"Yes. I was at the coast for a week. But I'm saving it up."

"Fine. Let me know when you are free and I'll take you out and show you some of the areas where there are no Mau-Mau. I'm due to meet the Hemingways down on the coast at Malindi."

"That would be great. Thanks." He already knew about this safari from Lalage. It sounded exciting.

Jonathan lay in bed uneasily, listening to the thunder rumbling and crashing and the growing and dying crescendo and diminuendo of the rain. He couldn't help thinking of the spear-head, because it had not struck him before how odd it was that people so primitive should be able to work metal. How did you set about it at the first attempt? Perhaps that was why the Bantu had conquered the poor bushmen and Hottentots who used to live, like the pigmies, in Central Africa, without iron. He must ask someone. But what a tragedy it was. Fire, the wheel, domesticated animals, the making of pigments, bone-needles, pottery, were all among the first discoveries of primitive people, and the first use of iron should be for stone-working chisels and cooking pots.

But then very quickly it was used for killing and maiming, cutting, stabbing and slashing at living flesh. You learnt about it at school, about those early people. This war. That war. Perhaps that was why *this* part of the world wasn't very glorious yet, because nobody had recorded the fact that the Masai had been cutting and slashing at the Kikuyu for hundreds of years, until the White Man came and taught them how to kill hygienically without having to throw or wield metal clumsily in the hands. Maybe it was one of those sleepless late night reflections that made no sense in the brave new light of morning, but all the same he thought that there was something crazy somewhere about teaching civilised children all those histories of wars. Perhaps if they took them all along to a busy mortuary once a year. Anyway most didn't do Greek, or even Latin any more, so they no longer had to learn about Greek and Roman wars.

Then Jonathan fell asleep and dreamed. It seemed to him

that it was morning, a very still peaceful morning, with the whole sky bleached a blinding white, although the sun was nowhere to be seen. And when he walked outside and looked over towards the hills they were not there any more and he saw that a huge rift had appeared during the night, and a huge chasm full of mist divided him from the rest of the world. With a feeling of panic, he walked down the farm track until he came to the place where the earth had slid away, and now the mist was clearing he could see down into a space for thousands of feet without seeing solid ground. Then he walked back to the farm wondering what to do, feeling utterly lost and alone and helpless. And there outside a hut was Sam, sitting high in the seat of a great yellow tractor with the engine roaring, and smoke pouring from it. "No sweat," he shouted and roared away.

Inside the hut a wireless blared out confused reports in various voices and languages. "New York, San Francisco and Chicago obliterated. The capitalist forces are wiped out. England smoulders and ceases to exist," a triumphant voice announced, to be interrupted by a clap of thunder and the calm, level tones of a BBC announcer. "Rockets have landed on Moscow, Kiev, Stalingrad, Omsk. Explosions are reported to have disrupted…"

Jonathan woke to find Tom Lerrick shaking him. "Are you all right?" he asked. "You've been throwing your arms about in your sleep," and Jonathan realised that his bed was so close to Tom that he had probably hit him, which made him feel foolish. Although it was still dark and raining steadily the impression of his dream or nightmare remained extraordinarily vivid, and he lay half asleep confusedly wondering what life would be like when the rest of the world had disintegrated. Sam would not have fuel for his tractor very long, but otherwise would life here be very different?

Tom's bed was empty when he woke again, and he did not return until long after the girls had organised breakfast. He had been trying, he said, to start the tractor, which had broken down in the hole they had seen, and been winched out by a neighbour.

Jonathan wandered towards the hut with running water, and with his mind on his dream, he sauntered inside. There was a bamboo screen at the entrance. As he rounded it he heard giggles, and then he was standing stock still, mouth wide open. Gillian was in the bath, Tom was brushing his teeth and Lalage was sitting on the edge of the bath smoking, with a very small towel in her lap, and nothing else. No one seemed to notice, or care, and went on chatting. Jonathan made an apologetic cough and retreated hurriedly backwards. As he went out he was sure he heard them giggle louder. "Damn," he said to himself. "But I suppose they all know each other since forever."

Sam and Gillian had taken the car and went into the nearest settlement post about twelve miles away, promising to be back for lunch. Tom took the horse and went to have a look at the land, leaving Jonathan to walk round the squatters huts with Lalage and Alison. No one said anything. "What..." Jonathan began, but Lalage put her finger on his lips "We are an odd lot, I know," she said with a beatific smile.

Already more bee-hive shaped huts had been built in the forest edge and Sam had put a fence up, so that, he explained, the natives would have to clear forest outside it.

"You can't blame him really." Lalage said. "After all, they've had this land for thousands of years and not been able to do anything with it, and even now they can move away to empty land if they want to."

There were about thirty families, and there seemed to be children all over the place, the usual big-eyed, appealing piccannins, clad in a knee length shirt of grubby khaki, sucking their fingers and peering at you shyly.

"Gillian will certainly be busy here," Alison said, and Lalage turned from her inspection of one of the huts with a serious look on her face and nodded silently. What could you really do, Jonathan thought, beyond a little rudimentary medicine? You could dig long drop lavatories and maybe pay a third-grade native teacher to teach the children, but none of their parents would earn more than five pounds a month unless they were the headman, tractor-driver or cook. And there were few free schools in the vicinity, or for that matter anywhere. It was a depressing morning, but Lalage didn't seem disheartened. This was something she could control she explained. "That is," she added," if we are allowed to farm the land for long enough."

"If they open the White Highlands to all comers," she explained, "you'll see the merchants buy up the mortgages and sell out the strugglers. Then there'll be farming for profit all right, and to hell with the labour."

"What about the big tea-growing people and the coffee growers?" Jonathan asked her. "Aren't they the basis of the whole country's economy after the farmers? Will they be expropriated by a native government? And what about African farmers?"

"Ah. There you are," she said. "I don't think any native government could just seize developed land on an enormous scale. Apart from farmers and planters, a lot of the town real estate is Indian owned. Sikhs own timber mills and garages for some reason. Throw them all out and all trade and commerce collapses."

"I don't understand," Alison said, as they walked back through the wet grass to the stockade, "Why, it matters if they open the White Highlands to all races? Surely only the bad farmers would go, and what difference does it make as a farmer, what race the owner is?"

Lalage stared at her. "Huh. Obviously you haven't met enough up-country farmers my dear. We'll meet some at the club this evening. You ask them then."

"I must say it baffles me too" Jonathan said, and Lalage turned on him impatiently.

"Oh, use your imagination, Jonathan dear. Can you see Sammy being stopped by an African policeman for speeding? Being fined by an African Magistrate. Losing his licence. That's what opening the Highlands to all races is going to mean. You can just see the happy Gujerati farmers standing round the bar at the Rift Valley Club with some jolly black Nandi stockmen, can't you?"

"Well, yes, I can." Jon muttered very quietly. So nobody could hear.

Tom came back and said it would cost a fortune to drain a lot of the land and Sam had better put his dam below his house site, because as planned it would take the house with it if it ever

311

broke.

Gillian and Sam came back with the car loaded and, after a merry lunch, Lalage announced that they would all go and visit the Settlement and maybe the Hullyers, and Sam would bring Gillian in to the little local club in the jeep. Sam took Jonathan aside and confided in him for the first time.

"I'm in a devil of a fix because Wayne Rossiter called to book a safari which was to be an extension of his honeymoon. I replied by telegram that I didn't think I could extend mine for more than two weeks. He always needs a month. I have located an old South African who could run the farm during my honeymoon I've ordered a new Land Rover. Can you test Lalage's reactions to that lot?"

"It's not Lala you should ask. Surely its Gillian? And her parents. And, maybe, Tom."

"Shit. Maybe you're right. Well hell man, I've got Bobo Howard also pestering me to take him out, and once either of them get taken out by one of the big safari firms, I'll never see them again. The first safari will pay for the kit and the second will furnish the damned house."

Some people have strange problems, in life Jonathan thought, as they drove down to the Settlement.

There wasn't much to the place beyond a couple of garages, two rows of seedy Indian shops, a small, old-fashioned hotel with a wooden verandah and a red, rusty corrugated iron roof; the local branch store of the Farmers' Co-operative. The native village huddled together in the lee of a police post and watchtower. They drove straight through after ringing up the Hullyers. There they had tea sitting on the lawn in the shade of striped umbrellas. They were in a different world already, to the primitive makeshifts of Sam's place, and Jonathan privately wondered whether Sam and Gillian would ever become staid and respectable like the Hullyers. Or whether they would go on living like gypsies, go whooping it up, down in Nairobi, and eventually go broke and split up.

"Had a word with Sammy, by the way," Lalage said, looking a bit shy. "Said it was time he knew that you and I ..." Jonathan looked up sharply.

312

"Don't worry," Sammy said, "Next time you come up here honey baby, you can have the bridal suite. Anyway. I guessed ages ago that you and he were an item. He's OK for a pom."

"Um." Jonathan said. "I think we'd better go slowly. That brother of yours is attached to his guns like – well like no one I ever saw." She laughed. "I can handle him. Worry not."

CHAPTER TWENTY FOUR

AMBUSH

"Everlasting peace is a dream, and not even a pleasant one; and
war is a necessary part of God's arrangement of the
world…Without war the world would deteriorate into
materialism."

Helmut von Moltke
1800-1891

The months had gone by so fast that it came as a shock to
receive a memo from Regimental H.Q. Which said that Second
Lieutenant Fitzpatrick J.X. had now completed twelve months
duty, and had performed satisfactorily, and was promoted to full
Lieutenant on a pay scale of sixty pounds per month plus
overseas allowances.

Then he got another to say that he was eligible for the
General Service Medal.

Finally Colonel Cormac sent for him, and presented him
with a document which stated that this Lieutenant was offered
the opportunity of enlisting as a regular officer. It suggested that
he could be promoted to Assistant Adjutant. Attached was a
letter of congratulation from Brigade-Major Corcoran.

Jonathan had a long talk with Tim.

"I thought that as you seem to like the place, you might
want to stay a bit longer. We won't be here much longer, but …"
He let it trail.

"I just don't know. But I sure am sick of tramping round the
bloody Aberdares. And the Rift is not much better."

"That's why we, er, the C.O. thought you might want to change to an office job for a while. Nothing to do with me."

"Of course not. Perish the thought."

"Think about it. Discuss it with that gorgeous girl friend of yours. Take your time. And by the way. We don't offer plum jobs to any old national service nig-nog."

"I am very flattered Sir. And you are both a scholar and a gentleman. Sir."

"Fall out, Fitzpatrick."

He didn't even mention it to Lalage. Although now very fit, his leg muscles were like spring steel. But, he was bone weary inside.

A month later he received another document. This time originating from the War Office. It stated that Lt. Jonathan Xavier Fitzpatrick had nearly completed his two years service. In another two months he would have two month's accrued leave. Then he was eligible for a one way ticket to his country of origin, troop transport permitting, etc, etc.

On one of the last days before he was eligible for this "demobilisation leave," he gave a farewell party in the mess to say goodbye to all those returning home with the regiment. He had permission to stay behind, he explained, and might take a year off in Kenya to decide whether to farm, to start a business or return to Ireland.

They met Governor Baring's staff at various cocktail parties. Now the Government House Administrator, Colonel Danvers, invited the Ranger officers to dinner with their ladies. Lalage was most impressed with this. Jonathan was very happy to take her. She wore a sensational evening dress which she had had made specially from a roll of deep blue sari silk. It was a foretaste of what social life could be in normal times.

He had kept quiet about her, never mentioning her to brother officers. They all, or nearly all, knew about her. But he had not flaunted her in front of his sex-starved brother officers. At the dinner she was a star. After it, everybody wondered who exactly she was. And what she did for a living. Jonathan was embarrassed. Tim kept his mouth shut.

In that last month two young subalterns, only a year out of

Sandhurst, who joined the Commando in the last month, were killed when their jeep ran off the road. Casualties through accidents can always happen in an active service role, but it all added to the cost of this so-called Emergency. More questions were being asked back in the House of Commons about the casualty rate. Jonathan had now done nearly thirteen months of patrolling, and his troop had lost only five men killed and twelve wounded. The Commando had however, lost six officers and forty-one men in three years.

Jonathan, leading his first patrol in the open country near Lake Naivasha, was just reflecting on how little activity there was, when he walked into an ambush. It was well placed on rising ground, so that the ambushers could shoot downwards from behind rocks and dense bush.

The trackers had been alongside him, but saw and heard nothing. The bullet that hit the Sergeant had missed Jonathan's right ear by an inch. Mac had just come up to ask him to stop for a ten minute rest. The bullet hit MacNamara's chest and knocked him flat. Everybody hit the ground and wriggled behind cover as a ragged volley whizzed over their heads.

They had a set drill for ambushes. They split, crawling left or right, then pushing forward aiming to get behind the ambush party. Some Mau-Mau knew this because they had been in the King's African Rifles, and they looked for these out-flankers. On this ambush the men were mostly not so skilled and their weapons were poor.

Jonathan, panting with effort, and tension, spotted something in a tree to his right. He lay on his side watching them tending to Mac. At the same time he was looking to see what would happen next. Then Flett caught up, got down behind his rifle and aimed. He had to wait until his hands were steady. He squeezed the trigger. Nothing happened. "Give me that."

Jonathan took very careful aim and very gently pulled the trigger. There was an agonised shout, a crash and a thump as the body fell. As the rest of the gang began to break cover, Jonathan yelled "Fire." But this shout gave away his location, and above the rattle of rifle and machine gun fire, he hardly noticed the ricochet which hit a stone near his right foot and broke up. One splinter ended up just above his left ankle.

"Grenades," he ordered. Flett had two, and hurled them forward. Behind them Noyk threw two more. That decided it. There was no more firing. Screams and shouts receded into the bush.

Five minutes later they had six corpses and one wounded with a broken leg. Jonathan handed command to Flett and Noyk and got up to see to MacNamara. They were still struggling to fix a wound dressing on his chest. The blood was that bright red with bubbles which meant a lung shot. They strapped the dressing on and got him to lie on his face. He wrenched the morphine syringe out and administered the whole dose. Mac had been shot before. He knew to be still until transport came. He opened one eye and grunted, "I'm cold." The older soldiers exchanged glances. They had heard that many times, just before the death rattle. In Normandy. At Arnhem. At the Rhine crossing.

Jonathan told the wireless operator to locate the Medivac helicopter. His leg felt numb, and when he looked down he was puzzled to see his whole jungle boot had turned red.

"Hey, Sir, you've copped one," Flett said. "Let's have a look."

He sat down and pulled out a knife, slit Jonathan's trouser leg and sloshed Dettol on it. Then he wiped the blade in a field dressing soaked in the Dettol, and said "Look away quick." As Jonathan did so, he felt a sharp pain and nearly screamed. Flett held up a piece of ragged metal like a thumbnail.

"Gotcha." He then sloshed more Dettol and bound another field dressing tight around the leg. Jonathan struggled to stand up.

"Don't move," Flett advised. Jonathan looked around. The men were well positioned and were firing only aimed single shots, to conserve ammunition. Incoming fire had stopped.

He let them help him along, as the pain was getting worse. Maguire had come up, as he was supposed to be his bodyguard. "They gotcha twice," he said.

"What?"

He pointed to Jonathan's arm, where a stain was appearing from near his left armpit. Never let them see you flinch, Tim had told him.

"Nothing," he said through clenched teeth, thinking "Bloody hell. How many more?"

When he regrouped the patrol they reported seeing fires on the horizon. The gang had European food and clothes with them, indicating that they had raided a farm house. They tied the wounded Mau-Mau to a dead one and went forward, watching for stragglers.

As they approached the burning buildings, Jonathan thought he recognised them. A terrified horse bleeding from panga slashes galloped past them. The first corpse they found was half burnt already in the kitchen, a stone building separate from the house. Two doors had been smashed through and as they pushed through a wrecked sitting room they saw through the smoke the legs hanging down from a bedroom window. Jonathan raced outside to pull the body away from the fire.

As he pulled he saw they had tried to hack off the head. The body clumped in a heap on to the garden flower bed. It was Alistair. They had taken his eyes. The signaller came, crunching over the broken glass. Jonathan turned to speak to him and vomited violently instead.

Training had paid off. Signals had gone out and battalion H.Q. sent two fifteen tonners for the wounded, surviving prisoners, and Alistair's corpse, wrapped in blankets. The men were quite subdued, worried that their sergeant was dying. Hating the whole business, each silently counting the days left of their national service. Muttering together sullenly, Jonathan saw that they needed leadership. Loudly he yelled at them to get moving.

"Come on. Come on, lads. Move your arses. Char and wads await at your favourite NAAFI. Let's get on with it. Let's have a cheery song from Marty." Maguire just looked at him, his eyes dead. "Sorry, Sorr. Fuck all to sing about today."

Tim Collins was there to buck them up on arrival, with Medical Officer, burial party, Intelligence Corps and the Quartermaster with his clipboard and regulation printed forms to count the unexpended ammunition. And list the dead and wounded.

He saw Tim have a quick word with Flett as he got them to

318

line up. He started to go through the after-action drills, but Tim came up and took over. He staggered over to Tim's Land Rover and sat on the bumper. Maguire same up and wordlessly scissored his shirt sleeve off. "Beg pardon," he said then, as he cut the whole thing loose, and started to mop down with gauze.

Tim came over. "Well done, lad. Up the bloody rebels." So no one could hear he whispered, "Proud of you, Jon. Now just relax and we'll get you back to an RAP."

At the Regimental Aid Post, just off the main road, they pulled off the field dressings and stitched the two ragged cuts where Flett had used his knife. Then Jonathan called Lalage and arranged for the ambulance to drop him at the Mayfair Hotel in Nairobi's outskirts. Lalage would meet him there.

She was furious when she saw the bandaging around his leg and arm. Someone had given him an old khaki bush jacket. That and the tattered remains of his bush pants and some American canvas boots were all he had. He hopped into her car, throwing his ammunition belt with water bottle and his Padgett on the back seat.

"Sorry," he said. She was speechless. After a while she said "This has got to stop. You are going to get killed. You have been doing this for quite long enough."

"I know. They will let me off the hook now, I'm sure."

She put him to bed, and rang Maguire to bring him a set of clothes. He didn't wake up until after midnight. She had laid out a cold meal in the kitchen. "I need a whiskey."

"Only a small one, my lad. They told you to take antibiotics, didn't they?"

"Hell. I forgot. And they gave me an anti-tetanus jab."

She packed him off to bed.

In the morning, he said he felt fine. But he hadn't told her that he had to report to the medical centre. He might need a blood transfusion. He did feel light-headed.

"Now," she began, "they have to do something about this. You must be overdue for leave. For God's sake, please, please." Her eyes filled with unshed tears. She choked up, pursing her lips, fighting back the tears. He stretched out towards her and

319

she half carried him to the sofa.

"Bloody hell," she sobbed out. "You've done your share. And I love you so, so very much. I can't bear this any longer. I really can't, Jon."

He hugged her wordlessly. His throat had choked up. To his horror he felt the tears warm and wet on his face. They were his as much as hers.

"For Christ's sweet sake, Jon, please. No more patrolling." She sobbed uncontrollably. He stroked her hair as his sisters had done to him when he was a child.

"It's all right now, darling. I'm a wreck anyway. I couldn't." He tried to laugh, but her shoulders heaved and she let out a high-pitched agonised cry like a wounded animal then a long shuddering sigh.

After a while she went out to make tea. "I can't take any more of this, Jon. I mean it. It's tearing me to pieces. Look at the state of you."

"Darling, I know. It's over now, honestly. I'm due for leave." After the tea he hugged her tight, and she was calmer. "You know, we two are getting to be like an old married couple. Except that we don't often have rows."

"Hmmm."

Then Maguire came with his uniform, and said the Colonel wanted to see him as soon as possible.

"Come straight back here," she ordered.

In the Land Rover. "I suppose I'll get a bollocking for being AWOL," Jon offered.

Marty grinned. "Don't think so, Sir. We reckon you done real well."

"For an amateur you mean?"

"No, Sir. You're one of us now."

The Colonel asked to see the damage. After looking at the leg and arm he said, "You know Jon, some of your men were with us on D-Day, in the Ardennes. Rhine crossing."

He paused. Jonathan looked puzzled.

"I mean, they know a good 'un when they see one. The report tells me that you look after your lads at all times. Led from the front. I want to thank you on behalf of the regiment. Now. I should not tell you this, but on condition you do not mention it to anyone at all, I can tell you that I shall be putting you up for a decoration. Don't say anything. Go now and report to the MO. And Jon. Thank you."

He came round his desk and shook Jonathan's hand.

When Jonathan next met with Lalage, he told her. "I'm quite flattered you know. The Rangers want to keep me."

"You're not going anywhere, my lad, until your leg is better."

"I know. I know. And, by the by, tonight is a mess night."

"Meaning?"

"Full dress and dine in."

"Nonsense."

Next day, she went out to the base. The gate guards did not want to let her in.

"Urgent for the Adjutant," she said. "I must see Captain Collins please."

"Yes Ma'am. Wait here."

"No. Tell him, Lalage Webb has an urgent … message."

They phoned, and straight away, Tim came out and saluted her. "Please come in."

She stood in front of his desk. "Do sit down," he said.

"This isn't a sit down thing. I want to ask you why you must send Jon out there all the damn time, right in front, where he is most likely to get killed…I…"

Tim remained standing too. "Lala. May I call you that? Jon is a bloody brave man. The job of a junior infantry officer is to lead his men. He did that. I'm sending him on sick leave. He wants to stay here if he can. And we want him too. He's a damn fine officer."

She gulped. "Thank you." She said. "Now I know." She held out her hand and he came round and shook it. Then she stood on tiptoes and kissed him on both cheeks."

"You're a pretty fine guy yourself," she said.

He grinned. "Thank you, Ma'am. It is a privilege to know you people."

CHAPTER TWENTY FIVE

HIGHLAND WEDDING

"When thou didst give thy love to me,
Asking no more of gods or men
I vow'd I would contented be
If Fate should grant us summers ten."

Bridges

The Lerrick-Webb wedding took place in mid-October in a stone church outside Nairobi that was one of the oldest buildings in the colony, dating from 1903. Sammy and Lalage's parents flew out from England, and their father went up to see the farm, leaving his nervous bright-eyed wife behind in Nairobi.

Lalage's mother had little of her daughter's vivaciousness and none of her energy. She spoke in a slow, quiet voice, smiling distantly and allowing herself to be directed completely by her husband or by Lalage. One very good reason for her not living in Africa was her notably fragile health. She suffered discomfort in the strong sun on the Lerricks' lawn after the wedding, to such an extent that she had to lie down in the house for the rest of the afternoon and evening.

Sam's mother turned up without her new husband. She was surprisingly slight, but you could see, tough as whipcord. Her arms and neck were the colour of mahogany. In South Africa she ran a stud farm. Obviously, she spent much of her time out in the sun.

A marquee was pitched on the lawn, English style, and gave the wedding a joyful air of sunny gaiety after the solemnity of the church. Not many guests had attended the ceremony, but the place seethed with them when the champagne was opened. It was a full dress wedding and most of the guests seemed uncomfortable, hot and ill-accustomed to best suits. The males of the younger set were obviously unhappy in ties and long trousers, as were some of the older people asked by Gillian's parents. Sammy made a short speech thanking his father for his foresight in buying the plot that enabled him to marry, and Gillian's father for his, in having first produced and then kept at home the prettiest girl in Kenya, long enough for him to get round to wooing her. He then got a bit confused about her mother, his mother and his step-mother's contribution to all this, gave up and drank to them all. Tom Lerrick made a dry, funny speech chiefly about the last minute deficiencies of the bridegroom's wardrobe.

There was a slight hubbub when it was rumoured that Sam had hired a plane to fly his bride off to their honeymoon which was going to be on the coast somewhere. This, it turned out, was perfectly true, but those who wagered that, judging by the bridegroom's consumption of alcohol, the marriage would be a very brief one, were slightly inaccurate. The Cessna belonged to an Ian Gredling who was going to fly it himself.

Jonathan limped amongst the guests, highly intrigued by the snippets of gossip he garnered, for few of the guests knew him sufficiently to guard their tongues. Lalage had been a bridesmaid and had not yet rejoined them.

"I say, have you seen the armoury old Sam's been given..."

"Can you see old Gill staying up in the sticks when Sam's out on safari? I bet we'll see plenty more of her down here yet."

"Hey, is that little white faced bird-woman Sam's Ma? You can see it is his father. Same build and jaw they've got. Never seen a brother and sister less alike. They say she's doing a line with some officer-type smoothie in a Brit Regiment...Queer family if you ask me, but she's a good looker all right, although I did hear..."

Jonathan moved on hastily and went over to talk to Gillian's parents, who he noticed had wisely given their daughter a refurbished Land Rover to boost her morale in the pioneering stages of her married life.

323

"I'm glad she was caught by a local lad really." Jane Lerrick told him shyly, and Jonathan thought surely she knows about Lalage by now. "But," she went on hastily, "It does make things so much simpler to have your children living near you. I do feel sorry for Sammy's parents, never seeing their children."

I wonder what she thinks about Alison and Tom, Jonathan thought, as he murmured agreement. Jane changed the subject as Sammy's step-mother approached.

"It is nice to see so many women here looking normal again, without pistols slung round them," she said brightly, before noticing how very pale indeed Mrs Webb looked. Jonathan stepped back as the two women talked in low voices together and then went off towards the house.

He found himself in a circle of hard drinking faces, and recognised by her voice first, June Dwent in a maternity jacket, surrounded by a group of young men.

"I hope," she was saying, "this party won't be as bad as ours. Hirshe Nel smashed his truck up at Dagoretti Corner and Julius knocked a munt down and kufa'd him on the Thika road."

"Have you seen Kobus?" somebody said. "Screechers he is, man."

"As long as nobody starts shooting," June said.

It was a great day for Jeha, resplendent in a new kanzu and fez, with many meals to prepare and many of the shenzi watu (scruffy people) from the shamba running in and out of the house. There had been nothing like it since Bwana Tom came back from the war, and it made Jeha a little sad to think of those days when there was no trouble and a man slept quietly at night, with no fear. But tonight there would be an ngoma, drum dances and a beer drink in the camp where the watu lived who worked the coffee shamba. And Bwana Sam had given him two hundred shillingi and there would be more if all went well and none of the extra house boys got drunk or broke too many glasses. He had always been slightly afraid of Bwana Sam, who was kali, (sharp). Unlike Bwana Tom or the Bwana M'kubwa. But he was a man to fear, for had he not captured Kathenge who Kabero had said would kill him if he broke the oath? But he was dead now they said, and so was Kabero and the oath had been washed away by a muthori (witch doctor) in the river. He was free again.

He was glad too that the Memsaab Kidogo had a husband now and would go away to a new shamba. Sometimes she was kali too and she made much work. Perhaps it was good that she was married before she shamed her father. She brought many young men to her father's house, and had lived a wild life in the strange manner of the young white women, driving herself in Bwana Tom's gharri and coming home late at night, waking the guard at the gate.

Soon perhaps Bwana Tom would take a woman, and then there would be a very big ngoma dance and many shillingi. It might be then that he would be able to buy a new wife when he went back to his village, for his two wives were getting old and would be unable to till the ground and carry wood and water to his new thingira. And men said there was much to do in the reserve now, with new villages, and a man had to plant his crops as the serikali (government) directed, and the number of his goats and his cattle were counted and written. But it could not be very bad because Karioki, his first born was a police askari at Nyeri and he would see that the plot was not lost. Both he and Muturi, his second son, who was an askari in the K.A.R., might get plots taken from the terrorists who had been killed in the forest. No. Things were not as bad as they had been, and soon he would be able to go back to the reserve again to see the plot and arrange with the chief to find him a new wife.

But of course, the Chief, Simon Wariuhu was dead, killed by a gangster in the hospital after his car had been ambushed. Well then, his son, if he could find him, and if not, the headman of the village would do. These days when his savings of two thousand shillings were gone, taken by Kabero for the Mau-Mau funds, it was not as if he, Jeha son of Gakuru, would cut the figure he once hoped. But Mau-Mau was dying, that was something, and a man's life was safe and was his to order again.

Samson came up to him, very maridadi (smart) in a new khaki suit with brass buttons, a collar and tie and a new khaki topee with the brass lion of the serikali, glinting on it. He looked like a station-master, Jeha thought scornfully, rather than a mere neopara, the head man of a shamba. For he was jealous of

Samson, who, being a Christian, had attended the church for the bridal oaths. And had not Bwana Lerrick himself attended the wedding of Samson's son in his village in Limuru? Perhaps he too should have become a Christian, but the thought gave him another pang, for the question was so close in his mind to the Mau-Mau oath he had taken. For at first Jomo Kenyatta had said that if a man wanted to be a Christian and keep his wives, he should join the Free Kikuyu Church, and when he had joined it he found that it was nothing but Mau-Mau.

"I must have Cheroge," Samson said, "he is in the house."

"There are three Cheroges in the house today," Jeha said irritably.

"Cheroge the Sais," Samson said. "There are three horses here that have been given to Bwana Sam and Memsaab Sillian." Samson could not pronounce her name any more than Jeha, and this weakness made Jeha relent, for he had been quite ready to argue that there was too much kazi (work) in the house and there were many lazy watu who could surely give food and carry water to horses.

"I will tell him," Jeha said pompously and turned to go into the house which Samson never entered except with the Bwana or Memsaab M'kubwa. It was time he went round to the kitchen anyway, to see that none of the watu were stealing or getting drunk on the dregs of the glasses. If only the old mpishi (cook) had not been so drunk, then, when it was found he had taken two oaths, he might still have stayed and not be down at the prison camp in Mackinnon road at this moment. This new mpishi was sly, as those coast Swahili were and although he could cook well, he was no friend of the Kikuyu, and while his own family grew fatter and fatter, the pickings for the others were thin.

Cheroge was furtively emptying a glass into a bowl inside a cupboard door. Seeing Jeha he stood up grinning, with his back to the door.

"Go outside," Jeha told him curtly. "Samson wants you at the stables."

Cheroge turned round, picked up the bowl and drained it, impudently smacking his lips. "Shenzi (savage)," Jeha hissed at him. "Kwenda upesi. (Get going)." Cheroge laughed and swore at him. "Mbichi," Jeha said bitterly as Cheroge ran out to the compound.

"But why do you have to go on with it now?" Alison said to Tom Lerrick. "Why can't you leave it to the professionals? When I read in the papers about surrender talks, and people going into the forest unarmed to talk to them. Well. I've visited several camps, and seen the really bad hardcore ones. I just can't believe that you could trust them. I know it's selfish but I just can't bear to think of you up there in the Aberdares talking to them."

She shuddered. "And how can you trust the terrorists you take with you? I don't understand." There was a tremulous note in her voice as she spoke. She gulped at her champagne glass.

"Please don't imagine too much, honey." Tom said gently. "It isn't as bad as it sounds. But we've got to finish this thing now. There are only about three thousand left. That means there are about eighty thousand being screened and rehabilitated in the camps. But the ones left in the forest are the hard core, and this is the only way to finish it."

Alison put out her hand suddenly and touched his arm. A lock of blonde hair had escaped from under the pert little white hat she wore.

"But Tom," she began imploringly.

"Let's go and sit down somewhere and talk," Tom interrupted. They moved in silence across the lawn to the verandah steps, where for the time being there were no guests.

"You see," he said, as they sat down, "this is the crucial time, and we are on to the right idea. But there are lots of people with other ideas. You've heard of some of them. The boys who want to challenge Dedan Kimathi to a duel. The magic schemes with coloured smoke and recorded voices shouting through loudspeakers from spotter planes. Well now we've got the Army doing sweeps and cordons and now we know where to look. We don't just trust ex-terrorists blindly. For one thing they can't go back any more once we capture them. The others know their faces by now. But we pick the ones we want, the ones with grudges and the ones who have seen Kimathi strangle their relatives and so on. We convince them first, psychologically, that we can shoot better than they can, and track nearly as well.

We take them up in planes and frighten them. We keep them apart and don't let them wash so they don't smell of civilisation when they go back. And you would be amazed how well they co-operate. They even make wigs of hair for us, plaited like their own, so they can get at the lice. But you can't organise them on European lines.

"I know I'm boring you, but this..."

She reached out a hand to his arm. "Go on. It's important." She meant for him to get it off his chest.

"You have to understand the Kikuyu mentality, and speak some of their language, and that's where people like myself are essential. We can test them by giving them rendezvous to keep after carrying letters into the forest and that sort of thing, but someone had to go with them to make them effective. You know why the surrender talks failed?" Alison shook her head. "The papers just said they had happened and that the remaining leaders refused to surrender."

"Because some gangster found an Asian prayerbook near a fig tree and the witchdoctors told Kimathi that it was sent by Ngai, the Kikuyu god, who lives on Mount Kenya. And now they say that a white man must be sacrificed in the forest to appease a curse."

Alison winced and Tom put his arm round her.

"Sorry, sweet, but I'm just trying to explain. We know what goes on now before it happens, and this is the only way to do it. We've had the bombing by the R.A.F. stopped now. One very good thing. You should see the condition of some of the game, elephant, rhino and buffalo with shrapnel wounds, mad with fear, wandering thousands of feet away from their natural level in the forest. Now the rains are nearly over the gangs will come lower down out of the mists to trap small game, and this is the time to catch them. We've all learnt a lot from the ex-terrorists now and we know the Mau-Mau habits. I've learnt a lot myself about tracking. Their skill is unbelievable. They say game never charge you if you smell of the forest. Some ex-Mau-Mau are sick if they ride in a vehicle because of the stench of petrol. They know more of the forest than any of us. So we must go on with the pseudo-gangs until we get the leaders. Until we do there will be no peace. I wish you could have been here when there was peace."

He paused for a moment as two children in party clothes went into the house, playing with a ridgeback pup.

"It must seem a helluva place to you now with all the barbed wire and security regulations. I don't know what went wrong." He stopped and Alison looked at him, thinking he looked more miserable than she had ever seen him. He had taken his arm away. She took his hand and squeezed it.

"It will be all right, Tom, won't it?" she said, haltingly. "After all this, I mean. Everything will have to change, won't it?"

"People will have to change," he said bitterly. "They'll have to wake up and realise this isn't the place to come when you are tired of life in civilised places. People like Pa came out here because they were begged to come. But they worked hard and were respected. They weren't get-rich-quick merchants. And they had no trouble with the African in his raw state. They can handle the modern African too, but not many people can. Africans aren't just black Europeans. They're a more difficult lot to understand than Chinese, Russians, Indians, Malays."

His voice tailed off into silence. "Let's go and get a drink," he said more cheerfully, getting to his feet. "And some time soon I'll take you down to the coast and forget about Kikuyu. We could take the old box-body and go via the Northern Frontier District. Then I can show you some of the old Africa, still unchanged. Would you like that?"

"A safari." Alison said, her eyes sparkling. "Lalage talks about safaris and the bush, so if she likes it, I would. Gillian is enthusiastic too."

"She's a menace in the bush, that girl," Tom said, laughing. "Poor old Sammy will find out if he takes her out with any of his clients."

Sam Webb and his bride, dressed for a three hour flight in a light plane, drove off the Lerrick premises in a swirl of dust, accompanied by a shower of thunder-flashes and smoke canisters.

All the Africans on the farm assembled to share the

excitement and add to the din. Since all the local police were there, and were not likely to object, a good many revolvers were fired, and even a burst of Padgett. Jonathan saw Jane's face suddenly contort with a spasm of grief at the parting, but her husband gripped her shoulder, and she recovered, turning to go into the house to see to Lalage's mother.

Lalage had been sitting with her, and she came out now and asked a few of the wilder bloods if they could stop making a racket. Jonathan took her to the marquee for a drink, where they bumped into Sean and Tim talking to the Dwents. Sean had just returned from a fortnight's leave in Rhodesia.

"You know, the charming thing about Kenya," he was telling June Dwent, who was looking at him with a cautious expression, "compared with further south, I mean, is that there isn't any class problem." Everybody looked a little puzzled. "No," he went on, it's quite simple. Here you just have colour. Workers are black, middle classes brown, and the upper classes are white. That's why our soldiers don't fit in. "

He looked round him with a dazzling smile on his face. He was a little tight.

"Oh, no. I don't think ..." Henry Dwent began, but Brian forged on. "Oh, yes. The people who insist on separate cinemas and different queues in post offices, are the white people, who work in shops, garages, on building sites. They insist on serving you first in the shops full of Africans. Frightfully class-conscious. Fearful snobs. You don't get it here because it's nearly always Indians who serve in the shops. It makes for a very much more relaxed air. Like Ireland. No one really cares who the hell you are. Don't you think so?" he threw out towards Jonathan and Lalage. June Dwent didn't have to speak to make her opinion clear.

"I've never been to Ireland, dear," Lalage said, in the tone one would use to a fractious child. She accepted a cigarette from Henry Dwent, and when he had lit it for her Jonathan watched fascinated as she gave that quick, characteristic flick of her head before exhaling sharply a thick, blown plume of smoke.

"Party tonight?" June asked Lalage, who sipped at her glass and looked coolly at June before replying.

"The bride's brother is supposed to be taking the bridegroom's sister out, but he hasn't done anything about it yet."

"Shall I volunteer?" Tim Collins offered, with a side glance at Jonathan.

"Where can we get some more girls from?" Lalage mused.

"You may well ask." Sean said dryly. "The question is posed in our mess occasionally."

"I'll come," June said brightly.

"There's Angela I suppose," Lalage said.

"Any of that left?" Sean said to Tim, peering hopefully into a bottle on the table. As they discussed meeting later in the evening, Jonathan reflected that the wedding might focus attention on Lalage and himself. And now her parents were here, and he had only exchanged pleasantries with them.

When Jonathan went to change he sat down and thought hard. The problem of his immediate future weighed on him, smothering him, nagging with a persistent ache. And Lalage refused to come to London until the Emergency was over and the camps were emptied and the Mau-Mau who were not irreconcilable were all returned to the reserves. Tom said there would be seventy thousand, of which three thousand hard core, oath-givers, witch-doctors and gang-leaders who had taken the advanced oaths, were expected to be irreconcilable.

On impulse he went over to the house as soon as he had changed and talked to Lalage's father. He came out and saw her most years on his way to do business in South Africa. Sometimes her mother would come. They both wanted her to come to London. Jonathan sensed that there was something unsaid in the background, something connected with Andrew, perhaps. He detected a reluctance in Mr Webb to discuss his daughter at all. There was little resemblance between father and daughter. He was a burly man with Sam's black hair, short nose, square jaw and ebullient manner. Jonathan found him rather offhand, as though he considered that he had done his best by his children and now they were no affair of his.

"I am very fond of your daughter," he said. "Best of luck. It's a great country," her father had said and emptied his glass, while avoiding Jonathan's eye. Angered, Jonathan said, "I am asking your permission to marry your daughter." He paused, and added, "Sir."

"Granted." Carton Webb grunted. Jon, unable to speak, left him there.

After dinner Jonathan sat in a window seat with Lalage and began by asking her abruptly if she would visit London when he went back.

"Why go back at all?" she said gravely.

"To talk to my family. Maybe get a job. That could send me back here. Lala, can't you see I'm as alien here as a... a barefoot Kikuyu would be in Piccadilly. I'm very fond of this country, and of you. You know that. I never understand what you have against Europe. But what do you have against London?" She didn't answer for a while, but picked at a seam on her dress.

"Because there is nothing there for me. I have to have something real to do." She clasped her hands around one knee and gazed upwards at the ceiling, smiling wryly.

"I'm afraid I would only make a good wife here in Africa, Jonathan." She looked straight at him and said. "If we two have a future, it is here. That's it, Jon darling. That's it."

Tom came over and said that if Jonathan had his leave coming in a month or two he was planning to go down to the coast. "You should come with us, Lala."

"I'll see if Angela can spare me when Gillian gets back."

They left it like that.

Later Lalage took him out into the garden. "You should see some of the other parts of this country, young man. Not just the bloody Aberdares, and Naivasha. We can show you the coast, Mombasa, Malindi, Lamu, the northern frontier, and the tea plantations at Kericho, the wheat farms up in the Highlands and the views down into the Masai Mara and the Serengeti." Jonathan gulped.

"How?"

"Take leave, whatever. Go out with Sam hunting. See a bit of life. He will take you, he said, if you don't mind being sort of assistant camp manager. He's taking out Wayne and Marie-Lou, a few days from now. Big game stuff. He needs someone with him, and he can't find anyone suitable. You'll be terrified, but you'll be OK. How's your foot?"

"Oh my God," Jonathan interrupted, "with names like Wayne and Marie-Lou, I'm not so damn sure that I…"

She cut him short. "Don't get smart, big boy. Just we have more wilderness and big game here than anywhere on earth. Go with Sam. I'll fix it now. It will be something you will never see anywhere else. Something you'll remember for ever. Then you might understand me a bit better too. I'm too busy to go. In case you ask."

She took him by the arm, then wrapped both arms around him in a bear hug.

"We are strange people, we Africans," she said as she bundled him into her car. They went to her flat and she confessed that she had planned a surprise dinner. with shrimp from Mombasa, kudu steak, and the most expensive wine she could find in Nairobi. Angela's cook had been there for hours. There was nothing to do but to open the wine. They got royally sloshed and fell into bed before midnight. She woke him hours later.

"Stop snoring," she commanded, "and earn your keep." He rolled over, and as they made love he whispered, "I didn't know that paradise was like this."

She grunted, "No talk. Just make love. So I can feel it tingle right down to my toes."

Jon went back to the regimental camp. Tim said, "I'll let you go for a month. You've bloody well earned it. MacNamara says you are a damn good soldier. I sent him home by air yesterday. He said to tell you may have saved his life. You should stay on. Anyway, I told the Orderly Room. You're on compassionate leave unpaid. No paper. I'll list you as sick and unfit for combat duties. Look after Lala. Fall out."

CHAPTER TWENTY SIX

HUNTING SAFARI

"Anayetaka hachoki, hata achichoka keshapata."
"There is nothing weary in desire. Weariness is only desire
realised."

Swahili proverb

Eddie Haymer was waiting for the same plane as Sammy Webb.
It was ten-thirty on a Sunday morning just after the Long Rains
in June. Eddie was an assistant hunter to a well-known
professional who worked for one of the three main hunting
syndicates. He was slim and dapper in his new khaki drill, and
with his good-looking, slightly girlish face, his finely formed
hands and lithe movements, he seemed more like a pianist than
the ruthless, tough young man Sammy knew him to be.

"Didn't know your outfit had started up again," Sammy told
him.

"Hasn't really. I'm meeting a couple of Germans who only
want to hunt in Tanganyika. The boss knew one of them there
before the war. I got out of the police a week ago. Reckon I'll get
going before the rush starts and get a full licence if I can."

"Good luck to you," Sammy said, strolling away. It looked
like the hunting business would revive when the Emergency was
really over. So few of the former clients could afford it. It was
interesting to hear that Germans were coming out. Since the end
of the war in Europe very few clients had been anything but
Americans or Saudis, and he had heard of only one Englishman.
He was glad it was Wayne who was coming out, and not
someone he had never met. The new wife might be a snag, but if

she was like the rest she would push off after a few days and go down south sightseeing or shopping in Johannesburg. And it was better than Bobo Howard too, because Gillian wouldn't have liked him. He was far too rich and far too successful with women, and he didn't want her to be upset the first time she met one of his clients.

Wayne Rossiter had his faults but one of them wasn't getting drunk and fooling with other peoples' wives. So far he had shown a preference for selecting his wives from unmarried candidates, and presumably he wouldn't be drunk when he did. The third would probably be something very sleek and hard and high-powered, because Wayne never suffered fools gladly, and he always wanted the best of all things.

The plane came in and taxied; the passengers were stepping down, looking rather dazed, with their cameras and bags slung around them. Sammy made his client out, big and husky in his light blue suit, with a hat swathed in a checked band. The woman he escorted was small beside him, plump and pretty and hatless. As they got nearer he saw that she was more than pretty, but she didn't look the ultra smart, lacquered, Stork Club and Madison Avenue sort he had expected, and he was slightly relieved. Wayne came through the barrier and gave that quiet grin that softened his craggy, rough cut features, and introduced Sammy to his wife Marie-Lou. She seemed almost shy and said nothing, so he and Wayne turned to the business of entry permits, smallpox, yellow fever and enteric certificates. He had brought a .270 Winchester with him, and the Customs were not very happy about it. Eventually they were cleared, and Sammy loaded them into the new Land Rover and headed for the Lerricks' house. Wayne knew Gillian's father well, as his own father had hunted with him once, and they would stay there three days while they decided on routes and got licences and all the last minute items. As they drove along, Marie-Lou gazed round her with big round eyes like a child, and Sammy felt more reassured because a lot of trouble would be saved if his mother and Gillian liked her.

After the honeymoon, Gillian had been pleased to leave the

new farm, and rejoin her parents. Things had been coming along well now, and the new house was beginning to look like home with the furniture and other wedding presents scattered about. She had felt that old Lutz Potgieter, the Afrikaner whom they had hired, wouldn't look after them, and had insisted on bringing a tin-trunk full of valuables down to Nairobi with them.

"Looks kinda like an old Mid-West boom town," Marie-Lou said as they left Nairobi. "Just look at that old Mamma with her piccaninnies. Kinda reminds me too of Carolina. Real Deep South stuff." Wayne's head swivelled round to her and then back to Sammy.

"She'll learn." He said. "How're your old Mau-Maus doing, Sam? She kept asking me on the plane, and I told her they didn't have 'em in Tanganyika, and I thought you had 'em corralled up by now in Kenya."

"They keep in the forests mostly," Sam told them. "We had a few wander into the Rift Valley farming area and across the escarpment into the Masai, but there won't be any in the Serengeti. The danger areas are closed to hunting anyway."

"Pity," Wayne said, "I kind of fancied a left and right at 'em with that .470 you lent me last time."

"Wayne," Marie-Lou said sharply. "You just cut that sort of talk right out, now."

"Take it easy, honey," Wayne said, and Sam smiled faintly. People didn't talk to Wayne Rossiter in that tone very often. This one had spirit all right. Sam hoped she wouldn't come out with them or she'd be giving her opinions on the hunting, and that could wreck any safari. Sam hastily told them about how some gangs followed in the wake of elephant driven up into the forest by the noise of the firing, and by bombs. The gangs, he explained, knew that the game wouldn't go near any troops, and the game tracks hid their own spoor unless it was wet underfoot.

Gillian Webb sat on the steps of the verandah of their parent's house waiting for them. Wayne said in his letters that he didn't know how his wife would react to Africa, but he wanted her to see the Nairobi Game Park, and then go down to Kilimanjaro and stay at the Amboseli Park a couple of days. If she liked that then they would go on to the Ngongoro crater, which was carpeted with new grass at this season and full of the game that went there from the arid savannah country of the Serengeti plains. After that he and Sam would go down to Arusha and start hunting from there. Meanwhile Gillian had got one of the rondavels ready for them to stay a few days at the new farm. Now she was feeling distinctly nervous at meeting her husband's first clients, because if she hated them, as she half expected to, then there would be a big fight with Sam about the next lot, and so on, every time he took a safari out.

But Wayne's new wife tripped out of the Land Rover an excited smile on her face, and took both her hands in hers and said, "My, you sure are real pretty, Gillian," and still holding her hands, swung round and looked at her husband and Sammy while she explained, "Sam here wrote Wayne and said you were a honey. I guess I thought you'd be a big tough corn-fed gal with muscles or something." They all laughed, partly with relief, as the boys unloaded their luggage, Marie-Lou went running over to a hibiscus and snapped off a blossom, tucking it behind her ear. She leant over a frangipani and put her face to the flower, then straightened up and gazed at the garden, the grass still green after the rains, with a scarlet spathedia and cannae lilies rioting under the flame trees, and bougainvillaea swarming everywhere. She exhaled an enormous sigh, and Wayne went over to her and put an arm round her gently. "Tired, baby?" She nodded, leaning against him, and Wayne took her over to Gillian, who led the way into the house.

The Lerricks welcomed Sammy's clients with the old-style Kenyan hospitality, dating from the time when people came down in ox-carts to Nairobi and stayed a week or a month in the guest house. Marie-Lou couldn't keep still, and went out to look round with Gillian and her mother, determined to keep awake until after lunch. Wayne sat and talked hunting with Sam and Henry Lerrick until lunch, and afterwards the guests went to sleep off the effects of their seven thousand mile journey.

Gillian went to wake Marie-Lou at six o'clock. Wayne had already got up and was on the shamba with her father. Marie-Lou lay under her mosquito net with her mouth slightly open and her neat helmet of chestnut hair puffed over her brow. There

337

wasn't any real need for the nets, but Mrs Lerrick put them in the rondavels for visitors, who at first regarded every moth and flying ant as potentially lethal. Looking at her, Gillian wondered whether she was much older than herself. She could have been anything between twenty-two and twenty-six.

She touched her arm lightly and Marie-Lou leapt upright with a startled expression on her face. Focusing on Gillian she gulped and said 'Oh', sleepily and fell back on the pillows, closing her eyes. "Sorry," she murmured with the slight drawl that Gillian found attractive. "I'm apprehensive, I guess, after all the animal talk at lunch. Where's Wayne?" Gillian told her, watching her rubbing her eyes, muzzy with sleep. She picked up the Flit gun and sprayed round the doors and windows. "Do you have many crawlies around?" Marie-Lou asked. "Well they do this in the hotels, but we usually forget." Gillian replied.

"Oh, we have them in California. Plenty. I'm not too scared of them when I know what they are. Don't you have to shake your shoes out, in case of scorpions or something?"

"Not here. Maybe in the bush." Gillian smiled reassuringly. "You'll find it a bit chilly outside when it gets dark, so you'll need a coat."

"I want to get out of here before it gets dark," Marie-Lou said quickly.

"I'm scared of the dark, too," she added merrily, getting out of bed.

"I'll stay here till you're ready if you like." Gillian said, thinking that for anyone else she might not have offered, but there was something delightfully appealing and disarming about the American woman's frankness. It looked though, as if she wouldn't stay out with Wayne very long, which meant that she would have to be entertained, and that would be a problem, if her husband wanted to hunt for six weeks or so.

On Monday morning Wayne spent all morning checking itineraries and supply points with Sam, and approving the bookings for various areas. He wanted a topi and sable which meant Southern Tanganyika and he was going to take out an elephant licence in case they came across a good one. Mostly, like many long-term hunters, he just wanted to improve on the heads he had. Get a good rhino, and then if possible, a bongo and a sitatunga deer. Bongo was the most elusive game, rarely seen, and the sitatunga area would probably be closed. After lunch they went down to the Game Department to check on hunting areas and to get Wayne's visitor's licence, which cost him £50, an elephant licence, £75, rhinoceros, £20 and leopard in case they met one and had to shoot it, £25. Lion and buffalo were on the General licence, but Wayne took out a Masai lion licence for £20, as they would be in the Masai quite a lot.

The PHA – Professional Hunters Association liked to have a back-up hunter if two people were hunting. Sam wanted Jonathan to have a chance to hunt. They chose René Babault, who had just returned from three years with Desert Locust Control. Belgian father, Irish mother, he was a crack shot, knew every animal and bird in the region, and was later to become the best and highest paid hunter in Africa. They were lucky to get him before he set up on his own.

Jonathan turned up in the safari gear that Lalage had made him buy. Long whipcord trousers and a bush jacket to match. On the left hand side instead of a breast pocket she had the tailor stitch in bullet loops. At his protest she said "Got to look the part, me boyo. And Sam will expect you to shoot for the pot while he's away from camp."

"If Tim sees me dressed like this he'll shoot me."

They took Marie-Lou with them to an Indian tailor to have khaki bush shirts and trousers made, and then called on the Firearms Bureau for Sam to have his guns sent up from the Gigil Armoury, where they all had to be kept. Then they went round to a gunsmith's to choose ammunition; soft-nose for deer and leopard and lion, and solids for elephant, rhino and buffalo. Sam had dropped a driver off to collect the Bedford three-tonner he had hired, and they met it at the little Indian store where Chotabhai Patel had the tinned food and other stores on order. Chotabhai gave Sam credit and lent him containers, arranged the hire of tents and a large kerosene refrigerator. He had a cousin with a duka in Arusha, where they could stock up later before starting to hunt, and there they could fill drums with petrol for the Land Rover as well. Wayne chose a lot of tins that he and

Marie-Lou preferred, but luckily he wasn't the type who would want fresh strawberries flown from Switzerland, and he hadn't ordered any hampers from Fortnum and Mason. One large item was mealie-meal for the nine boys who would accompany them. They would get meat from the game that was shot, and only green stuff was a problem. Sam checked the stores with Nganga, who had been promoted to head man for the safari, and Chotabhai's boys loaded them on the truck. Gillian had already taken the Rossiters home in the Land Rover.

That night they all went out for their last civilised evening and next morning they set out down the Tanganyika Road for lunch at the Namanga Hotel. By evening they had bumped across the grey dusty track towards the 19,000 feet mountain of Kilimanjaro, and as they raced across the dried salt flats at Amboseli, the long processions of wildebeest (gnus to Marie-Lou) were moving across to water, with the ice-cap of the mountain towering over the clouds that hung around the forests in the foothills.

Jonathan watched intently as the night camp went up, fires lit, the cooks got to work, guest drinks on a linen tablecloth. "In future," Sam said, "You get to get this perfect – every time. Limp or no limp."

"Screw you," Jonathan said under his breath.

Next day Sam went down the Mombasa Road to Sultan Hamud to collect six of the camp boys they needed. He had brought a cook from the farm, Chepkoin, and a gun-bearer, a Kamba called Kiteme, who had worked for Tom Lerrick, and was fairly certain not to run away at the wrong moment. At Sultan Hamud there were two dozen professionals waiting to be taken on, and Sam picked out a spare cook and driver, two good trackers and a skinner. They all carried references from the safaris they had been with before, and they were all keen to go out again, as on top of above-average wages they could expect generous tips for good heads and trophies. Apart from that, they liked hunting as much as any anyone, African or American, and most of them were poachers when they had the opportunity. They would travel with the lorry, and their real work wouldn't start until they left Arusha, since there were wooden camps in the Amboseli and Ngongoro Crater game reserves.

They were up before dawn the next morning and watched from the Land Rover as the elephants lumbered unperturbed to and from the swamp water holes, taking no notice of the vehicle. There were several Indian families there and two carloads of Swiss tourists, but the game in the area were accustomed to cars and took no notice at all. It was very still amongst the smashed down trees where the elephants browsed, and the enormous silence was pierced only by the shrillings of bush-shrikes, the chattering of weaver-birds, and the occasional raucous shriek of a toucan. At the water holes the smaller animals waited until the larger ones had drunk and when the zebra and giraffe had gone and antelope slaked their thirst, the flamingos and cranes took possession again. To be disturbed only by a few late-comers such as a comical family of bush-pig, who waddled suspiciously up, gulped down their fill and disappeared back into the scrub at a nervous trot.

As the sun rose, activity dwindled and only a few langorous giraffes moped out into the sun, browsing among the green tops of camel thorn and acacia trees. The elephants trumpeted to each other as they slithered into their mud wallows, hidden from view by the thick green vegetation of the swamps. The noise rang out clearly amongst the desolate trees, and echoed into the forest that climbed up towards the towering mountain, shrouded now in steamy mist and cloud.

Gillian had stayed behind with Jonathan to attend to breakfast, and when they arrived at the camp she told them that a game warden had called to say that a photographer was going next day to Ngongoro to attempt night photography of lion. Marie-Lou, who by now had dropped into a trance of fascination, just gulped and nodded dumbly. She told Gillian how amazed she had been to be so near the elephants, and how horrified to meet Masai herdsmen walking about cheerfully in a blanket with a little spear amongst all those savage beasts, and what was that red stuff they did their hair-dos with? Mutton-fat and red mud to keep the lice down and look dandified, Gillian told her.

"They sure looked cute to me," Marie-Lou said

breathlessly. "Kind of proud and superior and pitying. They walk like mannequins, and they don't look like Africans at all, not like any nig... blacks I ever saw. I saw a couple of girls with almond eyes, all dressed up in blue beads and copper wire. Gee, they were real beauties."

"Did you get close enough to see the flies round their eyes and mouths?" Gillian asked her, but she went on chattering about the old camp scout she saw as they left camp who had his prayer mat down and was bent double on it with his arms out towards the east.

They slept through the heat and went out again at four to watch the great herds of wildebeest and zebra filing towards the water. "The Masai hate the game," Sam explained, "because they want all the water for their cattle. On the Tanganyika side of the mountain the Wachagga have big coffee plantations and made four million pounds sterling last year. But no Masai would ever cultivate land. The southern slopes have a dozen or so European wheat farms but the Masai would never do anything with the land if it were all given to them, except multiply their tiny cattle. It would cost millions to clear the scrub and utilise the mountain water-shed, apart from the fact that it would mean that all the game would perish of thirst."

They waited around the water holes until dark, and got up again at dawn next morning to see if they could find lion, as there were vultures flying over a nearby kill, but they had no luck. They managed to photograph Gert and Daisy, the two photogenic rhino cows, who ambled about on the edge of the salt-pan, with their nose-horns grown out grotesquely to a tapering curve like bent spears about three feet long.

Then in the late afternoon they headed back across the blinding salt flats towards Namanga river, meeting the first trickle of antelope stirring from their day long doze under the umbrella thorns. They met two or three small herds of eland and hartebeest, a troop of baboons, several herds of wildebeest, Grants and Thompson's gazelle, and here and there a solitary water buck. As they approached Namanga and the road, they heard trumpeting and just before the park gates at dusk, a couple of elephant, looming enormous in the fading light, lumbered across the track towards the river. They stayed overnight at the rambling, reed-thatched hotel.

At about midnight there was a loud roaring from hunting lions, and Marie-Lou woke up and tried to turn a light on. But the power had been turned off. She insisted on lights, and Sam had to get up and get the night guards to turn the generator back on. Breakfast was a little tense, and next morning while Marie-Lou inspected the aviary of brilliant-hued sunbirds, weavers, bee-eaters and birds of paradise, Sam and Jonathan went to see Chotabai's cousin and order some supplies to be sent on.

Then they repacked and set off on the terrible road to Ngongoro. Lorries had ploughed it up in the rains and the ruts were a foot deep in places. Jonathan rode in the three-tonner with René, who never said much. You had to prise the words out of him. Very African, only his brown face was European.

Sam arranged for another truck to go down to Arusha and load stores and fill up the drums with petrol. At the Kenya - Tanganyika border the road changed to tarmac, as a change from lurching over stony tracks in a cloud of acrid lava dust. On the left the snow-streaked peak of Kilimanjaro towered out of the plain, unbelievably huge and remote, glittering in the strong sunshine, a hundred miles away.

The game at the side of the road knew that on the left was the safety of the game park, while on the right was a shooting area, and on seeing the Land Rover, they scampered across to the left. A bloated hyena slunk across the road, mangy and obscene, glancing evilly at them as it slunk into the scrub. They ran over several snakes, mostly dead, that had been basking on the warm tarmac, and just before they turned off on to the Ngongoro track they stopped to talk to a lorry-driver who had a load of four large crates, each of which contained a baby rhinoceros. They belonged to an internationally known game-catcher who had just spent three weeks on the southern slopes of the mountain trapping them by chasing them away from their mothers and lassooing them. There was a plague of rhinos on the plantations there, and they had to be thinned out. If these animals survived, Gillian explained, they would fetch up to £4,000 each in European zoos.

343

They turned off the tarmac and began to climb towards the lip of the extinct crater of the volcano, Ngongoro, bumping and lurching on the pot-holed track. After twenty minutes, rounding a bend they saw at the side of the road a table spread with a bright tablecloth, with several Africans in white kanzus, standing around a lorry. There was a cooking fire nearby and over the table a tent fly sheet had been erected. Another fly sheet was stretched out from the side of the truck, with deck-chairs set under it. Jonathan stood apart under an acacia tree.

"Say!" Wayne exclaimed. "Some characters do things in style round here."

"Some damned Maharajah or something," Sam commented archly. At the same time he swung the wheel over and drew up. An African ran over to them and bowed solemnly. "Jambo, Bwana." Then Nganga's face split into an ecstatic smile.

"Hey, what goes on, Sammy? That's Nganga." The Africans were having difficulty in suppressing their mirth by now, but when Wayne turned on Sammy and slapped him on the back, they all howled with laughter at the joke. "Gillian's idea," Sammy explained.

"Oh gee, I get it, "Marie-Lou said. "It's our lunch. All these boys look the same to me."

"Big deal," Wayne said admiringly. "Bully for you Gillian gal. I'm glad someone round here has got some brains."

"You be careful, big boy. You told me you married me for mine."

"It's a long way home to mother, honey," Wayne told his wife.

There was guinea-fowl for lunch, that Sammy had shot near the hotel that morning, and mangoes bought from the kitchen garden there. After lunch they had a short siesta and the boys packed up the truck to go down to Arusha. They set off again at three, with just one boy riding in the back of the Land Rover with Gillian.

The game lodge was high up on the lip of the Ngongoro crater. Sammy explained how the game migrated every year after the rains when the enormous flat floor of the crater held plentiful water and while the Serengeti plains dried rapidly, the grass here stayed longer, and grew higher. Every year before the rains the Masai burnt the old grass and scrub when the animals had left. Shooting in the crater was forbidden, which was an added attraction for game.

The photographer from Amboseli had a special box-body truck fitted for game observation. He had room for two more observers and so the second night Marie-Lou and Wayne went out with him to a water-hole. The warden had found a dead impala, a lion's kill, which he had salvaged from the jackals and hyenas and dragged around the water-hole to give a good scent. At dusk, they parked near the carcass and waited. Cicadas filled the air with their clicking whistle, and now and again a hyena howled and broke into a demoniacal cackle, at which Marie-Lou clutched at Wayne, hugging herself to him. The first thing they heard was a throaty, rasping "Churr." Marie-Lou gripped Wayne's arm. "Leopard," the warden said. A series of "Churrs" broke the silence, moving in a circle. "I think a mother is teaching her cubs to hunt," the warden whispered. Suddenly there was an outburst of high-pitched barking, a loud "Churr" and a final, screaming yap. Marie-Lou's nails dug into Wayne's arm. "You don't have to do that, honey, we're safe," Wayne told her. "Wha...what was it?" she asked penitently. "Leopard killing baboon," the photographer told them.

Nothing happened for some time, and Marie-Lou found relief for her nervous system by brewing some coffee. As she was handing it round, a heavy padding footfall sounded outside and the photographer stiffened, waved away the cup and got behind his tripod. The warden whispered something in his ear and he relaxed. They all craned out of the window towards the kill, and there was a lioness sniffing the dead impala, its legs stuck out rigidly from its bloated belly. The lioness let out a soft tremulous growl and three cubs padded out from the scrub. All four began to tear at the impala. When the flash-bulb illuminated them, they looked up, but took no notice, and resumed their tearing and crunching. After about five minutes, there was the sound of more heavy, padding steps and a black-maned, fully-grown lion approached the group. The lioness stood up and put up one paw towards him gently. The lion let out an angry growl that made Marie-Lou grab Wayne tightly with both arms, then he cuffed her aside, strode to the kill and the cubs scattered out of his way.

This time when the flash bulb went, the lion, who was facing the camera, stood up and swished his tail, but resumed eating immediately. "Why doesn't he get suspicious?" Marie-Lou whispered.

"Probably thinks it's lightning," the warden explained, "But animals are not usually afraid of lights in the bush. They don't connect them with danger, any more than they connect the smell of petrol and this truck with humans. We'll switch the lights on before they go, and I don't think they'll move, but they would if we started the engine probably, although lion might not, because they haven't anything to be afraid of in their natural state."

When the photographer had flashed for a while, the lion got tired of eating, picked the remains up and went off with it. They started the engine up and put the headlights on, and as they turned, they caught sight of the lioness and cubs trooping along disconsolately in the wake of the lion. "Lazy blighters lions," the warden said. "They let the lioness do all the killing. In the Nairobi Park we have to drive some away from their mates and the cubs because they pinch their food every day."

After another day watching the game in the crater bowl Wayne said he was getting his eye in, and getting used to the distances. Jonathan kept very quiet and just watched everything as carefully as he knew how. "I shall want you to flight sand grouse later," Sam said, "They make a good first toastie. So I hope you poms know how." Jonathan faked a nice smile.

The edges of the crater looked like a ring of hills all around them, and objects shimmered hazily in the short grass, with nothing to give any perspective but the crater lips.

"You cruel yahoo," Marie-Lou told Wayne. "You're as bad as that lion we saw killing that poor zebra last night. Just look at those giraffe moving. I just love the way their necks bob and those great long legs all swinging along."

"I ain't going to shoot any giraffes," Wayne said testily.

"You've got to understand that animals are getting themselves killed all the time out here. Every time some Masai or someone kills a lion or poisons a leopard, it means that two or three hundred zebra and antelope don't get killed. Someone's got to even the score and every year a couple of thousand elephants have to be killed by the Game Control boys. Isn't that so, Sam?" Sam nodded.

"Is that so?" Marie-Lou said. "Well, what about when you go and shoot some poor lion. Do you have to kill a couple of hundred other animals to even it up too?" Wayne looked at Sam blankly. "Muffinhead," he threw at her, and left it at that.

They went back to the Safari Hotel at Arusha the next evening, and the next day Sammy put the Land Rover in for an overhaul and a new set of tyres. Marie-Lou firmly refused to go back to Nairobi with Gillian, which put Sammy out slightly, because with only one hunting truck the girls would have to stay in camp most of the day, and he had already hired a car to take them back. "Wait till we bring in the tusks all covered in blood," Wayne said. "You'll yowl then. And what about those scorpions you're so scared of?"

"You just drop dead, big boy. We can hire a hunting car here, can't we, and another driver?"

"The name is Rossiter, not Rockefeller, honey."

"I'll cost you plenty up in little old Nairobi. Gillian was going to take me down to the coast some place too." Wayne sighed. "Do they have an American Express agency here, Sam?" "No but old Patel will find us a vehicle, and we can pay him in Nairobi."

"Well, I guess we'll take the old lady along. At least I've got my eye on her here."

Marie-Lou's arms snaked round his neck. She kissed him lovingly on the cheek and purred. Then she bit his ear hard and leapt away. "Big tough guy," she mocked, "Come on, Gillian let's go buy some big wide hats and bug chasers. Africa here I come. I'm just crazy about all this space. I don't ever want to see Times Square again. Just bush and a few honey-baby giraffes and a zebra or two."

"Where's this bar where they have Ernest Hemingway's

record kudu horns?" Wayne demanded. "Hold hard and I'll take you," Sam said and they disappeared on foot.

At dawn, Jonathan went out to a waterhole. In the half light there were lots of nocturnal animals sneaking off home, monitor lizards, foxes, warthog families. And the smaller game who had watered before the big cats woke up. He took Sam's loader with him, a Muslim whose job it was to "halal" the throats of birds before they died, or pretend to do it, so that the cooks could not object. If they had not been bled with a knife they were unclean. A daft notion in the bush, Jonathan thought, but had learnt to keep his mouth shut and as Babault said "act like a limey butler."

The sand grouse came in flights of fifty or more. It was not sporting, Sam said, to shoot them on the water. You had to get them as they wheeled to settle. Then Hamid had to jump in and fish them out. You needed at least four per person, grilled on toast, the cook said.

Wayne went out with Sam and the trackers and loaders to get their trophies. One elephant had tusks that weighed nearly a hundred kilos each. The other pair was much smaller, but they had to fire or they would have been trampled, so Sam said. They had been hacked out of the dead beasts with axes, and were bloody for three feet from the tooth end. Jonathan kept away from the cleaning process. His job was to see the tents were properly equipped, the cooks sober and the waiters clean; booze cold, and glasses shining.

Jonathan went out day after day to shoot for the pot, missing kudu after kudu. Having been reduced to just guinea fowl, which were easier to kill, Sam came back with Wayne's lion slung in the back of the truck. "Get it skinned Jon." Sam growled and went off to get a cold beer,

"What's for dinner?" Sam asked.

"Guinea fowl," Jon answered.

"Bugger that," Sam said, and said something very fast to René. He grabbed his nine millimetre. "Kiteme," he yelled, "Kuja hapa pesi-pesi. Ninataka kwenda piga chakula.(Come with me. I'm going to kill some meat)." He stalked off.

"What was that?" Jon asked Gillian. "Him Bwana go shoot

little deer for din-dins," she laughed and swallowed her gin and tonic. But sure enough just as it got dark, they heard one shot. René re-appeared, walking very fast, and behind him Kiteme with a kudu slung over his back. Gillian took out a silver tray and served him a large Tusker beer and one for Wayne. She pulled Jonathan away. "Let's see the cooks cut it up properly." she hissed. "And you make damn sure the Bwana has hot water for his bafu or he'll have your balls for breakfast."

"Watch it, girl," Jonathan said, "I am not the bloody head waiter."

Gillian left to Nairobi, and Wayne went out day after day with Sam and René. Jonathan pretended to be busy, but spent much time just reading, Hemingway mostly. Marie-Lou got bored, and started to look at him oddly. She gave up wearing trousers and changed to skirts and shirts, which showed off her fine plump figure. Her cleavage started to become more prominent, and she gave up wearing bras. She called for drinks with lunch and after it went for long siestas. Her lunchtime martinis got bigger and bigger. Jonathan watched without comment. Wayne, Sam and René came and went. The days got hotter. Rain seemed to threaten. Marie-Lou was getting bored.

Then the day came Jonathan had dreaded. Marie-Lou had about six martinis at lunch and stumbled as she went to her tent. Jonathan went to his, sleepy after a large beer. He was woken by Marie-Lou, sitting on his bed. "Hey," she said muzzily, "you know you are real cute?".

Jonathan shook off sleep and sat up, gulping. "Let's have a bit of you-know-what," she purred, putting her arms around him. The camp bed creaked. Jon tried to get off it, but he was trapped. She slipped off her purple satin dressing gown, and of course she was naked. Chestnut hair all loose, her heavy breasts swinging in his face. As she flung her body on top of him, the bed collapsed and she giggled as Jonathan fell on top of her, struggling.

Sam's words went through his head as their limbs thrashed. "Camp managers get do a load of lousy jobs. Screwing the clients' bored girlfriends is on the list. Just shut your eyes and screw for Kenya."

Angry now, Jonathan wriggled out of the tent, grabbing shorts, shirt and sandals as he went. Sure enough one of the cooks was watching as he wrenched on his clothes. He went back to the tent for his shotgun and strode off to the salt pan where the sand grouse flighted. He was too early for them, but there might be guinea fowl at this time of day.

He waited for the sand grouse until sunset, returning to camp with all his pockets bulging with dead birds. He would dress up formally for dinner, he thought, and pretend it never happened. This plan was aborted when he found Marie-Lou still asleep on the bent remains of his bed. He dragged out the suitcase with his uniform in it. The Rangers made even national servicemen buy the Number One dress, a dark green jacket with a high-buttoned collar and tightish trousers with a black stripe. As he struggled into the short black chukka boots, she woke up. "Wrong tent, darling," he said, and left her to re-assemble herself. He had to go back several times to make sure she got into her own tent.

This, as it turned out was just as well, because, although she did not appear at dinner, Wayne, René and Sam returned unexpectedly about 8pm. "Where is she?" Wayne asked.

"Dunno," Jonathan said, swallowing his second gin and tonic, pretending to read a book.

Write to me, Lalage had asked, and Jonathan, with time on his hands, wrote about the hunting and the animals, and how he spent his day. He also did a lot of thinking about the future. He had written a piece for the East African Standard, on the scenery around the Aberdares. They had published it.

After they had been gone for a three weeks, an envelope was hand-delivered to Lalage, from the base, with no address, just "To L with love." She ripped it open. There were two sheets of paper. The first said just. "This is to tell you how I miss you. And why I shall always come back to you. Only later I can tell you how."

The second was headed,

"REMEMBRANCE."

"There was a blue lake, cupped in an old crater,
And just you silent standing there.
Below us, Africa burns in the dry plains.
I see your face still in that high thin air.
From the volcano-wasted streams of water flow
Down into the dust and thorns below
Here only the birds and the clouds
Reign high over the shimmering plain.
Because I have lived with you
In my heart so long now, it is a rare
And dreary hour that is not pierced
By some memory that we share.
In the high wild wilderness of the Aberdare
I see your face in the bracken and the briars
Hear your voice in the sigh of the leleshwa
The surge and swish of the bamboo groves.
Because I move with you in my heart
My soldiers think that I walk without fear.
They don't know that with death so near
I see only the firelight glitter in your hair. "

CHAPTER TWENTY SEVEN

THE ENEFDEE – NORTHERN FRONTIER DISTRICT

"Leave thy father,
Leave thy mother
And thy brother;
Leave the black tents of your tribe apart!
Am I not thy father and thy brother,
And thy mother?
And thou – what needest thou with thy tribe's black tents
Who hast the red pavilion of my heart?"

Francis Thompson

As planned in early December, Lerrick arranged for a month's leave. He intended to spend most of it doing a survey of game movements in the Northern Frontier District, ending up with a week at Malindi for Christmas, a holiday resort seventy miles north of Mombasa. The Hemingways were to be there recuperating after their two plane crashes. Jonathan applied for the "embarkation leave," due to him, and Angela Gynne unwillingly let both Lalage and Alison go. By this time she had acquired two more assistants.

"I need to show you more of what we have to offer here," Lalage explained.

"Mm," Jonathan said, thinking, Bugger it, I'll have to write a letter to Joanna. No. I won't. I'll just tell her when I get back, so sod it. He was getting hardened to the Kenya way of just getting on with life and to hell with it.

Tom borrowed a big safari car with two rows of bench seats, and with all the usual paraphernalia. With a flat-bottomed boat on the roof and two native boys they set off for Mount Kenya. The first day they drove straight through Nanyuki, the market town on the western shoulder of the mountain, to spend the night at Isiolo, a settlement containing about thirty assorted officials and their families, and a platoon of the King's African Rifles. The country gradually thinned out to scrub-covered savannah, once past the cedar forest of the foothills, the road sloped down from 8,000 to 4,000 feet.

As they drove, Tom explained, "I reckon the Mau Mau are over. I want to see places I have not been able to visit for five years. It's a non-shooting safari. We all deserve a bit of R. and R!"

It was strange for Jonathan to look back and see behind him the other side of the mountain he knew so well, a sharp, jagged peak towering up 17,000 feet, blue-black and menacing in the evening light, capped with a cone of perpetual snow. There was the home of Ngai, the Kikuyu god who had forsaken the tribe; the mysterious place where the cold "white stone," barafu, (ice), glittered forever on the peak in the equatorial sun. The other side of the mountain seemed a very different place from the lush greenery of the Kikuyu Reserve, with its contour terracing and crooked red-murram roads. For him the mountain and the Aberdare forest were places of blood and spilled guts smelling of burnt flesh. Memories he wanted to forget. Mount Kenya was for him a place of horror. *Le mal d'Afrique.* For him, the place of ambush, anxiety, fear of the unknown and the unexpected.

Ahead of them the road stretched on downwards towards a desert. A buff-white-yellow plain scattered with bare white rocks and isolated flat-topped umbrella thorn. In the distance a solitary mountain stood up from the plain, and over to the right, some low, lonely-looking hills. The colours were elemental under a sky, sea-green without any cloud. As they approached the bleak little settlement of Isiolo in the fading light, clouds sprung up on the horizon, ballooning upward in great woolly, viscid shapes. The plain took on pastel shades of red and orange, dust grey, chocolate brown, black and pink. The sky paled and the clear light hazed.

353

He looked back through the dust trail thrown up by the car. The dust so finely churned, rose up twenty feet in the air and dissipated only slowly. There were clouds gathering around the base of the mountain, which was black now except where the light caught the summit from the far western side, turning the peak to a burning glow of red-gold. The sky behind it caught tints of blood-red, and then became streaked with huge, tattered bands of burning coppery light.

Isiolo settlement was just a row of Indian shops on both sides of the road, with a government boma at the end where the Administration offices were. The road ended in a barrier and a police post. Ahead, the road went straight on to the Ethiopian border three hundred miles away. A battered signpost said "Wajir, Moyale." They turned left and dived down into the dried-up course of a river and up the hill to where the bungalows of the Europeans were scattered amongst the thorn trees.

Jasper Thorpe, their host, was the Intelligence Officer for the whole area, from the Uganda and Sudan borders to the north-west, the Somalia border and the sea to the east, and Ethiopia to the north. 150,000 square miles of sand, camels, scrub, dust and rock. With an inland sea 150 miles long, Lake Rudolf is in an area larger than Britain, populated by a few thousand itinerant Somali and a few small Stone Age tribes on the fringes.

Jasper was a giant of a man, black-bearded with a bald, freckled cranium, and a deep bass voice. A chest so wide you thought he must have padding underneath his shirt, and a confident manner that showed immediately how little daunted he was by the huge complexity of his task.

He was known as 'The Sultan', Tom explained, and by a lot of other less complimentary names. He had spent almost his whole life in Somalia, Ethiopia and the Northern Frontier District of Kenya. The bald head contrasted with the huge black beard. Jonathan whispered to Lalage, "He's got his face on upside down." He dodged her elbow

They parked beside Jasper's immaculate, ancient blue Land Rover under a matting screen, and a horde of sharp-nosed, slit-eyed natives wearing blue kilembe head-dresses descended on

354

the truck, and despite the protests of Tom's two boys, Matt and Mzee, took every single thing out of it. "We'll pack you up properly tomorrow," Jasper boomed, and his laugh echoed from the scrub-covered hill behind the bungalow. "Glad to see you Tom. Where's your fiancée?"

Tom had announced his engagement a week before. Tom introduced Alison, who winced as her hand was shaken. Lalage noticed, and said, "Gently now. I met you once before with Sammy, my brother. Do you remember?"

"Sorry. No."

Lalage started to say something and then stopped. Sam had had a bit of bother with the D.C. – the District Commissioner, who was boss here.

Jasper, calling for his houseboys, roared again so loudly that the gecko lizard clinging to the wall in search of insects gave a violent start and fell off. "Anyway," he said, "our big White Chief wanted to know what the hell you were doing swanning up here with two Memsaabs, so I told him you were doing a job for me and the Memsaabs were both relations. Also mentioned you were Papa Hemingway's hunter, and he was expecting you."

A boy arrived with a message from another bungalow, and Jasper read it, and told them that they were all invited for a sundowner at "The Club." After a wash they all piled into Jasper's Land Rover and lurched down the washed-out track to a tiny thatched clubhouse where practically everybody was assembled to celebrate the return of the District Officer from leave. It was just like a large family gathering, since everybody there knew everybody else's Christian name, and everybody, Police, Veterinary, Colonial Service, Game Department, Public Works Department, and Hides and Skins Improvement Officers wore more or less the same khaki shirts and shorts.

Conversation was all local gossip. How the hyena and leopard were being a nuisance in the gardens again. Mrs X had had her fences smashed by elephant. Mrs Y had called out a vet to go up the hill to see her pet lion that turned out to be constipated and had to be given an enema and carried down on a stretcher by six natives. The D.O. had been posted to Moyale, a frontier post established to keep the peace amongst the Boran tribesmen who herded cattle on the Ethiopian border and crossed from side to side at will. He would have for company a European policeman and a long range wireless, a handful of native policemen, and if he was lucky an occasional visit from an official buyer of hides, skins or cattle.

They had to stay until nearly ten, and when they reached Jasper's house he merely said a few quiet words to his head-boy and dinner appeared at once.

"We don't keep civilised hours here," he said apologetically. "Probably because," he paused for thought, and added, "because we're not very civilised." He stroked his beard reflectively and looked at each of them in turn, silently.

"Can you give me a rough idea of where you are going on your game survey, and when?" he asked Tom a few mouthfuls later. "I have to let the patrols know and I can wire ahead and arrange petrol. Also we do have patrols out, in case Mau-Mau come down off the mountain."

"I thought of going up to the border," Tom said, "Or anyway as far as Marsabit, and then back by Garissa to Malindi, spending a week or two on the Tana on the way."

Jasper's head shot up. "What would you be doing on the Tana? I saw your boat."

Tom smiled, "I thought we might pot the odd croc. Alison would like a handbag."

"I never mentioned a handbag," Alison said indignantly.

"Never mind. As long as we know," Jasper said, "I thought it wouldn't be like you to lounge about in the bush doing nothing. Well let's see. Marsabit is 380 miles return. Two days there, that's four. Back here Saturday, leave here Monday for Garba Tula, via Mudi Gashi, or will you go up to Habbaswein?" Tom shook his head. There seemed to be some private joke about Habbaswein.

"Well, Garba Tula is about seventy from here, a slow seventy a day. The Tana is another day, about fifty, but the track along the river to Saka is terrible. I'd go straight to Saka, eighty, then Garissa is only forty and there's petrol there. Malindi is a good two hundred from Garissa. If you spend a week on the

Tana, the whole trip will take you three weeks less a day or two. We'd better see Mohammed about grub. Today's the third, you'll be back on the seventh, off on the ninth, Tana by the eleventh, a week there, the eighteenth, one day to re-fit in Garissa, so you should reach Malindi by the twenty-first in time for Christmas. OK?"

"You know it has to be, you old bear. Is the bridge at Bura intact?"

"Yes, but the Garba Tula – Saka stretch is bad. Wash-outs all the way. You must have four wheel drive and low reduction if possible."

"We have it," Tom said.

Jasper explained about Mohammed, the local duka wallah. "There isn't a bank in Isiolo, so the Indian traders finance most things from film safari provisions to tiny Somali dukas in mud-hut villages. The Indians, who are more often than not related and Muslims, provide the lorries to carry stores, stocks of ironmongery, rations and safari equipment. Once a pal of mine was buying Boran cattle up on the border and he needed two thousand quid. He sent a message down and two days later a babu arrived with the cash in a Gladstone bag." After a few more such stories they went to bed to dream of the oases on the road to Wajir, El Wak and Mandera, of the Blue Pool at Buffalo Springs and the emptiness of the desert.

Next morning Jasper said, "We should go and see the Adamsons. As Tom knows, George is the game warden for the NFD. They keep catching lion cubs and trying to tame them. He's lived here all his life. She's a bit odd. Austrian, I think. Calls herself Joy. Takes a lot of photos."

The Webbs, Lalage explained were not friends of the Adamsons. "Sammy had a run in with George. He had been charged by a bull with miserable ivory, and had shot it. The local district officer and the then Game Warden, knowing Sammy, had overlooked it, but someone else reported it and Sammy had had to count it on his licence. Then a week later the same man who had shopped Sammy reported having shot a bull carrying tusks of eighty-six and ninety pounds, but he admitted to having had to shoot at another one in self-defence. A scout found it over thirty miles away from the first one, with one bullet in its head, and vehicle tracks near it. Meaning that it hadn't just wandered there alone. So Sammy's rival lost both his licences for the year. And bad-mouthed Sammy as a result. In a small place these matters were known to all."

When they got to the Adamsons' house, they were asked if they would like to see the lion cub. It was out for a walk. Jonathan said he had to rest his leg a bit. Joy served him tea.

"You know," she said, "my husband gets paid only about a thousand pounds a year. You white hunters get paid thousands for just one safari, don't you?" Jonathan let her go on. She was really bitter. Suddenly, he thought he'd better tell her.

"I'm just a soldier. I get paid even less." She didn't comment. Just looked grim. Within ten years she was a very wealthy woman.

Later he followed lion spoor to the top of a small hill. There was an African game warden there, with the cub chained to his wrist. He sat with a rifle between his knees.

"What's the chain for?" he asked George.

"Well, when Elsa here sees a herd of elephant or whatever, she tries to run after them and to hamstring them. That's because she has not been taught by her mother what to kill, and how to do it."

"So what's the gun for?"

"If Cheroge here can't hold her, he fires one in the air. That scares the beasts off and tells me to come running."

Jonathan went up to stroke the cub. It licked his bare knees. "Ow!" he yelped as he felt hairs being pulled out by the roots. "That hurts."

"Do not flinch or jerk away. They can misinterpret sudden movements." George said. "Not their fault their tongue is designed to rasp meat off bones."

He liked George, who was very calm and peaceful, with a grizzled beard and the usual battered bush hat. It was years later that Elsa became famous through Joy's book and photographs; and became so very rich.

Years later they recalled that day when they first saw," Elsa the Lioness," film star.

African voices woke them next morning. The clicking, nasal sound of Somali mixed with the staccato music of Swahili. Jasper had their truck loaded and breakfast ready by eight. At nine they passed the police barrier and by ten they had crossed the Uaso Nyiro River and stopped at Buffalo Springs for a swim. The pool had been blasted out of the rock by South African troops on their way up to Addis Ababa with Wingate in 1943. For some reason or other the water was a deep turquoise, although all the surrounding rock was a blinding white. They shooed a few curious Somalis away and plunged in. Lalage was quite prepared to swim with the men, but after discussion with Alison she agreed to wait, as none of them had unpacked costumes. The cases with Malindi hotel clothes were deep inside the truck.

"I did one of my film extra bits here." Lalage said "As Sam kindly told you. Remember? I stood in for Ava Gardner. Swimming in the raw in this very pool." Jonathan remembered. Tom had said there was only half an hour, as they had to be through Archer's Post by eleven, with another hundred and fifty miles to go to Marsabit. "No time to rummage for bathing gear." So they all plunged in together. Jon felt a bit embarrassed, but tried not to show it. Lalage grinned at him, as she caught him sneaking a look at Allison's curves.

The girls got into the back with their hair still dripping and they bumped back on to the road. Flocks of vulturine guinea fowl dotted the sides of the road. They had the bare necks of vultures with a ruff of blue feathers at the base and their backs were spotted blue and white. Tom made Jonathan take the wheel and with one cartridge shot two birds for their evening meal. Mzee, who professed to be Muslim, fired with holy zeal amongst so many Mahommadans, cut off their heads with a knife before he gutted them.

The road was just a camel track scraped flat with a mechanical scraper. Every few miles there was a wash-out across the road, and the vehicle had to slow down to avoid breaking springs. No one was allowed on it during the rains, so that its surface was not as rutted or as corrugated as many of the main roads further south.

Gradually the country became more and more arid, until all that could be seen for miles around was a huge expanse of undulating sandy desolation with sparse dust-covered scrub. At noon they stopped at a rough hut on the side of the road, that had been used by Desert Locust Control to store poison bait. They stretched out inside it on a tarpaulin, while Mzee and Matt squatted outside under a tree and unpacked the lunch that Jasper had provided.

At one-thirty they started again, with four to five hours driving ahead of them. Lalage insisted on driving and Jonathan sat beside here to warn her of wash-outs and keep her awake by talking to her. After half an hour with the tyres singing monotonously in the thick dust, they came to a collection of huts around a water-pump where a camel caravan had stopped to water. A herd of Boran cattle were milling round an almost dry water-pan scooped out of the ground. These had travelled three hundred miles already from the Ethiopian border on their way to the cattle sales at Nanyuki, accompanied by the dingbats and dukabahs; Somali scouts who rode their camels, slung with long oblong water-cans, keeping the herd of two thousand or so head, on the track. The scrub, Tom explained was full of protein, although it didn't look it, and the zebu cattle with their hump-backs, sagging dewlaps and scruffy, tan and white skins, were used to the minimum of nutrition. The farmers would cross them with imported Hereford and Jersey bulls and their calves would be resistant to heat and to most diseases as well, apart from growing to a much larger size than the diminutive Boran cattle.

After that they saw nothing for hours, except a few bleached bones of dead cattle, until Lalage, exhausted with fighting the wheel to keep the heavy vehicle out of the storm drains, handed over to Jonathan.

He saw nothing ahead of him at first except the blinding track, a few stunted fever trees. No tree, even the cactus-like euphorbia, like a twisted candelabra, grew more than a few feet high. After another thirty miles however he began to see ahead of him what looked like a sugar-loaf mountain springing straight out of the surrounding plains. As he drove nearer it looked as though the mountain, mirage or whatever it was, had a halo of clouds around its summit. The others were all dozing, but in his excitement he shouted back to Tom, "There's a mountain ahead. Marsabit?" Tom stirred and shook the dust from his hat.

"Yes. Another couple of hours now. Amazing, isn't it? The moisture condenses on the slopes and it's so high that clouds going over, rain on it. It must have just been a rock once, and now its completely afforested, with plenty of water, and there's nothing but desert for hundreds of miles around, except for Lake Rudolf, about ninety miles over there." He pointed towards the west.

They arrived at the game lodge an hour before dark. It was strange to see trees and green shrubs again. Everywhere there were elephant droppings and spoor of smaller game. It was a perfect, natural game reserve, and formed a much needed oasis for all species. Looking down at the plain from the slopes, it looked as though the sea had receded, leaving this island thrust up inexplicably. Jonathan was reminded of Mont St Michel, with the salt flats and quicksands uncovered at low tide. The Lodge hadn't been used for tourists since the Emergency, and Matt and Mzee cleaned it out and unloaded while Alison and Lalage cooked supper.

"We'll go and pay our respects to Mohammed tomorrow," Tom said.

"Who?" Alison asked.

"It's an old bull elephant," Lalage told her. "Everyone knows him, or says they do, and for a lone bull, he's pretty affable."

"They say his tusks must be enormous, but I don't know," Tom said. "Last time I was close to him, about five years ago, I'd say only about 130 pounds a side, although he is probably nearer 150 in years. One of the tips was broken off too. I'd like to see them when he does die, all the same."

"Won't he go away and hide before he dies, to an elephant graveyard or somewhere?" Alison asked.

"I don't think so. All animals go somewhere to hide before they die, if they have time. They say the Lorian swamp is a place where they go. It's beyond Habbaswein, so we might visit it. But even if it was you wouldn't find any ivory, because porcupines, for example, love it, and ants eat ivory too."

"So much," Jonathan said, "for the myths about ivory in elephant graveyards."

They intended to get up before dawn, climb as high as they could and watch the sun rise out of the Indian Ocean, over five hundred miles away across the nothingness of Somalia.

It was nearly light when Jonathan woke, and knowing it was too late he went outside to see what there was left of the sunrise. As he sat there on a log watching, he heard a rustle and turned to see Lalage in a sweater and slacks, almost beside him. She smiled and sat down silently. He put out his hand and touched hers, and she answered by clasping it, and leaned over so her head rested on his arm.

"Wonderful, isn't it?" she whispered. "Terrible emptiness and silence. Nobody at all. It's like the sea. Endless and meaningless and frightening. So pointless and useless and empty and dead. But we love it."

Jonathan nodded. He had been thinking of the hermits who went out in the desert, because now for the first time he was glimpsing their reason. There was just the sun and the sky, and nothing to distract. When Lalage said "empty," he was going to say, "except for God, perhaps," but he didn't want to break the mood. She considered his attitude to God as priggish. There had been arguments before. A jackal slunk on noiseless feet, gliding through the short scrub below. Three vultures hovered in the distance. A cloud of grey-green sand grouse whirred overhead, and from the trees behind he could hear guinea-fowl calling.

"Over there," Lalage pointed south-east, "that's the Tana. Just think. One day there will be a dam, and instead of all the soil from the reserve going down the river into the sea, the water will spread, maybe right over to here. All that soil needs to be fertile, is water."

"You've been listening to old Lerrick," he teased her.

"Wait till you see the Tana. Red with mud the whole year. Terrible. One day there'll be a line of pylons stretching from the dam to here, and we'll have a town here, saw-mills, mines, factories."

"What a weird thought; also devastating. And sad."

"I was thinking of Sammy and the animals. Tom wouldn't mind if it was good for Kenya, but Sammy would hate it if it meant less room for the animals. I'm afraid my dear brother isn't very progressive. He wants Kenya to be kept as a wild place, just as it is. No dams or new towns."

"That's what René Babault says too. He wants all of East Africa and beyond as one glorious hunting reserve."

"I see his point. Right here, for example, there is not much else you can do."

They watched the scene below them in silence for a while. As the sun rose higher, there was less and less movement. A tattered-looking Marabou Stork, looking like a seedy old waiter, glided heavily along and alighted at a respectful distance from the lodge. The sand grouse flew back from where they had been watering, and as the heat grew, movement ceased.

Lalage went over to wake the boys, and soon a sharp smell of coffee floated in the air. She came back and they laid a table outside. Tom appeared, apologising for having overslept.

"I suppose you can't blame people like Sammy," Lalage mused. "After all, he doesn't know about anything else except this part of Africa."

"What's all this?" Tom asked.

"Just saying how Sammy wouldn't want this place changed."

"Nor would I."

"Developed, I mean. Dams, irrigation, hydro-electric schemes."

"There's plenty of land half-developed now. Look at the reserves. Look at Sam's place."

"One thing I will agree with you, Lala. Some of these huge estates in the Rift and round the mountain should be split up and developed, especially those where the owners are absentees. I grant you that would help with the land-hunger. But think of the panic that would cause amongst the successful farmers. Who would buy land off them if they wanted to sell?"

"Politics before breakfast? Awfully boring." Alison

363

appeared, looking terribly English behind her sun-glasses, and in her neat bush slacks and a sweater. Everyone else being in tatty shorts and an old shirt.

"Nice to see your early-in-the-morning-face, dear, after these argumentative men." Lalage said.

"Aren't we going to see Mohammed this morning, Tom?" Alison asked.

"He'll be in the trees by now, but we'll look."

Five days later, after a re-fit at Isiolo, and a visit to the Lorian swamp, they reached the belt of tall riverine trees along the edge of the Tana, and camped in the long grass under a huge tree. The tree had long grey pods like massive liver sausages hanging from it. Mzee's red, rheumy eyes lit up, and he was seen splitting several of them in half. "The next thing," Tom said, "is, he'll follow a honey-guide bird and get some wild honey and make a fearful brew of raw spirit with those pods. If we aren't careful he'll be drunk for a week."

The river was wide and shallow, and full of hippos and crocodile. Elephant and buffalo browsed in the thickly entangled bushes at the water's edge. In the morning and evening there was a constant procession of animals drinking. On the two sides of the river different species of the same animal existed, although in places it would be easy to cross over the shallows, stepping on rocks. "On the northern side," Tom explained, "Grevy's zebras are larger than the southern kind, with bigger, squarer stripes and tiny round ears. The giraffe on the north bank are reticulated with better defined patches than the ordinary. And the oryx, with their beautiful, spectacularly curved horns keep apart. Callotis on the north, Beisa on the south bank."

Tom took the boat down from the truck roof and let it float while he rigged up a spot-light in the bows and connected it to a six-volt battery. Matt went off with some of the rough salt brought to preserve the skins, and traded it with the locals for maize. Jonathan went out with Lalage to shoot a gazelle to make a curry. Getting out of the truck near a herd of Grant's gazelle, he took Tom's Winchester .270, while Lalage carried the .475, in case they blundered into a rhino. "Get downwind first, you clot,"

Lalage hissed and Jonathan groaned inwardly at his ineptitude. As they crept over to the right, a gerenuk started up, a red flash, and was gone, luckily, away from the gazelle. A few minutes later a pair of dik-dik appeared and stood there trembling, looking at them with their big, soft eyes. Lalage stopped and gazed at them until suddenly they streaked away on their delicate, stick-like legs.

There were traces of rhino about, shallow grooves in the soil at the roots of bushes, showing where they had been rubbing their horns. Just as they got within range of the gazelle, a flock of bustards got up, and the herd they were stalking moved on. They went back to the car and drove slowly on, seeing several water-buck, which they ignored, since the meat is unpalatable. Jonathan then stalked a bull oryx without success, until he was half a mile from the car, when it finally moved far out of range. They returned thoughtfully to the car and Lalage drove back towards camp. After a few minutes she stopped suddenly, grabbed the .270 and moved off into some thick bush. Two shots rang out before Jonathan and Mzee had caught up with her. Mzee ran forward knife in hand to slit the throat of a young impala that lay kicking on the side of a slope about 150 yards away.

"Well done," Jonathan said, still rather shaken by Lalage's sudden move.

"It's either that or hunger," she said quietly, watching Mzee pick the beautiful dead animal up and sling it across his shoulders. Jonathan didn't say anything, but her cool bushcraft amazed him. How many women could not only handle a high velocity rifle, but stalk a wild animal and kill it cleanly?

That afternoon Tom tried out the outboard engine, and an hour before dusk Jonathan and Matt joined him with an axe, a shotgun and the .270, and they chugged upstream. As it grew dark Tom cut the engine and turned the boat round. As they did so, three shiny black shapes, low in the water, erupted with a tremendous splash and violent indignant snorts. Jonathan froze with fright as the three hippos plunged towards the bank and blundered through the undergrowth. "If we are upset ever," Tom remarked gently, "swim downstream under water. Get on to the bank." He began to swing the light from its pivot in the prow, leaving Jonathan to wonder what happened when the water was only a foot deep when the boat overturned.

Tom explained, "The idea here is that we only bother when the eyes are about a foot apart. Then we know that the croc is big enough to have a decent skin. No use shooting little 'uns. No one will buy the skin."

As they drifted downstream, Matt guiding with a paddle, the light caught here and there the wicked red eyes of crocodiles close to the bank. They paid no attention to the light, but if Matt knocked the paddle on the side of the boat they disappeared in a flash. "There's a big 'un, if it isn't a hippo," Tom whispered. "Sit still for the first one and just balance the boat." Jonathan, petrified, nodded dumbly. As they approached the bank Tom stood up in the bows with the shot-gun in the crook of his arm, holding the light with the other. As they got within ten feet, the twin red orbs disappeared. "Feeding," Tom whispered, "Get ready to hand Matt the axe, will you?"

Jonathan, delighted to have something to do to relieve the tension, groped carefully for it. Matt, he noticed, was squatting with the gaff across his thighs, holding the boat steady, with the paddle in both hands. The eyes re-appeared and a blast of red flame split the darkness, the recoil rocking the boat. Tom leapt over the side, grabbing the axe as he went, and Matt gaffed the dying croc under the jaw-bone. Tom, standing in three feet of water, smashed the croc on the head with the axe. "Kwisha, Bwana," Matt murmured, and Tom climbed back as Matt hauled the carcass over the side. They paddled to the bank and threw it out.

"Collect that in the morning," Tom said. "Next time, you whack it on the head. I may get out and grab its tail, as they sink quickly and float away if you don't. If the water is deep then I won't of course, so you might have to give Matt a hand to hold it on the gaff, or, even better, balance the boat." Jonathan's mouth was too dry to reply. He was calculating how far it was back to the camp, and how soon they would reach it. Tom loaded another heavy S.S.G. shot cartridge and Matt swung the boat out into the sluggish current.

It was ten minutes before they saw another with eyes far enough apart to justify shooting, but before they reached it, the boat stuck on a sand bank and they all got out to push. Jonathan felt sure that at any moment his bare foot would contact a slimy, scaly skin, and his ankle would be gripped in a pair of vice-like jaws. He hopped back into the boat the minute the water reached his knees. His nerves had had no time to recover from this when Tom focused on a pair of eyes which floated across the river in front of them. Jonathan could feel his heart thumping as Tom slowly stood up. "Take the light," he whispered, and lifted the rifle slowly to his shoulder. The rifle meant a large croc, he had told Jonathan, who wondered as he felt a hot, quivering throb rise nearer and nearer his throat, whether it could have anything to do with the primitive instinct to hunt.

The rifle exploded and the croc submerged, its tail threshing viciously, almost hitting the lurching boat. Tom, poised and tense, kept his eye glued to the sights while Jonathan raked the water with the light. Tom fired again at a patch of bubbles and a white, clawed foot flapped above the surface. A second later a greenish-white belly floated up and Matt paddled over to it and leapt out. "Good one," Tom said, handing a stake out to Matt who was tying a cord to the neck of the carcass.

"We have to stake the big ones and come up and skin them in the morning."

On the way back to the camp they got two more eight-footers, keeping the last one in the boat. There was a peculiar sour odour from the carcass, which increased Jonathan's loathing no little.

Lalage and Alison had hot coffee and a curry waiting for them beside a blazing fire. "How was it?," Lalage asked.

"Not bad at all," Tom said. "Four."

"Terrible," Jonathan said. "Just terrible." His hand shook as he gulped at his coffee.

"And don't say I'll get used to it. I won't."

"I sympathise," Alison said. "I'll never want another pair of crocodile shoes, ever, after seeing that horrible thing." Matt was busy skinning it in the light of another fire near the truck.

"Averaging six bob an inch, there's twenty-five quid there already," Tom said. "If the big one hasn't got buttons, that is."

"Buttons?" Alison asked.

"Hard spots in the belly-skin that leave holes when the skin is tanned. Some are nipples. Not all. Instead of twelve bob an inch, you only get two bob, if that."

"Ugh. I still think they are quite the most revolting beasts I've ever seen." Alison shivered.

"The first stages of shoe-leather aren't pretty, you know." Tom told her. "I haven't finished my curry," Lalage protested.

Jonathan pulled his net aside to watch the dawn sky. They were sleeping without tents. The sun was already behind the dom-palms on the other bank, and in a clearing, two waterbuck were aureoled against the growing light. A slight wind blew upriver, ruffling the water, and a few great whirls of cloud ballooned higher and drifted away over the trees, leaving the sky a blue palette for the spreading light. A baboon screamed, breaking the stillness, and a tree crackled and rustled as a whole school of monkeys poured down from it and scampered away. Far down river an elephant trumpeted, and then the baboon cackled again, and a squeakier voice answered it. "Curse that dirty old baboon," Lalage grumbled sleepily.

"Why do they have to start their sex lives at this hour?"

"It hadn't occurred to me," Jonathan admitted.

"Huh. It's rape of course, you innocent. You'd better wake Tom. He'll want to get out to his corpses before the sun gets at 'em."

"Or the other crocs?"

"No. They don't start eating their relations until they're nice and high."

Presumably you couldn't live with Sammy for twenty odd years without picking up these unpleasant facts. He was seeing a side of Lalage that he had half guessed at. The tough, bush-whacking side, which she very sensibly preferred to conceal as a rule. Yesterday he had realised fully the enormous gap between himself and her personality. And between any two people brought up, one in Europe, the other in Africa, regardless of race.

He wondered if Alison felt the same, but perhaps she was accustomed to living in different places with her father, and expected to settle out of Europe. And maybe it was easier for a woman to adapt herself when she didn't have to compete daily with people of another tradition. Tom's mother had succeeded. But then Lalage's mother had not.

He gave it up, and lay watching a Bateleur eagle gliding lazily above his head, until he heard Lalage talking to the boys and got up to wake Tom.

Tom was sleeping very heavily. It was the lack of responsibility, he said, on his first holiday for three years. After breakfast they took the boat upstream to skin the three crocs they had left, and later they took the truck down river to a swamp area where Tom wanted to see how the elephant and buffalo there were faring. Papa Hemingway had asked for a report.

In the evening they sat watching the sunset. Alison wanted to see if there was really a "green flash" as the last of the sun's rim dipped below the horizon, so they went out to a knoll away from the river and sat in the cool shade of a baobab with a view over the plain. A river of sand a hundred yards wide, that carried the storm water in the rains, passed round the side of the hill. They lay under the tree drinking in the emptiness and peace.

"What day is it?" Lalage asked dreamily. Nobody knew, except that it was about the 13th. "We'll have to be at Garissa in about four days," Tom said.

"Oh, don't calculate, Tom, just relax," Lalage told him. She had arranged that they all had their own tents. This solved the who sleeps with who problem. She went to Jonathan's tent every night. They had both given up on any pretence.

The wind rose a little, wafting the few puffy clouds towards the sea, three hundred miles away. The western sky turned slowly violet, with a band of sea-green near the horizon. As the sun sank, the sky became mauve, streaked with blood-red, and in a few minutes the first stars appeared, with a glowing red planet low down on the horizon. The moon came up in a crescent below Venus, and one by one the stars of the Southern Cross pricked the clear, velvety blue.

Silently they climbed back into the truck and drove to the

camp. Tom woke Jonathan at four and they floated downstream this time, to Jonathan's relief, without seeing many crocodiles, and shooting only one. As it got light the larger animals came down to the water, and they had a magnificent view of a small herd of elephant watering. They were all covered in grey mud and the light caught on the clean patches of their tusks as their wet trunks rubbed against them. Once they startled a giraffe which was drinking with its neck pushed out and down between its two unbelievably stretched-out front legs.

They tied the boat up at some rapids and walked along the bank. Tom saw a croc lying on a rock in a pool, and stalked from behind, but, when shot, it fell into the water. He took the gaff from Matt and waded waist-deep into the pool. Jonathan stood watching with his teeth clenched, holding the rifle unsteadily. After what seemed like several minutes Tom let out a cry of "Got 'im" and retreated. Seeing Jonathan's drawn face he said laughing,

"You've always got a minute or so clear. The thing to look for is the blood in the bubbles, to see that the one you're fishing for is really dead."

After that they walked away from the river, Tom setting a terrific pace, threading his way through the bush, until after half an hour they reached a group of tents in a clearing. "How on earth did you know where to find this?" Jonathan asked, astonished. "Saka Police Camp," Tom replied blandly."A mile west of the rapids."

The days went by like that, to be remembered ever after, by Jonathan at least, as the Day of the Kudu; the Day of the Leopard's visit; the Day of the Buffalo. Finally they broke camp and moved down to Garissa to replenish stores. Garissa was a caravanserai, shopkeepers speaking only Somali and Arabic, ill-equipped to supply Europeans. Tom handed in his salt-pickled skins to be taken back to the Nairobi Tannery, and collected the drum of petrol Jasper had arranged for them. Lalage had run out of cigarettes, and while she was buying some, Jonathan watched an African filling his snuff horn with a mixture called by a native name, that she said meant "Not for Children." It seemed to be a mixture of soda and black tobacco, roughly ground.

Although the stores sold the very minimum of essential goods nearly all stocked one of the cola drinks.

They spent the night in a rest house, and the next day did 150 miles across rocky, washed-out tracks alongside the river, crossing it at a place the natives called "the empty or useless place" and camping at a dried-out river that flowed into the Tana. They had to put stones and branches down to get over it next morning, but they reached the coast after five hours driving. They could smell the sea, and the green coastal vegetation for the last thirty miles, where the road dropped downhill and the temperature and humidity rapidly climbed. The road now ran along parallel with the Indian Ocean.

By five o'clock they were waiting for the Mambrui ferry to cross the Galana, and then there was only ten miles to go to Malindi. The ferry consisted of two flat boats which were pulled across on chains by a gang of chanting natives, who stamped rhythmically and paused frequently to rest, argue or wave at the audience on either bank. They had a special turn for tourists, the refrain of which went:

"'Bwana Mkubwa, Kwenda Malindi" – The big Bwana, goes to Malindi

"Toka Kipini, Bwana Mkubwa " – (Leaves Kipini, the Big Bwana)

"Kwaheri Bwana, Kwaheri Sana" – (Goodbye Bwana, Goodbye very much.)

This was reversed should the Bwana be going in the opposite direction. Great gasping heaves and groans accompanied this, ending with the team leader, who danced up and down the line, drumming his feet loudly in front of the visitor, and holding out his brimless trilby for the coins.

The warm damp heat was stifling, bringing out a sweat all over the body, to which the white coral dust adhered as it blew off the road. It was a different world to the sand and rock of the interior, a world of dense green foliage, flowering shrubs, monstrous baobabs, wild date palms, aloes, azaleas and acacias, with an all-pervading smell of salt and scorching greenery.

Half an hour before dusk they rattled along the crushed coral road into Malindi, between the first isolated houses. Tom

371

parked in front of the Sinbad Hotel, that was built Arab style, with white Moorish arches and white pillars. Through the portico, a great doorless arch, there was a dining-room leading straight out to a dance floor, and beyond it there was the ocean and the sky. Lalage rummaged frantically in her bag. "I'm going to get into that water before I do anything else. Jonathan, please go and find out where our rooms are. Tom has to take the truck away and fix somewhere for Matt and Mzee to pitch camp." She knew the owners, she told Jonathan, and would ask for a double right on the beach for them. Digging her bathing things out of a case, she went off to the beach with Alison.

They met in the bar afterwards for a long iced drink of fresh orange juice. Jonathan noticed a much more relaxed atmosphere compared with up-country, which even included the friendly Afro-Arab barman. Voices seemed pitched lower, tempers more even. No one carried a gun and nearly everybody lounged in shorts and an open shirt. The evening breeze blew in through the glass-less arches of the windows, and there were no bars, grilles or barbed wire meshes. Farmer spoke to official, policemen to tobacco salesmen in the anonymity conferred by coastal dress. Everybody seemed relaxed, tanned, fit and happy. There were even Christmas decorations over the bar, managing not to look too tinselly and tawdry, though somewhat drooping in the moist atmosphere.

End of journey, Jonathan thought, looking around him contentedly, smiling at Lalage over his glass. Then his eye caught a face in the archway. It was a woman's face, bronzed and framed with a mass of chestnut hair. She was talking to a girl beside here, smaller, wearing a floral shirt with the sleeves rolled right up, her arms and face tanned as deeply as the first. Lalage turned to see what he was staring at, his eyes wide and a strained expression on his face. And then Gillian turned to face them.

"Tom," she cried and rushed towards him with arms outstretched. "Isn't this wonderful?" she laughed, kissing him. "This is Lou Rossiter." She introduced Marie-Lou to everybody. "Sammy is flying down tomorrow with Lou's husband."

"Leastwise we hope so," Marie-Lou said. "Or Mama is in

more trouble. Oh hi there, Jonathan. Howya doin'?"

Jonathan gulped and his mouth opened, but no words came out. Lalage looked at him narrowly. Gillian prattled on.

"Lou came back from the States especially to help me with…oh, did you know, I'm having a baby?" Tom whooped and grabbed her to kiss her again, and Lalage and Alison hugged her in their turn. Jonathan hastily went off to get another round of orange juice, this time with vodka in his.

"Wayne was real mad," Marie-Lou told them. "We went back in early November, and New York was good and cold, so when Gillian wrote I just said to Wayne at breakfast, 'I'm going back there. Who's your travel agent?' He thought I was kidding till he found my note next morning. I called him long distance from Nairobi and told him I'd be back for Christmas. He just got out himself a day ago."

"Sammy was shaken too," Gillian said. "We had to build a rondavel in record time."

"The mud was still wet," Marie-Lou chimed in. "And there was old Wayne writing to ask if the plumbing in the hotel was OK."

CHAPTER TWENTY EIGHT

MALINDI BEACH

Who shall have my faire lady?
Who shall have my faire lady?
Who but I, who but I, who but I?
Under the leaves grene!"

Anon.

"First off," Tom said, "Is find Bwana Hemingway. You heard about the crashes?

"Vaguely," Lalage said, "Tell us."

"He was up on the Uganda border, and Ray Marsh flew them over Murchison Falls to see how the Nile develops out of Lake Victoria. One version is that Ray hit a telegraph wire, which clipped the tail and put the elevators out. My guess is that Papa yelled "Go lower," to see the crocs there. Anyway they had to land as Ray couldn't steer. They hit the ground quite hard, but they were OK. Bruised and shook up. No fire or anything. Somehow they managed to contact Entebbe Airport, and a de Havilland came to pick them up. It landed all right, on a bush landing strip, and they all got on. Papa was careful to load the Gordon's gin and Grand MacNish, and some Carlsberg. On take off, they crashed again and this time they started to burn. Papa shoved his way out through the fuselage somehow, using his left shoulder, as he had dislocated the right one in the first crash.

"Poor old Papa," Lalage burst out.

"Worse. This time he ruptured a kidney, and did something to his liver, not to mention his left arm, shoulder and head.

374

That's why he came down here to rest."

"And Miss Mary?"

"Ray got her out the front way complete with vanity case."

"Is he bad?" Jonathan asked.

"Don't know, but we'll soon find out. I heard he wrote about it already for 'Look' magazine, and mentioned how the Gordon's made the only really good bang when the bottles blew."

Next day they smelt smoke, and thought nothing of it, as it could be burning rubbish, or just clearing bush.

When Tom went down to buy provisions in Malindi, he heard that the fire was being blown towards the coast, and he came back very fast.

"We'd better go help," he shouted, "Chuck towels in anything that holds water, and let's be off. I've got shovels." They all piled into one Land Rover and made for the fire. Alison had gone to see Sheikh Ahmed, with Doug Collins, a hunter friend of Tom's who lived locally.

Malindi did not have a fire brigade. It was a question of everybody going out with brooms and spades and doing what they could to make a fire break and put out the small fires caused by the wind blowing burning bits of palm tree towards the sea. They worked for three hours and Lalage was sent to buy bottles of water, as they were all very hot and thirsty. When she returned, she had two passengers.

"Tom," she shouted, "Jon. Over here, damn quick."

Unbelievably, it was Ernest and Miss Mary. He had insisted on going out to fight the fire. He had fallen into some burning bush and burnt his hand and arm. Tom grabbed his first aid kit and started to pull off the old T-shirt that Miss Mary had wound round his hand. Their clothes were smoke-smeared and Ernest's shirt was half burned off.

"What the bloody hell were you doing, Hem?" he said, as the blackened Hemingway gritted his teeth when Tom applied the Dettol with a sponge. "Don't answer," he added as the singed old warrior just grunted. Miss Mary sat slumped on the running board. Lalage came up and cradled her as the tough old journalist crumpled up, hiding her tears, unable, for once, to speak. Lalage watched Tom work. Poor old Papa had lost most of his beard, some of his white hair and his eyebrows. Jonathan stood wide–eyed examining the famous old man. He had hoped to speak to him, to ask about his hunting days with Denis Zaphiro and Philip Percival. And a thousand other things.

After a while, when everyone had recovered a little, Lalage whispered to Miss Mary, "Where are you staying?" They made the two scorched old people comfortable and took them to the house they had rented on the beach. "I need some whisky," Ernest croaked to his wife, as the houseboys came tumbling out into the garden to help.

"Get into the bath right now, you old…"

Hemingway obeyed her, but as he passed Tom, he hissed, "In the kitchen." Tom went there to get scissors to cut off Ernest's burnt clothes. He waited until Miss Mary had left Papa in the bath, and then he sneaked in with half a tumbler of Grand MacNish with a drop or two of water. Lalage had put Miss Mary to bed and told the cook to make soup. Jonathan was sent to find a doctor at the Sinbad Hotel. When he came they all left.

Papa's farewell words were. "Damn good fishing here Tom. Not as good as Bimini or Cuba, but a good few fighting sailfish. Plenty marlin further out. Goddam shark took my best one."

"Come on, Hem," Miss Mary said anxiously, emerging from the bedroom, the doc's waiting."

In the back of the Land Rover Jonathan said, "That's a damn nuisance. I wanted to talk to him. Ask him loads of questions. They will have to fly him out now, just as I got to meet the old fellow."

"Bad luck for you me boy," Lalage said. "But worse luck for him after all that crashing up in Uganda. He's accident-prone. Did you see the big scar on the right hand side of his forehead?"

"Yes. What animal did that?"

"He told me that a window fell on him in Paris. But he is covered in scars anyway. Right from his legs up."

"How well did you know him?"

"Me not, but Tom was assistant hunter to Denis after Percival retired. Tom took a month's leave to back up Denis last year. Ask him about it. He knows Patrick too, who is the middle son. He's out here now. Papa said once that Patrick loves Africa as though Africa were a girl."

Jonathan made a wry face, and Lalage raised her eyebrows and stared him out.

"If you really love her you'd live anywhere," Alison said. Jonathan rolled over on to his stomach. The white coral sand covered his oiled back like powder.

"It works the other way too," he said, "I've got to go back to England anyway. To Rangers H.Q. to be demobbed. Then to Ireland to the folks. I'm not trained for a thing, and I haven't got the capital to farm here. Africa is a wonderful place, and I'd like to stay but… apart from the Immigration authorities ideas on the subject, it isn't a very good time to decide. Most firms have surplus staff in the security forces, and the big ones all recruit in England. What is there besides selling tobacco, petrol, insurance or planting tea or coffee?"

"Lala said that the Commando want you to stay."

"Umm." He stared glumly out to where Tom and Lalage were goggling near the reef.

"You know what Lalage feels Jon. She wants to help get Stone age people modernised. She isn't too interested in anything else. Except you." she added quickly.

Jonathan was silent. He was thinking that in a few weeks he would be gone, whatever happened. He had no very good idea of what life as a civilian would be like, here or anywhere else, except that it would be fuller and richer with the black-haired girl out there in the sea. And empty and slightly pointless without her. But it had to be decided soon before he left. Maybe he would accept the Commando's offer and stay with them. But it still meant a return trip to the barracks in Ballykinlar, for the paperwork.

"Love is always difficult," she said. "It breaks the weak sooner or later. Better sooner."

"Mmmm," Jon said. But dear God, did it have to be as difficult as this?

Lately he had been resisting the growth of another enchantment. Africa was drawing him steadily and certainly, the more he saw of the emptiness of it's enormous space. What was that which Ishak said to Hassan in Flecker's book? "I will try the barren road and listen for the voice of the emptiness of earth. And you shall walk beside me." There was something that every great deserted place on earth seemed to say to the soul. He remembered about the Eskimo interviewed by Knud Rasmussen.

"All wisdom," he said, "is to be found in the great solitudes, far from the dwellings of men."

It was true, he felt, not just the absence of comfort and convenience. Something in the vast African spaces gripped the heart forever and would be there long afterwards, undiminished. To return in unlikely moments.

Then there was Lala's argument. There was so much to put right, and so much undeveloped, so much ignorance and blindness, black and white. If you felt it at all, then shouldn't you help to put it right? To this he had objected. "I'm not a doctor, an agronomist, an engineer, a geologist, a chemist, or even a lawyer. I ain't got no specialised knowledge. Am a half-baked soldier." To Alison he explained," If I went back to Europe and became a Colonial Service cadet, I would already be twenty-five after a year's training. As a junior District Officer, even if I was posted to Africa afterwards, I wouldn't be earning much more than I am as a subaltern. We have to consider such things," he said.

"You could live on your wife, for a time. No?"

"If one had one."

"God." she laughed. "You are so bloody serious."

She went off to the sea and plunged in.

Later, she walked up the beach out of the sea with Tom, and flung her goggles and snorkel down beside Jonathan.

"To think," she said, "that before someone invented these things, no white folks had ever seen those fish. Go and look, Jon. It's like being in an aviary, only they are much brighter than birds. Fantastic colouring. Hardly any of them are one colour, and the water makes them bright like jewels; blue and yellow, green and black, white and purple. And the coral growths are weird, like huge vegetables, cauliflowers and things.Wonderful, Tom, wasn't it?" Tom nodded. He was engrossed in some whispering with Alison.

Lalage pulled off her cap and combed her hair out, holding her head on one side to let it hang. Her face was radiant as she smiled at Jonathan. He had hardly ever seen her so enthusiastically happy. "I love the coast. I would like to live here when I'm old. We'd better buy a plot quick. The Lerricks have got one. We could build a big, cool house like the Arabs have now, with big wide arches and a verandah all round it and a flat, open roof. You must come and see Sheikh Ahmed one day. He keeps his wives in the village, all shuttered away, but on his plantations he has a big, airy place, built of crushed coral and you sit on the floor and his boys bring you coconuts and cut the tops off for you to drink the juice."

"Sounds interesting," Jonathan said, dully.

"He is." Tom added. "He talks about things not usual for a Coast Arab. Schools for his children and welfare for the watu. He built a huge well once, and when I asked him why not a bore-hole, which would have been much cheaper, he said, 'A well is for the watu what a club is for you. When I am dead that will always be Sheikh Ahmed's Well.'

"I like him. He's so different from most people. The local Swahili and Indians buy their wives a few rings and jewels and an American car for themselves, but Arabs have more soul somehow. We'll visit him. Alison wants to see him again. Now go and goggle. Keep that shirt on or you'll get burnt."

The days passed like that, goggling, lying on the beach, visiting the ruins of Gedi, that no one could explain; visiting Sheikh Ahmed in the middle of his plantation, a patchwork of cotton, oranges, figs, pineapple, bananas, paw-paw and cashew nuts; watching the native fishermen, and the dhows going down to Zanzibar.

One morning they got up in the dark and drove out to a place called the Blue Lagoon where there were motor-boats for hire. Arriving there at first light they loaded the boat and chugged out just beyond the reef. Tom and Lalage sat in the stern with a harness to which the rod was clipped on a chain. The boat moved at about four knots, and the bright metal spinner at the end of the line could just be seen, trawled about fifty yards out. After twenty minutes both reels screamed out at once, and the second the line stopped moving they put the tips of their rods down and reeled in, lifting the tips upwards as they stopped reeling, to keep the pressure on and rest at the same time. The African boatman had cut the engine and got ready with a gaff, his mate with a club. "Anyone want to take over?" Lalage said after five or six minutes of constant reeling, interrupted by a fresh drive from the fish, pulling the line out again.

"Put a harness on first, Jon," Tom advised. "Then take the rod and let her clip it to the rings under your arms." Jonathan did so, and immediately the fish dived again and the line went screaming out.

"Pump it," Tom said. "Pull the rod tip up, reel in, letting the tip down, pull it up and reel again." His fish had started trying to circle the boat. The Africans said something excitedly. "Barracuda." Tom said. "What a pity,"

Lalage said, "You can't eat those horrible things." Eventually both the exhausted fish came close enough to be gaffed, clubbed on the head and heaved inboard to slap the decking viciously with their tails. They were both barracuda with sharp teeth like an Alsatian dog, only more pointed.

The next fish Tom hooked was taken by a shark just as the Africans were going to gaff it. The shark slipped up from behind, and all that could be seen was a flash of white as it turned sideways, opening its mouth. It took the spinner and trace as well.

Lalage hooked something heavy and could not reel it in at all. Alison was on the other rod, and Tom told her to reel in so her line didn't tangle Lalage's. Then he took the rod and pulled at the fish. A hundred yards away a sailfish curved out of the sea in a powerful slow surge, its sail fanned out high on its back, sliding gracefully back into the water in a neat arc.

"Better take the spinner off the other line and get ready to splice it on to this. We may need it." He veered the rod out towards the fish, although most of the time Jonathan couldn't see where it was. The fish jumped five or six times and then went down, but the line was long enough and after twenty minutes work it appeared on the surface again, trying to circle the boat. Tom kept the tip of the rod down and reeled steadily. The sun was up high enough to be hot now, and there was a blinding dazzle from the water. The fish came closer, saw the boat and plunged again, but Tom held it and next time it came up the boatman leant out and gaffed it. The other boy grabbed the fish's sword with one hand wrapped in a rag, and pounded its head with the club in the other. Jonathan grabbed another gaff and they heaved it over the side threshing wildly. It was a magnificent sight, eight feet long, with a dark green iridescent sheen, and a wide forked tail. Soon it was still and the sheen dulled in a few minutes to a neutral, dullish grey.

After that Alison caught a flat, round rock-fish, scarlet with a gaping mouth, like a small grouper. Then the sun was too high and there were no more bites, and they got out the flasks and slaked their thirsts, keeping out of the glare under the boat's canopy.

The truck broke down on the way back, and they left Tom with the fish already smelling, and hitched a lift on a cotton lorry back to Malindi. Jonathan went to the one and only garage for a mechanic who drove the girls back to the hotel.

The truck was towed in and as they got back to the village they saw the blue Piper Cruiser which Sammy had flown up to Lamu, come swooping down over the beach, skim along the sea and curl back over the hotel towards the landing strip. It reminded Jonathan that it was Christmas Eve.

Tom Lerrick gave a party in the Rossiters' rooms that evening. The room faced on to the beach, and there was a loggia that opened straight on to the sand. They moved the beds out there so that they looked something like snow covered firs with the moon shining on the mosquito nets. The girls looked strangely dark-skinned against the light colour of their dresses, with the effect of a few days sun reflected off the white sand. Jonathan's legs stung inside the trousers of his blue patrols. Tom had asked a couple of lonely looking bachelors from Nairobi, and June Dwent arrived and asked herself. She soon had one of the young men in a corner and while the other captured Lalage, Jonathan found himself talking to Henry Dwent whose conversation was always laboured, and tonight centred on the rocketing prices of coastal building plots.

The Rossiters rescued him, and Marie-Lou must have been discussing him with Gillian, he suspected, because she steered her away first towards another group. "You sure look hot in that rig," she told him. Jonathan grinned, "No, there is hardly anything underneath." She looked at him a touch too long.

"You staying out here?" Wayne asked.

"Considering it," Jonathan admitted.

"Hunt?"

"No," Jonathan smiled at the idea. "I don't know anything about that."

"You must have had some shooting. They tell me there was trouble, and you did some?"

"Of a sort, yes. But you need to be born here to hunt professionally."

Wayne looked dubious. His glance wandered over Jonathan's build.

"There's money in it. Next year it'll open up. The New York agents are advertising already. You're young enough. Jump in, boy, that's my advice. It's a great life."

"I wouldn't be any good at it," Jonathan said, with a firmness that surprised him. "I have too much imagination or something. I get lost as it is. I'd forget the ammunition, run out of petrol."

"Brits," Marie-Lou said. "They always have to be so darned modest. Colonials are nice and brash. I like them for it."

Jonathan smiled, trying not to look condescending. "I can't even shoot straight. Just ask Lalage."

They ate, laughing at the jokes hilariously, with the breeze blowing hard through the dining room, and later the band went out to the dance floor and the wind blew the music in over their heads. They went back to the Rossiters' room for coffee out on the loggia. Jonathan, pleasantly mellow with wine, walked hand in hand with Lalage down to the edge of the sea. Spider-crabs, naked white in the moonlight, scuttled out of their way with a dry, whispering sound like the noise palm-fronds made brushing together. They sat on the sand, watching the sea, and the fringe of lights that followed the curve of the bay down past the three other hotels to the native village.

"I want you to come to Ireland to meet my parents," Jonathan said suddenly. "Will you?" Lalage lay back, gazing at the sky, without answering.

"Europe is so cold and grey Then my mother always tries to make me stay." She paused again. "You know, its odd. People don't seem to regard this as a country at all. Look at Marie-Lou. Can't tell her husband she's pregnant. She daren't tell Wayne because he'd take her home. To an American it's unthinkable to have a child in Africa. It's the same with Angela's American pals in Nairobi. When their wives get pregnant, that's the last they see of them until they join them in the States."

"Will you come?" Jonathan repeated gently.

"It's unfair to ask me now, but I might. Let's go and dance. Look at that floor. There's something that floodlit bougainvillaea does that nothing else can. We must go along to the Eden Roc later and the Blue Marlin. They have screens all round the floor at the Marlin and palms over it."

"At midnight," Jonathan said, "we can go to church."

"OK. It is Christmas." She paused. "We need a word about that, young man. Come here." She led the way down to edge of the sea.

"It is, of course, sheer sentiment," she said. "But it does make it more like Christmas." Jonathan's heart lifted. She never admitted to any colonial failings in her patriotism, and hadn't she once said, "God is something like face-powder that I feel no need for, and do not use."

Now she was quite solemn. "My darling soldier," she began, "you know we are really living in sin. So ..." He kissed her to stop the words.

"I know. Do I not know. I should do something about it. It worries me. If I had been killed...I was not in a state of grace. Thank God I don't have to go back to the bloody Aberdares. But I don't think God minds too much if you are really in love. Does He?"

"I don't know much about Him. Theology was not on my school list. The Greek Orthodox are pretty relaxed about it. Our priests are married, you know. We must get married soon."

"I have asked you that, my love, several times."

There was a long silence.

They met carol singers on the way, the white eyes glinting lustrously in the shining black faces. They carried torches of tallow-wrapped branches. A White Father led them, and they sang in English as they marched.

"Poor things," Lalage commented. "I must say I admire those priests of yours."

After mass they didn't feel like re-entering the noise, and walked along the beach together in silence.

"I would feel alone now, with you, if we were with other people," she said softly. "Would you?"

"I know what you mean. I feel like that often. Alone, I mean, and separate, from all you strange Africans, black and white."

"Are we so strange?" she asked, stopping and sitting down. He looked at her sitting there, with the sea wind blowing her hair. Strange? he was thinking. The ruins at Gedi for example. No one knew who had lived there, or why. Tom said there were ruins at Kilwa in south Tanganyika, quite different, and no one knew anything about them either, except that there had probably been a port there once. Someone had suggested that the Zimbabwe ruins in Rhodesia were connected with Kilwa. Zimbabwe had brick walls still standing, towering out of the bush, that no African in the area could build now. So it was said that the Queen of Sheba had mined gold there and Kilwa was the port from which she sent it to King Solomon.

"I was thinking about Gedi," he explained, "And how everything here is in its infancy."

"You think too much," she said, and he put an arm around her and drew her to him and kissed her. For a while they forgot about Africa, and about everything else.

"Africa," Lalage murmured eventually, "is a damned beautiful place."

"But," Jonathan began.

"Quiet, pommie," she said, putting her fingers to his mouth. "America had natives in it too, didn't it? We haven't shot all ours…"

"Well, if you do, for God's sake don't go on making films

about it," Jonathan interrupted.

"Don't be flippant. Africa is one great big, beautiful place."
She stood up and pulled him to his feet.

"Big and beautiful," she sang out happily, pivoting on his arm. "And one day soon, all the stupid bigoted people will go rushing off home, or down south, and leave the ones who understand. As you say, there are far more coloured people in the world than white. Won't everyone be surprised when China and Africa and India are the Big Three?" She laughed and swung her arms and skipped out in front of him. Jonathan was touched to see her like that, completely happy with her fantasy, like a little girl.

"Europe is so old and dull and stuffy. You are going to come out here and stay, aren't you darling?"

She stretched out her hands and her palms on his cheeks, she kissed him, and he swung her off her feet and held her tight.

"And then you will be a white Sheba." She frowned and wriggled.

"White? Was she white? You're colour conscious you…you…" She struggled in his arms, while Jonathan laughed, his laughter incensing her further. He grabbed her hand as she escaped, "Listen, Lala. I didn't mean it. I just thought of her as a dusky sort of maiden, that's all."

"Did you?" Lalage snorted, "You bloody superior Bwana, you." Jonathan let out a yell, half-exasperation, half-amusement.

"All right, a dusky, un-white, polyglot, multi-racial Sheba, if you like. A Greek Sheba. A beautiful, seductive…"

"Get on to the next bit for heaven's sake," she interrupted, calming down a trifle.

"I've lost my thread," he complained. "What thread I had."

"Well, weren't you going to go on about Solomon. Wasn't he a sort of economist?"

"Modesty forbids me to suggest it."

"Modest old pommie." She rubbed her hand along the tunic of his "Postman Suit," as she called his green Rangers Number Ones.

'Not Solomon in all his glory…'

"Wasn't there something about that? Even he didn't get

round to walking on this beach in such nice shiny buttons, with his Sheba."

She nuzzled her head under his chin.

"It may seem rather eccentric to you, but the cloth is very light, and it's less trouble than a dinner jacket."

"Silly boy. I didn't mean the uniform. I meant that with all his glory he never got his Sheba, did he?"

"I don't know." Jonathan felt suddenly sad about it all. Very soon he would be gone, and she would become a very far-away, unattainable Sheba.

"What are you thinking about? Something sad?"

"Why?"

"I can tell by your mouth when you are sad. I know a lot about you, my Jonathan."

He was a little startled, as always, when she showed such intuitive perception. It was a side of her which clashed with her matter-of-fact, practical briskness. But it was there, with all its ability to pierce him. He would never totally understand her, but then who was so brash as to imagine that they understood another being? Unpredictable as she was, there was a centre in her life, which was her love for Africa, and how many people had such a focus?

"I was thinking about you and about Africa."

"Darling. Don't worry about it. We have to live here. After about twenty years you begin to understand a little about it, if your brain isn't fuddled by then. We changed how Africans live. So now they need us. When they trust you, then there is something in life. You understand?"

"A little bit. But you see I think that there are so many people, of all colours, who don't."

"It doesn't matter. I can't do anything for the women shopping in Knightsbridge and Oxford Street, but here I can do a lot that needs doing, and it doesn't matter that I won't get any thanks for it, and that one day they'll tell me to go to hell. Then I can go shopping with the others. But now I have this to make me a person. Don't you see?"

Jonathan took her in his arms again and squeezed her, because he could not find the words to speak. Her mouth sought his as though to comfort him, and for the first time he felt that he was the weak one, and she the strong.

"If you really love me," she said, "you will come back. And I know that you will."

He let her go and they walked on until the quiet swish and lap of the surf drowned the notes of music from the hotels. The white beach glimmered softly, sweeping out in a long slow curve in front of them, without a single light to be seen anywhere except the glitter of the Southern Cross and the soft silver of the moon.

In Limerick a week later Jonathan received a letter from Nairobi.

Darling,
I enclose something which appeared today in the 'Sunday Post.' I wondered why you said to read the Sunday Post. Of course only I knew it was from you. Well, Sam and Gill might. If they ever read the Sunday papers. 'Farewell from a soldier,' indeed. What an odd thing to do."

The enclosure was a newspaper cutting.

To L with all my love

FAREWELL FROM A SOLDIER

'You turned your shining raven head,
"Goodbye, and thanks for everything," you said.
I saw only mistily the lovely face, the sweep of hair:
I thought I saw your tears that were not there.
Those last few minutes tortured me before the plane,
That brings me back to people I must love again
Ireland – our soft green mother shell
A gentle empty witness to a private hell.
Often I see the forests of the Aberdare,
I hear your voice that taught me how to care
For life on the high moors, the wind in the bamboo,
Those precious local leaves, and joy of holding you.

We said goodbye to Sam and Gill. The empty bottles stand
On your veranda, and as I shook each friendly hand,
I tried to laugh and say I longed to see
My folks at home and the old country.
I should have said my heart had nearly died that day,
When you said "Goodbye, My Love," and quickly turned
away.'

The letter ended.

*"When I told Sam and Gill they and everybody said to me,
'Wonderful, wonderful. That lovely man, and when is he due back?*
'

I love you. Come back soon. Soon.

Lalage."

GLOSSARY

Ki-Swahili	English
Askari	Soldier
Bwana	Master, Sir
Baraf	Ice
Bibi	Woman
Bunduki	Rifle
Chakula	Food
Duka	Shop
Effendi	Sir, military
Fisi	Hyena
Gharri	Vehicle
Habari	News
Hapana	No, none
Hodi	Anyone in?
Kahawa	Coffee
Kabisa	Completely
Kazi	Work
Kanzu	Gown
Kifaru	Rhino
Kufa	Kill
Kwaheri	Goodbye
Kwenda	Go
Jambo	Hello
Leti	Bring
Maji	Water
Maridadi	Dressed up
Mbaya	Bad

Mbichi	Raw, wild
Memsaab	Madam
Mingi	Many
Mkubwa	Large, elder, Chief
Mrefu	Long, tall
Murori	Witch Doctor
Mzuri	Good
Ndege	Bird – aircraft
Ndio	Yes
Ndugu	Brother
Neopara	Head man
Ngoma	Dance
Nyoka	Snake
Nyama	Meat
Rafiki	Friend
Rooinek (Afrikaans)	Redneck
Sana	Very
Serikali	Government
Shamba	Farm
Shauri	Discussion, affair
Shenzi	Bad, poor
Tafadali	Please
Tchui	Leopard
Tembo	Lion
Thingira	Hut, house
Upesi	Quick
Yako	Your